I WILL MAKE COURT TO YOU IN A COURT SOME DAY!

LEWIS RAND

By MARY JOHNSTON
AUTHOR OF
"TO HAVE AND TO HOLD," "PRISONERS OF HOPE,"
ETC.

WITH ILLUSTRATIONS BY F. C. YOHN

BOSTON AND NEW YORK
HOUGHTON MIFFLIN COMPANY
The Riverside Press Cambridge

COPYRIGHT 1908 BY MARY JOHNSTON AND
HOUGHTON MIFFLIN COMPANY

ALL RIGHTS RESERVED

Published October 1908

The Riverside Press
CAMBRIDGE · MASSACHUSETTS
U · S · A

THIS BOOK IS INSCRIBED
TO THE MEMORY OF
JOHN TYLER MORGAN
FOR THIRTY YEARS
UNITED STATES SENATOR
AND THROUGHOUT THE COURSE
OF A LONG LIFE
A GOOD MAN AND A PATRIOT

CONTENTS

I.	THE ROAD TO RICHMOND	1
II.	MR. JEFFERSON	14
III.	FONTENOY	28
IV.	THE TWO CANDIDATES	39
V.	MONTICELLO	56
VI.	RAND COMES TO FONTENOY	70
VII.	THE BLUE ROOM	86
VIII.	CARY AND JACQUELINE	99
IX.	EXPOSTULATION	108
X.	TO ALTHEA	116
XI.	IN THE GARDEN	133
XII.	A MARRIAGE AT SAINT MARGARET'S	144
XIII.	THE THREE-NOTCHED ROAD	162
XIV.	THE LAW OFFICE	183
XV.	COMPANY TO SUPPER	194
XVI.	AT LYNCH'S	214
XVII.	FAIRFAX AND UNITY	230
XVIII.	THE GREEN DOOR	241
XIX.	MONTICELLO AGAIN	257
XX.	THE NINETEENTH OF FEBRUARY	270
XXI.	THE CEDAR WOOD	282

CONTENTS

XXII.	Major Edward	295
XXIII.	A Challenge	311
XXIV.	The Duel	323
XXV.	Old Saint John's	336
XXVI.	The Trial of Aaron Burr	348
XXVII.	The Letter	363
XXVIII.	Rand and Mocket	373
XXIX.	The River Road	383
XXX.	Homeward	396
XXXI.	Husband and Wife	406
XXXII.	The Brothers	417
XXXIII.	Greenwood	427
XXXIV.	Fairfax Cary	440
XXXV.	The Image	455
XXXVI.	In Pursuit	466
XXXVII.	The Simple Right	475
XXXVIII.	M. de Pincornet	480
XXXIX.	Unity and Jacqueline	493
XL.	The Way of the Transgressor	503

ILLUSTRATIONS

I WILL MAKE COURT TO YOU IN A COURT SOME DAY (page 198) . . . . *Frontispiece*

YOU ARE A SCOUNDREL 138

CARY SAW AND FLUNG OUT HIS ARM, SWERVING HIS HORSE, BUT TOO LATE 394

DRINK TO ME ONLY WITH THINE EYES 506

LEWIS RAND

CHAPTER I

THE ROAD TO RICHMOND

THE tobacco-roller and his son pitched their camp beneath a gum tree upon the edge of the wood. It was October, and the gum was the colour of blood. Behind it rolled the autumn forest; before it stretched a level of broom-sedge, bright ochre in the light of the setting sun. The road ran across this golden plain, and disappeared in a league-deep wood of pine. From an invisible clearing came a cawing of crows. The sky was cloudless, and the evening wind had not begun to blow. The small, shining leaves of the gum did not stir, and the flame of the camp-fire rose straight as a lance. The tobacco cask, transfixed by the trunk of a young oak and drawn by strong horses, had come to rest upon the turf by the roadside. Gideon Rand unharnessed the team, and from the platform built in the front of the cask took fodder for the horses, then tossed upon the grass a bag of meal, a piece of bacon, and a frying-pan. The boy collected the dry wood with which the earth was strewn, then struck flint and steel, guarded the spark within the tinder, fanned the flame, and with a sigh of satisfaction stood back from the leaping fire. His father tossed him a bucket, and with it swinging from his hand, he made through the wood towards a music of water. Goldenrod and farewell-summer and the red plumes of the sumach lined his path, while far overhead the hickories and maples reared a fretted, red-gold roof. Underfoot were moss and coloured leaves, and to the right and left the squirrels watched him with bright eyes. He found the stream where it rippled between banks of fern and mint. As he knelt to fill the pail, the red haw and the purple ironweed met above his head.

Below him was a little mirror-like pool, and it gave him back himself with such distinctness that, startled, he dropped the pail, and bending nearer, began to study the image in the water. Back in Albemarle, in his dead mother's room, there hung a looking-glass, but it was cracked and blurred, and he seldom gazed within it. This chance mirror of the woods was more to the purpose. The moments slipped away while he studied the stranger and familiar in the pool below him. The image was not formed or coloured like young Narcissus, of whom he had never heard, but he observed it with interest. He was fourteen, and old for his years. The eyes reflected in the stream were brooding, the mouth had lost its boyish curves, the sanguine cheek was thin, the jaw settling square. His imagination, slow to quicken, had, when aroused, quite a wizard might. He sank deeper amid the ironweed, forgot his errand, and began to dream. He was the son of a tobacco-roller, untaught and unfriended, but he dreamed like a king. His imagination began to paint without hands images of power upon a blank and mighty wall, and it painted like a young Michael Angelo. It used the colours of immaturity, but it conceived with strength. "When I am a man — " he said aloud; and again, "When I am a man — " The eyes in the pool looked at him yearningly; the leaves from the golden hickories fell upon the water and hid him from himself. In the distance a fox barked, and Gideon Rand's deep voice came rolling through the wood: "Lewis! Lewis!"

The boy dipped the pail, lifted it brimming, and rose from his knees. As he did so, a man parted the bushes on the far side of the stream, glanced at the mossed and slippery stones rising from its bed, then with a light and steady foot crossed to the boy's side. He was a young man, wearing a fringed hunting-shirt and leggins and a coonskin cap, and carrying a long musket. Over his shoulder was slung a wild turkey, and at his heels came a hound. He smiled, showing very white teeth, and drew forward his bronze trophy.

"Supper," he said briefly.

The boy nodded. "I heard your gun. I've made a fire yonder beneath a black gum. Adam Gaudylock, I am well-nigh a man!"

"So you be, so you be," answered the other; "well-nigh a man."

The boy beat the air with a branch of sumach. "I want to be a man! But I don't want to be a tobacco-roller like my father, nor —"

"Nor a hunter like me," the other finished placidly. "Be the Governor of Virginia, then, or come with me and make yourself King of the Mississippi! I've watched you, boy! You're growing up ambitious, ambitious as What's-his-name — him that you read of?"

"Lucifer," answered the boy — "ambitious as Lucifer."

"Well, don't spill the water, my kingling," said the hunter good-naturedly. "Life's not so strange as is the way folk look at it. You and I, now, — we're different! What I care for is just every common day as it comes naturally along, with woods in it, and Indians, and an elk or two at gaze, and a boat to get through the rapids, and a drop of kill-devil rum, and some shooting, and a petticoat somewhere, and a hand at cards, — just every common day! But you build your house upon to-morrow. I care for the game, and you care for the prize. Don't go too fast and far, — I've seen men pass the prize on the road and never know it! Don't you be that kind, Lewis."

"I won't," said the boy. "But of course one plays to win. After supper, will you tell me about New Orleans and the Mississippi, and the French and the Spaniards, and the moss that hangs from the trees, and the oranges that grow like apples? I had rather be king of that country than Governor of Virginia."

The sun set, and the chill dusk of autumn wrapped the yellow sedge, the dusty road, and the pines upon the horizon. The heavens were high and cold, and the night wind had a message from the north. But it was warm beneath the gum tree where the fire leaped and roared. In the light the nearer leaves of the surrounding trees showed in strong relief; beyond that copper fretwork all was blackness. Out of the dark came the breathing of the horses, fastened near the tobacco-cask, the croaking of frogs in a marshy place, and all the stealthy, indefinable stir of the forest at night. At times the wind brought a swirl of dead leaves across the ring of light, an owl hooted, or one of the sleeping dogs stirred and raised his head, then sank to dreams again. The tobacco-roller, weary from the long day's travel, wrapped himself in a blanket and slept in the lee of his thousand pounds of bright leaf, but the boy and the hunter sat late by the fire.

"We crossed that swamp," said Gaudylock, "with the canes rattling above our heads, and a panther screaming in a cypress tree, and we came to a village of the Chickasaws —"

"In the night-time?"

"In the night-time, and a mockingbird singing like mad from a china tree, and the woods all level before us like a floor, — no brush at all, just fine grass, with flowers in it like pinks in a garden. So we smoked the peace pipe with the Chickasaws, and I hung a wampum belt with fine words, and we went on, the next day, walking over strawberries so thick that our moccasins were stained red. At noon we overtook a party of boatmen from the Ohio, — tall men they were, with beards, and dark and dirty as Indians, — and we kept company with them through the country of the Chickasaws and the Choctaws until we came to a high bluff, and saw the Mississippi before us, brown and full and marked with drifting trees, and up the river the white houses of Natchez. There we camped until we made out the flatboat, — General Wilkinson's boat, all laden with tobacco and flour and bacon, and just a few Kentucks with muskets, — that the Spaniards at Natchez had been fools enough to let pass! We hailed that boat, and it came up beneath the cottonwoods, and I went aboard with the letters from Louisville, and on we went, down the river, past the great woods and the strange little towns, and the cotton-fields and the sugar-canes, and the moss hanging like banners from taller trees than this gum, to New Orleans. And there the Intendant would have laid hands on our cargo and sent every mother's son of us packing, but Miro, that was governor, stood our friend, being frightened indeed of what Kentucky might do if put to it! And there, on the levee, we sold that tobacco and flour and bacon; and the tobacco which we sold at home for shillings and pence, we sold at New Orleans for joes and doubloons. Ay, ay, and not one picayune of duty did we pay! Ay, and we opened the Mississippi!"

The speaker paused to take from his pouch several leaves of tobacco, and to roll them deftly into a long cigar. The boy rose to throw more wood upon the fire, then sat again at the trader's feet, and with his chin in his hand stared into the glowing hollows.

"The West!" said Gaudylock, between slow puffs of smoke. "Kentucky and the Ohio and the Mississippi, and then Louisiana and all that lies beyond, and Mexico and its gold! Ha! the Mississippi open from its source — and the Lord in Heaven knows where that may be — to the last levee! and not a Spaniard to stop a pirogua, and right to trade in every port, and no lingo but plain English, and Mexico like a ripe apple, — just a touch of the bough, and there's the gold in hand! If I were a dreamer, I would dream of the West."

"Folk have always dreamed of the West," said the boy. "Sailors and kings, and men with their fortune to make. I've read about Cortez and Pizarro, — it would be fine to be like that!"

"I thought you wanted to study law."

"I do; but I could be a great soldier, too."

Gaudylock laughed. "You would trap all the creatures in the wood! Well, live long enough, and you'll hear a drum beat. They're restless, restless, yonder on the rivers! But they'll need the lawyers, too. Just see what the lawyers did when we fought the British! Mr. Henry and Mr. Jefferson — "

The boy put forth a sudden hand, gathered to him a pine bough, and with it smote the red coals of the fire. "Oh!" he cried, "from morn till night my father keeps me in the fields. It's tobacco! tobacco! tobacco! And I want to go to school — I want to go to school!"

"That's a queer wanting," said the other thoughtfully. "I've wanted fire when I was cold, and venison when I was hungry, and liquor when I was in company, and money when I was gaming, and a woman when the moon was shining and I wished to talk, — but I have never wanted to go to school. A schollard sees a wall every time he raises his head. I like the open."

"There are walls in the forest," answered the boy, "and I do not want to be a tobacco-roller! I want to study law!"

The hunter laughed. "Ho! A lawyer among the Rands! I reckon you take after your mother's folk!"

The boy looked at him wistfully. "I reckon I do," he assented. "But my name is Rand."

"There are worse folk than the Rands," said the woodsman. "I've never known one to let go, once he had man or beast by the throat! Silent and holdfast and deadly to anger — that's the Rands. If Gideon wants tobacco and you want learning, there'll be a tussle!"

"My father's a tyrant!" cried the boy passionately. "If he does n't keep his hands off me, I'll — I'll *kill* him!"

Gaudylock took the cigarro from his lips. "You're too fond of that word," he exclaimed, with some sternness. "All the wolves that the Rands ever hunted have somehow got into their blood. Suppose you try a little *un*learning? Great lawyers and great men and great conquerors and good hunters don't kill their fathers, Lewis, — no, nor any other man, excepting always in fair fight."

"I know — I know!" said Lewis. "Of course he's my father. But I never could stand for any one to get in my way!"

"That's just what the rattlesnake says — and after a while nobody does get in his way. But he must be a lonely creature."

"Do you think," asked the boy oddly, — "do you think I am really like that, — like a rattlesnake?"

Adam gave his mellow laugh. "No, I don't. I think you are just a poor human. I was always powerfully fond of you, Lewis, — and I never could abide a rattler! There's the moon, and it's a long march to-morrow, and folks sit up late in Richmond! Unroll the blankets, and let's to bed."

The boy obeyed, and the two lay down with the fire between them. The man's thoughts went back to the Mississippi, to cane-brakes and bayous and long levees; and the boy's mind perused the road before him.

"When I get to Richmond," he suddenly announced, "I am going to find a place where they sell books. I have a dollar."

The hunter put his hand in his pouch, drew out a shining coin, and tossed it across the fire. "There's another," he said. "Good Spanish! Buy your *Cæsars* and your *Pompeys*, and when you are a lawyer like Mr. Jefferson, come West — come West!"

Men and beasts slumbered through the autumn night, waked at dawn, and, breakfast eaten, took again the road. Revolving cask, horses, dogs, and men, they crossed the wet sedge and entered the pine wood, left that behind and traversed a waste of scrub and vine, low hills, and rain-washed gullies. Chinquapin bushes edged the road, the polished nut dark in the centre of each open burr; the persimmon trees showed their fruit, red-gold from the first frosts; the black haw and cedar overhung the ravines; there was much sassafras, and along the plashy streams the mint grew thick and pungent-sweet. In the deep and pure blue sky above them, fleecy clouds went past like galleons in a trade-wind.

The tobacco-roller was a taciturn man, and the boy, his son, never thought of disburdening his soul to his father. Each had the power to change for the other the aspect of the world, but they themselves were strangers. Gideon Rand, as he rode, thought of the bright leaf in the cask, of the Richmond warehouse, and fixed the price in his mind. His mind was in a state of sober jubilation. His only brother. a lonely, unloved, and avaricious merchant in a small way, had lately died, and had left him money. The hundred acres upon the Three-Notched Road that Gideon had tilled for another were in the market. The money would buy the land and the small, dilapidated house already occupied by the

THE ROAD TO RICHMOND

Rands. The purchase was in train, and in its own fashion Gideon's sluggish nature rejoiced. He was as land-mad as any other Virginian, but he had neither a lavish hand nor a climbing eye. What he loved was the black earth beneath the tobacco, and to walk between the rows and feel the thick leaves. For him it sufficed to rise at dawn and spend the day in the fields overseeing the hands, to come home at dusk to a supper of corn bread and bacon, to go to bed within the hour and sleep without a dream until cockcrow, to walk the fields again till dusk and supper-time. Church on Sunday, Charlottesville on Court Days, Richmond once a year, varied the monotony. The one passion, the one softness, showed in his love for horses. He broke the colts for half the county; there was no horse that he could not ride, and his great form and coal-black locks were looked for and found at every race. The mare that he was riding he had bought with his legacy, before he bought the land on the Three-Notched Road. He was now considering whether he could afford to buy in Richmond a likely negro to help him and Lewis in the fields. With all the stubbornness of a dull mind, he meant to keep Lewis in the fields. Long ago, when he was a handsome young giant, he had married above him. His wife was a beautiful and spirited woman, and when she married the son of her father's tenant, it was with every intention of raising him to her own level in life. But he was the stronger, and he dragged her down to his. As her beauty faded and her wit grew biting, he learned to hate her, and to hate learning because she had it, and the refinements of life because she practised them, and law because she came of a family of lawyers. She was dead and he was glad of it, — and now her son was always at a book, and wanted to be a lawyer! "I'll see him a slave-driver first!" said Gideon Rand to himself, and flecked his whip.

On the other side of the cask Adam Gaudylock whistled along the road. He, too, had business in Richmond, and problems not a few to solve, but as he was a man who never sacrificed the present to the past, and rarely to the future, he alone of the three really drank the wine of the morning air, saw how blue was the sky, and admired the crimson trailers that the dewberry spread across the road. When his gaze followed the floating down from a milkweed pod, or marked the scurry of a chipmunk at a white oak's root, or dwelt upon the fox-grape's swinging curtain, he would have said, if questioned, that life in the woods and in an Indian country taught a man the use of his eyes. "Love of Nature" was a phrase at which he would have looked blank, and a talisman which he did not know he possessed, and it may be doubted if he could have defined the word "Romance." He whistled as he rode, and presently, the sun rising higher and the clear wind blowing with force, he began to sing, —

> "From the Walnut Hills to the Silver Lake,
> Row, boatmen, row!
> Danger in the levee, danger in the brake,
> Row, boatmen, row!
> Yellow water rising, Indians on the shore!"

Lewis Rand, perched upon the platform before the cask, his feet dangling, his head thrown back against the wood, and his eyes upon the floating clouds, pursued inwardly and with a swelling heart the oft-broken, oft-renewed argument with his father. "I do not want to go to the fields. I want to go to school. Every chance I've had, I've learned, and I want to learn more and more. I do not want to be like you, nor your father, nor his father, and I do not want to be like Adam Gaudylock. I want to be like my mother's folk. You've no right to keep me planting and suckering and cutting and firing and planting again, as though I were a negro! Negroes don't care, but I care! I'm not your slave. Tobacco! I hate the sight of it, and the smell of it! There's too much tobacco raised in Virginia. You fought the old King because he was a tyrant, but you would make me spend my life in the tobacco-field! You are a tyrant, too. I'm to be a man just as you're a man. You went your way; well, I'm going mine! I'm going to be a lawyer, like — like Ludwell Cary at Greenwood. I'm not afraid of your horsewhip. Strike, and be damned to you! You can break every colt in the country, but you can't break me! I've seen you strike my mother, too!"

> "Way down in New Orleans,
>   Beneath an orange tree,
> Beside the lapping water,
>   Upon the old levee,
> A-laughing in the moonlight,
>   There sits the girl for me!"

sang Gaudylock.

> "She's sweeter than the jasmine,
>   Her name it is Delphine."

The day wore on, the land grew level, and the clearings more frequent. Stretches of stacked corn appeared like tented plains, brown and silent encampments of the autumn; and tobacco-houses rose from the fields whence the weed had been cut. Blue smoke hung in wreaths above the high roofs, for it was firing-time. Now and then they saw, far back from the road and shaded by noble trees, dwelling-houses of brick or wood. Behind the larger sort of these appeared barns and stables and negro quarters, all very cheerful in the sunny October weather. Once they passed a schoolhouse and a church, and twice they halted at crossroad taverns. The road was no longer solitary. Other slow-rolling casks of tobacco with retinue of men and boys were on their way to Richmond, and there were white-roofed wagons from the country beyond Staunton. Four strong horses drew each wagon, manes and tails tied with bright galloon, and harness hung with jingling bells. Whatever things the mountain folk might trade with were in the wagons, — butter, flour, and dried meat, skins of deer and bear, hemp, flaxseed, wax, ginseng, and maple sugar. Other vehicles used the road, growing more numerous as the day wore into the afternoon, and Richmond was no longer far away. Coach and chaise, curricle and stick-chair, were encountered, and horsemen were frequent.

In 1790 men spoke when they passed; moreover, Rand and Gaudylock were not entirely unknown. The giant figure of the one had been seen before upon that road; the other was recognized as a very able scout, hunter, and Indian trader, restless as quicksilver and daring beyond all reason. Men hailed the two cheerily, and asked for the news from Albemarle, and from Kentucky and the Mississippi.

"Mr. Jefferson is coming home," answered Rand; and "Spain is not so black as she is painted," said the trader.

"We hear," quoth the gentleman addressed, "that the Kentuckians make good Spanish subjects."

"Then you hear a damned lie," said Gaudylock imperturbably. "The boc:'s on the other foot. Ten years from now a Kentuckian may rule in New Orleans."

The gentleman laughed, settled back in his stick-chair, and spoke to his horse. "Mr. Jefferson is in Richmond," he remarked to Rand, and vanished in a cloud of dust.

The tobacco-cask and its guardians kept on by wood and stream, plantation, tavern, forge, and mill, now with companions and now upon a lonely road. At last, when the frogs were at vespers, and the wind had died into an evening stillness, and the last rays of the sun were staining the autumn foliage a yet deeper red, they came by way of Broad Street into Richmond. The cask of bright leaf must be deposited at Shockoe Warehouse; this they did, then as the stars were coming out, they betook themselves to where, at the foot of Church Hill, the Bird in Hand dispensed refreshment to man and beast.

CHAPTER II

MR. JEFFERSON

BY ten of the Capitol clock Gideon Rand had sold his tobacco and deposited the price in a well-filled wallet. "Eighteen shillings the hundred," he said, with grim satisfaction. "And the casks I sent by Mocket sold as well! Good leaf, good leaf! Tobacco pays, and learning don't. Put that in your pipe and smoke it, Lewis Rand!"

Father and son came out from the cool, dark store, upon the unpaved street, and joined Adam Gaudylock where he lounged beneath a sycamore. Up and down the street were wooden houses, shops of British merchants, prosperous taverns, and dwelling-houses sunk in shady gardens. An arrow-flight away brawled the river among bright islands. The sky above the bronze sycamores was very blue, the air crystal, the sunshine heavenly mild. The street was not crowded. A Quaker in a broad-brimmed hat went by, and then a pretty girl, and then a minister talking broad Scotch, and then a future chief justice who had been to market and had a green basket upon his arm. Gideon drew another breath of satisfaction. "I've been thinking this long time of buying a negro, and now I can do it! Mocket says there's a likely man for sale down by the market. Lewis, you go straight to Mocket now, and tell him I'll wait for him there! Are you coming with me, Adam Gaudylock?"

"Why," said Gaudylock, with candour, "I have business presently in Governor Street, and a man to meet at the Indian Queen. And I think I'll go now with Lewis. Somehow, the woods have spoiled me for seeing men bought and sold."

"They're black men," said Rand indifferently. "I'll see you, then, at dinner-time, at the Bird in Hand. I'm going home to-morrow. — Lewis, if you want to, you can look around this morning with Tom Mocket!" He glanced at his son's flushing face, and, being in high good humour, determined to give the colt a little rein. "Be off, and spend your dollar! See what sights you can, for we'll not be in Richmond again for many a day! They say there's a brig in from Barbadoes."

He put up his wallet, and with a nod to Gaudylock strode away in the direction of the market, but presently halted and turned his head. "Lewis!"

"Yes, father."

"Don't you be buying any more books! You hear me?"

He swung away, and his son stood under the sycamore tree and looked after him with a darkened face. Gaudylock put a hand upon his shoulder. "Never mind, Lewis! Before we part I'm going to talk to Gideon." He laughed. "Do you know what the Cherokees call me? They call me Golden-Tongue. Because, you see, I can persuade them to 'most anything, — always into the war-path, and sometimes out of it! Gideon may be obstinate, but he can't be as obstinate as an Indian. Now let's go to Mocket's."

The way to Mocket's lay down a steep hillside, and along the river-bank, under a drift of coloured leaves, and by the sound of falling water. Mocket dwelt in a small house, in a small green yard with a broken gate. A red creeper mantled the tiny porch, and lilac bushes, clucked under by a dozen hens, hedged the grassy yard. As the hunter and Lewis Rand approached, a little girl, brown and freckled, barefoot and dressed in linsey, sprang up from the stone before the gate, and began to run towards the house. Her foot caught in a trailing vine, and down she fell. Adam was beside her at once. "Why, you little partridge!" he exclaimed, and lifted her to her feet.

"It's Vinie Mocket," said his companion. "Vinie, where's your father?"

"I don't know, thir," answered Vinie. "Tom knows. Tom's down there, at the big ship. I'll tell him."

She slipped from Gaudylock's clasp and pattered off toward the river, where the brig from Barbadoes showed hull and masts. The hunter sat down upon the porch step, and drew out his tobacco pouch. "She's like a partridge," he said.

"She's just Vinie Mocket," answered the boy. "There's a girl who stays sometimes at Mrs. Selden's, on the Three-Notched Road. She's not freckled, and her eyes are big, and she never goes barefoot. I reckon it's silk she wears."

"What's her name?" asked the hunter, filling his pipe.

"Jacqueline — Jacqueline Churchill. She lives at Fontenoy."

"Fontenoy's a mighty fine place," remarked Gaudylock. "And the Churchills are mighty fine people. — Here's the partridge back, with another freckle-face."

"That's Tom Mocket," said Lewis. "If Vinie's a partridge, Tom's a weasel."

The weasel, sandy-haired and freckled, came up the path with long steps. "Hi, Lewis! Father's gone toward the market looking for your father. That's a brig from the Indies down there, and the captain's our cousin — ain't he, Vinie? I know who you are, sir. You're Adam Gaudylock, the great hunter!"

"So I am, so I am!" quoth Adam. "Look here, little partridge, at what I've got in my pouch!"

The partridge busied herself with the beaded thing, and

the two boys talked aside. "I've till dinner time to do what I like in," said Lewis Rand. "Have you got to work?"

"Not unless I want to," Young Mocket answered blissfully. "Father, he don't care! Besides" — he swelled with pride — "I don't work now at the wharf. I'm at Chancellor Wythe's."

"Chancellor Wythe's! What are you doing there?"

"Helping him. Maybe, by and by, I'll be a lawyer, too."

"Heugh!" said the other. "Do you mean you're reading law?"

"No-o, not just exactly. But I let people in — and I hear what they talk about. I like it better than the wharf, anyhow. I'll go with you and show you things. Is Mr. Gaudylock coming?"

"No," replied Adam. "I'll finish my pipe, and take a look at the ship down there, and then I'll meet a friend at the Indian Queen. Be off with you both! Vinie will stay and talk to me."

"Yeth, thir," said Vinie, her brown arm deep in the beaded pouch.

The two lads left behind the scarlet-clad porch, the hunter and Vinie, the little green yard and the broken gate. "Where first?" demanded Tom.

"Where is the best place in Richmond to buy books?"

Young Mocket considered. "There's a shop near the bridge. What do you want with books?"

"I want to read them. We'll go to the bridge first."

Tom hung back. "Don't you want to see the brig from Barbadoes? She's a beauty. There's a schooner from Baltimore, too, at the Rock Landing. You won't? Then let's go over to Widewilt's Island. Well, they whipped a man this morning and he's in the pillory now, down by the market.

Let's go look at him.—Pshaw! what's the use of books! Don't you want to see the Guard turn out at noon, and hear the trumpet blow? Well, come on to the bridge! Nancy, the apple-woman, is there too."

The shop near the bridge to which they resorted was dark and low, but learning was spread upon its counter, and a benevolent dragon of knowledge in horn spectacles ran over the wares for Lewis Rand. "De Jure Maritimo, six shillings eightpence, my lad. Burnet's History and Demosthenes' Orations, two crowns. Mr. Gibbon's Decline and Fall of the Roman Empire, a great book and dear! Common Sense — and that's Tom Paine's, and you may have it for two pistareens."

The boy shook his head. "I want a law-book."

The genie put forth The Principles of Equity, and named the price.

"'T is too dear."

A gentleman lounging against the counter closed the book into which he had been dipping, and drew nearer to the would-be purchaser.

"Equity is an expensive commodity, my lad," he said kindly. "How much law have you read?"

"I have read The Law of Virginia," answered the boy. "I borrowed it. I worked a week for Mr. Douglas, and read The Law of Nations rest-hours. Mrs. Selden, on the Three-Notched Road, gave me The Federalist. Are you a lawyer, sir?"

The gentleman laughed, and the genie behind the counter laughed. Young Mocket plucked Lewis Rand by the sleeve, but the latter was intent upon the personage before him and did not heed.

"Yes," said the gentleman, "I am a lawyer. Are you going to be one?"

"I am," said the boy. "Will you tell me what books I ought to buy? I have two dollars."

The other looked at him with keen light eyes. "That amount will not buy you many books," he said. "You should enter some lawyer's office where you may have access to his library. You spoke of the Three-Notched Road. Are you from Albemarle?"

"Yes, sir. I am Gideon Rand's son."

"Indeed! Gideon Rand! Then Mary Wayne was your mother?"

"Yes, sir."

"I remember," said the gentleman, "when she married your father. She was a beautiful woman. I heard of her death while I was in Paris."

The boy's regard, at first solely for the books, had been for some moments transferred to the gentleman who, it seemed, was a lawyer, and had known his people, and had been to Paris. He saw a tall man, of a spare and sinewy frame, with red hair, lightly powdered, and keen blue eyes. Lewis Rand's cheek grew red, and his eyes at once shy and eager. He stammered when he spoke. "Are you from Albemarle, sir?"

The other smiled, a bright and gracious smile, irradiating his ruddy, freckled face. "I am," he said.

"From — from Monticello?"

"From Monticello." The speaker, who loved his home with passion, never uttered its name without a softening of the voice. "From Monticello," he said again. "There are books enough there, my lad. Some day you shall ride over from the Three-Notched Road, and I will show you them."

"I will come," said Lewis Rand. The colour deepened in his face and a moisture troubled his vision. The shop, the littered counter, the guardian of the books, and President

Washington's Secretary of State wavered like the sunbeam at the door.

Jefferson ran his hand over the row of books. "Mr. Smith, give the lad old Coke, yes, and Locke on Government, and put them to my account. — Where do you go to school?"

The boy swallowed hard, straightened his shoulders, and looked his questioner in the face. "Nowhere, sir — not now. My father hates learning, and I work in the fields. I am very much obliged to you for the books, — and had I best buy Blackstone with the two dollars?"

The other smiled. "No, no, not Blackstone. Blackstone's frippery. You've got old Coke. Buy for yourself some book that shall mean much to you all your life. — Mr. Smith, give him Plutarch's Lives — Ossian, too. He's rich enough to buy Ossian. — As for law-books, my lad, if you will come to Monticello, I will lend you what you need. I like your spirit." He looked at his watch. "I have to dine at the Eagle with the Governor and Mr. Randolph. When do you return to Albemarle?"

"To-morrow, sir."

"Then I may overtake you on the road. Once I did your father a good turn, and I shall be glad to have a word with him now. He must not keep the son of Mary Wayne in the fields. Some day I will ride down the Three-Notched Road, and examine you on old Coke. Don't spare study; if you will be a lawyer, become a good one, not a smatterer. Good-day to you!"

He left the shop. The bookseller gazed after him, then nodded and smiled at the boy. "You look transfigured, my lad! Well, he's a great man, and he'll be a greater one yet. He's for the people, and one day the people will be for him! I'll tie up your books — and if you can make a friend of Mr. Jefferson, you do it!"

Lewis Rand came out into the sunlight with "old Coke" and Locke, Plutarch and Ossian, under his arm, and in his soul I know not what ardour of hero-worship, what surging resolve and aspiration. Young Mocket, at his elbow, regarded him with something like awe. "That was Mr. Jefferson," he said. "He knows General Washington and Marquis Lafayette and Doctor Franklin. He's just home from Paris, and they have made him Secretary of State — whatever that is. He wrote the Declaration of Independence. He's a rich man — he's a lawyer, too. He lives at a place named Monticello."

"I know," said Lewis Rand, "I've been to Monticello. When I am a man I am going to have a house like it, with a terrace and white pillars and a library. But I shall have a flower garden like the one at Fontenoy."

"Ho! your house! Is Fontenoy where Ludwell Cary lives?"

"No; he lives at Greenwood. The Churchills live at Fontenoy. — Now we'll go see the Guard turn out. Is that the apple-woman yonder? I've a half-a-bit left."

An hour later, having bought the apples, and seen the pillared Capitol, and respectfully considered the outside of Chancellor Wythe's law office, and having parted until the afternoon with Tom Mocket, who professed an engagement on the Barbadoes brig, young Lewis Rand betook himself to the Bird in Hand. There in the bare, not over clean chamber which had been assigned to the party from Albemarle, he deposited his precious parcel first in the depths of an ancient pair of saddle-bags, then, thinking better of it, underneath the straw mattress of a small bed. It was probable, he knew, that even there his father might discover the treasure. What would follow discovery he knew full well. The beating he could take; what he wouldn't stand would be, say,

Gideon's flinging the books into the fire. "He shan't, he shan't," said the boy's hot heart. "If he does, I'll — I'll —"

Through the window came Gaudylock's voice from the porch of the Bird in Hand. "You Stay-at-homes — you don't know what's in the wilderness! There's good and there's bad, and there's much beside. It's like the sea — it's uncharted."

Lewis Rand closed the door of the room, and went out upon the shady porch, where he found the hunter and a lounging wide-eyed knot of listeners to tales of Kentucky and the Mississippi. The dinner-bell rang. Adam fell pointedly silent, and his audience melted away. The hunter rose and stretched himself. "There is prime venison for dinner, and a quince tart and good apple brandy. Ha! I was always glad I was born in Virginia. Here is Gideon swinging down the hill — Gideon and his negro!"

The tobacco-roller joined them, and with a wave of the hand indicated his purchase of the morning. This was a tall and strong negro, young, supple, and of a cheerful countenance. Rand was in high good-humour. "He's a runaway, Mocket says, but I'll cure him of that! He's strong as an ox and as limber as a snake." Taking the negro's hand in his, he bent the fingers back. "Look at that! easy as a willow! He'll strip tobacco! His name is Joab."

The namesake of a prince in Israel looked blithely upon his new family. "Yaas, marster," he said, with candour. "Dat is my name — dat sho' is! Jes' Joab. An' I is strong as en ox, — don' know 'bout de snaik. Marster, is you gwine tek me 'way from Richmond?"

"Albemarle," said the tobacco-roller briefly. "To-morrow morning."

Joab studied the vine above the porch. "Kin I go tell my ole mammy good-bye? She's washin' yonder in de creek."

Rand nodded, and the negro swung off to where, upon the grassy common sloping to Shockoe Creek, dark washerwomen were spreading clothes. The bell of the Bird in Hand rang again, and the white men went to dinner.

Following the venison, the tart, and apple brandy came the short, bright afternoon, passed by Lewis Rand upon the brig from the Indies with Tom Mocket and little Vinie and a wrinkled skipper who talked of cocoanuts and strange birds and red-handkerchiefed pirates, and spent by Gideon first in business with the elder Mocket, and then in conversation with Adam Gaudylock. Lewis, returning at supper-time to the Bird in Hand, found the hunter altered no whit from his habitual tawny lightness, but his father in a mood that he knew, sullen and silent. "Adam's been talking to him," thought the boy. "And it's just the same as when Mrs. Selden talks to him. Let me go — not he!"

In the morning, at six of the clock, the two Rands, the negro Joab, the horses, and the dogs took the homeward road to Albemarle. Adam Gaudylock was not returning with them; he had trader's business with the merchants in Main Street, hunter's business with certain cronies at the Indian Queen, able scout and man-of-information business in Governor Street, and business of his own upon the elm-shaded walk above the river. Over level autumn fields and up and down the wooded hills, father and son and the slave travelled briskly toward the west. As the twilight fell, they came up with three white wagons, Staunton bound, and convoyed by mountaineers. That night they camped with these men in an expanse of scrub and sassafras, but left them at dawn and went on toward Albemarle. A day of coloured woods, of infrequent clearings, and of streams to ford, ended in an evening of cool wind and rosy sky. They descended a hill, halted, and built their fire in a grassy space beside a river. Joab tethered the horses and made the fire, and fried the bacon and baked the hoecake. As he worked he sang:—

> "David an' Cephas, an' ole brer Mingo,
> Saul an' Paul, an' de w'ite folk sinners —
> Oh, my chillern, follow de Lawd!"

Supper was eaten in silence. When it was over, Gideon Rand sat with his back against a pine and smoked his pipe. His son went down to the river and stretched his length upon a mossed and lichened boulder. The deep water below the stone did not give him back himself as had done the streamlet five days before. This was a river, marred with eddies and with drifting wood, and red with the soil. The evening wind was blowing, and the sycamore above him cast its bronze leaves into the flood which sucked them under, or bore them with it on its way to the larger river and the ultimate sea. This stream had no babbling voice; its note was low and grave. Youth and mountain sources forgotten, it hearkened before the time to ocean voices. The boy, idle upon the lichened stone, listened too, to distant utterances, to the sirens singing beyond the shadowy cape. The earth soothed him; he lay with half shut eyes, and after the day's hot communion with old wrongs, he felt a sudden peace. He was at the turn; the brute within him quiet behind the eternal bars; the savage receding, the man beckoning, the after man watching from afar. The inner stage was cleared and set for a new act. He had lowered the light, he had rested, and he had filled the interval with forms and determinations beautiful and vague, vague as the mists, the sounds, the tossed arms of the Ossian he had dared to open last night, before his father, by the camp-fire of the mountaineers. In the twilight of his theatre he rested; a shadowy figure, full of mysteries, full of possibilities, a boy in the grasp of the man within him, neither boy nor man unlovable, nor wholly unadmirable, both seen, and seeing, "through a glass darkly."

He turned on his side, and the light went up sharply. A man riding a beautiful and spirited horse was coming over the hilltop. Horse and rider paused a moment upon the crest, standing clear against the eastern sky. In the crystal air and the sunset glow they crowned the hill like a horse and rider nobly done in bronze. A moment thus, then they began to pick their way down the rocky road. Lewis Rand looked, and started to his feet. That horse had been bred in Albemarle, and that horseman he had met in Richmond. The boy's heart beat fast and the colour surged to his cheek. There was little, since the hour in the bookshop, that he would not have done or suffered for the approaching figure. All along the road from Richmond his imagination had conjured up a score of fantastic instances, in each of which he had rescued, or died for, or had in some impossibly romantic and magnificent fashion been the benefactor of the man who was drawing near to the river and camp-fire. As superbly generous as any other youth, he was, at present, in his progress through life, in the land of shrines. He must have his idol, must worship and follow after some visible hero, some older, higher, stronger, more subtle-fine and far-ahead adventurer. Heretofore, in his limited world, Adam Gaudylock had seemed nearest the gates of escape. But Adam, he thought, was of the woods and the earth, even as his father was, and as the tobacco was, and as he himself was. His enormous need was for some one to follow whose feet were above the fat, red fields and the leafy trails. All this was present with him as he watched the oncoming figure. Great men kept their word. Had not Mr. Jefferson said that he would overtake them? — and there he was! He was coming down to the camp-fire, he was going to stop and talk to the surly giant, like Giant Despair, who sat and smoked beside it.

Lewis Rand left the river and the windy sycamore and hastened across the sere grass. "Father, father!" he cried. "Do you know who that is?" In his young voice there was both warning and appeal. Adam Gaudylock, he knew, had spoken to his father, but Gideon had given no sign. Suppose, no matter *who* spoke, his father would give, forever, no other sign than that oft seen and always hated jerk of the head toward the tobacco-fields?

Gideon Rand took his pipe from his lips. "It's Mr. Jefferson," he answered laconically. "He's the one man in this country to whom I'd listen."

Jefferson rode up to the group about the camp-fire, checked his horse, and gave the tobacco-roller and his son a plain man's greeting to plain men. The eagerness of the boy's face did not escape him; when he dismounted, flung the reins of Wildair to his groom, and crossed the bit of turf to the fire beneath the pines, he knew that he was pleasing a young heart. He loved youth, and to the young he was always nobly kind.

"Good-evening, Mr. Rand," he said. "You are homeward bound, as I am. It is good to see Albemarle faces after years of the French. I had the pleasure of making your son's acquaintance yesterday. It is a great thing to be the father of a son, for so one ceases to be a loose end and becomes a link in the great chain. Your son, I think, will do you honour. And, man to man, you must pay him in the same coin. We on a lower rung of the ladder must keep our hands from the ankles of the climbers above us! Make room for me on that log, my lad! Your father and I will talk awhile."

Thus it was that an able lawyer took up the case of young Lewis Rand. It was the lawyer's pleasure to give aid to youth, and to mould the mind of youth. He had many protégés, to all of whom he was invariably kind, invariably generous. The only return he exacted was that of homage. The yoke was not heavy, for, after all, the homage was to Ideas, to large, sagacious, and far-reaching Thought. It was in the year 1790 that he broke Gideon Rand's resistance to his son's devotion to other gods than those of the Rands. The year that followed that evening on the Albemarle road found Lewis Rand reading law in an office in Charlottesville. A few more years, and he was called to the bar; a little longer, and his name began to be an oft-spoken one in his native county, and not unknown throughout Virginia.

CHAPTER III

FONTENOY

IN the springtime of the year 1804 the spectacle of human conduct ranged from grave to gay, from gay to grave again much as it had done in any other springtime of any other year. In France the consular chrysalis was about to develop imperial wings. The British Lion and the Russian Bear were cheek by jowl, and every Englishman turned his spyglass toward Boulogne, where was gathered Buonaparte's army of invasion. In the New World Spanish troops were reluctantly withdrawing from the vast territory sold by a Corsican to a Virginian, while to the eastward of that movement seventeen of the United States of America pursued the uneven tenor of their way. Washington had been dead five years. Alexander Hamilton was yet the leading spirit of the Federalist party, while Thomas Jefferson was the idol of the Democrat-Republicans.

In the sovereign State of Virginia politics was the staple of conversation as tobacco was the staple of trade. Party feeling ran high. The President of the Union was a Virginian and a Republican; the Chief Justice was a Virginian and a Federalist. Old friends looked askance, or crossed the road to avoid a meeting, and hot bloods went a-duelling. The note of the time was Ambition; the noun most in use the name of Napoleon Buonaparte. It seemed written across the firmament; to some in letters of light and to others in hell fire. With that sign in the skies, men might shudder and turn to a private hearth, or they might give loosest rein to desire for Fame. In the columns of the newspapers, above the name of every Roman patriot, each party found voice. From a lurid background of Moreau's conspiracy and d'Enghien's death, of a moribund English King and Premier, of Hayti aflame, and Tripoli insolent, they thundered, like Cassandra, of home woes. To the Federalist, reverencing the dead Washington, still looking for leadership to Hamilton, now so near that fatal Field of Honour, unconsciously nourishing love for that mother country from which he had righteously torn himself, the name of Democrat-Republican and all that it implied was a stench in the nostrils. On the other hand, the lover of Jefferson, the believer in the French Revolution and that rider of the whirlwind whom it had bred, the far-sighted iconoclast, and the poor bawler for simplicity and red breeches, all found the Federalist a mere burnished fly in the country's pot of ointment. Nowhere might be found a man so sober or so dull as to cry, "A plague o' both your houses!"

In the county of Albemarle April was blending with May. The days were soft and sunshiny, apt to be broken by a hurry of clouds, of slanting trees, and silver rain. When the sun came out again, it painted a great bow in the heavens. Beneath that bright token bloomed a thousand orchards; and the wheat and the young corn waved in the wet breeze. The land was rolling and red in colour, with beautiful trees and narrow rivers. Eastward it descended to misty plains, westward the mountains rose, bounding a noble landscape of field and forest. For many years the axe had swung and trees had fallen, but the forest yet descended to the narrow roads, observed itself in winding streams, gloomed upon the sunlit clearings where negroes sang as they tilled the soil. In the all-surrounding green the plantations showed like intaglios. From pleasant hillsides, shady groves, and hamlets of offices and quarters, the sedate red-brick, white-porticoed "great houses" looked easily forth upon a world which interested them mightily.

Upon a morning in late April of the year 1804, the early sunshine, overflowing such a plantation, dipped at last into a hollow halfway between the house and the lower gates, and overtook two young creatures playing at make-believe, their drama of the moment being that of the runaway servant.

"Oh, the sun!" wailed Deb. "We can't pretend it's dark any longer! God has gone and made another day! We'll see you running away, — all of us white folk, and the overseer and Mammy Chloe! If you climb this willow, the dogs will tree you like they did Aunt Dinah's Jim! Lie down and I'll cover you with leaves like the babes in the wood!"

Miranda, a slim black limb of Satan in a blue cotton gown, flung herself with promptitude upon the ground. "Heap de beech leaves an' de oak leaves upon dis heah po' los' niggah. Oh, my lan'! don' you heah 'um comin'?"

Dead leaves fell upon her in a shower, and her accomplice gathered more with frantic haste. "Oh, it's the ghost in the tobacco-house! it's a rock rolling down the mountain! it's — it's something splashing in the swamp!"

"Is I a-hidin' in de swamp? Den don' th'ow no oak leaves on dis niggah, for dey don' grow dyar. Gawd A'moughty, lis'en to de river roarin'! I's hidin' by de river — I's hidin' by de river! I's hidin' by de river Jordan!"

Deb swayed to and fro, beating her hands in her excitement. "I see a boat — a great big boat! It's as big as the Ark! The finders are in it, and the dogs and the guns! Let us pray! O Jesus, save Miranda, even though it is a scarlet sin to run away! O Jesus, don't let them take her to the Court House! O Jesus, let them take me —"

Miranda reared herself from her leafy bed. "Humph! what you gwine do at de Co'te House? Answer me dat.

I knows what de Lawd gwine say. He gwine say, 'Run for it, niggah!' Yaas, Lawd, I sholy gwine do what *you* say — I gwine run to de very aidge of de yearth.

> "Oh, I fool you, Mister Oberseer Man!
> Oh, I fool you, my ole Marster!
> Cotch de mockin'bird co'tin' in de locus',
> Cotch de bullfrog gruntin' in de ma'sh,
> Cotch de black snake trabellin' 'long his road,
> But you ain' gwine see dis niggah enny mo'!

Miss Deb, ef I gets to de big gate fust, you gwine lemme hoi' dat doll baby Marse Edward gin you?"

Deb brushed the last oak leaf from the skirt of her green gown, tossed her yellow hair out of her brown eyes, and scrambled up the steep side of the dell to a level of lawn and flowers. Her handmaiden followed her, and they paused for breath beneath the white blooms of a mighty catalpa. A hundred yards away, across an expanse of dewy turf, rose the great house, bathed in sunlight. Box, syringa, and honeysuckle environed it, and a row of poplars made a background of living green. It had tall white pillars, and shallow steps leading down to a gravelled drive. The drive was overarched by elm and locust, and between the trees was planted purple lilac. All of fresh and fair and tender met in the late April weather, in the bright and song-filled morning, in the dew and in the flowers. Upon the steps, between the white pillars, were gathered several muslined figures, flowery bright to match the morning. In the drive below, two horsemen, booted and spurred, clad in many-caped riding-coats and attended by a negro groom, were in the act of lifting tall hats to the ladies of the house they were quitting.

"Hi!" panted Miranda. "Marse Ludwell Cary, Marse Fairfax Cary, an' dat brack niggah Eli! Whar dey gwine dis mawnin'?"

"To the Court House — to the election," answered Deb. "I know all about it, for I asked Uncle Edward. If the Federalists win, the crops will be good, and General Washington and my father and my grandfather will lie quiet in their graves. We are Federalists. If the Republicans win, the country will go to the devil."

"Hi, dat so?" said Miranda. "Le's run open de big gate. Dey two gent'men moughty free wid dey money."

Racing over the jewelled turf, mistress and maid arrived at the big gate in time to swing it open before the approaching riders. Young Fairfax Cary laughed and tossed a coin to Miranda, who bobbed and showed her teeth, while his elder brother stooped gallantly to the pretty child of the house he was leaving. "Do you know what you are like in your narrow green gown and your blowing, yellow hair? You are like a daffodil in your sister's garden."

"If you were to swing me up from the ground," said Deb meditatively, "I could stand upon the toe of your boot, and hold by Pluto's mane, and ride with you as far as the creek. — What flower is Jacqueline like?"

"Like no flower that blooms," said Mr. Ludwell Cary. "Ah, well sprung, Proserpina! Now shall we go fast as the wind?"

They went fast as the wind to the creek, and then went like the wind back to the gate, where Ludwell Cary swung the child down to earth and the waiting Miranda.

Deb curtsied to him. "Wish me good luck, Daffy-down-Dilly!" he said, with his charming smile.

"I do," she answered earnestly. "I hope that you will kill the Devil."

He looked puzzled. "Is that feasible? I don't know where to find him."

"Are n't you going to fight him at the Court House?

Uncle Edward said that you were going to put down Lucifer."

The two brothers broke into laughter. "I say, Fair!" cried the elder. "Has Lewis Rand a cloven hoof? I've scarcely seen him, you know, since I went to England!"

"He's all cloven hoof, damn him!" the other answered cheerfully. "Best ride on. He'll have been at the Court House this hour!"

Ludwell Cary glanced at his watch. "Early or late, the result will be the same. The county's going for him twice over!"

"A damned tobacco-roller's son!" growled the other.

The elder brother laughed. "'A man's a man for a' that,' Fair. I dare say old Gideon rolled tobacco with all his might. As for his son, his worst enemy — and I don't know that I am that — could n't deny him courage and energy."

"He's a dangerous man —"

"Most men are who have won by fighting. But I don't think he loves violence. Well, well, I'm coming! Good-bye, little one!"

Deb curtsied and Miranda bobbed, the gentlemen touched their hats, black Eli grinned, the horses began to canter, and, the leafy road bending sharply, the party for the Court House passed suddenly from view as though the earth had swallowed them up.

Miranda bent her eyes upon her mistress. "Hit's time you wuz in de schoolroom. An' Lan' o' Goshen! Jes' look at yo' wet shoes! I reckon Mammy Chloe gwine whup me!"

Deb considered her stockings and slippers. "There's no school to-day. Mr. Drew's going to the Court House to vote. Uncle Edward says it is the duty of every gentleman to vote against this damned upstart and the Democrat-Republican party. The damned upstart's other name is

Lewis Rand. I'll ask Jacqueline to beg Mammy Chloe not to whip you. I like wet feet."

The parlour at Fontenoy was large and high and cool, hung with green paper, touched with the dull gold of old mirrors, of a carved console or two, of oval frames enclosing dim portraits. Long windows opened to the April breeze, and from above the high mantel a Churchill in lovelocks and plumed hat looked down upon Jacqueline seated at her harp. She was playing Water parted from the Sea, playing it dreamily, with an absent mind. Deb, hearing the music from the hall, came and stood beside her sister. They were orphans, dwelling with an uncle.

"Jacqueline," said the child, "do you believe in the Devil?"

Jacqueline played on, but turned a lovely face upon her sister. "I don't know, honey," she said. "I suppose we must, but I had rather not."

"Uncle Edward does n't. He says 'What the Devil!' but he does n't believe in the Devil. Then why do he and Uncle Dick call Mr. Lewis Rand the Devil?"

Jacqueline's hands left the strings. "They neither say nor mean that, Deb. Uncle Dick and Uncle Edward are Federalists. They do not like Republicans, nor Mr. Jefferson, nor Mr. Jefferson's friends. Mr. Lewis Rand is Mr. Jefferson's friend, and he is his party's candidate for the General Assembly, and so they do not like him. But they do not call him such names as that."

"Mr. Ludwell Cary does n't like him either," said Deb. "Why, Jacqueline?"

"Mr. Ludwell Cary is his political opponent."

"And Mr. Fairfax Cary called him a damned tobacco-roller's son."

Jacqueline reddened. "Mr. Fairfax Cary might be thankful to have so informed a mind and heart. It is well to blame a man for his birth!"

"Mr. Ludwell Cary said, 'A man's a man for a' that.' What does that mean, Jacqueline?"

"It means," said Jacqueline, "that — that man stamps the guinea, but God sees the gold."

"Won't you tell me a story?" demanded Deb. "Tell me about the time when you were a little girl and you used to stay at Cousin Jane Selden's. And about the poor boy who lived on the next place — and the apple tree and the little stream where you played, and the mockingbird he gave you. And how his father was a cruel man, and you cried because he had to work so hard all day in the hot fields. You have n't told me that story for a long time."

"I have forgotten it, Deb."

"Then tell me about summer before last, when you were at Cousin Jane Selden's again, and you were grown, and you saw the poor boy again — only he was a man — and his father was dead, and he talked to you in Cousin Jane Selden's flower garden. You never told me that story but once."

"I have forgotten that one too."

"Why does your breath come long like that, Jacqueline? I have gotten my feet wet. Will you tell Mammy Chloe not to whip Miranda? Here is Uncle Edward!"

Major Edward Churchill entered from the garden, for which he had an attachment almost comparable to his love for the old Fontenoy library and the Fontenoy stables. He was a gentleman of the old school, slight, withered, high-nosed and hawk-eyed, dressed with precision and carrying an empty sleeve. The arm he had lost at Yorktown; a temper too hot to hold he daily lost, but he had the art to keep his friends. There were duels to his account, as well as a reputation for great courage and coolness during the late war. Under the name of Horatius he contributed to The Virginia Federalist diatribes of a polished ferocity against the Democrat-Republicans and their chief, and he owned Mustapha, the noblest race-horse of the day. He was a bachelor, a member of the Cincinnati, a Black Cockade, a friend of Alexander Hamilton, a scholar, and a sceptic; a proud, high, fiery man, who had watched at the death-bed of many things. He made his home with his brother, the master of Fontenoy; and his niece Jacqueline, the daughter of a younger, long dead brother, was to him youth, colour, music, and romance.

"The moss-rose is in bloom," he announced, standing in the parlour door. "Come see it, Jacqueline."

They went out into the garden and stood before the moss-rose bush. "Oh, beautiful!" exclaimed Jacqueline, and touched the rose with her lips. It was sunny in the garden, and the box smelled strong and sweet. The Major plucked a sprig and studied it as though box were a rarity. "I have found," he said, "Ludwell Cary's visit highly agreeable. He has come home to Virginia as likely a man as one could find in a summer day. He adorns the state. I predict for him a long and successful career."

"Yes, indeed," assented Jacqueline. "I like him very much. How well he talks! And travel has not made him forget the old days here."

The Major plucked another sprig of box. "In the old days, my dear, your father and your Uncle Dick and I used to plan — well, well, castles in Spain! castles in Spain! But he's a handsome fellow!"

"He is indeed," said Jacqueline. "His eyes are especially fine. I like that clear grey — frank and kind."

"He has sense and principle — he has mind."

"That is evident," answered his niece. "He does everything admirably. Last night after supper he read to Unity and me. He reads extremely well. The book was the Death of Wallenstein. He made me see that murder! My heart stood still."

"He is to be admired for standing up to-day against that damned demagogue, Lewis Rand! No matter if he is defeated. Every gentleman applauds him. You women adore victory, but let me tell you, a vanquished Federalist is still the conqueror of any ranting Republican!"

"Did I tell you," asked Jacqueline, "that Mr. Pincornet holds the dancing class at Fontenoy this week?"

"The dancing class be damned! Ludwell Cary is a man and a gentleman, Jacqueline —"

"Yes," said Jacqueline.

The Major threw away his sprig of box. "The Sphinx was a woman, and every woman is an incarnate riddle! Why don't you care for him, Jacqueline?"

"I do care for him. I like him very much."

"Pshaw!" said the Major irritably. "Don't look at that rose any longer! It's cankered! And it's time that Dick and I were off. We vote —" he put his shapely, nervous hand upon his niece's shoulder — "we vote, Jacqueline, for Ludwell Cary."

"Yes, uncle," said Jacqueline. "I know — I know."

Colonel Dick Churchill, large and beaming, and Major Edward Churchill, thin and saturnine, rode away, and from between the white pillars Deb and Jacqueline watched them go. Colonel Dick's wife was an invalid, and lay always in the cool and spacious "chamber," between dimity bed curtains, with her key basket on the counterpane.

"Jacqueline," said Deb, "whom do you vote for?"

"Women do not vote, honey."

"But if you *did* vote, Jacqueline?"

"Do you remember," asked Jacqueline, "how Lady Mary Wortley Montagu offended Mr. Alexander Pope?"

"Ah," said Deb. "I'm little, and I ask questions, but I'm not crooked! Will Mr. Lewis Rand ever come to Fontenoy, Jacqueline?"

"You are going to wear your blue gown to the dancing class," said Jacqueline. "Unity is going to wear her yellow jaconet, and I shall wear white. I will make you a wreath of syringa like stars. And you may wear your gloves."

"Oh-h!" breathed Deb. "And my cornelian ring — and the flowered scarf — and — and your fan, Jacqueline?"

"Yes," said Jacqueline. "I am tired this morning, Deb. The sunlight is so strong. I think I'll go darken my room, and lie down upon my bed."

"Does your head ache?"

"Yes, my head," said Jacqueline, and went into the house.

CHAPTER IV

THE TWO CANDIDATES

THE town, established forty years before this April morning, had been named for a Princess of Mecklenburg-Strelitz, lately become Queen of England. During the Revolution it had been the scene of a raid of Tarleton's and a camp of detention for British prisoners. It was the county seat to which three successive presidents of the United States must travel to cast their votes; and somewhat later than the period of this story it was to rub elbows with a great institution of learning. No city even in our own time, it was, a hundred years ago, slight enough in size to suit the genius for tempered solitude characteristic of a tobacco-growing State.

A few dwelling-houses of frame and brick rose from an emerald mist of gardens, and there were taverns, much at the service of all who came to town with money in their purse. The Swan allured the gentlefolk of the county, the coach-and-four people, Jehus of light curricles, and riders of blooded horses. The Eagle had the stage-coach patronage, and thrice a week blew a lusty horn. Besides the inns and the dwelling-houses there were stores and a half-built church, the Court House, and the shady Court House yard.

For a great part of the time, the Court House, the centre of gravity for the county, appeared to doze in the sunshine. At stated intervals, however, it awoke, and the drowsy town with it. Once awake, both became very wide awake indeed. Court days doubled the population; an election made a beehive of the place.

It was the fourth Wednesday in April, and election day. A man was to be sent to the House of Delegates at Richmond. All likelihood was upon the side of the candidate of the Democrat-Republicans, but the Federalists had a fighting chance. There were reasons why this especial election was of great interest to the county, and the motto of both parties was "No malingering!" Early in the morning, by the Three-Notched Road, the Barracks Road, and the Secretary's Road, through the shady Thoroughfare, over the misty Rivanna, the Hardware, and the Rapidan, the county began to pour electors into Charlottesville. They came upon wheels, on horseback, and afoot; the strong and the weak, the halt and the blind, the sick and the well, the old and the young, all the free men of Albemarle, all alert, all pleasurably excited over the prospect of the fight.

Without the Court House yard, under the locust trees to the right of the open gate, were placed long tables, and on them three mighty punch-bowls, flanked by drinking-cups and guarded by house servants of venerable appearance and stately manners. Here good Federalists refreshed themselves. To the left of the gate, upon the trampled grass beneath a mulberry, appeared other punch-bowls, and in addition a barrel of whiskey, ready broached for all good Democrat-Republicans. The sunny street was filled with horses, vehicles, and servants; the broad path between the trees, the turf on either hand, and the Court House steps were crowded with riotous voters. All ranks of society, all ages, occupations, and opinions, met in the genial weather, beneath the trees where sang every bird of spring.

Within the Court House the throng, slight at first, was rapidly increasing. The building was not large, and from end to end, and on the high window-sills beneath the long green blinds, the people pushed and shoved and stood a-tiptoe.

THE TWO CANDIDATES

It was yet early morning, and for some unexplained reason the Federalist candidate had not arrived.

Upon the Justice's Bench, raised high above the crowded floor, sat the candidate of the Democrat-Republicans — the Republicans, pure and simple, as they were beginning to be called. Near him stood the sheriff and the deputy-sheriff; around him pressed committee-men, heelers with tallies, vociferous well-wishers, and prophets of victory, and a few, a very few, personal and private friends. On the other hand, strongly gathering and impatiently awaiting their candidate, his foes gloomed upon him. Everywhere was a buzzing of voices: farmers and townspeople voting loudly, the sheriff as loudly recording each vote, the clerk humming over his book, the crowd making excited comment. There was no ballot-voting; it was a *viva voce* matter, and each man knew his fellow's creed.

Lewis Rand sat at ease, a tall and personable man, with the head of a victor, and a face that had the charm of strength. The eye was keen and dark, the jaw square, the thick brown hair cut short, as was the Republican fashion. His dress was plain but good, worn with a certain sober effect, an "it pleases me," that rendered silk and fine ruffles superfluous. He was listening to a wide-girthed tavern-keeper and old soldier of the Revolution's loud declaration that Lewis Rand was the coming man, and that he was for Lewis Rand. The old county wanted no English-thinking young Federalist in Richmond. "Too many Federalists there a'ready! Mr. Lewis Rand, Mr. Sheriff!"

The Republicans applauded. The custom of the time required that the man voted for should thank the man who voted, and that aloud and aptly, with no slurring acknowledgment of service. Lewis Rand, a born speaker and familiar with his audience, was at no loss. "I thank you, Mr.

Fagg! May your shadow never grow less! The old county — Mr. Jefferson's county, gentlemen — may be trusted to hold its own, in Richmond or in Washington, in Heaven or in Hell! Mr. Fagg, I will drink your health in punch of the Eagle's brewing! Your very obliged friend and servant!"

From street and yard without came a noise of cheering, with cries of "Black Cockade! Black Cockade! The party of Washington — Washington forever! — The old county for Cary! — Albemarle for Cary! — The county for a *gentleman!*"

"Mr. Ludwell Cary has arrived," announced the sheriff.

"Here comes the gentleman!" cried a man from a window-sill. "Stand up, Lewis Rand, and show him a man!"

The throng at the door parted, and with a Federalist and distinguished following the two Carys entered, the elder quiet and smiling, the younger flushed, bright-eyed, and anxious. The attachment between these two brothers was very strong; it was to be seen in every glance that passed between them, in every tone of voice used by each to the other. The elder played fond Mentor, and the younger thought his brother a demi-god. They were men of an old name, an old place, an inherited charm. "Ludwell Cary!" cried a man. "Long live Ludwell Cary!"

Rand left the Justice's Bench, stepped forward, and greeted his opponent. The two touched hands. "I trust I see you in health, Mr. Cary?"

"Mr. Rand, I thank you, I am very well. You are early in the lists!"

"I am accustomed to early rising," answered Rand. "This morning I have ridden from the Wolf Trap. Will you sit?"

"Ah," said Cary, "I rode from Fontenoy. After you, sir!"

They sat down, side by side, upon the Justice's Bench, the Federalist very easy, the Republican, lacking the perfection of

THE TWO CANDIDATES

the other's manner, with a stiffness and constraint of which he was aware and which he hated in himself. He knew himself well enough to know that presently, in the excitement of the race, the ugly mantle would slip from the braced athlete, but at the moment he felt his disadvantage. Subtly and slowly, released from some deep, central tarn of his most secret self, a vapour of distaste and dislike began to darken the cells of clear thought. As a boy he had admired and envied Ludwell Cary; for his political antagonist, pure and simple, he had, unlike most around him, often the friendliest feeling; but now, sitting there on the Justice's Bench, he wondered if he were going to hate Cary. Suddenly an image came out of the vapour. "How long has he been at Fontenoy? Does he think he can win there, too?"

The younger Cary marched to the polls with his head held high, and voted loudly for his brother. The latter smiled upon him, and said with simplicity, "Thank you, Fair!" The Republican candidate looked attentively at the young man. The spirit and the fire, subdued in the elder brother, was in the younger as visible as lightning. Rand was quick at divining men, and now he thought, "This man would make a tireless enemy."

Following Fairfax Cary came another of the group who had entered with the Carys. "Mr. Peyton votes for Mr. Ludwell Cary!" cried the sheriff. The Federalists applauded, the Republicans groaned, the tallymen took note, and Cary bowed his thanks. "Mr. Peyton, your very humble servant! Mount Eagle and Greenwood are old comrades-at-arms!"

"I'll kill *your* vote, Craven Peyton!" came a voice. "I vote, Mr. Sheriff, for Lewis Rand!"

"Ludwell Cary!" cried another, "and there's a killer killed, Dick Carr!"

"I'll draw a bead on you, Gentry!" put in a third. "The best shot in the county, Mr. Sheriff, and that's Lewis Rand!"

"Lewis Rand stands ten ahead!" cried a committee-man; and the sheriff, "Gentlemen, gentlemen! order at the polls!"

A small, wizened man, middle-aged and elaborately dressed in much ancient and tarnished finery, came bowing through the crowd. A curled wig shadowed a narrow face, and lace ruffles fell over long-fingered hands, yellow as old ivory. The entire figure was fantastic, even a little grotesque, though after a pleasant fashion. In a mincing voice and with a strong French accent, M. Achille Pincornet, dancing-master and performer on the violin, intimated that he wished to vote for Mr. Ludwell Cary. Lewis Rand glanced sharply up, then made a sign to a sandy-haired and freckled man who, tally in hand, stood near him.

"I challenge that vote!" cried the man with the tally.

"Mr. Pincornet's vote is challenged!" shouted the sheriff. "Order, order, gentlemen! Your reason, Mr. Mocket?"

"The gentleman is a Frenchman and not a citizen of the United States! He is not even a citizen of the French Republic! He is an émigré. He has no vote. Mark off his name!"

"Sir!" cried the challenged voter, "I am a de Pincornet, cadet of a house well known in Gascony! If I left France, I left it to find a great and free country, a country where one gentleman may serve another!"

A roar of laughter, led by Mocket, arose from the younger and lower sort of Republicans. "But you do serve, Mr. Pincornet! You teach all the 'Well-born' how to dance!"

"Did n't you teach the Carys? They dance beautifully."

"Are brocaded coats still worn in Gascony?"

"*Ne sutor supra crepidam judicaret!* Caper all you please on a waxed floor, but leave Virginians to rule!"

THE TWO CANDIDATES

Fairfax Cary, hot and angry, put in an oar. "Mr. Sheriff, Mr. Sheriff! Mr. Pincornet has lived these twelve years in Albemarle! We have no more respected, no more esteemed citizen. His vote's as good as any man's — and rather better, I may remark, than that of some men!" He looked pointedly at Mocket.

Lewis Rand gave his henchman a second guiding glance.

"It is merely," said Mocket promptly, "a question of that Alien Law of which the 'Well-born' are so proud. Show your papers, Mr. Pincornet. If you are a citizen of the United States, you have papers to show for it."

"Yes, sir," agreed the sheriff. "That's right, Mr. Mocket. Let me see your papers, Mr. Pincornet."

"Papers, papers! I have no papers!" cried Mr. Pincornet. "But every gentleman here — and I have no care for the canaille — knows that I live in Albemarle, in a small house between Greenwood and Fontenoy! I have lived there since I left France in the abhorred year of '92, with tears of rage in my eyes! I came to this land, where, seeing that I must eat, and that my dancing was always admired, I said to myself, '*Tenez*, Achille, my friend, we will teach these Virginians to dance!' Mr. Fairfax Cary has been my pupil, and it gives me pleasure to vote for his brother to go make the laws for my adopted country —"

"I'm sorry, Mr. Pincornet," interrupted the sheriff, "but you have no vote. I'll have to ask you to stand aside."

"Come up here, Mr. Pincornet," said Cary, from the Justice's Bench. "I want to ask you about a gentleman of your name whom I had the honour to meet in London — M. le Vicomte de Pincornet, a very gallant man —"

"That," said the dancing master, "would be my cousin Alexandre. He escaped during the Terror hidden under a load of hay, his son driving in a blouse and red nightcap.

Will Mr. Cary honour me?" and out came a tortoise-shell snuff-box.

The voting quickened. "Rand is ahead — Rand is winning!" went from mouth to mouth. Fairfax Cary, caring much where his brother cared little, welcomed impetuously the wave of Federalists which that rumour brought in from the yard and street. "Ha, Mr. Gilmer, Mr. Carter, you are welcome! Who votes? Who votes as General Hamilton and Mr. Adams and Judge Marshall vote? Who votes as *Washington* would have voted?"

So many crowded to vote as Washington would have voted, that it almost seemed as though his shade might lead the Federalists to victory. But the dead Washington must cope with the living Jefferson; mild monarchism and stately rule with a spirit born of time, nursed by Voltaire and Jean-Jacques Rousseau, grown articulate in the French Revolution, and now full swing toward majority. When thrown, the Democrat-Republicans rose from the earth like Antæus. Much of the gentle blood and many of the prominent men of the county voted for Lewis Rand. Jefferson's personal following of friends and kinsmen was large; these accepted his man as a matter of course, while to the plain men of the county Lewis Rand was more even than the coming man: he was of them; he was a plain man. The clamour and excitement grew. "Here come the Three-Notched Road people!" cried a voice. "They all rolled tobacco with Gideon Rand!"

The Three-Notched Road people voted to a man for the son of Gideon Rand, and were promptly reinforced by a contingent of hot Republicans from the Ragged Mountains. At ten o'clock Lewis Rand was again well ahead, but at this hour there was a sharp rally of the Federalists. A cheering from without announced the arrival of some popular voter, and Colonel Churchill and his brother, Major Edward, and an array of Federalists from the Fontenoy district, entered the Court House.

"The Churchills are coming, Oho! Oho!" sang out a wag perched on the window-sill.

"Not to that tune," roared a Scot from the gallery. "Mon, they're Tories!"

"Gentlemen, gentlemen! order at the polls!" shouted the sheriff. "Colonel Churchill, for whom do you vote?"

"I vote, sir," cried the Colonel, "for Mr. Ludwell Cary, for a gentleman and a patriot, sir, and may the old county never be represented but by such!"

"Order, order at the polls! Colonel Churchill votes for Mr. Ludwell Cary! Major Edward Churchill, whom do you vote for?"

"For whom do you suppose, Mr. Sheriff?" said the Major. "For Mr. Ludwell Cary."

Cary rose from the bench and stepped forward to the edge of the platform. "Colonel Dick, Major Edward, I thank you both. May I deserve your confidence and your favour! Fontenoy is as dear to me as Greenwood."

"By God, you shall win, Ludwell!" cried Colonel Dick. "Here's a regiment of us to see you through!"

"Rome hasn't fallen yet," added Major Edward. "I don't hear the geese cackling."

"One's cackling now," smiled Cary, and Mr. Tom Mocket stepped up to the polls.

"It's not a goose; it's a turkey buzzard!"

"It's not feathered at all," said Fairfax Cary. "It's a mangy jackal to a mangy lion."

The young man had spoken loudly and contemptuously. Rand, on the Justice's Bench, and Mocket, in the act of voting, both heard, and both looked his way. Ludwell Cary knit his brows, and meeting his brother's eyes, slightly shook his head. Look and gesture said, "Leave abuse alone, Fair."

Mocket voted for Rand. "I challenge that vote!" cried Major Edward Churchill. "The man's been in prison."

Amid the noise that followed, the Jackal was heard to cry, "It's a lie! Lewis, tell them it's a lie! Major Churchill, you'd better be careful! I was acquitted, and you know it."

"Do I?" answered the Major coolly. "I know that you ought to be making shoes in the penitentiary! Mr. Sheriff, you should really have this courtroom sprinkled with vinegar. There's gaol fever in the air."

"I don't see, Mr. Sheriff," came Rand's voice from the Justice's Bench, "that any more vinegar is needed. Gentlemen, all — whether Federalist or Republican — I was Mr. Mocket's lawyer in the case referred to. Twelve good men and true — men of this county — pronounced him innocent. It is not surprising that my friends the Federalists should wish to gain time, — they are leagued with old Time, — but I protest against their gaining it by such means. This is not a matter of parties; it is a matter of a man being held innocent till he is proved guilty. A hundred men here can testify as to the verdict in this case. Mr. Mocket, gentlemen —" He paused and regarded the sandy-haired and freckled Tom, the brother of little Vinie, the sometime doorboy in Chancellor Wythe's law office, with a smile so broadly humorous, humane, and tolerant, that suddenly the courtroom smiled with him. "Tom Mocket, gentlemen, is a scamp, but he's not a scoundrel! The election proceeds, Mr. Sheriff."

"I vote for Lewis Rand!" shouted the scamp out of the uproar. "Richmond now, then Washington! We'll send Lewis Rand as high as he can go!"

THE TWO CANDIDATES

"As high as the gallows!" growled Major Edward Churchill.

"Send him," said a voice in the doorway, "out West. Mr. Jefferson gained Louisiana, but 't will take a stronger man to gain Mexico. Mexico wants a Buonaparte."

The day wore on with no lessening of heat and clamour. The Court House becoming too full, men betook themselves to the yard or to the street, where, mounted on chairs or on wagons from which the horses had been taken, they harangued their fellows. Public speaking came easily to this race. To-day good liquor and emulation pricked them on, and the spring in the blood. Under the locusts to the right of the gate Federalists apostrophized Washington, lauded Hamilton, the Judiciary, and the beauty of the English Constitution, denounced the French, denounced the Louisiana Purchase, denounced the Man of the People, and his every tool and parasite, and lifted to the skies the name of Ludwell Cary. To the left of the gate, under the locusts, the Republicans praised the President of the United States and all his doings, and poured oblation to Lewis Rand. From side to side of the path there were alarms and incursions. Before noon there had occurred a number of hand-to-hand fights, one, at least, accompanied by "gouging," and a couple of duels had been arranged.

In the courtroom the parties jostled each other at the polls, and the candidates, side by side upon the Justice's Bench, watched the day go now this way and now that. Their partisans they must acceptably thank, and they must be quick of wit with their adversaries. Fatigue did not count, nor hoarseness from much speaking, nor an undercurrent of consciousness that there were, after all, more parties than two, more principles than those they advocated, more colours than black and white, more epithets than hero and villain.

They must act in their moment, and accept its excitement. A colour burned in their cheeks, and the hair lay damp upon their foreheads. They must listen and answer to men saying loudly to their faces and before other men, "I hold with you, and your mind is brother to my mind"; or saying, "I hold not with you, and you and your mind are abominable to me! To outer darkness with you both!"

Sometimes they consulted with their committee-men, and sometimes punch was brought, and they drank with their friends. Occasionally they spoke to each other; when they did this, it was with extreme courtesy. Cary used the buttoned foil with polished ease. Rand's manner was less assured; there was something antique and laboured in his determined grasp at the amenities of the occasion. It was the only heaviness. To the other contest between them he brought an amazing sureness, a suppleness, power, and audacity beyond praise. He directed his battle, and at his elbow Tom Mocket, sandy-haired and ferret-eyed, did him yeoman service.

At one o'clock there was an adjournment for dinner. The principal Federalists betook themselves to the Swan; the principal Republicans to the Eagle. The commonalty ate from the packed baskets upon the trampled grass of the Court House yard. An hour later, when the polls were reopened, men returned to them flushed with drink and in the temper for a quarrel, the Republicans boisterous over a foreseen victory, the Federalists peppery from defeat. In the yard the constable had to part belligerents, in the courtroom the excitement mounted. The tide was set now for Lewis Rand. The Federalists watched it with angry eyes; the Republicans greeted with jubilation each new wave. The defeated found some relief in gibes. "Holoa! here's Citizen Bonhomme — red breeches, cockade, and Brutus crop!

"Ah, ça ira, ça ira, ça ira!"

THE TWO CANDIDATES

"That man ran away from Tarleton! — yes, you did, the very day that Mr. Jefferson — a-hem! — *absented* himself from Monticello!"

"Challenge that man — he deserted in the Indian War!
> "November the fourth, in the year ninety-one,
> We had a sore engagement near to Fort Jefferson!"

"Here's a traveller who has seen the mammoth and climbed the Salt Mountain!"

"Here's a tobacco-roller! Hey, my man, don't you miss old friends on the road?"

Under cover of the high words, laughter, and vituperation which made a babel of the courtroom, Cary spoke to his opponent. "Mr. Rand, do you remember that frosty morning, long ago, when you and I first met? I came upon you in the woods, and together we gathered chinquapins. Does it seem long to you since you were a boy?"

"Long enough!" answered Rand. "I remember that day very well."

"We told each other our names, I remember, and what each meant to do in the world. We hardly foresaw this day."

"It is not easy to foresee," said Rand slowly. "If we could, we might —"

"We might foresee our last meeting," smiled Cary, "as we remember our first." He took a glass of wine from a passing servant and put it to his lips, "To another meeting, in the wood!" he said, "since I may not quite drink to your victory."

"Ah, my victory!" answered Rand. "When I have it, I don't know that I shall care for it! That's a handsome youth, your brother — and he has worked for you like a Trojan! I'll drink to your brother!"

"Here are the Green Spring folk!" cried a voice. "They always vote like gentlemen!"

The Green Spring folk were a squadron, and they voted Cary again within sight of the goal. A man who had been standing just without the open door rested his long musket against the wall and advanced to the polls. "Last time I voted here," he said, "'t was for Mr. Jefferson. I reckon I'll have to vote to-day for Lewis Rand."

A tumult arose. "Adam Gaudylock belongs upon the Mississippi! — He isn't an Albemarle man! — He's a Kentuck — He's a Louisianian — He's a subject of Jefferson's new kingdom! — Challenged! — He can't vote in Albemarle!"

The hunter waited for the uproar to cease. "You Federalists are mighty poor shots!" he exclaimed at last. "You make no account of the wind. I am subject of no man's kingdom. I trade in New Orleans, and I travel on the great rivers, and I've friends in Kentucky, and I hunt where the hunting's good, but when I want to vote I come back to my own county where I was born, and where I grew up among you all, and where I've yet a pretty piece of land between here and the mountains. I voted here before, and I'll vote here again. The Gaudylocks may wander and wander, but their home is on the Three-Notched Road, and they vote in Albemarle."

The vote standing, and Adam being followed by a string of hunters, traders, and boatmen, the Republican candidate was again and finally in advance. The winds blew for him from the four quarters. In the last golden light of the afternoon there was a strong and sudden muster of Republicans. From all directions stragglers appeared, voice after voice proclaiming for the man who, regarded at first as merely a protégé of Jefferson, had come in the last two years to be regarded for himself. The power in him had ceased to be latent, and friend and foe were beginning to watch Lewis Rand and his doings with intentness.

THE TWO CANDIDATES

As the sun set behind the Ragged Mountains, the polls closed, and the sheriff proclaimed the election of the Republican candidate.

The Court House was quickly emptied, nor was the Court House yard far behind. The excitement had spent itself. The result, after all, had been foreknown. It drew on chilly with the April dusk, and men were eager to be at home, seated at their supper-tables, going over the day with captured friends and telling the women the news. On wheels, on horseback or afoot, drunk and sober, north, south, east, and west, they cantered, rolled, and trudged away from the brick Court House and the trampled grass, and the empty bowls beneath the locust trees.

The defeated candidate and the successful shook hands: Cary quiet and smiling, half dignified and half nonchalant; Rand with less control and certainty of himself. The one said with perfection the proper things, the other said them to the best of his ability. Young Fairfax Cary, standing by, twisting his riding-whip with angry fingers, curled his lip at the self-made man's awkwardness of phrase. Rand saw the smile, but went on with his speech. Colonel Churchill, who had been talking with Adam Gaudylock, left the hunter and came up to Cary. "Ludwell, you and Fair are not going to Greenwood to-night! I have orders from the ladies to bring you back to Fontenoy — alive or dead!"

"I find myself very much alive, Colonel!" answered Cary. "Thank you, I'll gladly spend the night at Fontenoy. Fontenoy would draw me, I think, if I *were* dead!"

"Dick has a middling Madeira," remarked Major Edward. "And after supper Jacqueline shall sing to us. Good-evening, Mr. Rand!"

"Good-evening to you, Major Churchill," said Rand. "Good-evening, Mr. Cary. Good-evening, gentlemen!"

"Here are Eli and Mingo with the horses," said Fairfax Cary, his back to the Republican. "Let's away, Ludwell!"

Colonel Churchill laughed. "Fontenoy draws you too, Fairfax? Well, my niece Unity is a pleasing minx — yes, by gad! Miss Dandridge is a handsome jade! Come away, come away, gentlemen!"

Federalists and Republicans exchanged the stiffest of bows, and the party for Fontenoy mounted and took the road. The Republicans whom they left behind had a few moments of laughter and jubilation, and then they also quitted the Court House yard and called to the servants for the horses.

"You'll spend the night at Edgehill, I hope, Mr. Rand?" cried one. "Mrs. Randolph expects you — she will wish to write to her father of your day —"

"No, no, come with me!" put in another. "There's all this business to talk over — and I've a letter to show you from Mr. Madison —"

"Best come to the Eagle!" cried a third. "No end of jolly fellows, and bumpers to next year —"

Rand shook his head. "Thank you, Colonel Randolph — but I am riding to Monticello. Mr. Jefferson has written for some papers from the library. Burwell will care for me to-night. Present, if you will, my humble services to Mrs. Randolph and the young ladies. By the same token I cannot go with you, Mr. Carr, nor to the Eagle, Mr. Jones. — My grateful thanks to you, one and all, gentlemen! I am a plain man — I can say no more. We will ride together as far as the creek."

The negro Joab brought his horse, a magnificent animal, the gift of Jefferson. He mounted and the party kept together as far as the creek, where their ways parted. Rand checked his horse, said good-bye, and watched the gentlemen who had given him their support ride cheerfully away

THE TWO CANDIDATES

toward the light of home. He himself was waiting for Adam Gaudylock, who was going with him to Monticello. After a moment's thought he decided not to wait there beside the creek, but to turn his horse and leave a message for Tom Mocket at a house which he had passed five minutes before.

CHAPTER V

MONTICELLO

THE house, a low frame one, stood back from the road, in a tangle of old, old flowering shrubs. Rand drew rein before the broken gate, and a young woman in a linsey gown rose from the porch step and came down the narrow path toward him. She carried an earthenware pitcher and cup. "It's water just from the well," she said, "fresh and cool. Won't you have some?"

"Yes, I will," answered Rand. "Vinie, why don't you mend that gate?"

"I don't know, thir," said Vinie. "Tom's always going to."

Rand laughed. "Don't call me 'thir'! Vinie, I'm elected."

Vinie set down her pitcher beside a clump of white phlox and wiped her hands on the skirt of her linsey dress. "Are you going away to Richmond?" she asked.

"Not until October. When I do I'll go see the little old house you used to live in, Vinie!"

"It's torn down," remarked Vinie soberly. "Here's Tom now, and — and —"

"Adam Gaudylock. Don't you remember Adam?"

The hunter and Tom Mocket came up together. "We beat them! we beat them, hey, Lewis!" grinned the scamp; and Gaudylock cried, "Why, if here isn't the little partridge again! Don't you want to see what I've got in my pouch?"

"Yeth, thir," said Vinie.

Rand and his lieutenant talked together in a low voice, Mocket leaning against black Selim's neck, Rand stooping a little, and with earnestness laying down the law of the case. They talked for ten minutes, and then Rand gathered up the reins, asked for another cup of water, and with a friendly "Good-bye, Vinie!" rode off toward Monticello, Adam Gaudylock going with him.

Brother and sister watched the riders down the road until the gathering dark and the shadow of the trees by the creek hid them from sight. "Just wait long enough and we'll see what we see," quoth Tom. "Lewis Rand's going to be a great man!"

"How great?" asked Vinie. "Not as great as Mr. Jefferson?"

"I don't know," the scamp answered sturdily. "He might be. One thing's certain, anyhow; he's not built like Mr. Madison or Mr. Monroe. He'll not be content to travel the President's road always. He'll have a road all his own." The scamp's imagination, not usually lively, bestirred itself under the influence of the day, of wine, and the still audible sound of horses' hoofs. "By George, Vinie! it will be a Roman road, hard, paved, and fit for triumphs! He thinks it won't, but he's mistaken. He does n't see himself!"

Vinie took the pitcher from beneath the white phlox. "It's getting dark. Tom, are n't we ever going to have that gate mended? — He's going away to Richmond in October."

The successful candidate and Adam Gaudylock, followed by Joab on a great bay horse, crossed Moore's Creek, and took the Monticello road. A red light yet burned in the west, but the trees were dark along the way, and the hollows filled with shadow. The dew was falling, the evening dank and charged with perfume.

"I asked you to come with me," said Rand, "because I

wanted to talk to some one out of the old life. Mocket's out of the old life too, he and Vinie. But —" he laughed. "They're afraid of me. Vinie calls me 'thir.'"

"Well, I'm not afraid of you," Adam said placidly. "No one at home at Monticello?"

"No, but Burwell keeps a room in readiness. I am often there on errands for Mr. Jefferson. Well, how go matters west of the mountains?"

"Christmas I spent at Louisville," answered Gaudylock, "and then went down the river to New Orleans. The city's like a hive before swarming. There are more boats at its wharves than buds on yonder Judas tree. And back from the river the cotton's blooming now."

"Ah!" said Rand, "I should like to see that land! When you have done a thing, Adam, a thing that you have striven with all your might to do, does it at once seem to you a small thing to have done? It does to me — tasteless, soulless, and poor, not worth a man's while. Where lies the land of satisfaction?"

"No," answered Adam, "I don't look at things that way. But then I'm not ambitious. Last year, in New Orleans, I watched a man gaming. He won a handful of French crowns. 'Ha!' says he, 'they glittered, but they do not glitter now! Again!' — and this time he won doubloons. 'We'll double these,' says he, and so they did, and he won. 'This is a small matter,' he said. 'We'll play for double-eagles,' and so they did, and he won. 'Have n't you a tract of sugar-canes?' says he. 'Money's naught. Let us play for land!' and he won the sugar-canes. 'That girl, that red-lipped Jeanne of thine, that black eye in the Street of Flowers — I'll play for her! Deal the cards!' But he never won the girl, and he lost the sugar-canes and the gold."

"A man walks forward, or he walks backward. There's

no standing still in this world or the next. Where were you after New Orleans, before you turned homeward?"

"At Mr. Blennerhassett's island in the Ohio. And that's a pleasant place and a pleasant gentleman —"

"Listen!"

"Aye," answered the other; "I heard it some moments back. Some one is fiddling beyond that tulip tree."

They were now ascending the mountain, moving between great trees, fanned by a cooler wind than had blown in the valley. The road turned, showing them a bit of roadside grass, a giant tulip tree, and a vision of a moon just rising in the east. Upon a log, beneath the tree, appeared the dim brocade and the curled wig of M. Achille Pincornet, resting in the twilight and solacing his soul with the air of "Madelon Friquet." Around him sparkled the fireflies, and above were the thousand gold cups of the tulip tree. His bow achieved a long tremolo; he lowered the violin from his chin, stood up, and greeted the travellers.

"That was a pretty air, Mr. Pincornet," said Rand. "Why are you on the Monticello road? Your next dancing class is at Fontenoy."

"And how did you know that, sir?" demanded the Frenchman in his high, thin voice. As he spoke, he restored his fiddle to its case with great care, then as carefully brushed all leaf and mould from his faded silken clothes.

"I know — I know," replied Rand. He regarded the figure in dusty finery with a certain envy of any one who was going to Fontenoy, even as dancing master, even as a man no longer young. Mr. Pincornet looked, in the twilight, very pinched, very grey, very hungry. "Come on with me to Monticello," said the young man. "Burwell will give us supper, and find us a couple of bottles to boot."

"Sir," answered the Frenchman stiffly, but with an

inner vision of Monticello cheer, "I would not vote for you —"

Rand laughed. "I bear no malice, Mr. Pincornet. Opinion's but opinion. I'll cut no traveller's throat because he likes another road than mine! Come, come! Fish from the river, cakes and coffee, Mr. Pincornet — and afterwards wine on the terrace!"

The road climbed on. Between the stems of the tall trees, feathered with the green of mid-spring, the dogwood displayed its stars, and the fringe tree rose like a fountain. Everywhere was the sound of wind in the leaves. When the riders and the dancing master, who was afoot, reached the crest of the little mountain, shaven and planed by the hand of man into a fair plateau, the moon was shining brightly. In the silver light, across the dim lawns, classically simple, grave, and fair, rose the house that Jefferson had built. The gate clanged behind the party from Charlottesville, a dog barked, a light flared, voices of negroes were heard, and hurrying feet from the house quarter. Upon the lawn to the right and left of the mansion were two toy houses, tiny brick offices used by Jefferson for various matters. The door of one of these now opened, and Mr. Bacon, the overseer, hastening across the wet grass, greeted Rand and Gaudylock as they dismounted before the white portico.

"Evening, evening, Mr. Rand! I knew you'd be coming up, so I hurried on afore ye. Cæsar and Joab, you take the horses round! Glad to see you, Adam; you too, Mr. Pincornet! Well, Mr. Rand, you spoiled the Egyptians this day! I never saw a finer election! Me and Mr. Fagg were talking of you. 'His father was a fighter before him,' says Mr. Fagg, says he, 'and he's a fighter, too, damn him!' says he, 'and we'll send him higher yet. Damn the Federalists!' says he. 'He's a taller man than Ludwell Cary!'"

"I'm a mighty hungry man, Mr. Bacon," said Rand. "And so is Adam, and so is Mr. Pincornet! You'll take supper with us, I hope? We'll make Adam Gaudylock tell us stories of Louisiana."

"Thank'ee, Mr. Rand, I will. Your room's all ready, sir, and Burwell shall bring you a julep. I reckon you're pretty tired. Lord! I'd rather clear a mountain side and then plough it, than to have to sit there all day on that there Justice's Bench and listen to them Federalists! They're a lot! And that Fairfax Cary — he's a chip of the old block, he surely is! He'd have gone through fire to-day to see his brother win. This way, gentlemen! Sally'll have supper ready in a jiffy. I smell the coffee now. Well, well, Mr. Rand! to think of the way you used to trudge up here all weathers, snow or storm or hot sun, just for a book — and now you come riding in on Selim, elected to Richmond, over the heads of the Carys! Life's queer, ain't it? We'll hear of you at Fontenoy next!"

Rand smiled. "Life's not so queer as that, Mr. Bacon. I wish you might —" he broke off.

"Might what?" asked Bacon.

"Hear of me at Fontenoy," answered Rand, and entered the wide hall as one who was at home there. "I'll go bathe my face and hands," he said, and turned into the passage that led to the bedrooms.

A tall clock struck the hour, a bell rang cheerfully, and Burwell flung open the dining-room door. Rand, entering a moment later, found the overseer, the hunter, and the dancing master awaiting him. With a nod and a "Ha, Burwell!" for the old servant, he took his place at the table, and he took it like a prince, throwing his tall, vigorous figure into the armchair which marked the head of the board, seating himself before the other and older men. In the wave of his hand toward the three remaining places there was a condescension not the less remarkable that it was entirely unconscious. The life within him was moving with great rapidity. It was becoming increasingly natural for him to act, simply, without thought, as his inner man bade. What yesterday was uneasiness, and to-day seemed assurance, was apt by to-morrow to attain convincingness. It was not that he appeared to value himself too highly. Instead, he made no attempt at valuation; he went his way like wind or wave. He took the armchair at the head of the Monticello table with the simplicity of a child, and the bearing of a general who sups with his officers after a victorious field.

The unfolding of the petal was not missed by his companions. Adam Gaudylock, with a glance, half shrewd and half affectionate, for the man whom he had known from boyhood, sank into the opposite seat with a light and happy laugh. It mattered little to Adam where he sat in life, provided that it was before a window. The overseer, a worthy, plain man, had a thought of old Gideon Rand, but, remembering in time Mr. Jefferson's high opinion of the man now occupying his chair, sat down and unfolded his damask napkin with great care. Mr. Pincornet, indeed, raised his eyebrows and made a backward movement from the table, but at that moment a mulatto boy appeared with a plate of waffles. The light from the wax candles burned, too, in certain crimson decanters. "Sit down, sit down, Mr. Pincornet!" said Rand, and the dancing master took the remaining place.

An hour later Rand pushed back his heavy chair and rose from the table, ending the meal with as little ceremony as he had used in beginning it. "I shall go write to Mr. Jefferson," he announced, as the four passed into the hall. "You, Adam, what will you do?"

"First I'll smoke and then I'll sleep," said Adam. The

moonlight streamed in upon them through the open hall door. "I'll smoke outside. That's a southern moon.

> "Kiss me, kiss me, flower o' night!
> Madelon!
> 'Ware the voices, 'ware the light!
> Madelon!

Will you smoke with me, Mr. Bacon? I'd like to try the Monticello leaf."

"I have to go to the quarters for a bit," answered the overseer. "There's sickness there. I'll join you later, Mr. Gaudylock."

He went whistling away. Adam sat down upon the broad steps whitened by the moon, filled his pipe, struck a spark from his flint and steel, and was presently enveloped in fragrant smoke. The dancing-master, hesitating somewhat disconsolately in the hall, at last went also into the moonlight, where he walked slowly up and down upon the terrace, his thin, beruffled hands clasped behind his old brocaded coat. What with the moonlight and the ancient riches of his apparel, and a certain lost and straying air, he had the seeming of a phantom from some faint, bewigged, perfumed, and painted past.

Lewis Rand paused for a moment before the door, and looked out upon the splendid night, then turned and passed into the library, where he called for candles, and, sitting down at a desk, began to write. His letter was to the President of the United States, and it was written freely and boldly. "'T was thus they did — 't was so I did. We won, and I am glad; they lost, and that also is to my liking. As the party owes its victory to your name and your power, so I owe my personal victory to your ancient and continued kindness. May my name be abhorred if ever I forget it! The Federalists mustered strongly. Mr. Ludwell Cary is extremely 'well born,' and that younger brother of his is — I know not why, he troubles me. There is a breath of the future about him, and it breathes cold. Well! I have fought and I have won. 'Let the blast of the desert come: I shall be renowned in my day!' To-night, you see, I quote Ossian. The moon is flooding the terrace. Were you here in your loved home, we would talk together. Adam Gaudylock is with me. Lately he was in Louisiana, and then with a Mr. Blennerhassett upon the Ohio. General Wilkinson is at New Orleans. The Spaniards are leaving, the French well affected. The mighty tide of our people has topped the mountains and is descending into those plains of the Mississippi made ours by your prophetic vision and your seizure of occasion. The First Consul is a madman! He has sold to us an Empire! Empire! Emperor — Emperor of the West! The sound is stately. You laugh. We are citizens of a republic. Well! I am content. I aspire no higher. I am not Buonaparte. Your lilies are budding beneath the windows; the sweet williams are all in bloom. I have little news for you of town or country — Mrs. Randolph, doubtless, sends you all. Work goes on upon the church. For me, I worship in the fields with the other beasts of burden or of prey. The wheat looks well, and there will be this year a great yield of apples. Major Churchill's Mustapha won at Winchester. Colonel Churchill has cleared a large tract of woods behind Fontenoy and will use it for tobacco. I rode by his plant bed the other day, and the leaf is prime. I am a judge of tobacco. They are bitter, the Fontenoy men. Mr. Ludwell Cary will, I suppose, remain in the county. He is altering and refurnishing Greenwood. I suppose that he will marry. The rains have been frequent this spring, the roads heavy and the rivers turbid. The stream is much swollen by my house on the Three-Notched Road. We hear that the feeling grows between

General Hamilton and Aaron Burr. Should the occasion arise, pray commend me to the latter, whose acquaintance I had the honour to make last year when I visited New York. There, if you please, is a spirit restless and audacious! The mill on the Rockfish is grinding this spring. The murder case of which I wrote you will be tried next court day. One Fitch killed one Thomas Dole in North Garden; knocked at his door one night, called him out, and shot him down. Dole had thwarted Fitch in some project or other. I am retained by the State, and I mean to hang Fitch. Adam Gaudylock says there is a region of the Mississippi where the cotton grows taller than a man's head. We may find our gold of Ophir in that plant. To-night I am a victor. I salute you, so much oftener than I a victor! But victory is a mirage: this that I thought so fair is but a piece of the desert; the *magnum bonum* shines, looms, and beckons still ahead! Had I been defeated, I believe I should have been in better spirits. Now to the papers which you desired me to read and comment upon: I find —"

The quill travelled on, conveying to sheet after sheet the opinion upon certain vexed questions of a very able lawyer. The analysis was keen, the reasoning just, the judgment final, the advice sound. The years since that determinative hour in the Richmond book-shop had been well harvested. The paper when he had finished it would have pleased the ideal jurist.

He wrote until the clock struck ten; then folded, sealed, and superscribed his letter, pushed back the heavy hair from his forehead, and rose from the desk. The long windows opened upon the terrace, and through them came the moonbeams and the fragrance of the April night — music too, for Mr. Pincornet was playing the violin. The young man extinguished the candles, and stepped into the silvery world without the room. Adam Gaudylock had disappeared, and the overseer was gone to bed. Lights were out in the quarters; the house was as still and white as a mansion in a fairy tale. Mr. Pincornet was no skilled musician, but the air he played was old and sweet, and it served the hour. Below their mountain-top lay the misty valleys; to the east the moon-flooded plains; to the west the far line of the Blue Ridge. The night was cloudless.

Rand stood with his hands upon the balustrade, then walked down the terrace and paused before the dancing master. "Before he hurt his hand Mr. Jefferson played the violin beautifully," he said. "When I was younger, in the days when I tried to do everything that he did, I tried to learn it too. But I have no music in me."

"It is a solace," answered Mr. Pincornet. "I learned long ago, in the South."

"I like the harp," announced Rand abruptly.

"It is a becoming instrument to a woman," replied Mr. Pincornet, and in a somewhat ghostly fashion became vivacious. "Ah, a rounded arm, a white hand, the rise and fall of a bosom behind the gold wires — and the notes like water dropping, sweet, sweet! Ah, I, too, like the harp!"

"I have never heard it but twice," said Rand, and turned again to the balustrade. Below him lay the vast and shadowy landscape. Here and there showed a light — a pale earth-star shining from grey hill or vale. Rand looked toward Fontenoy, and he looked wistfully. Behind him the violin was telling of the springtime; from the garden came the smell of the syringas; the young man's desire was toward a woman. "Is she playing her harp to-night? Is she playing to Ludwell Cary?"

"Belle saison de ma jeunesse —
Beaux jours du printemps!"

sang the violin. A shot sounded near the house. Adam Gaudylock emerged from the shadow of the locust trees and crossed the moonlit lawn below the terrace. "I've shot that night-hawk. He'll maraud no more," he said, and passed on toward his quarter for the night.

Rand made a motion as if to follow, then checked himself. It was late, and it had been a day of strife, but his iron frame felt no fatigue and his mood was one of sombre exaltation. What was the use of going to bed, of wasting the moonlit hours? He turned to the Frenchman. "Play me," he commanded, "a conquering air! Play me the Marseillaise!"

Mr. Pincornet started violently. Down came the fiddle from his chin, the bow in his beruffled hand cut the air with a gesture of angry repudiation. When he was excited he forgot his English, and he now swore volubly in French; then, recovering himself, stepped back a pace, and regarded with high dudgeon his host of the night. "Sir," he cried, "before I became a dancing master I was a French gentleman! I served the King. I will teach you to dance, but — Morbleu! — I will not play you the Marseillaise!"

"I beg your pardon," said Rand. "I forgot that you could not be a Republican. Well, play me a fine Royalist air."

"Are you so indifferent?" asked the dancing master, not without a faded scorn. "Royalist or Republican — either air?"

"Indifferent?" repeated Rand. "I don't know that I am indifferent. Open-minded, perhaps, — though I don't know that that is calling it rightly. The airs the angels sing, and the thundering march of the damned through hell — why should I not listen to them both? I don't believe in hell, nor much in angels, save one, but I like the argument. Mr. Pincornet, I don't want to sleep. Suppose — suppose you teach me a minuet?"

He laughed as he spoke, but he spoke in earnest. "Knowledge! I want all kinds of knowledge. I know law, and I know what to do with a jury, and I know tobacco — worse luck! — but I don't know the little things, the little gracious things that — that make a man liked. If I were a Federalist, and if I did n't know so much about tobacco, I would go, Mr. Pincornet, to your dancing class at Fontenoy!" He laughed again. "I can't do that, can I? The Churchills would all draw their swords. Come! I have little time and few chances to acquire that which I have longed for always, — the grace of life. Teach me how to enter a drawing-room; how to — how to dance with a lady!"

His tone, imperious when he demanded the Marseillaise, was now genial, softened to a mellow persuasiveness. Mr. Pincornet shrugged his shoulders. He had been offended, but he was not unmagnanimous, and he had a high sense of the importance of his art. He had seen in France what came of uncultivated law-givers. If a man wanted knowledge, far be it from Achille de Pincornet to withhold his handful! "You cannot learn in a night," he said, "but I will show you the steps."

"I can manage a country dance, a reel or Congo," said Rand simply. "I want to know politer things."

They left the terrace, went into the drawing-room, and lit the candles. The floor, rubbed each morning until it shone, gave back the heart-shaped flames. The slight furniture they pushed aside. The dancing master tucked his violin under his chin, drew the bow across the strings, and began the lesson.

The candles burned clear, strains of the *minuet de la cour* rose and fell in the ample room, the member from Albemarle and Mr. Pincornet stepped, bent, and postured with the gravity of Indian sachems. The one moved through the minuet in top-boots and riding-coat, the other taught in what had been a red brocade. Rand, though tall and largely built, moved with the step and carriage, light and lithe, of one who has used the woods; the Frenchman had the suppleness of his profession and of an ancient courtier. Now they bowed one to the other, now each to an imaginary lady. Mr. Pincornet issued directions in the tone of a general ordering a charge, his pupil obeyed implicitly. In the silent house, raised high on a mountain-top above a sleeping world, in the lit room with many open windows, through which poured the fragrance of spring, they practised until midnight the *minuet de la cour*. The hour struck; they gravely ceased to dance, and after five minutes spent in mutual compliments, closed the long windows and put out the superfluous lights, then said good-night, and, bedroom candle in hand, repaired each to his own chamber. Rand had risen at dawn, and his day had been a battlefield, but before he lay down in the dimity-hung, four-post bed he sat long at the window of his small, white, quiet room. The moon shone brightly; the air was soft and sweet. In the distance a lamb bleated, then all was still again. The young man rested his chin on his hand, and studied the highest stars. That day a milestone had been passed. He saw his road stretching far, far before him, and he saw certain fellow travellers, but the companion whom his heart cried for he could not see.

"Her way and mine are far apart — are far apart. I had better marry Vinie Mocket." He spoke half aloud and with bitterness, looking from the window toward Fontenoy. Suddenly the water smarted in his eyes, and he stretched out his arms. "Oh, pardon, love!" he whispered, "I love but you — and I'll love you to the end!" His fancy dwelt on Fontenoy. It was for him enchanted land, the sleeping palace, strongly hedged. "But I am not the appointed man," he thought. "I am a pauper, and no prince. It is Ludwell Cary that goes in and out."

CHAPTER VI

RAND COMES TO FONTENOY

"I NEVER dance but by candlelight," remarked Unity. "A Congo in the heat of the afternoon, a jig before sunset, — la! I had rather plough by moonlight. As well be a grasshopper in a daisy field! Elegance by waxlight becomes rusticity in the sunshine, — and of all things I would not be rustic! Oh, Mr. Cary, I've caught my gown in this rosebush!"

Mr. Fairfax Cary knelt to release the muslin prisoner. "Rusticity becomes you so that if I were a king, you should dance with me the livelong day. But I'll not grumble if only you'll dance with me as soon as the candles are lit! Last night you were all for that booby, Ned Hunter!"

"He's no booby," said Miss Dandridge. "He is bashful — though, indeed, I think he is only bashful in company! We sat on the porch, and he told me the long history of his life."

"Confound his impudence —"

"Oh, it was interesting as — as the Mysteries of Udolpho! You are a long time over that briar, Mr. Cary. There! thank you! Listen to Mr. Pincornet's fiddle. Scrape, scrape, scrape! The children are dancing, and Jacqueline is helping them. Jacqueline is always helping some one. But Mr. Pincornet thinks it is because she is in love with him. He is sorry for her because he rather prefers me. I am in love with him too. So is Molly Carter, so is Anne Page, and so will be little Deb as soon as she is old enough. He is fifty, and French, and a dancing master, and he wears an old, old, lace cravat and a powdered wig! When are we going back to the house, Mr. Cary?"

"Let us walk a little farther!" pleaded the gentleman. "It is cool and pleasant, with no fuss, and no Ned Hunter, with the history of his life, confound him! Other men have histories as well as he! Your gown looks so pretty against the leaves. Let us walk down to the lower gate."

Unity pursed her red lips, and considered the distance with velvety black eyes. "I have on my dancing shoes,— but perhaps you will help me across the brook!"

"I will," declared Fairfax Cary, and, when the brook was reached, was as good as his word.

"I shall tell Uncle Dick to put safer stepping-stones," quoth Miss Dandridge, with heightened colour. "How thick the mint grows here! We are at the gate, Mr. Cary."

"Let us walk to the bend of the road! The wild honeysuckle is in bloom there; I noticed it riding to Charlottesville the other morning. It is just the colour of your gown."

"Then it must be beautiful," said Miss Dandridge, "for this rose-coloured muslin came from London. Ah, you looked so angry and so beaten on Wednesday, when you came back from Charlottesville!"

"I was not angry, and I was not beaten."

"Fie! You mean that your brother was."

"I mean nothing of the kind!" cried the younger Cary hotly. "My brother, at the importunity of his friends, and for the good of the county, consented to stand against this pet of Jefferson's, this — this *vaurien* Lewis Rand. Some one had to stand. He knew what the result would be. 'T was but a skirmish — just a seat in a tri-colour Republican House of Delegates! My faith! the honour's not great. But wait awhile, Miss Dandridge! The real battle's not yet. Beaten! Rands, Miss Dandridge, don't beat Carys!"

"La, so warm!" exclaimed Unity. "I have never seen a man love a brother so!"

"Ludwell Cary is worthy of any man's love —or any woman's either!"

"The pair of you ought to be put in the wax-works, and labelled 'The Loving Brothers.' When you marry, there'll be no love left for your wife."

"Just you try and see."

"The man whom I marry," said Miss Dandridge, "must have no thought but for me. He must swoon if I frown, laugh if I smile, weep if I sigh, be altogether desperate if I look another way. I am like Falkland in The Rivals. Heigho! this is the bend of the road, Mr. Cary."

"I am altogether desperate when you look another way. When you looked at Ned Hunter last night, I wanted to blow his brains out. He hasn't any, but I should like to try."

"Then you would have been hanged for murder," remarked Miss Dandridge. "Think how terrible that would be for us all! — Did you know that Mr. Hunter once dined with General Washington?"

"You are a royal coquette. See, there is the honeysuckle! If I gather it for you, will you wear one spray to-night?"

"It is a very stiff flower," said Unity thoughtfully, "and I have an idea that Mr. Hunter will bring me violets. But — I will see if I can find a place for one small spray."

She sat down upon a fallen tree, took her round chin into her hand, and studied the point of her morocco shoe, while her cavalier, not without detriment to his pumps and silk stockings, scrambled up the red bank to the rosy flowers.

The honeysuckles did not grow upon the main road, but upon a rough and narrow cross-country track, little used except by horsemen pressed for time. Now, clear through the still afternoon, a sound of hoofs gave warning that riders were coming down the steep and dangerous hill beyond the turn. Unity looked up with interest, and Fairfax Cary paused with his hand upon a coral bough. Suddenly there was a change in the beat, then a frightened shout, and a sound of rolling stones and a wild clatter of hoofs. Unity sprang to her feet; Cary came down the bank at a run, tossed her his armful of blossoms, and was in the middle of the road in time to seize by the bridle the riderless horse which came plunging around the bend.

Fairfax Cary was strong, the black horse not quite mad with terror, and the man mastered the brute. "Whose is he?" he asked. "If you will hold him — he is quite quiet now — I will go see."

A negro came panting around the turn. "Gawd-a-moughty, marster! did you cotch dat horse? You, Selim, I's gwine lam' you, I's gwine teach you er lesson — dancin' roun' on yo' two foots 'cause you sees er scrap of paper! R'arin' an' pitchin' an' flingin' white folks on er heap of stones! I'll larn you! Yo' marster was a-dreamin', or you'd never th'owed him! You jes wait twel I git you home! Marse Fairfax Cary, dis debbil done th'owed my marster, an' he lyin' by de roadside, an' I don' know whether he live or daid!"

"I know you now," exclaimed the younger Cary. "You're Mr. Lewis Rand's servant. Had n't you better stay here, Miss Dandridge, until I see what really is the matter? Here, boy, stop chattering your teeth! Your master's not killed. Was it at the top of the hill?"

"Halfway down, Marse Fairfax, whar de footpath goes down through de papaw bushes. Joab'll show you."

"I'm coming too," said Miss Dandridge. "I'll lead Selim."

Without more ado the four rounded the bend of the road and began to climb the hill. Halfway up, as Joab had stated, they found their man. He lay beside the papaw bushes, among the loose stones, and he lay very still. One arm was doubled under him. His head was thrown back, and his brown hair was matted with blood.

"Oh!" cried Unity pitifully, and went down upon her knees beside the unfortunate.

Cary examined the cut in the head. "Well, he's not dead, but he's had a pretty fall! What's to be done? Joab —"

"Joab," commanded Miss Dandridge, "ride straight to Fontenoy and tell Colonel Dick to send Big Jim and a couple of men with the old litter! — and then ride to Charlottesville and bring Dr. Gilmer —"

"Are you going to take him to Fontenoy?" asked the younger Cary.

"Why not?" flashed Miss Dandridge. "Would you leave him to bleed to death by the roadside? 'My enemy's dog —' and so forth. Hurry, Joab!"

The negro mounted his horse that had been grazing by the papaw bushes, and was off at a gallop, leaving Unity and Cary with the luckless rider. Cary brought water from the brook that brawled at the foot of the steep hillside, and Unity wet the brow and lips of the unconscious man, but he had given no sign of life when the relief party arrived from Fontenoy. This consisted of four stout negroes bearing the litter, and of Colonel Dick Churchill and Mr. Ned Hunter.

"Tut, tut!" cried Colonel Dick. "What's this? what's this? Damn this place! My mare Nelly threw me here thirty years ago! — I was coming home from a wedding. Senseless and cut across the head! — and I don't like the way that arm's bent. — Ned Hunter, you take Big Jim's corner of the litter for a minute. Now, Big Jim, you lift Mr. Rand. — So! we'll have him at Fontenoy in a jiffy, and in bed in the blue room. Run ahead, Unity, and tell Jacqueline and Mammy Chloe to make ready. His boy's gone for Gilmer. Easy now, men! Yes, 't was at this very spot my mare Nelly threw me! — it was Maria Erskine's wedding."

The sun was low in the heavens when the good Samaritans and the unconscious man arrived at the foot of the wide, white-pillared Fontenoy porch. The arrival had many witnesses; for on hearing of the accident the large party assembled for the dancing class had at once dropped all employment and flocked to various coigns of vantage. A bevy of young girls looked from one parlour window, and another framed Mr. Pincornet's face and wig and flowered coat. In the hall and on the porch the elders gathered, while on the broad porch steps young men in holiday dress waited to see if they might be of help. Around the corner of the house peered the house negroes, pleasurably excited by any catastrophe and any procession, even that of a wounded man borne on a litter.

The cortège arrived. In the midst of much ejaculation, and accompanied by a fire of directions from Colonel Dick, Lewis Rand was borne up the steps and across the porch into the cool, wide hall. Here the litter was met by Jacqueline Churchill. She came down the shadowy staircase in a white gown, with a salver and a glass in her hand. "The room is ready, Uncle Dick," she said, in a steady voice. "The blue room. Aunt Nancy says you must make him take this cordial. I have lint and bandages all ready. This way, Big Jim. Mind the wall!"

She turned and preceded the men up the stair, along a hallway and into a pleasant chamber hung with blue and white. "Turn down the sheet, Mammy Chloe," she directed a negro woman standing beside the bed. "Quick! quick! he is bleeding so."

Rand was laid upon the bed, and as the men drew their arms from beneath him, he moved his head, and his lips parted. A moment later he opened his eyes. Colonel Dick heaved a sigh of relief. "He'll do now! Gilmer shall come and bleed him, and he'll be out again before you can say Jack Robinson! I'll have that place in the road mended to-morrow. Yes, yes, Mr. Rand, you've had an accident. Lie still! you're with friends. Hey, what did you say?"

Rand had said nothing articulate. His eyes were upon Jacqueline, standing at the foot of the bed. The room was in the western wing of the house, and where she stood she was bathed in the light of the sinking sun. It made her brown hair golden and like a nimbus. Rand made a straying motion with his hand. "I did not believe in heaven," he muttered. "If I have erred — "

"Lie still, lie still!" said Jacqueline. In a moment she turned, left the room, and went downstairs. "He is better," she told her cousin Unity, who with Fairfax Cary was waiting in the lower hall; then went on to the library, opened the door, and closed it softly behind her.

The room was dim, and she thought it vacant. There was an old leather chair which she loved, which had always stood beside the glass doors that gave upon the sunset, in whose worn depths she had, as a child, told herself fairy tales, and found escape from childish woes. She went straight to it now, sank into its old arms, and pressed her cheek against the cool leather. She closed her eyes, and sat very still, and tried to ease the throbbing of her heart. Some one coughed, and she looked up to find her Uncle Edward regarding her from his own favourite chair.

"I did not know you were there," she exclaimed. "I thought the room was empty. What are you reading?"

"A Treatise on Hospitality," answered Major Churchill, with great dryness. "I suppose Dick is making posset in his best racing cup? How is the interesting patient?"

Jacqueline coloured. "Uncle Dick —"

"Uncle Dick," interrupted the Major, "is the best of fellows, but he is not perspicacious. I am, and I say again, why the deuce did this damned Republican get himself thrown at our very gates? In my day a horse might act a little gaily, but a man kept his seat!"

Jacqueline coloured more deeply. "It was that bad place on the hill road. I do not suppose that Mr. Rand is a poor horseman."

"Who said that he was?" demanded the Major testily. "A poor horseman! He and his old wolf of a father used to break all the colts for twenty miles round! That place in the road! Pshaw! I've ridden by that place in the road for forty years, but I never had the indecency to be brought on a litter into a gentleman's house who was not of my way of thinking! And every man and woman on the place — barring poor Nancy — out to receive him! I am not at home among fools, so I came here — though the Lord knows there's many a fool to be found in a library! — Well, are any bones broken?"

"Dr. Gilmer will tell us — oh, he looked like death!"

"Who? — William Gilmer?" demanded Uncle Edward with asperity. "Your pronoun 'he' stands for your antecedent 'Gilmer.' But what's the English tongue when we have a Jacobin in the house! Women like strange animals, and they are vastly fond of pitying. But you were always a home body, Jacqueline, and left Unity to run after the sea lions and learned pigs! And now you sit there as white as your gown!"

Jacqueline smiled. "Perhaps I am of those who pity. I

hear a horse upon the road! It may be Dr. Gilmer!" and up she started.

"The horse has gone by," said Uncle Edward. "Gilmer cannot possibly be here for an hour. Sit down, child, and don't waste your pity. The Rands are used to hard knocks. I've seen old Gideon in the ring, black and blue and blind with blood, demanding proof that he was beaten. The gentleman upstairs will take care of himself. Bah!— Where is Ludwell Cary this afternoon?"

"He rode, I think, to Charlottesville."

"You think! Don't you know?— What woman was ever straightforward!"

Major Churchill opened his book, looked at it, and tossed it aside; took The Virginia Federalist from the table, and for perhaps sixty seconds appeared absorbed in its contents, then with a loud "Pshaw!" threw it down, and rising walked to a bookcase. "I am reading Swift," he said, and brought a calf-bound volume to the window. "There was a man who knew hatred and the *risus sardonicus!* Listen to this, Jacqueline."

Major Churchill read well, and it was his habit to read aloud to Jacqueline, whose habit it was to listen. Now she sat before the window, in the old leather chair, her slender face and form in profile, and her eyes upon the sunset sky. It was her accustomed attitude, and Uncle Edward read on with growing satisfaction, finding that he was upon a passage which gave Democracy its due. He turned a page, then another, glanced from the book, and discovered that his niece was not attending. "Jacqueline!"

Jacqueline withdrew her eyes from the fading gold, and, turning in her chair, faced her uncle with a faint smile. She loved him dearly, and he loved her, and they had not many secrets from each other. Now she looked at him with a wavering light upon her face, shook her head as if in answer to some dim question of her own, and broke into silent weeping.

"Bless my soul!" cried Uncle Edward, and started up in alarm. He had a contemptuous horror of women's tears; but Jacqueline was different, Jacqueline was not like other women. He could not remember having seen Jacqueline cry since she was a child, and the sight troubled him immensely. She wept as though she were used to weeping. He crossed to the chair by the window and touched her bowed head with his wrinkled hand. "What is it, child?" he asked. "Tell Uncle Edward."

But Jacqueline, it appeared, had nothing to tell. After a little she wiped her eyes, and brokenly laughed at herself; and then, a sound coming through the window, she started to her feet. "That is Dr. Gilmer! I hear his horse at the gate. Joab must have met him upon the road!"

"Joab?"

"Mr. Rand's servant."

"You appear," said the Major, "to know a deal more than I do about Mr. Rand. Where did you learn so much?"

Jacqueline, halfway to the door, turned upon him her candid eyes. "Don't you remember?" she answered, "the month that I spent, summer before last, at Cousin Jane Selden's, on the Three-Notched Road? I saw Mr. Rand very often that summer. Cousin Jane liked him, and he was welcome at her house. And when I used to stay there as a child I saw him then, and—and was sorry for him. Don't you remember? I told you at the time."

"No, I don't remember," replied Uncle Edward grimly. "I have other things to think of than the Rands. There should have been no association—though I am surprised at nothing which goes on beneath Jane Selden's roof. Jane

Selden has a most erratic mind. — Don't sympathize too much, Jacqueline, with that damned young Republican upstairs! He's an enemy." The Major walked to the window. "It is Gilmer, sure enough, and — ah, it is Ludwell Cary with him, riding Prince Rupert. Come look, Jacqueline!"

Receiving no answer, he turned to find that his niece had vanished and he was alone in the library. Presently he heard from the hall, through the half-open door, the doctor's voice and Ludwell Cary's expressions of concern, Jacqueline's low replies, a confusion of other voices, and finally, from the head of the stairs, Colonel Dick's hearty "Come up, Gilmer, come up! D'ye remember that damned place in the hill road where my mare Nelly threw me, coming home at dawn from Maria Erskine's wedding?"

Steps and voices died away. The evening shadows lengthened, and filled the library where Uncle Edward sat, propping his lean old chin upon his lean old hand, and staring at a dim old clock in the corner, as if it could tell him more than the time of day. He heard Mr. Pincornet's fiddle from the long parlour in the other wing. Since the doctor was come, the younger part of the gathering at Fontenoy had cheerfully returned to its business. The dancing class was not long neglected. Uncle Edward disliked France, disliked even monarchical and émigré France. And he disliked all music but Jacqueline's singing, and disliked the fiddle because Thomas Jefferson played it. He half rose to shut the door and so keep out Mr. Pincornet's Minuet from Ariadne, but reflected that the door would also keep out the doctor's descending voice and final dicta delivered at the stair-foot. Uncle Edward was as curious as a woman, and the door remained ajar. He tried to read, but the words conveyed no meaning to his mind, which became more and more frowningly intent upon the fact of Jacqueline's weeping. What had the child to weep for? He determined to send to Richmond to-morrow for a certain watch which he had in his mind, — plain gold with J. C. upon it in pearls. He reflected with satisfaction that Cary as well as Churchill began with a C.

The glass door led by a flight of steps down to the flower garden. Deb came up the steps and into the library. "Kiss me good-night, Uncle Edward. It's mos' seven o'clock. I've had my supper at the Quarter with Aunt Daphne. The scarlet beans over her door are in bloom, and Uncle Mingo told me about the rabbit and the fox. Miranda is going to put me to bed because Mammy Chloe is busy in the blue room with the doctor and the man whose horse threw him."

Uncle Edward put his one arm around the child and drew her close to his chair. Deb touched with her brown fingers the sleeve that was pinned across his coat. "Does your arm that is buried at Yorktown hurt you to-day, Uncle Edward? Tell me a story about General Washington."

"No; you tell me a story."

Deb considered. "I'll tell you a story about the man upstairs in the blue room."

"What do you know about the man in the blue room?"

"Jacqueline told me. She knows," answered Deb. "I am going to begin now, Uncle Edward."

"I am listening," said the Major.

"Once upon a time there lived on the Three-Notched Road a boy, a poor boy. He lived in a log house that was not so good as an overseer's house, and there were pine trees all around it, and wild flowers, but no other kinds of flowers. And in the trees there were owls, and in the bushes there were whip-poor-wills, and sometimes a mockingbird, but no other kinds of birds, and at night the fireflies were all about. And outside the pine trees, all around the house, the tobacco grew and grew. It grew so broad and high that the children might have played I-spy in it, — only there were n't any children. There was only the boy, and he hated tobacco. He was poor, and his father was a hard man. He had no time to play or to learn — he worked all day in the fields like a hand. He had to work like the men at the lower Quarter, like Domingo and Cato and Indian Jim. He worked all the time. I never saw the sun get up, but he saw it every day. In the long afternoons when it was hot, and we make the rooms cool and dark, and rest with a book, he was working, working like a friendless slave. And at night, when the moon rises, and we sit and watch it, and wonder, and remember all the battles that were ever won and lost, and all the songs that ever were sung, he could only stumble to his own poor corner, and sleep, and sleep, with a hot and heavy heart, and the blisters on his poor, poor hands!"

Major Churchill sank back in his chair and stared at his niece. "Good God, child! whose words are you using?"

"Jacqueline's," answered Deb, staring in her turn. "Jacqueline told it to me just that way, one hot night when I could not sleep, and there was heat lightning, and she took me in her lap and we sat by the window. Are you tired, Uncle Edward? Does your arm hurt? Suppose I finish the story to-morrow?"

"No, I'm not tired," said Uncle Edward. "Finish it now."

"The boy," went on Deb, using now her own and now Jacqueline's remembered words, — "the boy did not want to work all his life long in the tobacco-fields, working from morning to night, with his hands, at the thing he hated. He wanted books, he wanted to learn, and to work with his mind in the world beyond the Three-Notched Road. The older he grew the more he wanted it. And Jacqueline said that the mind finds a way, and that the boy got books together, and he studied hard. You see, Jacqueline knows, for when she was a little girl, she used to stay sometimes with Cousin Jane Selden on the Three-Notched Road. And Cousin Jane Selden's farm was next to where the boy lived. There was just a little stream between them. There were no children at Cousin Jane Selden's, and Jacqueline was lonely. And she used to sit under the apple tree on the bank of the little stream and send chip boats down it, just as Miranda and I do. Only she did n't have Miranda, and she was all by herself. And she could see the boy working on the other side of the stream, and there was n't any shade in the tobacco-field, and Jacqueline was so sorry for him. And one day he came down to the stream for water and they talked to each other. And Jacqueline told Cousin Jane Selden, and Cousin Jane Selden did not mind. She said she was sorry for the boy, and that she had given his father a piece of her mind, — only he would n't take it. So Jacqueline used to see the boy often and often, for she always played under the apple tree by the stream, and he had a little time to rest every day at noon, and he would come down to the shade on his side of the stream, and Jacqueline told him all about Fontenoy. And he told Jacqueline what he was going to do when he was a man, and he asked her if she had ever read Cæsar, and she had not, and he told her all about it. And Jacqueline told him fairy tales, but he said they were not true, and that a harp could not sing by itself, nor a hen lay golden eggs, nor a beanstalk grow a mile. He said he did not like lies, — which was n't very polite. He was older, you see, than Jacqueline, ever so much older. But she knew how to dance, and she was taking music lessons, and so she seemed older, and he liked Jacqueline very much. What is the matter, Uncle Edward?"

"Nothing. Go on, child."

"Then the summer was over, and Jacqueline came back to Fontenoy. But the next summer, when she went to Cousin Jane Selden's, there was the boy working in the tobacco on the other side of the stream. And Jacqueline called to him from under the apple tree. And then the month that she was to stay with Cousin Jane Selden went by, and she came back to Fontenoy. And the next summer she did n't go to the Three-Notched Road, but one day the boy came to Fontenoy."

"Ah!" said the Major.

"The boy's father sent him to pay some money that he owed to Uncle Dick. Jacqueline says his father was an honest man, though he was so unkind. And Uncle Dick sent for Jacqueline and said, 'Jacqueline, this is young Lewis Rand. Take him and show him the garden while I write this receipt!' So Jacqueline and the boy went into the flower garden, and she showed him the roses and the peacock and the sundial. And then he went away, and she did n't see him any more for years and years, not till she was grown, and everything was changed. And — and that is the end of the story. But the boy's name was Lewis Rand, and the man's name, up in the blue room, is Mr. Lewis Rand, and I heard Mr. Fairfax Cary say that Lewis Rand was the Devil, — but Jacqueline would n't have liked the Devil, would she, Uncle Edward?"

"No, child, no, no!" exclaimed Uncle Edward, with violence. He rose so suddenly from his chair, and he looked so grim and grey, that Deb was almost frightened.

"Did n't you like the story, Uncle Edward? I did like it so much when Jacqueline told it to me — only she would never tell it to me again."

"Yes, yes, I liked it, honey. Don't I like all your stories? But I don't like Mr. Rand."

"Will he stay always upstairs in the blue room?"

"The Lord forbid!" cried Major Churchill.

The door opened wide, and Mr. Ned Hunter put in an important face. "Are you there, Major? Here's the devil to pay. Rand's arm is broken and his ankle wrenched and his head cut open! The doctor says he mustn't be moved for at least a fortnight. I thought you'd like to know." He was gone to spread the news.

Major Churchill stood still for a moment, then turned to the table, placed with deliberation a marker between the leaves of Swift, took up the volume, and restored it to its proper shelf.

"It is getting dark — I must go to bed," said Deb. "Uncle Edward, who pays the devil?"

"His hosts, child," answered Uncle Edward, looking very grim and very old.

CHAPTER VII

THE BLUE ROOM

THE news of the accident to Lewis Rand spread far and wide. Both as a lawyer and as Mr. Jefferson's adjutant he had become in two years' time a marked man. Federalist and Republican were agreed that the recent election was but a foot in the stirrup. Another two years might see him — almost anywhere. He was likely to ride far and to ride fast. To the Federalists his progress from the tobacco-fields to the Elysian Heights of office was but another burning sign of the degeneracy of the times and the tendencies of Jefferson. On the other hand, the Republicans quoted the Rights of Man and the Declaration of Independence, and made the name of Lewis Rand as symbolic as a liberty pole. He was *bon enfant, bon Républicain.* Virginia, like Cornelia, numbered him among her starry gems. He was of the Gracchi. He was almost anything Roman, Revolutionary, and Patriotic that the mind of a perfervid poet could conjure up and fix in a corner of the Argus or the Examiner. Every newspaper in the state mentioned the accident, and in a letter from a Gentleman of Virginia, an account of it was read by the subscribers to the Aurora.

All this was somewhat later, when the stage-coach and the mail-rider had distributed the slow-travelling news. In the mean time Lewis Rand lay in the curtained bed in the blue room at Fontenoy, and wondered at that subtle force called Chance. The blue roses upon the hangings, the blue willows and impossible bridges of the china, the apple-cheeked moon surmounting the face of the loud-ticking clock were not more fantastically unnatural than that he, Lewis Rand, should be lying there between the linen sheets, in the sunny morning stillness of the fourth day after his fall, listening for the stir of the awakening house, for one step upon the stair, and for one voice. He was where he had desired to be; he was at Fontenoy; but the strangeness of his being there weighed upon him. He would hear the step and the voice; chance had brought him past every ward of a hostile house, and had laid him there in the blue room to be generously pitied and lavishly cared for; chance had given him leverage. To each the chaos of his own nature; if, with Rand, the Spirit brooded none too closely over the face of the deep, yet was there light enough to tread by. As he lay in the blue room, watching the early sunlight steal through the window and lay a golden finger on his bed, he had no sense of triumph, no smugness of satisfaction over the attainment of his dream. He thought of how often as a boy, working under the glare of the sun, in the shadeless tobacco-fields, he had dreamed of the poplars of Fontenoy, the cool porches, the cool rooms, the rest from labour, and the books, of all that the little girl named Jacqueline had told him, sitting under the apple tree beside the stream that flowed between a large and a small farm on the Three-Notched Road. As a boy, he would have been puzzled to choose between "Will you go to Heaven?" and "Will you go to Fontenoy?" The one seemed as remote, as unattainable, and as happy as the other. The advantage was possibly with Fontenoy, for he could picture that to himself. He could not have described the mansions in the skies, but, thanks to Jacqueline, he knew every room at Fontenoy. Before he was laid in it, he had known the blue room, the roses on the curtains, and the peacock-feathered mandarin forever climbing a dull yellow screen. The library should be below, with the bookshelves, and the glass door opening on the snowball bushes. Outside his window was the flower garden. He had seen the garden with his bodily eyes, for there was the morning he had spent at Fontenoy. In the desert of his hardly-treated, eager, and longing youth the place and the life of which the girl who came to Mrs. Selden's had told him was become the vision of an oasis and a paradise. The magic word was Fontenoy. If Gideon Rand or Adam Gaudylock chanced to pronounce it, it was as though the Captain of the Thieves had said, "Open Sesame!" The cave door opened, and he saw strange riches.

That day at Fontenoy! He tried to recall it, but it did not stand out in his memory; it was curiously without edge. Trying to remember was like remembering a dream, delicious and evasive. The child named Jacqueline had changed to a girl named Jacqueline. She had spoken to him shyly, and he had answered with much greater shyness, with a reddening cheek and a stumbling tongue. He remembered her dress, a soft blue stuff that he was afraid of touching, and he remembered how burning was his consciousness of his coarse shoes, his shirt of osnaburg, the disreputable hat upon his sunburnt hair. Then they had walked in the garden, and sat on the steps of a summer house, and he had been very happy after all. And then a black boy had come to tell him that the Colonel was ready with the receipt he was to carry back to the Three-Notched Road. He said good-bye with great awkwardness, and went away, and he saw the girl no more for a long, long time, for so long a time that insensibly her image faded. It was in the October of that year that he went to Richmond with Gideon, and met Mr. Jefferson in the bookshop by the bridge.

The years that followed that meeting! Rand, lying still upon his pillows, with his eyes upon the yellow mandarin, passed them in review,—well, they had not been wasted! Usually he saw the approximate truth about himself, and he knew that these years of toil and achievement were honourable to him. He thought of all those years, and then he turned his head upon the pillow and faced through widely opened windows the misty, fragrant morning. His mind turned with suddenness to a morning two summers past. His father, who had lived to take grim pride in the son he had been used to thwart, was six months dead, and he himself was living alone, as he yet lived alone, in the small house upon the Three-Notched Road. He lived there with his ambitions, which were many. That morning he had gone, without knowing why, down through the tobacco-field to the stream which parted his patrimony from his neighbour's grassy orchard. And there, beneath the apple tree, across the clear, brown water stood Jacqueline. He forgot her no more. "Fontenoy" was again the magic word, the "Open Sesame," but Jacqueline was the wealth of all the world. He was young, and he was a man of strong passions who had lived, perforce, a rigid, lonely, and ascetic life. He had dreamed of most things, and he had dreamed of love. It was the hectic vision of a lilied pool. Love, entered, proved to be the sea, boundless and strong, salt, clean, and the nurse of life. He loved Jacqueline to the end of his life; he never swerved from allegiance to the sea.

For a summer month he saw her almost every day,—twice or thrice beneath the apple tree beside the stream, and at other times in Mrs. Jane Selden's parlour, porch, or little friendly garden. He did not tell Jacqueline that he loved her; he had not dared so much. The fact that he was the son of Gideon Rand while she was a Churchill mattered little to his common sense and his Republicanism. His blood was clean. He had never heard of a Rand in prison or a beggar.

Moreover, he meant to make his name an honoured one. But he was a poor man, though he meant also to become a rich man, and he was a Republican, with no thought of changing his party. Politics might not matter, perhaps, to Miss Churchill, but they mattered decidedly to her uncles and guardians, whom she loved and obeyed. Wealth and birth mattered too, to them. Lewis Rand set no great store upon obedience for obedience' sake, but he divined that Miss Churchill rarely vexed those she loved. He had an iron will, and he set his lips, and resolved that this was not the time to speak of that ocean on whose shore he stood. He meant that the time should come. The probability of a rejection he looked full in the face, and found that he did not believe in it, though when he looked as fully at his assurance, that, too, became incredibly without foundation. Jacqueline's spirit might dwell in the mountains, and never dream of the sea; she gave him no sign, and he could not tell. The summer month went by; she returned to Fontenoy, and he saw her no more for a long time. When she was gone, he fell upon work like a bereaved lion upon his prey. As best he might, he would make that hunting do. He worked at first with lonely fury, though at last with zest. Only by this road, he knew, could he enter the gates of Fontenoy. Success begets success; let him make himself a name, and the gates might open! When he was not in court, or not most diligently preparing a case, or not instructing Tom Mocket, who was on the way to become his partner, or not busied with affairs of his patron, or not keenly observant of the methods of the poor whites whom he hired to tend his tobacco, he read. He read history: Clarendon, Gibbon, and Hume; Aristotle, Bacon, Machiavelli, Shakespeare, and Voltaire, Rousseau, and Tom Paine. His Ossian, Cæsar, and Plutarch belonged to his younger days. A translation of the Divina Commedia fell into his hands, and once he chanced to take up, and then read with the closest attention, Godwin's Caleb Williams. From Monticello he received the hot and clamorous journals of the day, Federalist and Republican. He studied the conditions they portrayed with the intentness of a gladiator surveying his arena. The Examiner, the Argus, the Aurora, the Gazette gave, besides the home conflict, the foreign news. He missed no step of Buonaparte's.

Thrice in these two years he had seen Jacqueline. Once he rode to church at Saint Anne's that he might see her. She had been at the great race when Major Churchill's Mustapha won over Nonpareil and Buckeye. The third time was a month ago in Charlottesville. She was walking, and Ludwell Cary was with her. When she bowed to Rand, Cary had looked surprised, but his hat was instantly off. Rand bowed in return, and passed them, going on to the Court House. He had not seen her again until four days ago, when he opened his eyes upon her face. The golden finger on his bed became a shining lance that struck across to the wall. There were ivy and a climbing rose about the window through which he looked to the shimmering poplars and the distant hills. Many birds were singing, and from the direction of the quarters sounded the faint blowing of a horn. A bee came droning in to the pansies in a bowl. Rand's dark eyes made a journey through the room, from the flowered curtains to the mandarin on the screen, from the screen to the willowed china and the easy chair, from the chair to the picture of General Washington on the wall, the vases on the mantel-shelf, and the green hemlock branches masking for the summer the fireplace below. Over all the blue room and the landscape without was a sense of home, of order and familiar sweetness. It struck to the soul of a too lonely and too self-reliant man. Suddenly, without warning, tears were in his eyes. Raising his uninjured arm, he brushed them away, settled his bandaged head upon the pillows, and stared at the clock. The half-shut door of a small adjoining room opened very slowly and softly, and Joab entered on tiptoe, elaborate caution surrounding him like an atmosphere.

"You, Joab," said Rand. "It's time you were in the field."

Joab's preternaturally lengthened countenance became short, broad, and genial. He threw back his head and breathed relief. "Dar now! What I tell em? Cyarn Selim nor no urr hoss kill you, Marse Lewis! Mornin', sah. I reckon hit is time I wuz in de field, but I reckon I got to stay heah to tek care of you. How yo ahm, Marse Lewis?"

"It's not so bad."

"You sho wuz ressless in yo sleep — a-talkin' an' a-turnin' an' sayin' you must n't keep de cote waitin'. I done sit by you ter keep de kivers on twill de cock crow. What you reckon you said to me? You said, 'Is dat you, Gineral Buonaparte?'"

Rand laughed, "Did you say, 'Yes, sire my brother?'"

"No, sah, I say, 'Hit's Joab, Marse Lewis.' I gwine now ter git de water to shave you ef dar's fire in de kitchen. Folks git up moughty late at Fontenoy. I don' know when I gwine git yo breakfast."

An hour later appeared the master of the house, red and jovial, solicitous for his guest's comfort, and prodigal of suggestions for his ease and entertainment. Not until Rand was well and gone from Fontenoy would Colonel Dick let his mind rest upon the indubitable fact that here had been an upstart and an enemy. Hard upon the Colonel's steps came the doctor. Arm and ankle and wounded head were doing well — there was no fever to speak of — Mr. Rand had an unabused constitution and would make a rapid recovery.

THE BLUE ROOM

For precaution's sake, best let a little blood. Rest, gruel, and quiet, and in a few days Mr. Rand would be downstairs with the ladies. The blood was let, and the doctor rode away. Joab and the culprit Selim went on Rand's errands to the town and to the home on the Three-Notched Road. Mammy Chloe, in white apron and kerchief and coloured turban, presented herself with a curtsy, delivered kindly messages from the ladies of the house, and sat down with her sewing in the little adjoining room. The morning advanced, sunny and peaceful, with vague sounds, faint laughter from distant rooms, droning of bees, and rustling of cool poplar leaves.

Rand, lying high upon his pillows, stopped his work of writing with his left hand to listen to a step coming up the polished stairway and along the passage leading to his room. His ear was almost as quick and accurate as was Adam Gaudylock's, and he rightly thought he knew the step. A somewhat strange smile was on his lips when Ludwell Cary knocked lightly at the blue room door. "Come in!" called Rand, and Cary, entering, closed the door behind him and came up to the bed with an outstretched hand and a pleasant light upon his handsome face.

"Ah, Mr. Rand," he said, smiling, "I see my revenge. I shall sit each day by your bedside, and read you the Federalist! How is the arm? Your right! That's bad!"

"It will heal," answered Rand. "Will you not take a chair?"

Cary pushed the easy chair nearer the bed, and sat down. "The ladies charge me," he said pleasantly, "with more messages of sympathy and hopes for your recovery than I can remember. Miss Dandridge vows that you have supplanted in her affections the hero of her favourite romance. 'T was she and my brother, you know, who found you upon the road. Colonel Churchill and the county must mend that turn where you came to grief. It is a dangerous place."

"I was not attentive," said Rand, "and my horse is a masterful brute. Pray assure Miss Dandridge and your brother of my gratitude. I am under deep obligation to all at Fontenoy."

"It is a kindly place," said Cary simply. He looked about him. "The blue room! When I was a boy and came a-visiting, they always put me here. That screen would set me dreaming — and the blue roses — and the moon clock. I used to lie in that bed and send myself to sleep with more tales than are in the Arabian Nights. There's a rift in the poplars through which you can see a very bright star — Sirius, I believe. May you have pleasant dreams, Mr. Rand, in my old bed!" He glanced from Rand's flushed face to the papers strewn upon the counterpane. "You have been writing? Would Dr. Gilmer approve?"

Rand looked somewhat ruefully at the scrawled sheets and the ink upon his fingers. "It is a necessary paper of instructions," he said. "I was retained by the State for the North Garden murder case. It is to be tried next week — and here am I, laid by the heels! My associate must handle it." He made a movement of impatience. "He's skilful enough, but he's not the sort to convince a jury — especially in Albemarle, where they don't like to hang people. If he's left to himself, Fitch may go free."

"The murderer?"

"Yes, the murderer. These," he laid his hand upon the papers, "are the points that must be made. If Mocket follows instructions, the State will win. But I wish that Selim had not chosen to break my right arm — it is difficult to write with the left hand."

"Could not Mr. Mocket take his instructions directly from you?"

Rand moved again impatiently, and with a quick sigh. "I sent him word not to come. I will not bring a friend or ally where I myself must seem an intruder and a most unwelcome guest. There's a fine irony in human affairs! Selim might have thrown me before Edgehill or Dunlora — but to choose Fontenoy!" He looked at Cary with a certain appeal. "I shall, of course, remove myself as soon as possible. In the meantime, if you could assure me that Colonel Churchill and his family understand —"

"Set your mind at rest," said Cary at once. "Colonel Churchill is the soul of kindness and hospitality, and the ladies of Fontenoy are all angels. You must not think yourself an unwelcome guest." He glanced again at the papers. "I am sure you should not try to write. Will you not accept me as amanuensis? The matter is not private?"

"Not at all: but —"

"Then let me write from your dictation. I have nothing at all to do for the next two hours, — I am staying in the house, you know, — and it will give me genuine pleasure to help you. You have no business with such labour. Dr. Gilmer, I know, must have forbidden it. Come! I write a very fair clerkly hand."

"You don't know the imposition," said Rand, with an answering smile. "It is nothing less than a Treatise on Murder."

"I shall be glad," replied Cary, "to hear what you have to say on the subject. Come! here are blank sheets and a new quill and an attentive secretary!"

Rand smiled. "It's the strangest post for you! — but all life's a dream just now. I confess that writing is uphill work! Well — since you are so good."

He began to dictate. At first his words came slowly, with some stiffness and self-consciousness. This passed; he forgot himself, thought only of his subject, and utterance became quiet, grave, and fluent. He did not speak as though he were addressing a jury. Gesture was impossible, and his voice must not carry beyond the blue room. He spoke as to himself, as giving reasons to a high intelligence for the invalidity of murder. For an infusion of sentiment and rhetoric he knew he might trust Mocket's unaided powers, but the basis of the matter he would furnish. He spoke of murder as the check the savage gives to social order, as the costliest error, the last injustice, the monstrousness beyond the brute, the debt without surety, the destruction by a fool of that which he knows not how to create. He spoke for society, without animus and without sentiment; in a level voice marshalling fact and example, and moving unfalteringly toward the doom of the transgressor. Turning to the case in hand, he wove strand by strand a rope for the guilty wretch in question; then laid it for the nonce aside and spoke of murder more deeply with a sombre force and a red glow of imagery. Then followed three minutes of slow words which laid the finished and tested rope in the sheriff's hand. Rand's voice ceased, and he lay staring at the poplar leaves without the window.

Cary laid the pen softly down, sat still and upright in his chair for a minute, then leaned back with a long breath. "The poor wretch!" he said.

"Poor enough," assented Rand abruptly. "But Nature does not, and Society must not, think of that. As he brewed, so let him drink, and the measure that he meted, let it be meted to him again. There is on earth no place for him." He fell silent again, his eyes upon the dancing leaves.

"You will make your mark," said Cary slowly. "This

THE BLUE ROOM

is more than able work. You have before you a great future."

Rand looked at him half eagerly, half wistfully. "Do you really think that?"

"I cannot think otherwise," Cary answered. "I saw it plainly in the courtroom the other day." He smiled. "I deplore your political principles, Mr. Rand, but I rejoice that my conqueror is no lesser man. I must to work against the next time we encounter."

"You have been long out of the county," said Rand. "I had the start of you, that is all. You were trained to the law. Will you practise it, or will Greenwood take all your time?"

"I shall practise. A man's life is larger than a few acres, a house, and slaves. But first I must put Greenwood in order, and I must —" He did not finish the sentence, but sat looking about the blue room. "The old moon clock! I used to listen to it in the night and dream of twenty thousand things, and never once of what I dream of now! What a strange young savage is a boy!" He gathered the written sheets together. "You will want to look these over? I shall be very glad to see that they reach Mr. Mocket safely, or to serve you in any way. Just now I am very idle, and I will be your secretary every day with pleasure." He rose. "And now you must rest, or we will have a rating from Dr. Gilmer. Is there any message I may take for you?"

"My devotion and my thanks to the ladies of the house," replied Rand — "to Mrs. Churchill and Miss Dandridge and to Miss Churchill. For these" — he put his hand upon the papers — "I shall look them over, and Joab will take them to Charlottesville to Mocket. I cannot sufficiently thank you for your aid and for your kindness."

Cary went, and Rand lay back upon his pillows, weary enough, though with a smile upon his lips. He valued Cary's visit, valued the opinion of his fellow lawyer and fellow thinker. He valued praise from almost any source, though this was a hidden thirst. Where he loved, there he valued good opinion most; but also he strongly desired that his enemies should think highly of him. To be justly feared was one thing, to be contemned quite another. Apparently Ludwell Cary neither feared nor contemned. As, a few days before on the Justice's Bench, Rand had wondered if he were going to hate Cary, so now, lying in the quiet blue room, weakened by pain and loss of blood, softened by exquisite kindness, and touched by approbation, he wondered if he were going to like Cary. Something of the old charm, the old appeal, the old recognition, with no mean envy, of a golden nature moving in harmonious circumstance, stirred in Lewis Rand's breast. He sighed and lay still, his eyes upon the pansies on the table beside his bed. The moon clock ticked; the sunshine entered softly through the veil of poplar leaves; upon the bough that brushed the window, a cicada shrilled of the approaching summer. Rand put out his uninjured arm and took a pansy from the bowl. The little face, brave and friendly, looked at him from the white counterpane where he laid it. He studied it for a while, touching it gently, with the thought in his mind that Jacqueline might have gathered the pansies, and then he left it there, took up his papers, and turned to the argument which must hang Fitch.

CHAPTER VIII

CARY AND JACQUELINE

AT supper table that evening at Fontenoy, Ludwell Cary said something complimentary to the prisoner in the blue room. Fairfax Cary fired up. "You are too easy, Ludwell! Lewis Rand, I warn you, is a dangerous man! Serve him once, and you serve him once too often! — begging your pardon, Colonel Churchill!"

"We could hardly have left him, you know," reasoned his host good-naturedly, "on the roadside, and Dick Wood's the nearest house! And once within a man's doors, every attention, of course, must be shown. But, as you say, he is a dangerous fellow."

"Dangerous fiddlesticks!" growled Major Churchill from the other side of the table, where he sat at Jacqueline's right hand. "I would have as soon called old Gideon Rand dangerous! Like father, like son. You may be sure that this fellow's spirit rolls tobacco. Maybe now and then it breaks a colt."

"'Dangerous' implies power to be dangerous," said Cary, "and conversely power to be humane. A turn, and all the strength of the man may flow toward good."

"A fool and his doctrine!" snapped Major Edward. "I do not expect grapes from thistles, or a silk purse from a sow's ear."

"Tut, tut, Ned! The man who carries this county may be a damned Republican, but he is not a fool," pronounced Colonel Dick. "Jacqueline, my dear, another cup of coffee."

"If we were all as good as gold," said Unity pensively, "and as wise as — as Socrates, and wore black cockades, and cared only for the Washington March, and hated Buonaparte, and the Devil, how tiresome life would be! — Myself, I like variety and the Marseillaise!"

"Then you differ from the other rogues only in liking the Rogue's March," said Uncle Edward. "Jacqueline, more sugar!"

The younger Cary rushed to Miss Dandridge's defence. "Well, sir, in itself the Marseillaise is a very noble air. It is better than Jefferson's March!"

"Oh, a very good air to go to the gallows by!" snapped Uncle Edward. "Jacqueline, some cream!"

"Well, well," said his brother amicably, from the head of the table, "we must care for a man when he's wounded at our door, friend or foe, Federalist or damned Republican. *Noblesse oblige.* I was glad enough the night my mare Nelly threw me, coming home from Maria Erskine's wedding, to hear Bob Carter's voice behind me! And if Gideon Rand was a surly old heathen, he broke colts well, and he rolled tobacco well. We'll treat his son like a Christian."

"And he'll repay you like a Turk!" broke out Major Edward. "I tell you it is bred in the bone —"

"Mr. Rand is our guest," said Jacqueline, in a clear voice, from her place behind the coffee urn. Her hands made a little noise amid the rosebud china. "Mr. Cary, may I not pour you another cup? — Caleb, Mr. Cary's cup. — Bring more waffles, Scipio."

"The work at Greenwood is nearly finished, sir," remarked Ludwell Cary, addressing his host. "I rode over this afternoon, and the men assure me that the house will soon be habitable. Fair and I have no excuse for staying longer."

"Then stay without excuse," answered Colonel Dick

heartily. "Fontenoy will miss you — eh, Unity, eh, Jacqueline?"

"It will indeed," said Jacqueline, with a smile; and Unity, "Will I have time to order a black scarf from Baltimore? Will you leave us mourning rings?"

"If Miss Dandridge would accept another fashion of ring!" cried Fairfax Cary, and all at table laughed.

Scipio took away the rosebud china, and laid the purple dessert service for the strawberries and floating island and Betty Custis cake. Caleb placed the decanters of claret and Madeira, and the Fontenoy men began to talk of horse-racing, of Mustapha, Nonpareil, York, and Victor.

Jacqueline and Unity, leaving the gentlemen at their wine, came out into the broad hall and stood at the front door looking out at the coloured clouds above the hills. They supped early at Fontenoy, and the evening was yet rosy.

"He is going to speak to-night," said Unity, with conviction. "It is written in his eye."

"If you mean Mr. Cary —"

"Whom else should I mean? What are you going to say to him, Jacqueline? I want you to say Yes, and I want you to say No."

"Don't, Unity —"

"If you say Yes, you will have Greenwood and the most charming husband in the world, and be envied of every girl in the county; and if you say No, I'll have you still —"

"I shall say No."

"What ails you, Jacqueline? I could swear that you're in love, and yet I don't believe you are in love with Ludwell Cary! — though I am sure you ought to be. It's not Mr. Lee, nor Mr. Page, nor Jack Martin, nor — you're never in love with Fairfax Cary?"

Jacqueline laughed, "How absurd, Unity! — though may be some day I shall love him as a cousin!"

Unity regarded her with a puzzled gathering of black brows. "There's no one else that by any stretch of imagination I can believe you in love with — unless it's Mr. Pincornet!"

"Oh, now you certainly have it!" cried Jacqueline, with another tremulous laugh. She released herself from her cousin's arm. "I am going to tell Deb good-night. And Unity — I don't want Mr. Cary to speak to-night, nor to-morrow night, nor any other night! I'll stay at Fontenoy — I'll stay at Fontenoy and care for Aunt Nancy and Deb and Uncle Dick and Uncle Edward. I'll dance at your wedding, Unity, but you'll not dance at mine!"

She was gone. Unity sat down upon the porch steps and began to name upon her fingers the eligible young men of three counties. In her anxiety to account for Jacqueline's pallor and the dark beneath her eyes, she went far afield, but she met with no success. "It's not one of them!" she sighed at last. "And yet, she's changed —"

Jacqueline went slowly upstairs, a slender figure in white, touching with her hand the polished balustrade. When she reached the long and wide upper hall, she passed steadily along it, but she turned her eyes upon a door at the far end, the door of the blue room. Arrived in her own cool and fragrant chamber, she found Deb already asleep in the small bed, her yellow hair spread upon the pillow, her gown open at the throat, a rag doll in the hollow of her arm. Upon the floor, with her head against the bed, sat Miranda, as fast asleep as her mistress. At Jacqueline's touch she awoke, smiled widely, and was on her feet with a spring. "Yaas, Miss Jacqueline, I done put Miss Deb to bed. Mammy Chloe say dat niggah Joab don' know nothin' 'bout er broken ahm, an' she too busy in de blue room. Yaas'm, I done mek Miss Deb wash her face an' say her prayers. Kin I go now?"

Alone, Jacqueline stood for a minute beside the sleeping child, then bent and kissed Deb's brown neck. Moving to a window, she sat down before it, resting her arm upon the sill and her head upon her arm. Outside the window grew a giant fir tree, shading the room, and giving it at times an aspect too cold and northern. But Jacqueline loved the tree, and loved and fed the birds that in winter perched upon the dark boughs. Now, between the needles, the eastern sky looked blue and cold. Jacqueline, sitting idle, felt her eyes fill with slow tears. They did not fall. She was not lacking in self-control, and she told herself that of late she had wept too often. She sat very still, her head bowed upon her listless arm, while the moments passed, bearing with them pictures seen through unshed tears. She was living over the days of the Three-Notched Road, and she beheld each shifting scene by the light of a passion that she believed to be unreasonable, unnatural, secret, and without hope. Her uncle's voice came to her from the hall below. "Jacqueline, Jacqueline!" She arose, bathed her eyes, and went downstairs.

It was the custom of the family to gather after supper upon the great white pillared porch, and to sit through the twilight. The men smoked slowly and reflectively, the women sat with folded hands, watching the last glow upon the hills, and the brightening of the evening star; dreamily listening to the choir of frogs, the faint tinkle of cowbells, the bleating of folded lambs, and the continual rustle of the poplar leaves.

Jacqueline took her seat beside Unity. Colonel Churchill, in his especial chair, was smoking like a benevolent volcano; at a small table Major Edward was playing Patience. On the broad porch steps below Jacqueline and Unity half sat, half lay, the two Carys. The fireflies were beginning to show, and out of the distance came a plaintive *Whip-poor-will — Whip-poor-will!*

"I shall have," said Ludwell Cary, "the vines at Greenwood trained like these. There could be no better way."

"Is the drawing-room finished?" asked Unity.

"Almost finished. The paper came to-day from Baltimore. The ground is silver, and there are garlands of roses and a host of piping shepherds."

"Oh, lovely!" cried Unity. "But no shepherdesses?"

"Yes, in among the roses. It is quite Arcadian. When will the princesses come to see the shepherdesses?"

He looked at them both. "The Princess and her waiting-maid," said Unity demurely, "will come very soon." She rose from the green bench. "The waiting-maid is going now to her harpsichord!" Her eyes rested upon the younger Cary. "Will you be so very good as to turn the leaves for me?"

Fairfax Cary embracing with alacrity the chance of goodness, the two went into the house. The dusk deepened; the odour of honeysuckle and syringa grew heavier, and white moths sailed by on their way to the lighted windows.

> "Since love — since love is blissful sorrow,
> Then bid the lad — then bid the lad —
> Then bid the lad a fair good morrow!"

flowed in soprano from the parlour.

Colonel Churchill laid down his pipe and lifted his burly figure from the great chair. "I forgot," he remarked to Jacqueline, "to tell your Aunt Nancy that Charles Carter is going to marry Miss Lewis," and he left the porch. The rose in the sky turned to pearl, the fireflies grew brilliant, and the wind brought the murmur of streams and the louder rustling of the poplar leaves. "It is too dark to see the cards," said Major Edward. "I'll go read what the Gazette has to say of Burr and the Massachusetts secession fools. Don't move, Cary!" He deftly gathered up the cards, and went indoors.

"When I was green in years, and every month was May" —
sang Unity.

"With Phyllis and with Chloe made I holiday!"

"It is dark night," said Jacqueline. "Shall we not go in?"

Cary put out an appealing hand. "Don't rise! May we not stay like this a little longer? — Miss Churchill, there is something that I ardently wish to say to you."

"Yes, Mr. Cary?"

"It is too soon to speak, I know, — it must seem too soon to you. But to-day I said, 'The spring is flying — I'll put my fortune to the touch!' I think that you must guess the thing I wish to say —"

"Yes, I know. I wish that you would leave it unsaid."

"I love you. On the day, three months ago, when I saw you after my return and found the lovely child I remembered changed into the loveliest of all women, I loved you. If then, what now, when I have seen you, day by day? — I love you, and I shall never cease to love you."

"Oh, with all my heart I wish that you did not!"

"I ask you to be my wife. I beg you to let me prove throughout my life the depth of my love, of my solicitude for your happiness —"

"Ah, happiness!" cried Jacqueline sharply. "I do not see it in my life. The best that you can do is to forget me quite."

"I will remember you when I draw my dying breath. And if we remember after death, I will remember you then. With all my strength I love you."

"I am sorry — I am sorry!" she cried. "Oh, I hoped 't was but a fancy, and that you would not speak! I do not love you —"

"Let me wait," said Cary, after a pause. "I said that I was speaking too soon. Let me wait — let me prove to you. Your heart may turn."

She shook her head. "It will not change."

"Is there," asked Cary, in a low voice, "is there another before me?"

She looked at him strangely. "You have no right to question me. I do not think that I shall ever marry. For you, you will live long and be happy. You deserve happiness. If I have wounded you, may it soon heal! Forget this night, and me."

"Forget!" said Cary. "I am not so lightly made! But neither will I despair. I will wait. If there is no man before me, I will win you yet! There is little reason, God knows, why you should care for me, but I shall strive to make that reason greater!"

"There is reason," answered Jacqueline. "I think highly, highly of you! You would make a woman happy; — all her life she would travel a sunny road! I prize your friendship — I am loth to lose it. But as for me," — she locked her hands against her breast, — "there is that within me that cries, *The shadowed road! — the shadowed road!*"

She rose, and Cary rose with her. "Forgive me," she said. "Is it not cruel that we hurt each other so? Forgive — forget."

"I would forgive you," he answered, with emotion, "the suffering and the sorrow of a thousand lives. But forget you — never! I'll love you well and I'll love you long. Nor will I despair. To-night is dark, but the sun may shine to-morrow. Think of me as of one who will love you to the end."

CARY AND JACQUELINE 107

He took her hand and kissed it, then stood aside, saying, "I will not face the lights quite yet." She passed into the hall and up the stairway, and he turned and went down the porch steps into the May night.

CHAPTER IX

EXPOSTULATION

THE next morning Ludwell Cary rose early, ordered his horse, and opened the door of his brother's room.

"Fair," he said, as the younger Cary sat up in bed, with a nightcap wonderfully askew upon his handsome head, "I am off for Greenwood. Make my excuses, will you, to Colonel Churchill and the ladies? I will not be back till supper-time." He turned to leave the room. "And Fair — if you have anything to say to Miss Dandridge, this is the shepherd's hour. We go home to-morrow."

"What the Devil?" — began the younger Cary.

"No, not the Devil," said the other, with a twist of the lip half humorous, half piteous. "Just woman."

He was gone. Fairfax Cary looked at his watch, then rose from his bed and looked out of the window at the rose and dew of the dawn. "What the Devil!" he said again to himself; and then, with a forehead of perplexity, "He was up late last night — out in the garden alone. He rides off to Greenwood with the dawn, and we go home to-morrow. She can't have refused him — that's not possible!" He went back to bed to study matters over. At last, "The jade!" he exclaimed with conviction, and two hours later, when he came down to breakfast, wished Miss Churchill good-morning with glacial courtesy.

Jacqueline, behind the coffee urn, had heavy-lidded eyes, and her smile was tremulous. Unity, brilliant and watchful, regarded the universe and the hauteur of young Mr. Cary with lifted brows. Major Churchill, when he appeared,

EXPOSTULATION

shot one glance at the place that was Ludwell Cary's, another at his niece, then sat heavily down, and in a querulous voice demanded coffee. Colonel Dick wore a frown. Deb, who before breakfast had visited a new foal in the long pasture, kept for a time the ball of conversation rolling; but the dulness and the chill in the air presently enwrapped her also. The meal came to an end with only one hazard as to what could have taken Ludwell Cary to Greenwood for the entire day. That was Unity's, who remarked that pains must be bestowed upon the hanging of a drawing-room paper, else the shepherds and the shepherdesses would not match.

Fairfax Cary asked after Lewis Rand and his broken arm, and Colonel Dick responded with absent-mindedness that the arm did very well, and that its owner would soon be going about his business with all the rest of the damned Republican mischief-makers: then, "Scipio, did you take that julep and bird up to the blue room?"

"Yaas, marster," answered Scipio. "The gent'man say tell you 'Thank you.' He say he ain't gwine trouble you much longer, an' he cyarn never forgit what Fontenoy's done fer him."

"Deb!" said Uncle Edward, with great sharpness, "you are spilling that cup of milk. Look what you are doing, child!"

The uncomfortable meal came to an end. Outside the dining-room door Uncle Dick mentioned to Unity that her aunt wanted her in the chamber to cut off linsey gowns for the house servants, and Uncle Edward inquired if it would be troublesome to Fairfax Cary to ride over to Tom Wood's and take a look at that black stallion Tom bragged of. Unity went to her aunt's chamber; the younger Cary walked away somewhat stiffly to the stables; Uncle Edward sent Deb to her lessons, and Uncle Dick told Jacqueline to come in half an hour to the library. Edward and he wanted to speak to her.

Jacqueline gave her directions, or her aunt's directions, to Scipio, then crossed the paved way to the kitchen and talked of dinner and supper with the turbaned cook; opened with her keys the smokehouse door, and in the storeroom superintended the weighing of flour and sugar and the measuring of Java coffee, and finally saw that the drawing-room was properly darkened against the sunny morning, and that the water was fresh in the bowls of flowers. She leaned for a moment against her harp, one hand upon its strings, her forehead resting upon her bare arm; then she turned from the room and entered the library, where she found her uncles waiting for her, Uncle Dick upon the hearth rug and Uncle Edward at the table.

"Jacqueline," began the first, then, "Edward, I never could talk to a woman! Ask her what all this damned nonsense means!"

"Your uncle doesn't mean that it is all damned nonsense, Jacqueline," said Uncle Edward, with gentleness. "Not perhaps from your point of view, my dear. But both he and I are greatly grieved and disappointed—"

"It was all arranged ages ago!" broke in the elder brother. "Fauquier Cary and your dear father, my brother Henry, settled it when you were born and Fauquier's son was a lad at Maury's school! When Henry died, and Fauquier Cary died, my brother Edward here and I said to each other that we would see the matter out! So we will, by God!"

"Gently, Dick! Jacqueline, child, you know how dear you are to us, and how the future and the happiness of you and of Unity and of Deb is our jealous care—"

"Fauquier Cary was as noble a man as ever breathed,"

EXPOSTULATION

cried the other, "and his son's his image! There's no better blood in Virginia — and the land beside —"

"It does not matter about the land, Jacqueline," said Uncle Edward, "though God forbid that I should depreciate good land —"

"Land's land," quoth Colonel Dick, "and good blood's gospel truth!"

"Bah! it's nature's truth!" said Uncle Edward. "Jacqueline, my dear, our hearts are set on this match. Mr. Ludwell Cary asked your uncle's permission to speak to you, and your uncle gave it gladly, and neither he nor I ever dreamed —"

"Of course we did n't," broke in the other. "We did n't dream that Jacqueline could be unreasonable or ungrateful, and we don't dream it now! Nor blind. Ludwell Cary's a man and a gentleman, and the woman who gets him is lucky!"

"We approved his suit, Jacqueline, and we hoped to be happy to-day in your happiness —"

"And in he comes at midnight last night, with his father's own look on his face, and what does he say to Edward and me, sitting here, waiting, with a thousand fancies in our heads? 'Miss Churchill will not have me,' says he, 'and you who have been so good to me, are to be good still, and not by word or look reproach her or distress her. The heart goes its own way, and loves where it must. She is an angel, and to-night I am a poor beaten and weary mortal. I thank you again, both of you, and wish you good-night.' And off he goes before a man could say Jack Robinson! Those were his very words, were n't they, Edward?"

"Yes," answered Edward. "He is a brave and gallant gentleman, Jacqueline. I love you, child, more than my old tongue can say. My Castle in Spain is Greenwood with you and Ludwell Cary and the children of you both."

"Oh, cruel!" cried Jacqueline. "He is brave and good — He is all that you say. But I shall never live at Greenwood!"

"It was your father's dearest wish," said the Major. "It is ours — Richard's and mine. We are not men who give up easily. God forbid, child, that I should hint to you, who are the darling of us all, of obligation — and yet I put it to you if obedience is not owed —"

"Yes, yes," answered Jacqueline. "It is owed. I am not ungrateful — I am mad — perhaps I am wicked! I wish that I were dead!"

"The Churchills," said Uncle Edward, "have never in their marriages set vulgar store by money. Blood we ask, of course, and honourable position, and the right way of thinking. Individually I am a stickler for mind. To his wealth and to his name and his great personal advantages Ludwell Cary adds intellect. He may become a power in his country and his time. You would so aid him, child! I am called a woman-hater, but once, Jacqueline, I loved too well. For all that I am a sorry old bachelor, I know whereof I speak. With a man, a woman to fight for is not half the battle — it is all the battle."

"He is all that you say," answered Jacqueline. "But I do not love him."

"You like him. You admire him."

"Yes, yes. That is not love."

"It is mighty near kin," said Uncle Dick. "No end of happy folk begin with esteem and go on like turtle doves. My little Jack, you shall have the prettiest wedding gown! It's all a mistake and a misunderstanding, and the good Lord knows there's too much of both in this old world! You'll think better of it all, and you'll find that you did n't know your own mind, — and there'll be a smile for poor Cary when he comes riding back to-night?"

"No, no," cried Jacqueline. "There is no mistake and no misunderstanding. Love cannot be forced, and I'll not marry where I do not love!"

"You don't," said Colonel Churchill slowly, "you don't by any chance love some one else? What does that colour mean, Jacqueline? Don't stammer! Speak out!"

But Jacqueline, standing by the old leather chair, bowed her head upon its high green back, and neither could nor would "speak out." The two men, grey and withered, obstinate and imperious in a day and generation that subordinated youth to the councils of the old, gazed at their niece with perplexity and anger. With the simpler of the two the perplexity was the greater, with the other anger. A fear was knocking at Major Churchill's heart. He would not admit it, strove not to listen to it, or to listen with contemptuous incredulity. "It's not possible," he said to himself. "Not a thousand summers at Jane Selden's would make her so forget herself! Jacqueline in love with that damned Jacobin demagogue upstairs! Pshaw!" But the fear knocked on.

Jacqueline lifted her head. "Be good to me, Uncle Dick! If I could love, if I could marry Mr. Cary, I would — I would indeed! But I cannot. Please let me go!"

"Not till I know more than I know now," said Colonel Churchill. "If it's George Lee, Jacqueline, I'll not say a word, sorry as I am for Cary. But if it's Will Allen, I'll see you dead before I give my consent! He's a spendthrift and a Republican!"

"I care neither for Mr. Lee nor Mr. Allen," said Jacqueline, with a burning cheek. "Oh, Uncle Edward, make Uncle Dick let me go!"

"It is not wise," Major Churchill considered within himself, "to push a woman too far. I'm a suspicious fool to think this thing of Jacqueline. It's all some girl's fancy or other, and if we go easily Cary will yet win — by God, he shall win! This damned Yahoo upstairs is neither here nor there!"

He spoke aloud to his brother. "Best let the child go think it over, Dick. She knows her duty — and that we expect her compliance. She doesn't want to wound us cruelly, to make us unhappy, to prove herself blind and ingrate. Give her a kiss and let her go."

"You come down and sing to us to-night, my little Jack, in your blue gown," quoth Uncle Dick. "Don't you ever let a time come when your singing won't be the sweetest sound in the world to me! Now go, and think of what we have said, and of poor Cary, ridden off to Greenwood!"

Jacqueline gazed at the two for a moment, and made as if to speak, but the words died in her throat. She uttered a broken cry, turned, groped a little for the door, found and opened it, and was gone. They heard the click of her slippers upon the stairs, and presently the closing of a blind in the room that was hers.

The brothers sat heavily on in the sunshine-flooded library, the elder red and fuming, the younger silent and saturnine. At last Colonel Dick broke out, "What the devil ails her, Edward? Every decent young fellow in the county comes to Fontenoy straight as a bee to the honey-pot! I've heard them sighing for her and Unity, but I never could see that she favoured one man more than another, — and she's no coquette like Unity! Except for that fine blush of hers, I'd never have thought. What do you think, Edward?"

"The ways of women are past my finding out," said Edward. "Let it rest for a while, Dick." He rose from his chair stiffly, like an old man. "Let Cary go home to-morrow as he intends. 'Absence makes the heart grow fonder,' they say. She may find that she misses him, and may look for him when he comes riding over. Never fear but he'll ride over often! He must n't guess, of course, that you have spoken to her. And that's all we can do, Dick, except —" Major Edward walked stiffly across the floor and paused before the portrait of his brother Henry, dead and gone these many years. The face looked imperiously down upon him. Henry had stood for something before he died, — for grace and manly beauty, pride and fire. The Major's eyes suddenly smarted. "Poor white trash," he said between his teeth, "and Henry's daughter!" He turned and came back to the table. "Dick! just as soon as you can, you clear the house of old Gideon Rand's son!"

"What's he got to do with it?" asked Colonel Dick.

"I don't know," said the other. "But I want him out of the blue room, and out of Fontenoy! and now, Dick, I've got a piece to write this morning on the designs of Aaron Burr."

At five in the afternoon Cary returned, quiet and handsome, ready with his account of matters at Greenwood, from the stable, upon which Major Churchill must pronounce, to the drawing-room paper, which awaited Miss Dandridge's sentence. His behaviour was perfection, but "He's hard hit," said his brother to himself. "What, pray, would Miss Churchill have?" And Unity, "The shepherds and shepherdesses don't match. How can she have the heart?" And Major Churchill, "Are women blind? This is Hyperion to a satyr." And Jacqueline, "Oh, miserable me! Is he writing or reading, or is he lying thinking, there in the blue room?"

CHAPTER X

TO ALTHEA

ADAM GAUDYLOCK came, when his leisure served him, to Fontenoy as he went everywhere, by virtue of his quality of free lance and golden-tongued narrator of western news. The stress of thought at the moment was to the West and the empire that had been purchased there; and a man from beyond Kentucky, with tales to tell of the Mississippi Territory, brought his own welcome to town, tavern, and plantation. If this were true of all, it was trebly true of Adam, who had been born open-eyed. As the magnet draws the filings, so he drew all manner of tidings. News came to him as by a thousand carrier pigeons. He took toll of the solitary in the brown and pathless woods, of the boatmen upon fifty rivers, of the Indian braves about the council-fire, of hunters, trappers, traders, and long lines of Conestoga wagons, of soldiers on frontier posts, Jesuit missionaries upon the Ohio, camp-meeting orators by the Kentucky and the upper James, martial emissaries of three governments, village lawyers, gamblers, dealers in lotteries, and militia colonels, Spanish intendants, French agents, American settlers, wild Irish, thrifty Germans, Creoles, Indians, Mestizos, Quadroons, Congo blacks, — from the hunter in the forest to the slave in the fields, and from the Governor of the vast new territory to the boatman upon a Mississippi ark, not a type of the restless time but imparted to Adam something of its view of life and of the winds that vexed its sea. He was a skilful compounder, and when, forever wandering, he wandered back by wood and stream to the sunny, settled lands east of the Blue Ridge, he gave to the thirsty in plantation and town bright globules of hard fact in a heady elixir of fancy. While he talked all men were adventurers, and all women admired him. Adam liked this life and this world; asked nothing better than to journey through a hundred such.

Now, sitting at his ease in the blue room, a fortnight after Rand's accident, he delivered a score of messages from the Republicans of the county, gentle and simple, whom he had chanced to encounter since the accident to their representative.

"Colonel Randolph says the President has bad luck with the horses he gives — young Mr. Carr was thrown by a bay mare from Shadwell. Old Jowett swears that a trooper of Tarleton's broke his neck at that identical place — says you can hear him any dark night swearing like the Hessian he was. They drank your health at the Eagle, the night they heard of the accident, with bumpers — drank it just after Mr. Jefferson's and before the memory of Washington. 'Congress next!' they said. 'Hurrah! He'll scatter the Black Cockades — he'll make the Well-born cry King's Cruse! Hip, hip, hurrah! What's he doing at Fontenoy? They'll put poison in his cup! Hurrah!'"

"Fontenoy will not put poison in my cup," said Rand. "I hope some one was there to say as much."

"I said it," answered Adam. "They are a noisy lot. Tom Mocket made a speech and compared you to Moses. He wept when he made it, and they had to hold him steady on his feet. When they broke up, I took him home to the Partridge. I'll tell you one speech that he never made by himself, and that's the speech that's going to hang Fitch."

"No," said Rand. "I wrote it. You were at the trial?"

"Ay. It would have hung Abel, so poor Cain had no chance. Mr. Eppes says Mr. Jefferson counts upon your becoming a power in the state. I don't know — but it seems to me there's power enough in these regions! It's getting crowded. First thing you know, you'll be jealous of Mr. Jefferson, or he'll be jealous of you. If I were you, I'd look to the West."

"The old song!" exclaimed Rand. "What should I do in the West?"

"Rule it," said Adam.

Rand shot a glance at the hunter where he lounged against the window, a figure straight and lithe as an Indian, not tall, but gifted with a pantherish grace, and breathing a certain tawny brightness as of sunshine through pine needles. "You're daft!" he said; then after a moment, "Are you serious?"

"Why should I not be serious?" asked Adam. "My faith! it's a restless land, the West, and it's a far cry from the Mississippi to the Potomac. The West does n't like the East anyhow. But it wants a picked man from the East. It will get one too! The wind's blowing hard from the full to the empty, from the parcelled-out to the virgin land!"

"Yes," said Rand.

"Why should n't you be the man?" demanded Gaudylock. "Just as well you as Claiborne — Wilkinson's naught, I don't count him — or any one still East, like — like — Aaron Burr."

"Aaron Burr?"

"Well, I just instance him. He's ambitious enough, and there does n't seem much room for him back here. If Adam Gaudylock was ambitious and was anything but just an uneducated hunter with a taste for danger — I tell you, Lewis, I can see the blazed trees, I can see them with my eyes shut, stretching clean from anywhere — stretching from this room, say — beyond the Ohio, and beyond the

Mississippi, and beyond Mexico to where the sun strikes the water! It's a trail for fine treading and a strong man, but it leads — it leads —"

"It might lead," said Rand, "to the Tarpeian Rock."

"Where's that?"

"It's where they put to death a sort of folk called traitors — Benedict Arnolds and such."

"Pshaw!" exclaimed Adam. "Traitors! Benedict Arnold *was* a traitor. This is not like that. America's large enough for a mort of countries. All the states are countries — federated countries. Say some man is big enough to *make* a country west of the Mississippi — Well, one day we may federate too. Eh, Lewis, 'twould be a powerful country — great as Rome, I reckon! And we'd smoke the calumet with old Virginia — and she'd rule East and we'd rule West. D'you think it's a dream? — Well, men make dreams come true."

"Yes: Corsicans," answered Rand. "Aaron Burr is not a Corsican." He looked at his left hand, lying upon the arm of his chair, raised it, shut and opened it, gazing curiously at its vein and sinew. "You are talking midsummer madness," he said at last. "Let's leave the blazed trees for a while — though we'll talk of them again some time. Have you been along the Three-Notched Road?"

"Yes," replied Adam, turning easily. "Your tobacco's prime, the wheat, too, and the fencing is all mended and whitewashed. It's not the tumble-down place it was in Gideon's time — you've done wonders with it. The morning-glories were blooming over the porch, and your white cat washing itself in the sun."

"It's but a poor home," said Rand, and he said it wistfully. He wished for a splendid house, a home so splendid that any woman must love it.

"It's not so fine as Fontenoy," quoth Adam, "nor Monticello, nor Mr. Blennerhasset's island in the Ohio, but a man might be happy in a poorer spot. Home's home, as I can testify who have n't any. I've known a Cherokee to die of homesickness for a skin stretched between two saplings. How long before you are back upon the Three-Notched Road?"

Rand moved restlessly. "The doctor says I may go downstairs to-day. I shall leave Fontenoy almost immediately. They cannot want me here."

"Have you seen Mr. Ludwell Cary?"

"He and his brother left Fontenoy some time ago. But he rides over nearly every day. Usually I see him."

"He is making a fine place of Greenwood. And he has taken a law office in Charlottesville — the brick house by the Swan."

"Yes. He told me he would not be idle."

Adam rose, and took up the gun which it was his whim to carry. "I'll go talk ginseng and maple sugar to Colonel Churchill for a bit, and then I'll go back to the Eagle. As soon as you are on the Three-Notched Road again I'll come to see you there."

"Adam," said Rand, "in the woods, when chance makes an Indian your host, an Indian of a hostile tribe, an Indian whom you know the next week may see upon the war-path against you — and there is in his lodge a thing, no matter what, that you desire with all your mind and all your heart and all your soul, and he will not barter with you, and the thing is not entirely his own nor highly valued by him, while it is more than life to you, and moreover you believe it to be sought by one who is your foe — would you, Adam, having eaten that Indian's bread, go back into the forest, and leave behind, untouched, unspoken of, that precious thing your soul longed for? The trail you take may never lead again to that lodge. Would you leave it?"

"Yes," answered Adam. "But my trail *should* lead that way again. It is a hostile tribe. I would come back, not in peace paint, but in war paint. I would fairly warn the Indian, and then I would take the bauble."

"Here is Mammy Chloe," said the other. "What have you there, mammy — a dish of red pottage?"

"No, sah," said Mammy. "Hit's a baked apple an' whipped cream an' nutmeg. Ole Miss she say Gineral Lafayette sho' did favour baked apples wunst when he wuz laid up wid a cold at her father's house in Williamsburgh. An' de little posy, Miss Deb she done gather hit outer her square in de gyarden. De Cun'l he say de fambly gwine expect de honour of yo' company dis evenin' in de drawin'-room."

Adam said good-bye and went away. An hour later, going down the Fontenoy road, he came upon a small brown figure, seated, hands over knees, among the blackberry bushes.

"Why, you partridge!" he exclaimed. "You little brown prairie-hen, what are you doing so far from home? Blackberries are n't ripe."

"No," said Vinie. "I was just a-walking down the road, and I just walked on. I was n't tired. I always think the country's prettier down this way. Did you come from Fontenoy, Mr. Adam?"

"Yes," replied Adam, sitting down beside her. "I went to see Lewis Rand — not that I don't like all the people there anyway. They're always mighty nice to me."

Vinie dug the point of her dusty shoe into the dusty road.

"How ith Mr. Rand, Mr. Adam?"

"He 'ith' almost well," answered Adam. "He's going

down into the parlour to-night, and pretty soon he's going home, and then he'll be riding into town to his office."

He looked kindly into the small, freckled, pretty face. The heat of the day stood in moisture on Vinie's brow, she had pushed back her sunbonnet, and the breeze stirred the damp tendrils of her hair. "Tom must miss him," said the hunter.

"Yeth, Tom does." Vinie drew toward her a blackberry branch, and studied the white bloom. "Which do you think is the prettiest, Mr. Adam,— Miss Unity or Miss Jacqueline?"

"Why, I don't know," answered Adam. "They are both mighty pretty."

"I think Miss Unity's the prettiest," said Vinie. "It's time I was walking back to Charlottesville." She rose and stood for a moment in the dusty road below the blackberry bushes, looking toward Fontenoy. "I don't suppose he asked after Tom and me, Mr. Adam?"

"Why, surely!" protested Adam, with cheerful mendacity. "He asked after you both particularly. He said he certainly would like a cup of water from your well."

"Did he?" asked Vinie, and grew pink. "That water's mighty cold."

"I'd like a cup of it myself," said Adam. "Since we are both walking to town, we might as well walk together. Don't you want me to break some cherry blossoms for your parlour?"

"Yeth, if you please," replied Vinie, and the two went up the sunny road to Charlottesville.

Back at Fontenoy, in the blue room, Rand, resting in the easy chair beside the window, left the consideration of Adam and Adam's talk, and gave his mind to the approaching hour in the Fontenoy drawing-room. He both desired and dreaded that encounter. Would Miss Churchill be there? Aided by the homely friendliness of her cousin's house on the Three-Notched Road, he had met her and conversed with her without being greatly conscious of any circumstance other than that she was altogether beautiful, and that he loved her. But this was not Mrs. Selden's, this was Fontenoy. He had stood here hat in hand, within Miss Churchill's memory — certainly within the memory of the men of her family. Well! He was, thank God! an American citizen. The hat was now out of his hand and upon his head. The conditions of his boyhood might, he thought, be forgotten in the conditions of his manhood. But — they would all be gathered in the drawing-room. Should he speak first to Colonel Churchill as his host, or first to the ladies of the house, to Miss Churchill and Miss Dandridge? If Miss Churchill or Miss Dandridge were at the harpsichord, should he wait at the door until the piece was ended? He had a vision of a great space of polished floor reflecting candlelight, and of himself crossing that trackless desert beneath the eyes of goddesses and men. The colour came into his face. There were twenty things he might have asked Mr. Pincornet that night at Monticello. He turned with hot impatience from the consideration of the usages of society, and fell to building with large and strong timbers the edifice of his future. He built on while the dusk gathered, and he built while Joab helped him to dress, and he was yet busy with beam and rafter when at eight o'clock, with some help from the negro, he descended the stairs and crossed the hall to the parlour door. How was he dressed? He was dressed in a high-collared coat of blue cloth with eagle buttons, in cloth breeches and silk stockings, in shoes with silver buckles, and a lawn neckcloth of many folds. His hair was innocent of powder, and cut short in what the period supposed to be the high Roman fashion. It was his chief touch of the Republican. In the matter of dress he had not his leader's courage. Abhorring slovenliness and the Jacobin motley, he would not affect them. He was dressed in his best for this evening; and if his attire was not chosen as Ludwell Cary would have chosen, it was yet the dress of a gentleman, and it was worn with dignity.

Music was playing, as he paused at the half-open door, — he could see Miss Dandridge at the harpsichord. The room seemed very light. For a moment he ceased to be the masterbuilder and sank to the estate of the apprentice, awkward and eaten with self-distrust; the next, with a characteristic abrupt motion of head and hand, he recovered himself, waved Joab aside, and boldly crossed the threshold.

Unity, at the harpsichord, was playing over, very rapidly, one after another, reels, hornpipes, jigs, and Congos, and looking, meanwhile, slyly out of velvet eyes at Fairfax Cary, who had asked for a particularly tender serenade. He stood beside her, and strove for injured dignity. It was a day of open courtship, and polite Albemarle watched with admiration the younger Cary's suit to Miss Dandridge. He had ridden alone to Fontenoy, his brother, who had business in Charlottesville, promising to join him later in the evening. Mr. Ned Hunter, too, was at Fontenoy, and he also would have been leaning over the harpsichord but for the fact that Colonel Dick had fastened upon him and was demonstrating with an impressive forefinger the feasibility of widening into a highway fit for a mail-coach a certain forest track running over the mountains and through the adjoining county. They stood upon the hearth, and Mr. Hunter could see Miss Dandridge only by much craning of the neck. "Yes, yes," he said vaguely, "it can easily be widened, sir."

Major Churchill, playing Patience at the small table, raised his head like a war-horse. "Nonsense! widen on one side and you will fall into the river; on the other, and a pretty cliff you'll have to climb! You could as well widen the way between Scylla and Charybdis — or Mahomet's Bridge to Paradise — or Thomas Jefferson's Natural Bridge! Pshaw!" He began to build from the five of clubs.

"A detour can be made," said Colonel Dick.

"Around the Blue Ridge?" asked the Major scornfully. "Pshaw! And it passes my comprehension what a stage-coach would do in that country. There are not ten houses on that cart track."

"Nonsense! there are fifty."

"Fifty-three, I assure you, sir."

The Major laid down his cards and turned in his chair. "I counted every structure the last time I was on that road. Taking in Fagg's Mill and Brown's Ferry and the Mountain Schoolhouse, there are just ten houses. It is my habit, sir, to reckon accurately."

Mr. Hunter grew red. "But, sir, the count was taken before the last election, and fifty-three —"

"Ten, sir!" said the Major, and placed the queen of diamonds.

"When did you ride that way, Edward?" queried his brother. "I don't believe you've been across the mountain since the war."

"I was on that road in '87," said the Major. "I rode that way on the sixth of April with Clark. And there are ten houses; I counted them."

"But good Lord, sir, this is 1804!"

The Major's hawk eyes, dark and bright beneath shaggy brows, regarded Mr. Ned Hunter with disfavour. "I am aware, sir, that this is 1804," he said, and placed the king of diamonds.

Jacqueline arose from her chair beside the open window,

softly crossed the floor, and touched Colonel Churchill upon the arm. "Uncle Dick," she murmured, and with the slightest of gestures indicated Rand standing in the door.

Colonel Churchill started, precipitantly left Mr. Hunter, and crossed the floor to his guest of two weeks. "My dear sir, you came in so quietly! I welcome you downstairs. Gilmer says you're a strong fighter. When I was thrown at that same turn coming home from a wedding, I believe I was in bed for a month! — Allow me to present you to my nieces — Miss Churchill, Miss Dandridge. My poor wife, you know, never leaves her chamber. Mr. Ned Hunter, Mr. Rand. Mr. Fairfax Cary I think you know, and my brother Edward."

The young men's greeting, if somewhat constrained, was courteous. Major Churchill played the card which he held in his hand, then slowly rose, came stiffly from behind the small table, and made an elaborate bow. There was in his acknowledgment of the honour of Mr. Rand's acquaintance so much accent, cruelty, and hauteur that the younger man flushed. "This is an enemy," said a voice within him. He bowed in return, and he no longer felt any distrust of himself. When Miss Dandridge, leaving the harpsichord, established herself upon the sofa before him and opened a lively fire of questions and comment, he answered with readiness. He thought her pretty figure in amber lutestring, and the turn of her ringleted head, and the play of her scarlet lips all very good to look at, and he looked without hesitation. The account which she demanded of the accident which had placed him there he gave with a free, bold, and pleasing touch, and the thanks that were her due as the immediate Samaritan he chivalrously paid. Unity made friends with all parties, and she now found, with some amusement, that she was going to like Lewis Rand.

Rand looked too, freely and quietly, at the young men, his fellow guests. Each, he knew, was arrogantly impatient of his presence there. Well, they had nothing to do with it! His sense of humour awoke, and Federalist hauteur ceased to fret him. Colonel Churchill, the most genial of men, pushed his chair into the Republican's neighbourhood, and plunged into talk. Conversation in Virginia, where men were concerned, opened with politics, crops, or horseflesh. Colonel Dick chose the second, and Rand, who had a first-hand knowledge of the subject, met him in the fields. The trinity of corn, wheat, and tobacco occupied them for a while, as did the fruit and an experiment in vine-growing. The horse then entered the conversation, and Rand asked after Goldenrod, that had won the cup at Fredericksburg. "I broke him for you, you know, sir, seven years ago."

Colonel Churchill, who in his own drawing-room would not for the world have mentioned this little fact to his guest, suddenly thought within his honest heart, "This is a man, even if he is a damned Republican!" He gave a circumstantial account of Goldenrod, and of Goldenrod's brother, Firefly, and he said to himself, "I'll keep off politics." Presently Rand began to speak of Adam Gaudylock's account of New Orleans.

"Ay, ay," said the Colonel, "there's a city! But it's not English — it is Spanish and French. And all that new land now! 'twill never be held — begging your pardon, Mr. Rand — by Thomas Jefferson and a lot of new-fangled notions! No Spaniard ever did believe that all men are born equal, and no Frenchman ever wanted liberty long — not unadorned liberty, anyway. As for our own people who are pouring over the mountains — well, English blood naturally likes pride and power and what was good enough for its grandparents! Louisiana is too big and too far away.

It takes a month to go from Washington to New Orleans. Rome could n't keep her countries that were far away, and Rome believed in armies and navies and proper taxation, and had no pernicious notions — begging your pardon again, Mr. Rand — about free trade and the abolishment of slavery! I tell you, this new country of ours will breed or import a leader — and then she 'll revolt and make him dictator — and then we 'll have an empire for neighbour, an empire without any queasy ideas as to majorities and natural rights! And Thomas Jefferson — begging your pardon, Mr. Rand — is acute enough to see the danger. He 's not bothering about majorities and natural rights either — for the country west of the Ohio! He 's preparing to govern the Mississippi Territory like a conquered province. Mark my words, Mr. Rand, she 'll find a Buonaparte — some young demagogue, some ambitious upstart without scruple or a hostage to fortune, some common soldier like Buonaparte or favourite like — like —"

"Like —" queried Rand. But the Colonel, who had suddenly grown very red, would not or could not continue his comparison. He floundered, drew out his snuff-box and restored it to his pocket, and finally was taken pity on by Unity, who with dancing eyes reëntered the conversation, and asked if Mr. Rand had read The Romance of the Forest. Fairfax Cary left the harpsichord, where he had been impatiently turning over the music, and, strolling to one of the long windows, stood now looking out into the gloomy night, and now staring with a frowning face at the lit room and at Miss Dandridge, in her amber gown, smiling upon Lewis Rand! Near him, Major Churchill, preternaturally grey and absorbed, played Patience. The cards fell from his hand with the sound of dead leaves. Beside a second window sat Jacqueline, looking, too, into the night. She sat in a low chair covered with dull green silk, and the straight window curtains, of the same colour and texture, half enshadowed her. Her dress was white, with coral about her throat and in her hair. She leaned her elbow on her knee, and with her chin in her hand looked upon the dark mass of the trees, and the stars between the hurrying clouds.

The younger Cary, at his window, leaned out into the night, listened a moment, then turned and left the room. "It is my brother, sir," he announced, as he passed Colonel Churchill. "I hear him at the gate."

Ten minutes later Ludwell Cary entered. He was in riding-dress, his handsome face a little worn and pale, but smiling, his bearing as usual, quiet, manly, and agreeable. "It is a sultry night, sir," he said to Colonel Churchill. "There is a storm brewing. — Miss Dandridge, your very humble servant! — Mr. Rand —" He held out his hand. "I am rejoiced to see you recovered!"

Rand stood up, and touched the extended hand. "Thank you," he said, with a smile. "I were a Turk if I did not recover here amidst all this goodness."

"Yes, yes, there's goodness," answered Cary, and moved on to the window where Jacqueline sat in the shadow of the curtains. Rand, looking after him, saw him speak to her, and saw her answer with a smile.

A pang ran through him, acrid and fiery. It was not like the vapour of distaste and dislike, of which he had been conscious on the day of the election. That had been cold and clinging; this was a burning and a poisoned arrow. It killed the softening, the consciousness of charm, the spell of Cary's kindness while he lay there helpless in the blue room. Not since the old days when his heart was hot against his father, had he felt such venom, such rancour. That had been a boy's wild revolt against injustice; this passion was the fury of the adolescent who sees his rival. He looked at Cary through a red mist. This cleared, but a seed that was in Rand's nature, buried far, far down in the ancestral earth, swelled a little where it lay in its dim chasm. The rift closed, the glow as of heated iron faded, and Rand bitterly told himself, "He will win; more than that, he deserves to win! As for you, you are here to behave like a gentleman." He turned more fully to Unity, and talked of books and of such matters as he thought might be pleasing to a lady.

Fairfax Cary entered, brushing the drops from his coatsleeve. "The rain is coming down," he said, and with deliberation seated himself beside Miss Dandridge.

"That's good!" exclaimed the Colonel. "Now things will grow! — Jacqueline, child, are n't you going to sing to us?"

Jacqueline rose, left the window, and went to her harp, Cary following her. She drew the harp toward her, then raised her clear face. "What shall I sing?" she asked.

Cary, struck by a note in her voice, glanced at her quickly where she now sat, full in the light of the candles. She had no colour ordinarily, but to-night the fine pale brown of her face was tinged with rose. Her eyes were lustrous. As she spoke she drew her hands across the strings, and there followed a sound, faint, far, and sweet. Cary wondered. He was not a vain man, nor over-sanguine, but he wondered, "Is the brightness for me?" The colour came into his own cheek, and a vigour touched him from head to heel. "I don't care what you sing!" he said. "Your songs are all the sweetest ever written. Sing To Althea!"

She sang. Rand watched her from the distance — the hands and the white arm seen behind the gold strings, the slender figure in a gown of filmy white, the warm, bare throat pouring melody, the face that showed the soul within. All the room watched her as she sang, —

TO ALTHEA

> "Stone walls do not a prison make,
>   Nor iron bars a cage;
> Minds innocent and quiet take
>   That for a hermitage."

Through the window came the sound of rain, the smell of wet box and of damask roses. Now and then the lightning flashed, showing the garden and the white bloom of locust trees.

> "Minds innocent and quiet take
>   That for a hermitage."

Rand's heart ached with passionate longing, passionate admiration. He thought that the voice to which he listened, the voice that brooded and dreamed, for all that it was so angel-sweet, would reach him past all the iron bars of time or of eternity. He thought that when he came to die he would wish to die listening to it. The voice sang to him like an angel voice singing to Ishmael in the wilderness.

The song came to an end, but after a moment Jacqueline sang again, sonorous and passionate words of a lover to his mistress. It was not now the Cavalier hymning of constancy; it was the Elizabethan breathing passion, and his cry was the more potent.

> "The thirst that from the soul doth rise
>   Doth ask a drink divine" —

Blinding lightning, followed by a tremendous crash, startled the singer from her harp and brought all in the room to their feet. "That struck!" exclaimed the Colonel. "Look out, Fairfax, and see if 't was the stables! I hear the dogs howling."

"'T was the big pine by the gate, I think, sir," answered Fairfax Cary, half in and half out of the window. "Gad! it is black!"

"You two cannot go home to-night," cried Colonel

Churchill, with satisfaction. "And here's Cato with the decanters! We might have a hand at Loo — eh, Unity? you and Fairfax, Ned Hunter and I. — The card-table, Cato!"

The four sat down, the card-table being so placed as to quite divide Jacqueline and Ludwell Cary, at the harp, from Major Edward's small table and Rand beside the sofa. "Edward!" said the Colonel. His brother nodded, gathered up his cards, and turned squarely to the entertainment of the Republican. "So, Mr. Rand, Mr. Monroe goes to Spain! What the Devil is he going to do there? I wish that your party, sir, would send Mr. Madison to Turkey and Colonel Burr to the Barbary States! And what, may I ask, are you going to do with the Mississippi now that you've got it? It's a damned expensive business buying from Buonaparte. Sixty millions for a *casus belli!* That's what you have paid, and that's what you have acquired, sir!"

"I don't think you can be certain that it's a *casus belli*, sir —"

"Sir," retorted the Major, "I may not know much, but what I know, I know damned well! You cry peace, but there'll be no peace. There'll be war, sir, war, war, war!"

Unity glanced from the card-table. "Sing again, Jacqueline, do! Sing something peaceful," and Jacqueline, still with a colour and with shining eyes, laughed, struck a sounding chord, and in her noble contralto sang Scots wha hae wi' Wallace bled.

CHAPTER XI

IN THE GARDEN

IN the forenoon of the next day Rand closed, for the second time that morning, the door of the blue room behind him, descended the stairs, and, passing through the quiet house, went out into the flower garden. He was going away that afternoon. Breakfast had been taken in his own room, but afterward, with some dubitation, he had gone downstairs. There Colonel Churchill met him heartily enough, but presently business with his overseer had taken the Colonel away. Rand found himself cornered by Major Edward and drawn into a discussion of the impeachment of Judge Chase. Rand could be moved to the blackest rage, but he had no surface irritability of temper. To his antagonists his self-command was often maddening. Major Churchill was as disputatious as Arthur Lee, and an adept at a quarrel, but the talk of the impeachment went tamely on. The Republican would not fight at Fontenoy, and at last the Major in a cold rage went away to the library — first, however, watching the young man well on his way up the stairs and toward the blue room. But Rand had not stayed in the blue room. Restless and unhappy, the garden, viewed through his window, invited him. He thought: "I'll walk in it once again; I'll find the summer-house where I sat beside her," and he had acted upon his impulse. No one was about. Within and without, the house seemed lapped in quiet. He had been given to understand that the ladies were busy with household matters, and he believed the Carys to have ridden to Greenwood. That afternoon he would mount Selim, and with Joab would go home to the house on the Three-Notched Road.

After the rain of the night before the garden was cool and sweet. The drops yet lay on the tangle of old-fashioned flowers, on the box and honeysuckle and the broad leaves of the trees where all the birds were singing. The gravel paths were wet and shining. Rand walked slowly, here and there, between the lines of box or under arching boughs, his mind now trying to bring back the day when he had walked there as a boy, now wondering with a wistful passion if he was to leave Fontenoy without again seeing Jacqueline. He meant to leave without one word that the world might not hear, but he thought it hard that he must go without a touch of the hand, without a " From my heart I thank you for your kindness. Good-bye, good-bye!" That would not be much; Fontenoy might give him that.

He reached an edge of the garden where a threadlike stream trickled under a bank of periwinkle, phlox, and ivy, and on through a little wood of cedars. The air was cool beneath the trees, and Rand raised his forehead to the blowing wind. The narrow pathway turned, and he came upon Deb and Miranda seated upon the bare, red earth and playing with flower dolls.

Deb had before her a parade of morning-glories, purple and white, pink and blue, while Miranda sat in a ring of marigolds and red columbines. Each was slowly swaying to and fro, murmuring to herself, and manipulating with small, darting fingers her rainbow throng of ladies. Rand, unseen, watched the manœuvres for a while, then coughed to let them know he was there, and presently sat down upon a root of cedar, and gave Deb his opinion of the flower people. Children and he were always at their ease together.

"Hollyhocks make the finest ladies," he announced

IN THE GARDEN

gravely. "Little Miss Randolph puts snapdragon caps upon them and gives them scarfs of ribbon grass."

"Hollyhocks are not in bloom," said Deb. "I use snapdragon for caps, too. — Now she has on a red and gold cap. This is a currant-leaf shawl."

"Do you name them?" asked Rand, poising a columbine upon the back of his hand.

"Of course," answered Deb. "All people have names. That is Sapphira."

Miranda advanced a flourishing zinnia. "Dishyer Miss Keren-Happuch — Marse Job's daughter."

Deb regarded with shining eyes a pale blue morning-glory with a little cap of white. "This is Ruth — I love her! The dark one is Hagar — she was dark, you know — and those two are Rachel and Leah."

"Ol' Miss Babylon!" said Miranda succinctly, and put forth a many-petalled red lady.

> "Babylon, Babylon,
> Red an' sinnin' Babylon,
> Wash her han's in Jordan flood,
> Still she's sinnin' Babylon!"

"And these three?" asked Rand.

"Faith, Hope, and Charity," answered Deb. "Faith is blue, Hope is pink, and that white one is Charity."

"She has a purple edge to her gown."

"Yes," said Deb, "and I am going to give her a crown, 'for the greatest of these is Charity!' That yellow lily is the Shulamite. Miranda and I are going now to gather more ladies." She looked at Rand with large child's eyes. "If you want somebody to talk to, my sister Jacqueline is reading over there in the summer-house."

The blood rushed to Rand's face. His heart beat so loud and fast that it stifled a voice within him. He did not even hear the voice. He rose at once, turned, and took the path that Deb's brown finger indicated. Had he been another man, had he been, perhaps, Ludwell Cary, he might not have gone. But he was Lewis Rand, the product and effect of causes inherited and self-planted, and his passion, rising suddenly, mastered him with a giant's grip. The only voice that he heard was the giant's urgent cry, and he went without protest.

The summer-house was a small, latticed place, overgrown with the Seven Sisters rose, and set in a breast-high ring of box opening here and there to the garden paths. A tulip tree towered above the gravel space before it, and two steps led to a floor chequered with light and shade, and to a rustic chair and table. Jacqueline was not within the summer-house; she sat in the doorway, upon the step. She was not reading. She sat bowed together, her head upon her folded arms, a figure still and tragic as a sphinx or sibyl. Rand's eyes upon her roused her from her brooding. She lifted her head, saw him, and her face, which had been drawn and weary, became like the face of the young dawn.

As Rand crossed the space between them, she rose. He saw the colour and the light, and he uttered only her name — "Jacqueline, Jacqueline!" A moment, and they were in each other's arms.

It was their golden hour. Neither thought of right or wrong, of the conditions of life beyond their ring of box, of wisdom or its contrary. It was as though they had met in the great void of space, the marvel called man and the wonder that is woman, each drawn to each over the endless fields and through the immeasurable ages. Each saw the other transfigured, and each wished for lover and companion the other shining one.

They moved to the summer-house, and sat down upon the

IN THE GARDEN

step. About them was the Seven Sisters rose, and above towered the tulip tree with a mockingbird singing in its branches. The place was filled with the odour of the box. To the end of their lives the smell of box brought back that hour in the Fontenoy garden. The green walls hid from view all without their little round. They had not heard step or voice when suddenly, having strolled that way by accident, there emerged from the winding path into the space about the summer-house Colonel Churchill and Ludwell Cary. There was a second's utter check, then, "Sir!" cried the Colonel, in wrathful amazement.

The hands of the lovers fell apart. Rand rose, but Jacqueline sat still, looking at her uncle with a paling cheek and a faint line between her brows. The mockingbird sang on, but the garden appeared to darken and grow cold. The place seemed filled with difficult breathing. Then, before a word was spoken, Cary turned, made a slight gesture with his hand, and went away, disappearing between the lines of box. The sound of his footsteps died in the direction of the stream and the dark wood. Colonel Churchill moistened his lips and spoke in a thick voice. "You scoundrel! Was it for this? You are a scoundrel, sir!"

"I have asked Miss Churchill to be my wife," said Rand, with steadiness. "She has consented. I love your niece, sir, with all my heart, most truly, most dearly! I will ask you to believe that it was not in my mind to speak to her to-day, or to speak at all without your knowledge. I confess the impropriety of my course. But we met unawares. It is not to be helped. In no way is she to blame."

Jacqueline rose, came to her uncle, and tried to take his hand. He repulsed her. "Is this true — what this man says?"

"Yes, yes," said Jacqueline. "It is true. Oh, forgive him!"

The Colonel struck down her outstretched hands. "I do not believe you are Henry's child! Your mother was a strange woman. You are not a Churchill. My God! Henry's child talking of marrying this — this — this *gentleman*. You are mad, or I am mad. Come away from him, Jacqueline!"

"I love him!" cried Jacqueline. "Oh, Uncle Dick, Uncle Dick! —"

"I loved your niece, sir, when I was a boy," said Rand; "and I love her now that I am a man. I grant that I should not have spoken to her to-day. I ask your pardon for what may seem to you insult and thanklessness. But the thing itself — is it so impossible? Why is it impossible that I should wed where I love with all my heart?" He broke a piece of the box beside him and drew it through his hands, then threw it away, and squarely faced the elder man. "I had my way to make in life. Well, I am making it fast. I am making it faster, perhaps, than any other man in the county, be he who he may! I am poor, but I am not so poor as once I was, and I shall be richer yet. My want of wealth is perhaps the least — why should I not say that I know it is the least objection in your mind? My party? Well, I shall become a leader of my party — and Republicans are white as well as Federalists. It is not forgery or murder to detest Pitt and George the Third, or to believe in France! Is it so poor a thing to become a leader of a party that has gained an empire, that has put an end to the Algerine piracy, that has reduced the debt, that has made easier every man's condition, and that stands for freedom of thought and deed and advance of all knowledge? Party! Now and then, even in Virginia, there is a marriage between the parties! My family — or my lack of family? The fact that my father rolled tobacco, and that now and then I broke a colt for you?" He smiled. "Well, you must allow that I broke them thoroughly — and Goldenrod was a very demon! Pshaw! This is America, and once we had an ideal! For the rest, though I do not go to church, I believe in God, and though I have been called an unscrupulous lawyer, I take no dirty money. Some say that I am a demagogue — I think that they are wrong. I love your niece, sir, and more than that — oh, much more than that! — she says that she loves me. She says that she will share my life. If I make not that sharing sweet to her, then indeed — But I will! I will give her wealth and name and place, and a heart to keep. Again I say that the fault of this meeting is all mine. I humbly beg your pardon, Colonel Churchill, and I beg your consent to my marriage with your niece —"

The Colonel, who had heard so far in stormy silence, broke in with, "Marry my niece, sir! I had rather see my niece dead and laid in her grave! Consent! I'd as soon consent to her death or dishonour! Name and place! you neither have them nor will have them!" He turned upon Jacqueline. "I'll forgive you," he said, breathing heavily, "there in the library, when you have written and signed a letter to Mr. Lewis Rand explaining that both he and you were mistaken in your sentiments towards him. I'll forgive you then, and I'll do my best to forget. But not else, Jacqueline, not else on God's earth! That's sworn. As for you, sir, I should think that your awakened sense of propriety might suggest —"

"I am going, sir," answered Rand. "I return to the house but to take my papers from the blue room. Joab shall saddle my horse at once. You shall not anger me, Colonel Churchill. I owe you too much. But your niece has said that she will be my wife, and before God, she shall be! And that's sworn, too, sir! I leave Fontenoy at once, as is just, but I shall write to your niece. Part us you cannot —"

"Jacqueline," cried the Colonel, "the sight of you there beside that man is death to my old heart. You used to care — you used to be a good child! I command you to leave him; I command you to say good-bye to him now, at once and forever! Tell him that you have been dreaming, but that now you are awake. God knows that I think that I am dreaming! Come, come, my little Jack!"

"Will you tell me that?" asked Rand. "Will you tell me that, Jacqueline?"

"No!" cried Jacqueline; "I will tell you only the truth! I love you — love you. Oh, my heart, my heart!" She turned from them both, sank down upon the summer-house step, and lay with her forehead on her arm.

There was a moment's silence, then, "You see," said Rand, not without gentleness, to the elder man.

Colonel Churchill leaned on his walking-stick, and his breath came heavily. He wondered where Edward was — Edward could always find words that would hurt. At last, "We part, Mr. Rand," he said, with dignity. "In parting I have but to say that your conduct has been such as I might have expected, and that I conceive it to be my duty to protect my misguided niece from the consequences of her folly. I warn you neither to write to her nor to attempt to see her. If she writes to you otherwise than as I shall dictate; if she does not, when she has bethought herself, break with you once and forever, — all's over between us! She is no niece of mine. She is dead to me. I'll not speak to her, nor willingly look upon her face again. I am a man of my word. I have the honour, sir, to bid you a very good-day." He drew out and looked at his ponderous watch. "I shall remain here with my niece for an hour. Perhaps in that time she will awaken to her old truth, her old duty; and perhaps you will require no more in which to gather your papers and remove yourself from Fontenoy?"

"I shall not need the hour," answered Rand. "I will be gone presently. God knows, sir, I had not thought to go this way." He turned from his host and bent for a moment over Jacqueline. "Good-bye," he said. "Good-bye for a little while! My heart is in your hands. I trust you for constancy. Good-bye — good-bye!"

He was gone, moving rapidly toward the house. Colonel Churchill drew a long sigh, wiped his face with his handkerchief, and looked miserably up to the green boughs where the mockingbird was singing. He wished again for Edward, and he wished that Henry had not died. He believed in Heaven, and he knew that Henry was there, but then the thought came into his mind that Henry was here, too, in the person of his child, prone on the summer-house steps. Henry, also, had been a man of his word, had known his own mind, and exercised his will. There, too, had been the veil of sweetness! The Colonel sighed more heavily, wished again impatiently for Edward, then marched to the summer-house, and, sitting down, began to reason with Henry's daughter.

Rand passed through the Fontenoy garden, in his heart a pain that was triumph, an exaltation that was pain. Mounting the porch steps, he found himself in the presence of Major Edward playing Patience in the shade of the climbing rose. The player started violently. "I thought, sir," he said, wheeling in his chair, "I thought you yet in the blue room! How the deuce! — I was on guard —" the Major caught himself. "I was waiting to renew our very interesting discussion. Where have you been?"

"I have been in the garden," said Rand. He hesitated,

standing by the table. There was a debate in his mind. "Should I speak to him, too? What is the use? He'll be no kinder to her!" He put out his hand uncertainly, and touched one of the Major's cards. "Is it an interesting game?"

"I find it so," answered the other dryly. "Else I should not play it."

"Why do you like it? It is poor amusement to play against yourself."

"I like it, sir," snapped the Major, "because I am assured of playing against a gentleman."

Rand let his hand fall from the table. "Major Churchill, I am leaving Fontenoy immediately. Perhaps I ought to tell you what I have just told your brother: I love Miss Churchill —"

The Major rose from his chair. "Have you spoken to her?"

"Yes, I have asked her to marry me."

"Indeed!" said the Major huskily. "May I ask what Miss Churchill replied?"

"Miss Churchill loves me," answered Rand. "She will do what I wish."

The silence grew painful. The words, acid and intolerable, that Rand expected, did not seem to come easily to the Major's dry lips. He looked small, thin, and frozen, grey and drawn of face, as though the basilisk had confronted him. When at last he spoke, it was in a curiously remote voice, lucid and emotionless. "Well, why not? All beliefs die — die and rot! A vain show — and this, too, was of the charnel!"

He turned upon Rand as if he would have struck him, then drew back, made in the air an abrupt and threatening gesture, and with a sound like a stifled cry passed the other and entered the house. Rand heard him go down the hall, and the closing of the library door.

The young man's heart was hot and sore. He went up

IN THE GARDEN

to the blue room, where he found Joab packing his portmanteau. A few peremptory words sent the man to the stables, while his master with rapid fingers collected and laid together the papers with which the room was strewn. The task finished, he threw himself for a moment into the great chair and looked about him. He was capable of great attachment to place, and he had loved this room. Now the mandarin smiled obliquely on him, and the moon-clock ticked the passing moments, the impossible blue roses flowered on thornless stems, and the picture of Washington looked calmly down from the opposite wall. He put his hand over his eyes, and sat still, trying to calm the storm within him. There were in his mind joy and gratitude, hurt pride and bitter indignation, and a thousand whirling thoughts as to ways and means, the overcoming of obstacles, and the building of a palace fit to shelter his happiness. The clock struck, and he started up. Not for much would he have overstayed his hour.

He left the room and passed through the silent house, mounted his horse, and rode away. A crowd had witnessed his arrival there; only a few wondering servants were gathered to see him depart. He gave them gold, but though they thanked him, they thanked him with a difference. He felt it, and that more keenly than he might have felt a greater thing. Could he not even give largesse like one to the manner born, or was it only that all the air was hostile? He rode away. From the saddle he could have seen the distant summer-house, but he forced himself not to look. The lawn fell away behind him, and the trees hid the house. The gleam of a white pillar kept with him for a while, but the driveway bent, and that too was hidden. With Joab behind him on the iron grey, he passed through the lower gate, and took the way that led to Mrs. Jane Selden's on the Three-Notched Road.

CHAPTER XII

A MARRIAGE AT SAINT MARGARET'S

"YES," said Unity. "That is just what the Argus says. 'On Thursday M. Jérôme Buonaparte, the younger brother of the First Consul, passed through Annapolis with his bride — lately the lively and agreeable Miss Elizabeth Patterson of Baltimore. M. Buonaparte's Secretary and Physician followed in a chaise, and the valets and *femmes-de-chambre* in a coach. The First Consul's brother wore —' I protest I don't care what the First Consul's brother wore! The Argus is not gallant. If you were the First Consul's brother —"

"The Argus should describe the bride's dress, not mine," said Fairfax Cary. "How lovely you would look, in that gown you have on, in a curricle drawn by grey horses! What is the stuff — roses and silver?"

"Heigho!" sighed Unity. "'T is a bridesmaid's gown. I am out with men. I shall never wear a bride's gown."

"Don't jest —"

"Jest! I never felt less like jesting! I laugh to keep from crying. Here is the coach."

The great Fontenoy coach with the Churchill arms on the panel drew up before the porch. It was drawn by four horses, and driven by old Philip in a wig and nosegay. Mingo was behind, and Phyllis's Jim and a little darky ran alongside to open the door and let down the steps. "All alone in that!" exclaimed Cary. "I shall ride with you as far as the old road to Greenwood. Don't say no! I'll hold your flowers."

A MARRIAGE AT SAINT MARGARET'S 145

Unity looked down upon the roses in her arms. "They should all be white," she said. "I feel as though I were going to see them bury Jacqueline." Her voice broke, but she bit her lip, forced back the tears, and tried to laugh. "I'm not. I'm going to her wedding — and people know their own business best — and she may be as happy as the day is long! He *is* fascinating, — he is dreadfully fascinating, — and we have no right to say he is not good — and everybody knows he is going to be great! Why shouldn't she be happy?"

"I don't know," answered Cary. "But I know she won't be."

"You say that," cried Unity, turning on him, "because you are a Federalist! Well, women are neither Federalists nor Republicans! They have no party and no soul of their own! They are just what the person they love is —"

"That's not so," said Cary.

"Oh, I know it's not so!" agreed Miss Dandridge, with impatience. "It's just one of those things that are said! But it remains that Jacqueline must be happy. I'll break my heart if she's not! And as long as I live, I'll say that Uncle Dick and Uncle Edward are to blame —"

"Where are they?"

"Oh, Uncle Dick is in the long field watching the threshing, and Uncle Edward is in the library reading Swift! And Aunt Nancy has ordered black scarfs to be put above the pictures of Uncle Henry and of Great-Aunt Jacqueline that Jacqueline's named for. Oh, oh!"

"And Deb?" asked the young man gently.

"Deb is at Cousin Jane Selden's. She has been there with Jacqueline a week — she and Miranda. Oh, I know — Uncle Dick is a just man! He does what he thinks is the just thing. Deb shall go visit her sister — every now and then! And all that Uncle Henry left Jacqueline goes with her — there are slaves and furniture and plate, and she has money, too. The Rands don't usually marry so well — There! I, too, am bitter! But Uncle Dick swears that he will never see Jacqueline again — and all the Churchills keep their word. Oh, family quarrels! Deb's coming back to Fontenoy to-morrow — poor little chick! Aunt Nancy's got to have those mourning scarfs taken away before she comes!"

Miss Dandridge descended the porch steps to the waiting coach. The younger Cary handed her in with great care of her flowers and gauzy draperies, and great reluctance in relinquishing her hand. "I may come too?" he asked, "just as far as the old Greenwood road? I hate to see you go alone."

"Oh, yes, yes!" answered Miss Dandridge absently, and, sinking into a corner, regarded through the window the July morning. "Those black scarfs hurt me," she said, and the July morning grew misty. "It's not death to marry the man one loves!"

The coach rolled down the drive to the gate, and out upon the sunny road. The dust rose in clouds, whitening the elder, the stickweed, and the blackberry bushes. The locusts shrilled in the parching trees. The sky was cloudless and intensely blue, marked only by the slow circling of a buzzard far above the pine-tops. There were many pines, and the heat drew out their fragrance, sharp and strong. The moss that thatched the red banks was burned, and all the ferns were shrivelling up. Everywhere butterflies fluttered, lizards basked in the sun, and the stridulation of innumerable insects vexed the ear. The way was long, and the coach lumbered heavily through the July weather. "I do not want to talk," sighed Unity. "My heart is too heavy."

"My own is not light," said Cary grimly. "I am sorry for my brother."

"We are all sorry for your brother," Unity answered gently, and then would speak no more, but sat in her silver and roses, looking out into the heat and light. The Greenwood road was reached in silence. Cary put his head out of the window and called to old Philip. The coach came slowly to a stop before a five-barred gate. Mingo opened the door, and the young man got out. "Unless you think I might go with you as far as the church —" he suggested, with his hand on the door. Unity shook her head. "You can't do that, you know! Besides, I am going first to Cousin Jane Selden's. Good-bye. Oh, it is going to be a happy marriage — it must be happy!"

"What is going to make it happy?" demanded Cary gloomily. "It's a match against nature! When I think of your cousin in that old whitewashed house, and every night Gideon Rand's ghost making tobacco around it! I am glad that Ludwell has gone to Richmond. He looks like a ghost himself."

"Oh, the world!" sighed Unity. "Tell Philip, please, to drive on."

"I'll ride over to Fontenoy to-morrow," said Fairfax Cary. "'Twill do you good to talk it over."

The coach went heavily on through the dust of the Three-Notched Road. The locusts shrilled, the pines gave no shade, in the angle of the snake fences pokeberry and sumach drooped their dusty leaves. The light air in the pine-tops sounded like the murmur of a distant sea, too far off for coolness. Unity sighed with the oppression of it all. The flowers were withering in her lap. After a long hour the road turned, discovering yellow wheat-fields and shady orchards, the gleam of a shrunken stream and a brick house embowered in wistaria. Around the horse-block and in the shade of a great willow were standing a coach or two, a chaise, and several saddle-horses. "All of them Republican," commented Unity.

At the door she was met by Cousin Jane Selden herself, a thin and dark old lady with shrewd eyes and a determined chin. "I'm glad to see you, Unity, though I should have been more glad to see Richard and Edward Churchill! 'Woe to a stiff-necked generation!' says the Bible. Well! you are fine enough, child, and I honour you for it! There are a few people in the parlour — just those who go to church with us. The clock has struck, and we'll start in half an hour. Jacqueline is in her room, and when she does n't look like an angel she looks like her mother. You had best go upstairs. Mammy Chloe dressed her."

Unity mounted the dark, polished stairs to an upper hall where stood a tall clock and a spindle-legged table with a vast jar of pot-pourri. A door opened, framing Jacqueline, dressed in white, and wearing her mother's wedding veil. "I knew your step," she said. "Oh, Unity, you are good to come!"

In the bedroom they embraced. "Wild horses could n't have kept me from coming!" declared Unity with resolute gaiety. "Whichever married first, the other was to be bridesmaid! — we arranged that somewhere in the dark ages! Oh, Jacqueline, you are like a princess in a picture-book!"

"And Uncle Dick and Uncle Edward?" asked Jacqueline, in a low voice.

"Well, the Churchills are obstinate folk, as we all know!" answered Unity cheerfully. "But I think time will help. They can't go on hating forever. Uncle Dick is in the fields, and Uncle Edward is in the library reading. There, there, honey!"

Mammy Chloe bore down upon them from the other end of the room. "Miss Unity, don' you mek my chile cry on her weddin' mahnin'! Hit ain't lucky to cry befo' de ring's on!"

"I'm not crying, Mammy," said Jacqueline. "I wish that I could cry. It is you, Unity, that are like a princess in your rose and silver, with your dear red lips, and your dear black eyes! Isn't she lovely, Mammy?" She came close to her cousin and pinned a small brooch in the misty folds above the white bosom. "This is my gift — it is mother's pearl brooch. Oh, Unity, don't think too ill of me!"

"Think ill!" cried Unity, with spirit. "I think only good of you. I think you are doing perfectly right! I'll wear your pearl always — you were always like a pearl to me!"

"Even pearls have a speck at heart," said Jacqueline. "And there's nothing perfectly right — or perfectly wrong. But most things cannot be helped. Some day, perhaps, at home — at Fontenoy — they will think of the time when they were young — and in love." She turned and took up her gloves from the dressing-table. "I have had a letter from Ludwell Cary," she said, then spoke over her shoulder with sudden fire. "He is the only one of all I know, the only one of all my people, who has been generous enough, and just enough, to praise the man I marry!"

"Oh, Jacqueline!" cried Unity, "I will praise him to the skies, if only he will make you happy! Does not every one say that he has a great future? and surely he deserves all credit for rising as he has done — and he is most able —"

"And *good*," said Jacqueline proudly. "Don't praise him any more, Unity." She put her hands on her cousin's shoulders and kissed her lightly on the forehead. "Now and then, my dear, will you come to see me on the Three-Notched Road? I shall have Deb one week out of six."

"I shall come," answered Unity. "Where is Deb?"

"She is asleep. She cried herself to sleep."

"Chillern cry jes' fer nothin' at all," put in Mammy Chloe. "Don' you worry, honey! Miss Deb's all right. I's gwine wake her now, an' wash her face, an' slip on her li'l white dress. She's gwine be jes' ez peart an' ez happy! My Lawd! Miss Deb jes' gainin' a brother!"

"Jacqueline," came Cousin Jane Selden's voice at the door. "It is almost time."

The coach of the day was an ark in capacity, and woman's dress as sheathlike as a candle flame. Jacqueline, Unity, Deb, Cousin Jane Selden, and a burly genial gentleman of wide family connections and Republican tenets travelled to church in the same vehicle and were not crowded. The coach was Cousin Jane Selden's; the gentleman was of some remote kinship, and had been Henry Churchill's schoolmate, and he was going to give Jacqueline away. He talked to Cousin Jane Selden about the possibilities of olive culture, and he showed Deb a golden turnip of a watch with jingling seals. Jacqueline and Unity sat in silence, Jacqueline's arm around Deb. Behind their coach came the small party gathered at Mrs. Selden's. The church was three miles down the road. It was now afternoon, and the heat lay like a veil upon wood and field and the foot-hills of the Blue Ridge. The dust rose behind the carriage, then sank upon and further whitened the milkweed and the love vine and the papaw bushes. The blaze of light, the incessant shrilling of the locusts, the shadeless pines, the drouth, the long, dusty road — all made, thought Unity, a dry and fierce monotony that seared the eyes and weighed upon the soul. She wondered of what Jacqueline was thinking.

The Church of Saint Margaret looked forth with a small, white-pillared face, from a grove of oaks. It had a flowery churchyard, and around it a white paling, keeping in the dead, and keeping out all roaming cattle. There was a small cracked bell, and the swallows forever circled above the eaves and in and out of the belfry. Without the yard, beneath the oaks, were a horserack and a shed for carriages. To-day there were horses at the rack and tied beneath the trees; coaches, chaises, and curricles, not a few, beneath the shed and scattered through the oak grove. The church within was all rustle and colour. Saint Margaret's had rarely seen such a gathering, or such a wholly amicable one, for to-day all the pews were of one party. The wedding was one to draw the curious, the resolutely Republican, the kindred and friends of Jefferson, — who, it was known, had sent the bride a valuable present and a long letter, — the interested in Rand, the inimical, for party and other reasons, to the Churchills and the Carys. The county knew that Miss Churchill might have had Greenwood. The knowledge added piquancy to the already piquant fact that she had chosen the house on the Three-Notched Road. Colonel Churchill and Major Edward, the county knew, would not come to the wedding; neither, of course, would the two Carys; neither, it appeared, would any other Federalist. The rustling pews looked to all four corners and saw only folk of one watchword. True, under the gallery was to be seen Mr. Pincornet, fadedly gorgeous in an old green velvet, but to this English stock Mr. Pincornet might give what word he chose; he remained a French dancing master. The rustling pews nodded and smiled to each other, waiting to see Jacqueline Churchill come up the aisle in bridal lace. Under the gallery, not far from Mr. Pincornet, sat Adam Gaudylock, easy and tawny, dressed as usual in his fringed hunting-frock, with his coonskin cap in his hand, and his gun at his feet. Beside him sat Vinie Mocket, dressed in her best. Vinie's eyes were downcast, and her hands clasped in her lap. She wondered — poor little partridge! — why she was there, why she had been so foolish as to let Mr. Adam persuade her into coming. Vinie was afraid she was going to cry. Yet not for worlds would she have left Saint Margaret's; she wanted, with painful curiosity, to see the figure in bridal lace. She wondered where Tom was. Tom was to have joined Mr. Adam and herself an hour ago. The bell began to ring, and all the gathering rustled loudly. "She's coming — she's coming!" whispered Vinie; and Adam, "Why, of course, of course, little partridge. Now don't you cry — you'll be walking up Saint Margaret's aisle yourself some day!"

The bell ceased to ring. Lewis Rand came from the vestry and stood beside the chancel rail. A sound at the door, a universal turning as though the wind bent every flower in a garden — and Jacqueline Churchill came up the aisle between the coloured lines. Her hand was upon the arm of her father's schoolmate; Unity and Deb followed her. Rand met her at the altar, and the old clergyman who had baptized her married them. It was over, from the "Dearly beloved, we are gathered here together," to the "Until Death shall them part!" Lewis and Jacqueline Rand wrote their names in the register, then turned to receive the congratulations of those who crowded around them, to smile, and say the expected thing. Rand stooped and kissed Deb, wrung Mrs. Selden's hand, then held out his own to Unity with something of appeal in his gesture and his eyes. Miss Dandridge promptly laid her hand in his, and looked at him with her frank and brilliant gaze. "Now that we are cousins," she said, "I do not find you a monster at all. Make her happy, and one day we'll all be friends." "I will — I will!" answered Rand, with emotion, pressed her hand warmly, and was claimed by others of his wedding guests. Jacqueline, too, had clung at first to Unity and Deb and Cousin Jane Selden, but now she also turned from the old life to the new, and greeted with a smiling face the people of her husband's party. Many, of course, she knew; only a difference of opinion stood between them and the Churchills; but others were strangers to her — strangers and curious. She felt it in the touch of their hands, in the stare of their eyes, and her heart was vaguely troubled. She saw her old dancing master, tiptoeing on the edge of the throng, and her smile brought Mr. Pincornet, his green velvet and powdered wig, to her side. He put his hand to his heart and bowed as to a princess.

"Ha! Mr. Pincornet," exclaimed Rand, "I remember our night at Monticello. Now I have a teacher who will be with me always! — Jacqueline, I want you to speak to my old friend, Adam Gaudylock."

"Ah, I know Mr. Gaudylock," answered Jacqueline, and gave the hunter both her hands. "We all know and admire and want to be friends with Adam Gaudylock!"

The picture that she made in her youth and beauty and bridal raiment was a dazzling one. Adam looked at her so fully and so long that she blushed a little. She could not read the thought behind his blue eyes. "You shall be my Queen if you like," he said at last, and Jacqueline laughed, thinking his speech the woodsman's attempt to say a pretty thing.

Rand drew forward with determination a small brown figure. "Jacqueline, this is another good friend of mine — Miss Lavinia Mocket, the sister of my law partner. — Vinie, Vinie, you *are* shyer than a partridge! You shan't scuttle away until you have spoken to my wife!"

"Yeth, thir," said Vinie, her hand in Jacqueline's. "I wish you well, ma'am."

Rand and Adam laughed. Jacqueline, with a sudden soft

kindliness for the small flushed face and startled eyes, bent her flower-crowned head and kissed Vinie. "Oh!" breathed Vinie. "Yeth, yeth, Mith Jacqueline, I thertainly wish you well!"

"Where's Tom?" asked Rand. "Tom should be here —" but Vinie had slipped from the ring about the bride. Adam followed; Mr. Pincornet had already faded away. More important folk claimed the attention of the newly wedded pair, and Mr. Mocket had not yet appeared when at last the gathering, bound for the wedding feast at Mrs. Selden's, deserted the interior of the church and flowed out under the portico and down the steps to the churchyard and the coaches waiting in the road. Lewis and Jacqueline Rand came down the path between the midsummer flowers. They were at the gate when the sight and sound of a horse coming at a gallop along the road drew from Rand an exclamation. "Tom Mocket — and his horse in a lather! There's news of some kind —"

It was so evident, when the horse and rider came to a stop before the church gate, that there was news of some kind, that the wedding guests, gentle and simple, left all talk and all employment to crowd the grassy space between the gate and the road and to demand enlightenment. Mocket's horse was spent, and Mocket's face was fiery red and eager. He gasped, and wiped his face with a great flowered handkerchief. "What is it, man?" cried a dozen voices.

Mocket rose in his stirrups and looked the assemblage over. "We're all Republicans — hip, hip, hurrah! Eh, Lewis Rand, I've brought you a wedding gift! The stage had just come in — I got the news at the Eagle! Hip, hip —"

"Tom," said Rand at his bridle rein, "you've been drinking. Steady, man. Now, what's the matter?"

A MARRIAGE AT SAINT MARGARET'S 155

"A wedding gift! a wedding gift!" repeated Tom, taken with his own conceit. "And I never was soberer, gentlemen, never 'pon honour! Hip, hip, hurrah! we're all good Republicans — but you'll never guess the news! — The Creole's dead!"

"No!" cried Rand.

There arose an uproar of excited voices. "Yes, yes, it's true!" shouted Mocket. "The stage brought it. He was challenged by Aaron Burr. They met at a place named Weehawken. Burr's first shot ended it. — Sandy'll trouble us no more!"

"It's rumour —"

"No, no, it's gospel truth! There's a messenger from the President, and letters from all quarters. He's dead, and Burr's in hiding! Gad! We'll have a rouse at the Eagle to-night! Blue lights for Assumption and Funding and the Sedition Bill and Taxes and Standing Armies and the British Alliance —

"Oh, Alexander, King of Macedon,
  Where is your namesake, Andy Hamilton?

In a hotter place, I hope, than Saint Kitts!"

"Hush!" said Rand. "Don't be ranting like a Mohawk! When a man's dead, it's time to let him rest."

He turned to the excited throng, and as he did so, he was aware that Jacqueline was standing white and frozen, and that Unity was trying to take her hand. He felt for her an infinite tenderness, and he promised himself to give Tom Mocket an old-time rating for at least one ill-advised expression. Such wedding gifts were not for Jacqueline. But as for the news — Rand felt his cheek grow hot and his eyes glow. In all the history of the country this was the decade in which political animosity, pure and simple, went its greatest length. Each party thought of the struggle as a battlefield; the Federalist strength was already broken, and now if the leader was down, it was not in fighting and Republican nature to restrain the wild cheer for the rout that must follow. Rand was a fighter too, and a captain of fighters, and the hundred whirling thoughts, the hundred chances, the sense of victory, and the savage joy in a foe's defeat — all the feeling that swelled his heart — left him unabashed. But he thought of Jacqueline, and he tried to choose his words. There would be now, he knew, no wedding feast at Mrs. Selden's. Randolphs, Carrs, Coles, Carters, Dabneys, Gordons, Meriwethers, and Minors — all would wish to hurry away. Plantation, office, or tavern, there would be letters waiting, journals to read, men to meet, committees, clamour, and debate. Of the ruder sort who had crowded to the church, many were already on the point of departure, mounting their horses, preparing for a race to the nearest tavern and newspaper. "Gentlemen," exclaimed Rand, "if it's true news — if we have indeed to deplore General Hamilton's death —"

"'Deplore!'" cried Mocket.

"'Deplore!'" echoed bluntly a Republican of prominence. "Don't let's be hypocrites, Mr. Rand. We'll leave the Federalists to 'deplore' —"

"Oh, I'll deplore him with pleasure!" cried a third. "It won't hurt to drop a tear — but for all that it's the greatest news since 1800!"

"Hip, hip, hurrah!"

"Weehawken! where's Weehawken? What's Burr in hiding for? Can't a gentleman fight a duel? Let him come down here, and we'll give him a triumph!"

"'Deplore!'" —

"I chose my word badly," said Rand, with the good-nature that always disarmed; "I shall not weep over my enemy, I only mean that I would not ignobly exult. Of course, sir, it is great news — the very greatest! And all here will now want the leisure of the day."

"Tell them, Lewis, that I'll excuse them," said Cousin Jane Selden. "We won't have a feast on the day of a funeral."

A little later, deep in the embrace of the old Selden coach, husband and wife began their journey to the house on the Three-Notched Road. In the minutes that followed the disposal of their wedding guests it had been settled that they would not return to Mrs. Selden's — it was best to go home instead. Cousin Jane would take Deb; Unity must return at once to Fontenoy. Hamilton and Edward Churchill had served together on Washington's staff; of late years they had seldom met, but the friendship remained. Unity knew, but would not speak of it, that Uncle Edward had finished, only the night before, a long letter to his old comrade-at-arms. With the exception of Deb, all the little party were aware that Jacqueline Rand's chances for forgiveness from her uncles were measurably slighter for this day's tidings. She seemed dazed, pale as her gown, but very quiet. She held Deb in her arms, and kissed Unity and Cousin Jane Selden. Her husband lifted her into the coach, wrung the others' hands, and followed her. "Good-bye, Lewis," said Mrs. Selden at the door. "I'll send a bowl of arrack to your men, and I'll ride over to-morrow to see Jacqueline. Good-bye, children, and God bless you both!"

The coach and four took the dusty road. A turn, and Saint Margaret's was hidden, another, and they were in a wood of beech and maple. The heat of the day was broken, and a wind was blowing. Rand took Jacqueline's hands, unclasped and chafed them. "So cold!" he said. "Why could we not have heard this news to-morrow!"

She shuddered strongly. "The noble — the great —" her voice broke.

"Is it so you think of him?" he asked. "Well — I, too, will call him noble and great — to-day.

> "No more for him the warmth of the bright sun;
> Nor blows upon his brow the wind of night!

He's gone — and we all shall go. But this is our wedding day. Let us forget — let us forget all else but that!"

"I grieve for the country," she said.

He kissed her hand. "Poor country! But her sons die every day. She is like Nature — she takes no heed. Let us, too, forget!"

"Oh, his poor wife —"

Rand drew her to him. "Will you mourn for me when I am dead?"

"No," she answered. "We will die together. — Oh, Lewis, Lewis, Lewis!"

"You promised that you would be happy," he said, and kissed her. "You promised you would not let Fontenoy and the things of Fontenoy stand like a spectre between us. Forget this, too. Everywhere there is dying. But it is our wedding day — and I love you madly — and life and the kingdoms of life lie before us! If you are not happy, how can I be so?"

"But I am!" she cried, and showed him a glowing face. "I am happier than the happiest!"

The wood thinned into glades where the shadows of beech and maple were beginning to be long upon the grass; then, in the afternoon light, the coach entered open country, fields of ox-eyed daisies, and tall pine trees standing singly.

"I never came this far," said Jacqueline. "I never saw the house."

"It is there where the smoke rises beyond that tobacco-field," answered Rand. "All the tobacco shall be changed into wheat."

They came in sight of the house, — a long storey-and-a-half structure of logs, with two small porches and a great earthen chimney. Pine trees gave a scanty shade. House and outbuildings and fencing had all been freshly whitewashed; over the porches flourished morning-glory and Madeira vines, and the little yard was bright with hollyhock and larkspur. Jacqueline put her hand in her husband's. Rand bent and kissed it with something in touch and manner formal and chivalrous. "It is a poor house for you. Very soon I shall build you a better."

"I want no better," she answered. "Have you not lived here all these years?"

"Adam called you Queen. You should have a palace —"

"If I am Queen, then you must be a King. I think it is a lovely palace. What is that tree by the gate — all feathery pink?"

"A mimosa. Mr. Jefferson gave it to me. It is like you — it does not belong on the Three-Notched Road. It should stand in a palace garden with dim alleys, fountains, and orange groves." He ended in a deeper tone, "Why not? One day we may plant a mimosa in such a garden, and smile and say, 'Do you remember the tree — do you remember our wedding day?' Who knows — who knows?"

"You shall stay in that palace all alone," said Jacqueline. "I like this one best."

The house stood back from the road in its clump of pines. The coach stopped, and Rand and Jacqueline, descending, crossed a strip of short grass tufted with fennel and velvet mullein to the gate beneath the mimosa, entered the gay little yard, and moved up the path to the larger of the two porches. They were at home. On the porch to welcome them they found the white man who worked on shares and oversaw the farm, Joab and three other slaves of Rand's, Mammy Chloe, Hannah, and the negro men who belonged to Jacqueline. These gave a noisy greeting. Rand put money into the hands of the slaves and sent them away happy to the tumble-down quarter behind the house. The white man took his leave, and Mammy Chloe and Hannah retired to the kitchen, where supper was in preparation. Rand and Jacqueline entered together the clean, bare rooms.

Later, when Hannah's supper had been praised and barely touched, the two came again to the porch, and presently, hand in hand, moved down the steps, and over the dry summer grass to the mimosa at the gate. Here they turned, and in the gathering dusk looked back at the house, the sleeping pines, and all the shadowy surrounding landscape.

"Hear the frogs in the marsh!" said Rand. "They are excited to-night. They know I have brought a princess home."

"Listen to the cow-bells," she said. "I love to hear them, faint and far like that. I love to think of you, a little barefoot boy, bringing home the cows — and never, never dreaming once of me!"

"When could that have been?" he asked. "I have always dreamed of you — even when 'twas pain to dream! — There is the first whip-poor-will. *Whip-poor-will!* Once it had the loneliest sound! The moon is growing brighter. The dark has come."

"I love you, Lewis."

"Darling, darling! Listen! that is the night horn. The lights are out in the quarter. Do you hear the stream — our stream — hurrying past the apple tree? It is hurrying to the sea — the great sea. We've put out to sea together — you and I, just you and I!"

"Just you and I!" she echoed. "Oh, bliss to be together!"

"Let us go," he whispered. "Let us go back to the house," and with his arm around her, they moved up the path between the flowers that had closed with the night.

CHAPTER XIII

THE THREE-NOTCHED ROAD

LEWIS RAND and his wife dwelt that summer and autumn in the house on the Three-Notched Road, and were happy there. If the ghost of Gideon Rand walked, the place, renovated, clean, bright, and homely sweet, showed no consciousness of any influence of the dark. Passers-by on the dusty road looked curiously at the gay little yard and the feathery mimosa and the house behind the pines. "Lewis Rand lives there," they said, and made their horses go more slowly.

The pines hid the porch where Jacqueline sat with her work, or, hands about her knees, dreamed the hours away. She was much alone, for after the first week Rand rode daily to his office in Charlottesville. There was no reconciliation with her people. All her things had been sent from Fontenoy. Linen that had been her mother's lay with bags of lavender in an old carved chest from Santo Domingo, and pieces of slender, inlaid furniture stood here and there in the room they called the parlour. Her candlesticks were upon the mantel, and her harp made the room's chief ornament. Her fortune, which was fair, had been formally made over to her and to Rand. She was glad it was no less; had it been vastly greater, she would only have thought, "This will aid him the more." The little place was very clean, very sweet, ordered, quiet, and lovable. She was a trained housewife as well as the princess of his story, and she made the man she loved believe in Paradise. Each afternoon when he left the jargon and wrangling of the courtroom his mind turned at once to his home and its genius. All the way through the town, beckoning him past the Eagle and past every other house or office which had for him an open door, he saw Jacqueline waiting beneath the mimosa at the gate, clad in white, her dark hair piled high, about her throat a string of coral or of amber. Out on the road, beneath the forest trees, in the radiance of the evening, he rode with his head high and a smile within his eyes. All the scheming, all the labour and strife of the day, fell from him like rusty armour, and his spirit bathed itself in the thought of that meeting. She did not always await him at the gate; sometimes he found her half a mile from home, sitting in the sunset light upon a stone beside the road. Then he dismounted, kissed her, and they walked together back to their nest in the tree of life. Supper-time would follow, with the lighted candles and the fragrance from Hannah's kitchen, and the little humorous talk with the old, fond, familiar servants, and the deeper words between husband and wife of things done or to be done; then quiet upon the porch, long silences, broken sentences of deep content, while the glow faded and the stars came out; then the candles again and his books and papers, while she read or sewed beside him. When his task was done she sang to him, and so drew on the hour when they put out the lights and entered the quiet, spotless chamber where the windows opened to the east.

Rand worked as he had not worked before. All the springs were running, all the bitter wells were sweet; to breathe was to draw in fulness of life, and all things were plastic to his touch. Love became genius, and dreaming accomplishment. In Albemarle, in Virginia, in the country at large, the time was one of excitement, fevered labour, and no mean reward. The election for President was drawing on. Undoubtedly the Republicans and Jefferson would sweep the country, but it behooved them to sweep it clean. The Federalist point of view was as simple. "Win! but we'll not make broad the paths before you! Winning shall be difficult." The parties worked like Trojans, and he who could speak spoke as often as any leader of heroic times.

At court house and at tavern banquets, at meetings here and meetings there, barbecues, dinners, races, militia musters, gatherings at crossroads and in the open fields, by daylight and by candlelight and by torchlight, Republican doctrine was expounded, and Federalist doctrine made answer. The clash of the brazen shields was loud. It was a forensic people and a plastic time. He who could best express his thought might well, if there were power in the thought, impress it so deeply that it would become the hall-mark of his age. His chance was good. Something more than fame of a day shone and beckoned before every more than able man. To stamp a movement of the human mind, to stamp an age, to give the design to one gold coin from the mint of Time, — what other prize worth striving for? The design? — one thought of moderate Liberty and the head of Washington, another thought of Liberty and the head of Jefferson, another of License and a head like Danton's, another of Empire and a conqueror's head.

In Albemarle, at all Republican gatherings the man most in demand was Lewis Rand; and the surrounding counties of Fluvanna, Amherst, Augusta, and Orange considered themselves happy if he could be drawn to this or that mass meeting. It was not easy to attract him. He never consciously said to himself, "Be chary of favours; they will be the more prized"; he said instead, "I'll not waste an arrow where there's no gold to hit." When he saw that it was worth his while to go, he went, and sent an arrow full into the gold. Amherst and Augusta, Fluvanna and Orange, broke into applause and prophecy, while upon each return home Republican Albemarle welcomed him with added rapture, and Federalist Albemarle hurled another phrase into its already comprehensive anathema. His reputation grew amain, both in his native section and in the state at large. Before the autumn his election to the House of Delegates, which in April seemed so great a thing, began to assume the appearance of a trifle in his fortunes. He would overtop that, and how highly no man was prepared to say. Through all the clashing of shields, through Republican attack and Federalist resistance, through the clamour over Hamilton's death, the denunciation and upholding of Burr, the impeachment of Chase, the situation in Louisiana, the gravitation towards France, and the check of England, the consciousness of Pitt and the obsession of Napoleon, — through all the commotion and fanfaronade of that summer Rand kept a steady hand and eye, and sent his arrows into the gold. In the law, as in politics, he was successful. A comprehensive knowledge and an infinite painstaking, a grasp wide and firm, a somewhat sombre eloquence, a personal magnetism virile and compelling, — these and other attributes began to make his name resound. He won his cases, until presently to say of a man, "He has Lewis Rand," was in effect to conclude the matter. He had no Federalist clients; that rift widened and deepened. Federalist Albemarle meant the Churchills and the Carys, their kinsmen, connections, and friends. The gulf seemed fixed.

Jacqueline, keeping at home in the house on the Three-Notched Road, saw very few from out her old life. Those who had been her girlhood friends kept aloof. If their defection pained her, she gave no sign — she had something of her father's pride. Among the Republican gentry she was of course made much of, and she saw something of the plainer sort of her husband's friends. Tom Mocket came occasionally on business with Rand, and once he brought Vinie with him. Jacqueline liked the sandy-haired and freckled scamp, and made friends with Vinie. In the first July days Adam Gaudylock often sat upon her porch, but now for weeks he had been wandering in the West. Once or twice Mr. Pincornet, straying that way, had delicately looked his pity for a lovely woman in a desert waste. Cousin Jane Selden remained her good neighbour and kind friend, and once Mr. Ned Hunter brought a message from Unity. Her old minister came to see her, and Dr. Gilmer, when illness called him in that direction, always drew rein at her gate. Ludwell Cary was out of the county, and Fairfax Cary never rode that way. Unity came whenever it was possible, and thrice, between July and October, Deb and Miranda and a horsehair trunk arrived for a blissful week. To Deb they were unshadowed days. The log house, the pine wood and singing stream, an owl that hooted each night, a row of tiger lilies and a thicket of blackberries, Jacqueline to tell her stories, Mammy Chloe and Hannah, the new brother who came home every evening riding a great bay horse and kissing Jacqueline beneath the mimosa tree,—the brother who showed her twenty unguessed treasures and gave her the Arabian Nights,—Deb thought the week on the Three-Notched Road a piece out of the book, and wept when she must go back to Fontenoy.

But Colonel Churchill and Major Edward never came, never wrote, never sent messages to Jacqueline, never, she forced Unity to tell her, mentioned her name or would hear it mentioned at Fontenoy. Only Aunt Nancy, lying always in the chamber, her key-basket beside her on the white counterpane, talked of her when she chose. "But she talks as though you were dead," acknowledged Unity; then, "Oh, Jacqueline, it must all come right some day! And as for him, he's talked of more and more,— everywhere one goes, one hears his name! He's head and front of his party here. Oh, what a party! Mrs. Adams writes that at Washington they eat soup with their fingers and still think *Ça Ira* the latest song! Cannot you convert him? They say the Mammoth's jealous, and that your husband and Colonel Burr correspond in cipher. Is that so?"

"I don't know," said Jacqueline. "I shall not try to convert him. I would have a man loyal to his beliefs — so would you, Unity! Suppose yourself of another party — would you change Fairfax Cary? You would wish him to stay always the Federalist that he is! So with me. I love my great Republican."

"I love you," said Unity. "Kiss me. Now, when do you go to Richmond?"

"Next month. Oh, Unity, if Uncle Dick and Uncle Edward would but make friends before we go!"

Unity, stopping for an hour at Cousin Jane Selden's, remarked to that lady, "Ah, she is happy! She does not know and she does not care what is said of Lewis Rand. They say dreadful things. The last Gazette—"

"She does n't hear a Federalist upon the subject," replied Cousin Jane. "The last Gazette! Pooh! who believes what a Federalist paper says of a Republican, or a Republican paper says of a Federalist? Most men and all newspapers are liars."

"It says that he is a Buonaparte ready to break the shell."

"Buonaparte's a great man, my dear."

"And that the Mammoth's alarmed —"

"Like the hen that hatched the eaglet —"

"And that Lewis Rand's no more Republican at heart than he is Federalist. He's just for Lewis Rand."

"Hm-m-m!"

"And that his name's known as far west as the Mississippi."

"There's no law against a man's name spreading. It's what every man strives for. One succeeds, and the birds that carried the news are indignant."

"And that he's an Atheist."

"Lewis Rand's no saint, child, but he's no fool either. You'll be telling me next that he mistreats his wife."

"Ah, he does not do that!" exclaimed Unity. "She's deep in love. He can't be so very bad, can he, Cousin Jane?"

"He's not a monster, child: he's just a man. — And now, Unity, I am making damson preserves to-day."

"I'll go," said Unity, rising. "But they believe these things at Fontenoy."

"Do they believe them at Greenwood?"

"I don't know. Ludwell Cary is still away—"

"When are you going to marry his brother?"

"Why, I don't know that I am going to marry his brother at all," answered Unity, her foot upon the coach step. "Good-bye, Cousin Jane. I wish I could make pot-pourri like yours."

"You must know what spices to use, and when to gather the roses," said Cousin Jane. "Good-bye, child! You read too many romances, but you're a loyal soul — and one of your gowns is prettier than another. Don't you believe all the world says of Lewis Rand. It's mighty prone to make mistakes. The man's just a sinner like the rest of us."

At Fontenoy, that September afternoon, Fairfax Cary, riding over from Greenwood, found Miss Dandridge seated upon the steps which ran down to the garden from the glass doors of the library. Her chin was in her hands, and her black eyes were suspiciously bright. "You were crying," exclaimed the younger Cary. "Why?"

"I've been reading about the Capulets and the Montagues."

"You are not one to cry for the dead," said the young man. "Tell me truly."

"No; I'm crying for the living. I've been talking to the Capulets. I've been giving Uncle Edward a piece of my mind."

"Which he would not take?"

"Just so. Oh, it was a battle royal! But I lost — I always lose. He is sitting there in triumphant misery, reading Swift. I brought my defeat out here. Now and then I am glad I am a woman."

"I'm glad all the time," said Fairfax Cary. "Don't dwell on lost battles. Unity, when are you going to let me fight all your battles?"

"I don't know," answered Miss Dandridge promptly. "I don't even know that I would like to have all my battles fought for me. I'm not lazy, and I believe my ancestors fought their own. Besides — would you fight this one?"

There was a pause; then, "Do you love your cousin so?" asked the young man.

"Love Jacqueline? Jacqueline is like my sister. If she is not happy, then neither am I!"

"But she is happy. She loved Lewis Rand, and she married him."

"Yes, yes. But a woman may marry her lover and yet be unhappy. If he takes her to a strange country, she may perish of homesickness."

"Has he taken her to a strange country?"

"Yes," cried Unity, with fire. "How can it but be a strange country?" Her eyes filled with tears. "Why, why did she not love your brother!"

"That," said the younger Cary grimly, "is what I do not

profess to understand. And I would fight for your cousin, but I will not fight for Lewis Rand. My brother's enemies are mine."

"You see. You would n't fight this battle, after all."

"Would Miss Dandridge wish me to?"

Unity regarded the sunset beyond the snowball bushes. "No," she said at last, with a sigh and a shake of her head, "no, I would n't. I had rather a man behaved like a man than like an angel."

"You are the angel. At least your cousin will not live much longer in that log house, with the pines and the tobacco and the ghost of old Gideon. Lewis Rand has bought Roselands."

"Roselands!"

"You knew it was for sale. Well, he's bought it. I had the news from the agent. It's to be put in order this winter, and in the spring Rand will come back from Richmond and take possession. It is strange to think of a Rand owning Roselands!"

"A Churchill will own it, too! It will have been bought with Churchill money. I am so glad! It can be made a lovely place. Jacqueline will have the garden and the old, long drawing-room! Deb and I can go there easily. It is all more fitting — I am glad!"

"It is too near Greenwood," said the other gloomily. "I think that Ludwell will stay in Richmond."

"I'm sorry," said Unity softly and brightly. "I wish, I wish — but what's the use in wishing? There! the sun has gone, and it is growing cold. I have sat here until I'm no longer angry with Uncle Edward. Poor man! to be reading Swift all this time! — I'll walk with you to the front porch."

"I thought," ventured the young man, "I thought that

perhaps you might ask me to stay to supper. It's so lonely at Greenwood."

"You stayed to supper last night," said Miss Dandridge pensively, "and you were here to dinner the day before, and you rode over the preceding afternoon, and the morning before that you read me Vathek. — Oh, stay to supper by all means!"

Cary picked up her scarf and handed her down the steps to the path that was beginning to be strewn with autumn leaves. "Miss Dandridge — Unity — it has been fourteen mortal days since I last asked you to marry me! You said I might ask you once a month —"

"I did n't," said Unity serenely. "I said once a month was too often."

"Are n't you ever going to love me?"

"Why, some day, yes!" replied Miss Dandridge. "When you've swum the Hellespont like Leander, or picked a glove out of the lion's den like the French knight, or battered down a haunted castle like Rinaldo, or taken the ring from a murderer's hand like Onofrio, or set free the Magician's daughter like Julio — perhaps — perhaps —"

"I must cast about to win my spurs!" said the younger Cary. "In the mean time I'll ask you again, come fourteen days."

Late September passed into October. The nuts ripened, the forests grew yellow and red, and the corn was stacked in the long, sere fields, above which, each morning, lay a white mist. Goldenrod and farewell-summer faded, but sumach and alder-berry still held the fence corners. The air was fragrant with wood smoke; all sound was softened, thin, and far away. A frost fell and the persimmons grew red gold. The song birds had gone south, but there were creatures enough left in the trees. Sometimes, through the thin forest, in the blue distance, deer were seen; bears began to approach the corn-cribs, and in the unbroken wilderness wolves were heard at night. Early and late the air struck cold, but each midday was a halcyon time. In the last of October, on a still and coloured morning, Rand and Jacqueline, having shaken hands with the overseer and the slaves they were leaving, caressed the dogs, and said good-bye to the cat, quitted the house on the Three-Notched Road. At the gate they turned, and, standing beneath the mimosa, looked back across the yard where the flowers had been touched by the frost, to the house and the sombre pines. They stood in silence. Jacqueline thought of the first evening beneath the mimosa, of the July dusk, and the cry of the whip-poor-will. Rand thought, suddenly and inconsequently, of his father and mother, standing here at the gate as he had often seen them stand. There was no mimosa then. — Jacqueline turned, caught his hand, and pressed it to her lips. He strained her in his arms and kissed her, and they entered the chaise which was to carry them to Richmond. Before them lay a hundred miles of sunny road, three days' companionship in the blue, autumnal weather. A few moments, and the house, the pines, and the hurrying stream were lost to view. "A long good-bye!" said Rand. "In the spring we'll enter Roselands!"

"You value it more than I," answered Jacqueline. "I loved the house behind us. Loved! I am speaking as though it were a thing of the long past. Farewells are always sad."

"I value it for you," said Rand. "Have I not chafed, ever since July, to see you in so poor a place? Roselands is not ideal, but it is a fairer nest for my bird than that we've left!"

Jacqueline laughed. "'Roselands is not ideal!' *I* think Roselands quite grand enough! Oh, Lewis, Lewis, how high you build! Take care of the upper winds!"

"I'll build firmly," he answered. "The winds may do their worst. Here is the old road to Greenwood. Now that the trees are bare, you can see the house."

They drove all day by field and woodland. At noon they paused for luncheon beside a bubbling spring in a dell strewn with red leaves, then drove on through the haze of afternoon. There were few leaves left upon the boughs. In the fields that they passed the stacked corn had the seeming of silent encampments, deserted tents of a vanished army, russet and empty wigwams drawn against a deep blue sky. Now and then, in the darker woods, there was a scurry of partridges, the red gleam of a fox, or a vision of antlers, and once a wild turkey, bronze and stately, crossed the road before the chaise. When they passed a smithy or a mill, the clink of iron, the rush of water, came to them faintly in the smoky air. That night they slept at the house of a wealthy planter and good Republican, where, after supper, all sat around a great fire, the children on footstools between the elders, and stories were told of hunting, of Indian warfare, and of Tarleton's raid. At ten they made a hall and danced for an hour to a negro's fiddling, then a bowl of punch was brought and the bedroom candles lighted.

In the morning Rand and Jacqueline went on towards Richmond, and at sunset they found themselves before a country tavern, not over clean or comfortable, but famous for good company. The centre of a large neighbourhood, it had been that day the scene of some Republican anniversary, and a number of gentlemen, sober and otherwise, had remained for supper and a ride home through the frosty moonlight. Among them were several lawyers of note, and a writer and thinker whose opinion Rand valued. Besides all these there were at the inn a group of small farmers, a party of boatmen from the James, the local schoolmaster and the parson, a

Scotch merchant or two, and the usual idle that a tavern draws. All were Republicans, and all knew their party's men. Rand descended from the chaise amidst a buzz of recognition, and after supper came a demand that he should speak from the tavern porch to an increasing crowd. He did not refuse. To his iron frame the fatigue of the day was as naught, and there were men in the throng whom he was willing to move. It came to him suddenly, also, that Jacqueline had never heard him speak. Well, he would speak to her to-night.

His was an universal mind. On occasion he could stoop to praise one party and vituperate another, but that was his tongue serving his worldly interest. The man himself dealt with humanity, wherever found and in whatever time, however differentiated, however allied, with its ancestry of the brute and its destiny of the spirit; with the root of the tree and the far-off flower and every intermediate development of stem and leaf; with the soil that sustained the marvellous growth, and with the unknown Gardener who for an unfathomable purpose had set the inexplicable seed in an unthinkable universe. From the ephemera to the star he accepted and conjectured, and while he often thought ill of the living, he had never yet thought ill of life. He had long been allied with a thinker who, with a low estimate of at least so much of human nature as ran counter to his purposes, yet believed with devoutness in the perfectibility of his species, and had of the future a large, calm, and noble vision. If Lewis Rand had not Jefferson's equanimity, his sane and wise belief in the satisfying power of common daylight, common pleasures, all the common relations of daily life; if some strangeness in his nature thrilled to the meteor's flight, craved the exotic, responded to clashing and barbaric music, yet the two preached the same doctrine. He believed in the doctrine, though he also believed that great men are not mastered by doctrine. They made doctrine their servant, their useful slave of the lamp. He knew — none better — that the genie might turn and rend; that there was always one last, one fatal thing that must not be asked. But his mind was supple, and he thought that he could fence with the genie. Usually, when he spoke, he believed all that he said, believed it with all the strength of his reason, and yet — he saw the kingdoms of the world. To-night, in the autumn air, pure and cold beneath the autumn stars, with the feeling and the fragrance of the forest day about him, in sympathy with his audience, and conscious in every fibre of the presence of the woman whom he loved, he saw no other kingdom than that of high and tranquil thought.

Jacqueline, seated at her open window, listened for the first time to any public utterance of her husband's. He was not a man who often spoke of the processes of his thought. Sometimes, in the house on the Three-Notched Road, he told her, briefly, his conclusions on such and such a matter, but he rarely described the road by which he travelled. She knew the conservative, the British, the Federal side of most questions. That was the cleared country, familiar, safe, and smiling; her husband's side was the strange forest which she had entered and must travel through. She was yet afraid of the forest, of its lights and its shadows, the rough places and the smooth, the stir of its air and the possibility of wild beasts. To her it was night-time there, and where the ground seemed fair and the light to play, she thought of the marsh and the will-o'-the-wisp. She could not but be loyal to the old, trodden ways. She had married Lewis Rand, not his party or its principles. But to-night, as she listened, the light seemed to grow until it was dawn in the forest, and the air to blow so cold, strong, and pure that she thought of mountain peaks and of the ocean which she had never seen. She was no longer afraid of the country in which she found herself.

Rand, standing in the red torchlight above the attentive crowd, preached a high doctrine, preached it austerely, boldly, and well. He did not speak to-night of the hundred party words, the flaunting banners, systems, expedients, and policies fit for this turn of the spiral, born to be disavowed, discarded, and thrown down by a higher, freer whorl; but he gave his voice for the larger Republicanism, for the undying battle-cry, and the ever-streaming battle-flag. He had no less a text than the Liberty and Happiness of the human race, and he made no straying from the subject.

Freedom! Happiness! What is freedom? What is happiness? Freedom is the maximum of self-government finally becoming automatic, and the minimum of government from without finally reduced to the vanishing-point. Happiness is the ultimate bourne, the Olympian goal, the intense and burning star towards which we travel. Does not its light even now fall upon us? even now we are palely happy. And how shall we know the road? and what if, in the night-time, we turn irremediably aside? How are they to be attained, true Liberty and true Happiness? Learn! Light the lamp, and the shadows will flee. — Self-government. Teach thyself temperance, foresight, and wise memory of the past. Thou thyself, in thine own body, art a community. See, then, that thy communal life is clean, that thy will is in right operation, and thy minds divide thee not to disaster. Thy very ego, is it not but thy president, the voice of all thy members, representative of all that thy race has made thee to be, effect of ten million causes, and cause of effects thou canst not see? Let thy ego strengthen itself, deal justly, rule wisely, that thy state fall not behind in this world-progress and be lost out of time and out of mind, in a night without a dawn. There have been such things: over against immortal gain there lies immortal loss. Work, then, while it is day, for if thou work not, the night will make no tarrying. Know thyself, and, knowing, rule that strange world of thine. Were it not a doom, were it not a frightful doom, that it should come to rule thee? . . . Government from without! Government of to-day, Government abroad as we see it in every journal, in every letter that we open — how heavy, how heavy is the ball and chain the nations wear! If we alone in this land go free, if for four golden years we have moved with lightness, look to it lest a gaoler come! Government! What is the ideal government? It is a man of business, worthy and esteemed, administering his client's affairs with thoroughness, economy, and honour. It is a wise judge, holding the balances with a steadfast hand, sitting there clothed reverently, to judge uprightly and to do no more. It is a skilled council, a picked band, an honourable Legion, chosen of the multitude, to determine the line of march for an advancing civilization; to make such laws as are according to reason and necessity and to make none that are not, and to provide for the keeping of the law that is made. The careful man of affairs, the upright judge, the honest maker of honest laws must needs present an account for maintenance and for that expenditure which shall give offence neither to generosity nor to justice; and the account must be paid, yea, and ungrudgingly! Let us pay, then, each man according to his ability, the tax that is right and fitting; and let us, moreover, give due honour to the vanguard of the people. It is there that the great flag waves with all the blazonry of the race. But we want no substituted banner, no private ensign, no conqueror's flapping eagles! Government! Honour the instrument by which we rule ourselves; but worship not a mechanical device, and call not a means an end! Admirable means, but oh, the sorry end! Therefore we'll have no usurping Prætorian, no juggling sophist, no bailiff extravagant and unjust, no spendthrift squandering on idleness that which would pay just debts! A ruler! There's no halo about a ruler's head. The people — the people are the sacred thing, for they are the seed whence the future is to spring. He who betrays his trust, which is to guard the seed, — what is that man — Emperor or President, Louis or George, Pharaoh or Cæsar — but a traitor and a breaker of the Law? He may die by the axe, or he may die in a purple robe of a surfeit, but he dies! The people live on, and his memory pays. He has been a tyrant and a pygmy, and the ages hold him in contempt. . . . War! There are righteous wars, and righteous men die in them, but the righteous man does not love war. Conquest! Conquest of ignorance, superstition, and indolence, conquest of the waste and void, of the forces of earth, air, and water, and of the dying beast within us, but no other conquest! We attained Louisiana by fair trade, for the benefit of unborn generations. Standing armies! We want them not. Navies! The sea is the mother of life; why call her that of death? Her highways are for merchant ships, for argosies carrying corn and oil, bearing travellers and the written thought of man; for voyages of discovery and happy intercourse, and all rich exchange from strand to strand. Why stain the ocean red? Is it not fairer when 't is blue? Guard coast-line and commerce, but we need no Armada for that. Make no quarrels and enter none; so we shall be the exemplar of the nations. . . . Free Trade. We are citizens and merchants of the world. No man or woman but lives by trade and barter. Long ago there was a marriage between the house of Give and the house of Take, and their child is Civilization. Sultan or Czar may say, "Buy here, sell there, and at this price. You are my slave. Obey!" But who, in this century and this land, shall say that to me — or to you? Are we free men? Then let us walk as such through the marts of the earth. "Trade where you will," saith Nature. "It was so I brought the tree to the barren isle, and scattered the life of the seas." Authority of law! Respect the law, and to that end let us have laws that are respectable. Laws are made to be kept, else we live in a house of chicane. But there is a danger that decrees may thicken until they form a dungeon grate for Freedom, until, like Gulliver, she is held down to earth by every several hair. Few laws and just, and those not lightly broken. The Contract between the States — let it be kept. It was pledged in good faith — the cup went around among equals. There is no more solemn covenant; we shall prosper but as we maintain it. Is it not for the welfare and the grandeur of the whole that each part should have its healthful life? The whole exists but by the glow within its parts. Shall we become dead members of a sickly soul? God forbid! but sister planets revolving in their orbits about one central Idea, which is Freedom by Coöperation. To each her own life, varied, rich, complete, and her communal life, large with service rendered and received! Each bound to other and to that central Thought by primal law, but each a sovereign orb, grave mistress of her own affairs! Slavery! Ay, I will give you that though you want it not! Slavery is abominable. There is a tree that grows in the tropics which they call the upas tree. All who lie in the shadow of its branches fall asleep, and die sleeping. To-day we lie under the upas tree — would that we were awake! I have heard that — in the tropics — the sons sometimes hew down that which the fathers have planted. I would that it were so in Virginia! Freedom of thought, of speech, and of pen. I will away with this cope of lead, this Ancient Authority, which is too often an Ancient Iniquity. Did it not have once a minority? was it not once a New Thought? Is not a man's thought to-day as potent, holy, and near the right as was his great-grandfather's thought which was born in a like manner, of the brain of a man, in a modern time? I will think freely and according to reason. When it seems wise to tell my mind I will speak; and with judgment I will write down my thought, and fear no man's censure. Knowledge! I was a poor boy, and I strove for learning, strove hard, and found it worth the striving. I know the hunger, and I know the rage when one asks for knowledge and asks in vain. Is it not a shameful thing that happy men, lodged warm and clear in the Interpreter's house, should hear the groping in the dark without, know that their fellows are searching, in pain and with shortness of breath, for the key which let the fortunate in, and make no stir to aid those luckless ones? Give of your abundance, or your abundance will decay in your hands and turn to that which shall cause you shuddering!

His words went on, magnetic as the man. He spoke for an hour, coming at the last to a consideration of those particular questions which hung in Virginian air. He dealt with these ably, and he subtly conciliated those of his audience who might differ with him. None could have called him flatterer, but when he ceased to speak his hearers, feeling for themselves a higher esteem, had for him a reflex glow. It was what he could always count upon, and it furthered his fortunes. Now they crowded about him, and it was late before, pleading the fatigue of his journey, he could escape from their friendly importunity. At last, it being towards midnight and the moon riding high, the neighbouring planters and their guests got to saddle and, after many and pressing offers of hospitality to Rand and his wife, galloped off to home and bed. The commonalty and the hangers-on faded too into the darkness, and the folk who were sleeping at the inn took their candles and said good-night. All was suddenly quiet, — a moonlit crossroads in Virginia, tranquil as the shaven fields and the endless columns of the pine.

Upstairs, in the low "best room," Rand found his wife still seated by the open window, her folded arms upon the sill, her eyes raised to the stars that shone despite the moon. He crossed to her and closed the window. "The night is cold. Dearest, have you been sitting here all this time?"

She rose, turning upon him a radiant face. "All this time. I was not cold. I was warm. I am so happy that I'm frightened."

"Did you like it?" he asked. "I hoped that you would. I thought of you — my star, my happiness!"

"I used to wonder," she said; "when they would come home to Fontenoy and say, 'Lewis Rand spoke to-day,' I used to wonder if I should ever hear you speak! And when they blamed you I said to my aching heart, 'They need not tell me! He's not ambitious, self-seeking, a leveller, a demagogue and Jacobin! — he is the man I met beneath the apple tree!' And I was right — I was right!"

"Am I that man?" he asked. "I will try to be, Jacqueline. Leveller, demagogue, and Jacobin I am not; but for the rest, who knows — who knows? Men are cloudy worlds — and I dream sometimes of a Pursuer."

The next morning the skies had changed, and Rand and Jacqueline fared forward through a sodden, grey, and windy day. The rain had ceased to fall when at twilight they came into Richmond by the Broad Street Road. Lights gleamed from the wet houses; high overhead grey clouds were parting, and in the west was a line of red. The wind was high, and the sycamores with which the town abounded rocked their speckled arms. The river was swollen and rolled hoarsely over the rocks beneath the red west. Rand had taken a house on Shockoe Hill, not far from the Chief Justice's, and to this he and Jacqueline came through the wet and windy freshness of the night. Smiling in the doorway were the servants — Joab and Mammy Chloe and Hannah — who had set out from Albemarle the day before their master and mistress. Rand and Jacqueline, leaving the mud-splashed chaise, were welcomed with loquacity and ushered into a cheerful room where there was a crackling fire and a loaded table.

"Mrs. Leigh's compliments, Miss Jacqueline, an' she done sont de rolls. Mrs. Fisher's best wishes, an' she moughty glad to hab a neighbour, an' she done sont de broiled chicken. An' Mr. Hay, he done sont de oysters wid he compliments — an' de two bottles Madeira Mr. Ritchie sont — an' Mr. Randolph lef' de birds, an' he gwine come roun' fust thing in de mawnin'—"

"We shall have friends," said Rand. "I am glad for you, sweetheart. But I wish that one Federalist had had the grace to remember that Jacqueline Churchill came to town to-day."

"Ah, once I would have cared," answered Jacqueline. "It does not matter now."

"There's a tear on your hand—"

Jacqueline laughed. "At least, it does n't matter much. — Is that all, Joab?"

"An' Marse Ludwell Cary, he ride erroun in de rain an' leave he compliments for Marse Lewis, an' he say will Miss Jacqueline 'cept dese yer flowers—"

"One remembered," said Rand, and watched his wife put the flowers in water.

CHAPTER XIV

THE LAW OFFICE

"IF you were not so damned particular—" said the weasel disconsolately.

"I'm not damned particular," answered Rand. "I've wanted wealth and I've wanted power ever since I went barefoot and suckered tobacco — as you know who know me better than almost any one else! But this" — he tapped the papers on the table before him—"this is cheating."

"Oh, you!" complained the scamp. "You are of the elect. What you want you'll take by main force. You are a strong man! You've taken a deal since that day we went into the bookshop by the bridge. But I'm no Samson or David — I'm just Tom Mocket — and still, why shouldn't I have my pennyworth?"

Rand paused in his walking up and down the office in Main Street. It was the late winter, a year and more from that evening when he and Jacqueline had first come to the house on Shockoe Hill. Standing by the rough deal table, he laid an authoritative hand upon the documents with which it was strewn. "You'll never get your pennyworth here. The scheme these gentry have afoot is just a Yazoo business. If these lands exist, they're only a hunting-ground of swamp, Indians, and buffalo. The survey is paper, the cleared fields a fable, the town Manoa, the scheme a bubble, the purchasers fools, and the sellers knaves,—and there's your legal opinion in a nutshell!"

"I didn't ask for a legal opinion," said Mocket. "I'm a lawyer myself. There's land there, you'll not deny, and a river, and plenty of game. If a Yankee does n't find it Paradise, he had no chance anyhow, and a Kentuck can care for himself! There's no sense in calling it a bubble, or being so damned scrupulous!"

Rand made a gesture of contempt. "You let Yazoo companies and the Promised Land alone! People are ceasing to be fools. To-day they demand a hair of the mammoth or a sample of the salt mountain."

Mocket ceased rustling the papers on the table, and turned to regard his chief more closely. "Lewis, I've heard you say things like that more than once lately. A year ago you were mighty respectful to Mr. Jefferson's salt mountain and strange bones and great elk and silk grass and all the rest of it. That was a curious letter of yours in the Examiner. If 't was meant to defend his neutrality doings, 't was a damned lukewarm defence! If I had n't known 't was yours, sink me if I would n't have thought it a damned piece of Federal sarcasm! — Did you send that paper to the President?"

"No, I did not send it."

"Lewis," said the scamp slowly, "are you breaking with Mr. Jefferson?"

Rand walked to the window and stood looking out upon the winter afternoon. It was snowing hard, and through the drifting veil the trees across the way could hardly be discerned. "Yes," he said deliberately. "Yes, — if you call it breaking with a man to have grown away from him. If he served me once — yes, and greatly! — have I not worked for him since, hand and foot? We are quits, I think. I shall not cease to esteem him."

Mocket breathed hard with excitement. "You have n't been natural for a long time — but I did n't know 't was this —"

"I am being natural now," said Rand somewhat sternly.

"I've told you, Tom, and now let it alone. Least said is soonest mended."

"But — but —" stammered the scamp, "are you going over to the other camp?"

Rand did not at once answer. From a plate on the window-sill he took a crust of bread, and, raising the sash, crumbled it upon the snow without. The sparrows came at once, alighting near his hand with a tameness that spoke of pleasing association with the providence above them. "No," said Rand at last, "I am not going over to the other camp — if by that you mean the Federalist camp. Must one forever sign under a captain? It is not my instinct to serve. — Now let it alone."

He closed the window and, turning again to the table, bent over an unrolled map which covered half its surface. The chart was a large one, showing the vast territory drained by the Ohio, the Missouri, and the Mississippi, and the imagination of the cartographer had made good his lack of information. Rivers and mountains appeared where nature had made no such provision, while the names, quaint and uncouth, with which Jefferson proposed to burden states yet in embryo sprawled in large letters across the yellow plain. "Assenispia — Polypotamia — Chersonesus — Michigania," read Rand. "Barbarous! I could name them better out of Ossian!" He traced with his finger the lower Ohio. "This is where Blennerhasset's island should be." The finger went on down the Mississippi. "What a river! When it is in flood, it is a sea. And the rich black fields on either side! Cotton! Our Fortunatus purse shall be spun of that. They call the creeks bayous. All these little towns — French and Spanish. To speak to them of Washington is to speak of the moon — so distant and so cold. Here are Indians. Here are settlers from the East, and the burden of their song is, 'We are so far from the Old Thirteen that we care not if we are farther yet!'"

"Hey!" exclaimed Mocket. "That's treason!"

"Here Adam Gaudylock met Wilkinson. The river narrows here, and runs deep and strong." Rand's hand rested on the coast-line. "New Orleans," he said, "but capable of becoming a new Rome. Here to the westward is the Perdido that they call the boundary, — then Mexico and the City of Mexico. If not New Orleans, then Mexico!" He straightened himself with a laugh. "I am dreaming, Tom — just as I used to dream in the fields! Ugh! I feel the hot sun, and the thick leaves draw through my hands! Let's get back to every day. To-morrow in the House I am going to carry the Albemarle Resolutions. The last debate is on. Wirt speaks first, and then I speak."

"Ludwell Cary is fighting you," said Mocket. "Fighting hard."

"Yes."

"Well, I'll be there to hear you speak. Lord! if I could speak like you, Lewis, and plan like you, and if whiskey would let me alone, and if I was n't afraid of the dark, I'd make a stir in the country — I'd go higher than a Franklin kite!"

"You might manage the rest," said Rand, with good-natured scorn; "but it does n't do to be afraid of the dark."

From the pegs behind the door he took his greatcoat and beaver. "I am going home now," he said. "I have company to supper."

"Who, then?" asked Mocket. "Adam Gaudylock? He's in town."

Rand laughed. "'Who, then?' Tom, Tom, you've the manners of the West Indian skippers you consort with! No, it's not Adam Gaudylock. It is —" He hesitated, then took up a pen and wrote two words. "That's his name — but you are to keep it dark."

THE LAW OFFICE

Mocket's tilted chair came noisily to the floor. "What! In Richmond! — he in Richmond! When did he come? Where's he staying?"

"He came last night, and he's staying quietly at Bowler's Tavern. It is n't known that he's here, and he is not anxious that it should be known. He's here on business, and he goes to-morrow. That is all — and you're to say no word of what I tell you."

"All right," quoth Tom. "I won't blab. But I'd mightily like to see the man who shot Alexander Hamilton."

"I've told you he's not anxious for company."

"Oh, I know!" said Tom, not without humility. "I'm small fry. Well, there are curious things said about him, and you and he are strange bedfellows! How did it happen?"

"Tom, Tom," answered Rand, "you ask too many questions! It was an accident, or it was predestined and foreordained when I was dust blown about by the wind. You may take your choice according to your theology! I'm going now. Be at the House early to-morrow."

"Are you going to take that Mathews case? Young Mathews was here yesterday, swearing that if he could n't get you, he would hang himself."

"I've said that I would take it."

"Ludwell Cary's for the other side."

"Yes, I know. I'll win."

"Well, you're fairly pitted. Half the town backs one and half the other. That letter signed 'Aurelius' in the Gazette — did you know 't was his?"

Rand dropped his hand from the latch. The colour rushed to his face, then ebbed as quickly. "No, I did not know," he said, in a voice that was not quite steady. "I thought of quite another man."

"It is Ludwell Cary's, and every Black Cockade in Richmond, and not a few Republicans, are quoting it. My certie! it was a commentary in caustic — and so damned courteous all the time!"

"I don't care for such courtesy," answered Rand. "Ludwell Cary had best look where he treads."

"Well, I thought I'd tell you," said his colleague. "I don't like the Carys, either! — And so I'm not to go into that land scheme?"

"No. It's a small thing, and not honest. Some day, Tom, I'll help you to a larger thing than that."

"And honest?" said Mocket shrewdly.

The other turned upon him with anger, black as it was sudden. "Honest! Yes, honest as this storm, honest as any struggle for any piece of earth wider than a coffin space! Who are you to question me? I give you warning —"

"Gently, gently!" exclaimed the scamp, and started back. "Lord, how Gideon peeps out of you now and then!"

"You need not say that, either," retorted Rand grimly. He stood for a moment, a cloudy presence in the darkening room, then with a short laugh recovered himself. "I thought the black dog was dead," he said. "It's this gloomy day — and I did not sleep last night. Honest! We're all indifferent honest!"

"Well, well," answered the pacific Tom, "I'll sink or swim with you. I've followed where you have led this many a day."

Outside the red brick office the snow lay deep. It was still falling steadily, in large flakes, grey in the upper air, feathery white and pure against the opposite houses and the boles of leafless trees. The day was closing in. Up and down the street merchants were putting up their shutters; customers had been few on such a snowy day. Here and there appeared a figure, booted and greatcoated, emerging from a tavern or from a law office such as Rand's. A sledge passed, laden with pine and hickory, drawn by mules with jangling bells; and a handful of boys loosed from school threw down their bags of books and fell to snowballing. A negro shuffled by with a spade on his shoulder, singing as he went, —

> "Did n't my Lawd deliber Daniel,
> Did n't my Lawd deliber Daniel,
> An' why not ebery man?
> He delibered Daniel from de lions' den,
> An' de Hebrew Chillern from de furnace,
> He delibered David from de han' of Saul,
> An' why not ebery man?"

Rand turned into Governor Street, climbed its white ascent, and struck across the Capitol Square. Above him every bough had its weight of snow, and seen through the drifting veil the pillared Capitol looked remote as that building of which it was a copy. He walked quickly, with a light and determined step, a handsome figure in a many-caped coat of bottle green, striding through the snow toward the cheer of home. In his outer man, at least, the eighteen months since his marriage had wrought a change. What was striking then was more striking now, — his ease and might of frame, the admirable poise of his head, and the force expressed in every feature, the air of power that was about him like an emanation. The difference was that what had been rude strength was now strength polished and restrained. The deeps might hide abrupt and violent things, but the surface had assumed a fine amenity. Where he wished to learn he was the aptest pupil, and from the days of the tobacco-field he had longed for this smooth lustre. Not Gideon, but the mother, spoke in the appreciation and the facility. Manner counted for much in Lewis Rand's day; the critical point was not what you did, but the way you did it. Rand set himself to learn from his wife all the passwords of the region native to her, but into which he had broken. She taught him that code with a courtesy and simplicity exquisitely high-minded and sweet, and he learned with quickness, gratitude, and lack of any false shame. What else he might have learned of her he dimly felt, but he had not covenanted with existence for qualities that would war with a hundred purposes of his brain and will. He and Jacqueline were lovers yet. At the sight of each other the delicate fire ran through their veins; in absence the mind felt along the wall and dreamed of the gardens within. If the woman who had given all was the more constant lover; if the man, while his passion sweetened all his life, yet bowed before his great idol and fought and slaved for Power, it was according to the nature of the two, and there was perhaps no help.

He left the Capitol Square and went on toward the house he had retaken for the second winter in Richmond. Few were afoot, though now and then a sleigh went by. Rand's mind as he walked was busy, not with the debate of to-morrow or the visitor of to-night, the Mathews trial or Tom Mocket's puerile schemes, but with the letter in the Gazette signed "Aurelius." It had been an attack, able beyond the common, certainly not upon Lewis Rand, but upon the party which, in the eyes of the generality, he yet most markedly represented. In the inflamed condition of public sentiment such attacks were of weekly occurrence; the wise man was he who put them by unmoved. For the most part Rand was wise. Federal diatribes upon the Tripoli war, the Florida purchase, the quarrel with Spain, Santo Domingo, Neutral Trade, and Jefferson's leanings toward France left him cold. This letter in the Gazette had not done so. It had gone to the sources of things, analyzing with a coolness and naming with a propriety the more remarkable that it acknowledged, on certain sides, a community of thought with the party attacked. The result was that, as in civil war, the quarrel, through understanding, was the more determined. The man who signed "Aurelius" had not spared to point out, with a certain melancholy sternness, the plague spots, the defenceless places. Moreover, throughout his exposition there ran a harsh and sombre thread, now felt in denunciation and now in ironic praise. There was more than unveiling of the weakness of any human policy or party; the letter was in part a commination of individual conduct. No name was used, no direct reference given or example quoted; but one with acumen might guess there was a man in mind when the writer sat in judgment. The writer himself was perhaps not aware of the fulness of this betrayal, but Lewis Rand was aware. The paper had angered him, and he had not lacked intention of discovering at whose door it was to be laid. He had enemies enough — but this one was a close observer. The subtlety of the rebuke shook him. How had the writer who signed "Aurelius" known or divined? He thought of Major Edward Churchill, but certain reasons made him sure the letter was not his. And now it seemed that it was Ludwell Cary's.

Rand's lips set closely. Ludwell Cary might not know where all his shafts were striking, but Rand felt the sting. Fair fight in the courtroom, — that was one thing, — but this paper was wrought of sterner stuff. There was in it even a solemnity of warning. Rand's soul, that was in the grasp of Giant Two-Ways, writhed for a moment, then lay still again. With his characteristic short laugh, he shook off the feeling that he mistook for weakness, dismissed the momentary abashment, and pursued his way through the snowy streets. The question now in his mind was whether or no he should make his resentment plain to Ludwell Cary. At long intervals, three or four times in the winter, perhaps, it was the latter's custom to lift the knocker of Rand's door, and to sit for an hour in Jacqueline's drawing-room. Sometimes Rand was there, sometimes not; Cary's coming had grown to be a habit of the house, quiet, ordered, and urbane as all its habits were. Its master now determined, after a moment's sharp debate, to say nothing that he might not have said before he knew the identity of that writer to the Gazette. He was conscious of no desire for immediate retaliation; these things settled themselves in the long run. He did not intend speaking of the matter to Jacqueline. Pride forbade his giving Cary reason to surmise that he had hit the truth. Rand was willing to believe that many of the shafts were chance-sent. The reflection hardly lessened his anger, but it enabled him to thrust the matter behind him to the limbo of old scores.

He was crossing Broad Street when the door of a house before him opened, and a young man, with a gay word of farewell to some one in the doorway, ran down the steps and into the snowy street. It was Fairfax Cary. Rand and he, passing, lifted their hats, but they did not speak. Had it been the elder Cary, there would have been a moment's tarrying, an exchange of courteous speech. But Fairfax Cary made no secret of his enmity. If he did not offensively publish it, if he was, indeed, for so young a man, somewhat grimly silent upon those frequent occasions when Rand was talked of, the hostility was defined, and at times frank. He went on now with his handsome head held high. Rand looked after him with a curious, even a wistful smile upon his lips. He was himself a man young in years and strength of passion, but older far in experience and in thought. He did not dislike Fairfax Cary; he thought indeed that the young man's spirit, bearing, and partisanship were admirable. His smile was for the thought that had lightened through his mind: "If in after years I could have a son like that!" He wanted children; he wanted a son. Rand sighed. The day had been vexatious, and there were heavy questions yet to settle before the evening closed. After all, what was the use, since Jacqueline cared nothing for baubles, and there was no child! Better live out his days at Roselands, a farmer and a country lawyer! He shook off the weight, summoned all his household troop of thoughts, and went on homewards through the falling snow.

CHAPTER XV

COMPANY TO SUPPER

JACQUELINE arranged the flowers, cut from her window stand, in the porcelain vase, and set the vase with care in the centre of the polished table. All was in order, from the heavy damask napkins and the Chelsea plates to the silver candlesticks and the old cut-glass. She turned her graceful head, and called to her husband, whose step she heard in the adjoining room. He came, and, standing beside her, surveyed the mahogany field. "Is there anything lacking?" she asked.

He turned and kissed her. "Only that you should be happy!" he said.

"If I am not," she answered, "he will never find it out! But when I see him, I shall hear that fatal shot!"

"He will make you quite forget it. All women like him."

"Then I shall be the exception. General Hamilton was Uncle Edward's friend. At Fontenoy they'll call it insult that I have talked with this man!"

"They will not know," Rand replied. "It was an honest duel fought nigh two years ago. Forget — forget! There's so much one must forget. Besides, others are forgiving. There is not now the old enmity between him and the Federalists."

"No?" said Jacqueline. "Why is that?"

"I cannot tell you, but old differences are being smoothed over. It is rather the Republicans who are out with him."

"I know that he is no friend to Mr. Jefferson."

"No, he is no friend to Mr. Jefferson. The room looks well, sweetheart. But some day you shall have a much grander one, all light and splendour, and larger flowers than these —"

His wife rested her head against his shoulder. "I don't want it, Lewis. It is only you who care for magnificence. Sometimes I wonder that you should so care."

"It is my mother in me," he answered. "She cared — poor soul. But I don't want magnificence for myself. I want it for you —"

"You must not want it for me," cried Jacqueline, with wistful passion. "I am happy here, and I am happy at Roselands — but I was happiest of all in the house on the Three-Notched Road!"

There was a moment's silence, then Rand spoke slowly. "I was not born for content. I am urged on — and on — and I cannot always tell right from wrong. There is a darkness within me — I wish it were light instead!" He laughed. "But if wishes were horses, beggars might ride! — And you've cut all your pretty bright flowers! After supper, before we begin our talk, you must sing to him. They say his daughter is an accomplished and beautiful woman. But you — you are Beauty, Jacqueline!"

The knocker sounded. "That is he," exclaimed Rand, and went into the hall to welcome his guest. Jacqueline returned to the drawing-room, and waited there before the fire. She was dressed in white, with bare neck and arms and her mother's amethysts around her throat. In a moment the two men entered. "This is my wife, Colonel Burr," said Rand.

Jacqueline curtsied. A small, slight, black-eyed, and smiling gentleman bowed low, and with much grace of manner took and kissed her hand. "Mr. Rand, now I understand the pride in your voice! Madam, I wish my daughter Theodosia were with me. She is *my* pride, and when I say that you two would be friends, I pay you both a compliment!"

"I have heard much of her," answered Jacqueline, "and nothing but good. My husband tells me that you have been in the South — and in Virginia we are welcoming you with a snowstorm!"

"The cold is all outside," said Colonel Burr. "Permit me —"

He handed his hostess to the green-striped sofa, and seated himself beside her with a sigh of appreciation for the warmth and soft light of the pleasant room, and the presence of woman. "Your harp!" he exclaimed. "I should have brought a sheaf of Spanish songs such as the ladies sing to the guitar in New Orleans! — My dear sir, your fair wife and my Theodosia must one day sing together, walk hand in hand together, in that richer, sweeter land! They shall use the mantilla and wield the fan. Crowns are too heavy — they shall wear black lace!"

He spoke with not unpleasant brusqueness, a military manner tempered with gallantry, and he looked at Rand with quick black eyes. "Yes, they must meet," said Rand simply. He spoke composedly, but he had nevertheless a moment's vision of Jacqueline, away from the snow and the storm, walking in beauty through the gardens of a far country. He saw her with a circlet of gold upon her head, a circlet of Mexican gold. Crowns were heavy, but men — ay, and women, too! — fought for them. Hers should be light and fanciful upon her head. She should wear black lace if she chose, — though always he liked her best in white, — in her kingdom, in the kingdom he was going to help Aaron Burr establish. — No! in the kingdom Aaron Burr should help Lewis Rand establish! His dream broke. He was not sure that he meant to come to an understanding with Burr. It depended — it depended. But still he saw Jacqueline in trailing robes, with the gold circlet on her head.

Joab at the door announced supper, and the three went into the dining-room, where the red geraniums glowed between the candles. Jacqueline took her place behind the coffee-urn, and Joab waited.

The meal went pleasantly on. Colonel Burr was accomplished in conversation, now supple and insinuating as a courtier, now direct, forceful, even plain, as became an old soldier of the Revolution, always agreeable, and always with a fine air of sincerity. The daughter of Henry Churchill did not lack wit, charm, and proper fire, and the Virginia hostess never showed her private feelings to a guest. She watched over the stranger's comfort with soft care, and met his talk with graceful readiness. He spoke to her of her family: of her grandfather, whose name had been widely known, of her father, whose praises he had heard sung, of Major Churchill, whom he had met in Philadelphia in General Washington's time. He spoke of her kinsmen with an admiration which went far toward including their opinions. Jacqueline marvelled. Surely this gentleman was a Democrat-Republican, lately the Vice-President of that party's electing. It was not two years since he had slain General Hamilton; and now, in a quiet, refined voice, he was talking of Federalists and Federal ways with all the familiarity, sympathy, and ease of one born in the fold and contented with his lot. She wondered if he had quarrelled with his party, and while he was talking she was proudly thinking, "The Federalists will not have him — no, not if he went on his knees to them!" And then she thought, "He is a man without a country."

Rand sat somewhat silent and distrait, his mind occupied in building, building, now laying the timbers this way and now that; but presently, upon his guest's referring to him some point for elucidation, he entered the conversation, and thenceforth, though he spoke not a great deal, his personality dominated it. The acute intelligence opposite him took faint alarm. "I am bargaining for a supporter," Burr told himself, "not for a rival," and became if possible more deferentially courteous than before. The talk went smoothly on, from Virginia politics to the triumphal march of Napoleon through Europe; from England and the death of Pitt to the Spanish intrigues, and so back to questions of the West; and to references, which Jacqueline did not understand, to the Spanish Minister, Casa Yrujo, to the English Mr. Merry, and to Messieurs Sauvé, Derbigny, and Jean Noël Destréhan of New Orleans.

Joab took away the Chelsea plates and dishes, brushed the mahogany, and placed before his master squat decanters of sherry and Madeira. The flowing talk took a warmer tone, and began to sing with the music of the South and the golden West; to be charged with Spanish, French, and Indian names, with the odour of strange flowers, the roll of the Mississippi, and the flashing of coloured wings. It was the two men now who spoke. Jacqueline, leaning back in her chair, half listened to the talk of the Territory of Orleans, the Perdido, and the road to Mexico, half dreamed of what they might be doing at Fontenoy this snowy night. The knocker sounded. "That is Adam Gaudylock," exclaimed Rand. "Joab, show Mr. Gaudylock in."

Jacqueline rose, and Colonel Burr sprang to open the door for her. "We may sit late, Jacqueline," said Rand, and their guest, "Madam, I will make court to you in a court some day!"

Gaudylock's voice floated in from the hall: "Is a little man with him? — a black-eyed man?" She passed into the drawing-room, and, pressing her brow against the window-pane, looked out into the night. The snow had ceased to fall, and the moon was struggling with the breaking clouds. The

COMPANY TO SUPPER

door opened to admit her husband, who came for a moment to her side. "It is not snowing now," he said. "A visitor will hardly knock on such a night. If by chance one should come, say that I am engaged with a client, make my excuses, and as soon as possible get rid of him. On no account — on no account, Jacqueline, would I have it known that Aaron Burr is here to-night. This is important. I will keep the doors shut, and we will not speak loudly." He turned to go, then hesitated. "On second thoughts, I will tell Joab to excuse us both at the door. For you — do not sit up, dear heart! It will be late before our business is done."

He was gone. Jacqueline went back to the fire and, sitting down beneath the high mantel, opened the fifth volume of Clarissa Harlowe. She read for a while, then closed the book, and with her chin in her hand fell to studying the ruddy hollows and the dropping coals. Perhaps half an hour passed. The door opened, and she looked up from her picture in the deep hollows to see Ludwell Cary smiling down upon her and holding out his hand. "Perhaps I should have drifted past with the snow," he said, "but the light in the window drew me, and I heard to-day from Fontenoy. Mr. Rand, I know, is at home."

"Yes," answered Jacqueline, rising, "but he is much engaged to-night with — with a friend. Did Joab not tell you?"

"Mammy Chloe let me in. I did not see Joab. I am sorry —"

He hesitated. There came a blast of wind that rattled the boughs of the maple outside the window. The fire leaped and the shadows danced in the corners of the room. Jacqueline knew that it was cold outside — her visitor's coat was wet with snow. Sitting there before the fire she had been lonely, and her heart was hungry for news from home.

"May I stay a few minutes?" asked Cary. "I will read you what Major Edward says of Fontenoy."

She was far from dreaming how little Rand would wish this visitor to know of his affairs that night. Her knowledge extended no further than the fact that for some reason Colonel Burr did not wish it known that he was in Richmond. She listened, but the walls were thick, and she heard no sound from the distant dining-room. Cary would know only what she told him, and in a few minutes he would be gone. "I should like to hear the letter," she said, and motioned to the armchair beside the hearth. He took it, and she seated herself opposite him, upon an old, embroidered tabouret. Between them the fire of hickory logs burned softly; without the curtained windows the maple branches, moved by the wind, struck at intervals against the eaves. Jacqueline faced the door. It was her intention, should she hear steps, to rise and speak to Lewis in the hall without.

The letter which Cary drew from his breast pocket was from Major Churchill. That he did not read it all was due to his correspondent's choice of subjects and great plainness of speech; but he read what the Major had to say of Fontenoy, of the winter weather and the ailing slaves, of Mustapha, of county deaths and marriages, of the books he had been reading, and the men to whom he wrote. Major Edward's strain was ironic, fine, and very humanly lonely. Jacqueline's eyes filled with tears, and all the flames of the fire ran together like shaken jewels.

"Almost all the rest," said Cary, "has to do with politics. I will not read you what he has to say of us slight, younger men and the puny times in which we live. But this will interest you — this is of general import."

He turned the page and read: "I have to-day a letter from G. Morris with the latest mischief from the North. Aaron

Burr is going West, but with, I warrant you, no thought of the setting sun. The Ancient Iniquity in Washington smiles with thin lips and pronounces that all men and Aaron Burr are unambitious, unselfish, and peace-loving — but none the less, he looks askance at the serpent's windings. The friends of Burr are not the friends of Jefferson. There are Federalists — 't is said they increase in numbers — who do not wish the former ill; myself I am not of them. Colonel Burr *desired* that duel; he lay in wait for the affront which should be his opportunity; he murdered Hamilton. He risked his own life — very true, the majority of murderers do the same. The one who does not is a dastard in addition — *voilà tout!*

"Burr quits the East, and all men know that the West, like Israel of old, is weary of an Idea and would like to have a King. If the world revolves this way much longer, the Man of the People will not be asked to write the next Declaration of Independence, and the country west of the Ohio will be celebrating not the Fourth of July but an eighteenth Prairial. Aaron Burr and his confederates intend an Empire. 'T is said there are five hundred men in his confidence here in the East, and that the chief of these wait but for a signal from him or from Wilkinson — whereupon they'll follow him and he'll make them dukes and princes.

"Like Macbeth, he has done his murder and is on his way to be crowned at Scone. He has not a wife, but he has a daughter ambitious as himself. She has a son. He sees his line secured. He has suborned other murderers and made traitors of honest men — and our Laputa philosopher at Washington smiles and says there is nothing amiss!

"May I be gathered soon out of this cap-and-bells democracy to some Walhalla where I may find Hamilton and General Washington and be at peace! This world is growing wearisome to me.

"G. Morris speaks of the bulk of his news as report merely, but I'll stake my head the report is true."

Cary ceased to read. Jacqueline sat motionless, and in the silence of the room they heard the wind outside and the tapping of the maple branches.

"If I were Mr. Jefferson," said Cary presently, "I would arrest Colonel Burr this side of the Ohio. He has been West too often; he is in the East now, and I would see to it that he remained here. But Mr. Jefferson will temporize, and Burr will make his dash for a throne. Well! he is neither Cæsar nor Buonaparte; he is only Aaron Burr. He is the adventurer, not the Emperor. The danger is that in all the motley he is enlisting there may be a Buonaparte. Then farewell to this poor schemer and any delusions he may yet nourish as to a peaceful, federated West! War and brazen clamour and the yelling eagles of a conqueror!"

He spoke with conviction, but now, as though to lighten his own mood, he laughed. "All this may not be so," he said. "It may be but a dream of our over-peaceful night."

Jacqueline rose, motioned him with a smile to keep his seat, and, moving to an escritoire standing near the door, wrote a line upon a sheet of paper, then rang the bell and when Joab appeared, put the paper into his hand. "Give this to your master," she said, and came back to Cary beside the fire. She smiled, but he saw with concern that she was very pale, and that the amethysts were trembling at her throat. "I should not have read you this letter," he exclaimed. "It is over-caustic, over-bitter. Do not let it trouble you. You have grown pale!"

She bent over the fire as if she were cold. "It is nothing. Yes, I was troubled — I am always troubled when I think of Fontenoy. But it is over now — and indeed I wanted to hear Uncle Edward's letter." She straightened herself and turned to him a smiling face. "And now tell me

COMPANY TO SUPPER

yourself! You are looking worn. Men work too hard in Richmond. Oh, for the Albemarle air! The snow will be white to-morrow on my fir tree, and Deb will have to throw crumbs for the birds. I have learned a new song. When next you come, I will sing it to you."

"Will you not," asked Cary, — "will you not sing it to me now?"

She shook her head. "Not now. How the branches strike against the roof to-night!"

As she spoke she moved restlessly, and Cary saw the amethysts stir again. A thought flashed through his mind. It had to do with Lewis Rand, of whom he often thought, sometimes with melancholy envy, sometimes with strong dislike, sometimes with unwilling admiration, and always with painful curiosity. Now, the substance of Major Churchill's letter strongly in mind, with senses rendered more acute and emotions heightened as they always were in the presence of the woman he had not ceased to love, troubled, too, by something in her demeanor, intangibly different from her usual frank welcome, he suddenly and vividly recalled a much-applauded speech that Rand had made three days before in a public gathering. It had included a noteworthy display of minute information of western conditions, extending to the physical features of the country and to every degree of its complex population. One sentence among many had caught Cary's attention, had perplexed him, and had remained in his memory to be considered afterwards, closely and thoughtfully. There was one possible meaning —

Cary crumpled the letter in his hand. Rand's speech perplexed him no longer. That was it — that was it! His breath came quickly. He had builded better — he had builded better than he knew, when he wrote that paper signed "Aurelius"!

With fingers that were not quite steady he smoothed and

refolded Major Churchill's letter. He was saying to himself, "What does she know? She grew pale. Thou suspicious fool! That was for thought of home. He will have told her nothing — nothing! Her soul is clear."

He pocketed his letter and, rising, spoke to her with a chivalrous gentleness. "I will go now. Do not let the thought of Fontenoy distress you. Do you remember the snow man we made there once, wreathing his head with holly? But I'll tell you a strange thing, — even on such a night as this, I always see Fontenoy bathed in summer weather!"

"Yes, yes," she answered. "I, too. Oh, home!"

He held out his hand. "You'll give my compliments to Mr. Rand?"

"Yes," she said. "He is busy to-night with a client from the country. He works too hard."

"Take him soon to Roselands and tie him there. Sing him To Althea and make him forget." He bent and kissed her hand. "Good-night — good-night!"

"Good-night," she answered, and moved with him to the door. Standing there, she watched him through the hall and out of the house, then turned and, going to the window, pressed her brow against the pane and watched him down the street. The night had cleared; there was a high wind and many stars.

In Rand's dining-room the three men sat late over the wine and the questions that had brought them together, but at last the conference was somewhat stormily over. Burr and Adam Gaudylock left the house together, the hunter volunteering to guide the stranger to his inn. It was midnight, and Colonel Burr did not see his hostess. He sent her courtly messages, and he pressed Rand's hand somewhat too closely, then with his most admirable military air and frankest smile, thrust his arm through Gaudylock's and marched away. Rand closed

COMPANY TO SUPPER

the door, put down the candle that he held, and turned into the drawing-room.

Before the dying fire he found Jacqueline in her white gown, the amethysts about her throat, and her scarf of silver gauze fallen from her hand upon the floor. In her young face and form there should have been no hint, no fleeting breath of tragedy, but to-night there was that hint and that breath. The fire over which she bent and brooded seemed to leave her cold. The room was no longer brightly lighted, and she appeared mournfully a part of the hovering shadows. Her spirit had power to step forth and clothe the flesh. Almost always she looked the thing she felt. Now, in the half light, bent above the fading coals, she looked old. Her husband, with his hand upon the mantel-shelf, gazed down upon her. "It was wise of you to send me that note. Burr and I might have walked in here, or we might have spoken loudly. I heard Cary when he went out. How did you manage?"

"He asked for you. I told him that you were engaged with a client from the country. Oh, Lewis!"

Rand stooped and kissed her. "It was the best thing you could say. I would not have had him guess our visitor to-night. You are trembling like a leaf!"

"The best that I could say! — I don't know that. I feel like a leaf in the wind! I did not understand — but I was afraid for you. It is done, but I prefer to tell the truth!"

"I prefer it for you," said Rand. "To-night was mere unluckiness. And he suspected nothing?"

"He went without knowing who was in the dining-room. Lewis, what is there to suspect?"

He stood looking down upon her with a glow in his dark eyes and an unwonted red in his cheek. "Suspect? There is nothing to suspect. But to expect — there might be expectations, my Queen!"

"As long as you live you are my King!" she said. "To-night I am afraid for my King. I do not like Colonel Burr!"

"I am sorry for that. He is said to be a favourite with women."

"Lewis!" she cried, "what does he want with you? Tell me!"

So appealing was her voice, so urgent the touch of her hand, that with a start Rand awoke from his visions to the fact of her emotion. His eye was hawklike, and his intuition unfailing. "What did Ludwell Cary say to you?" he demanded.

She took her scarf from the floor, wound her hands in it, and clasped them tightly before her. "When I told him, — Mammy Chloe let him in, — when I told him that you were busy with your client, he thought no more of it. And then we talked of Fontenoy, and he read me a letter from Uncle Edward. Much of the letter was about Colonel Burr, and — and suspicions that were aroused. Uncle Edward called him a traitor and a maker of traitors. That is an ugly name, is it not? Ludwell Cary did not think the rumour false. He said that if he were Mr. Jefferson, he would arrest Colonel Burr. He, also, called him traitor. I can tell you what he said. He said, 'But Mr. Jefferson will temporize, and Burr will make his dash for a throne. Well! he is neither Cæsar nor Buonaparte; he is only Aaron Burr. The danger is that in all the motley he is enlisting there may be a Buonaparte. Then farewell to this poor schemer and any delusions he may yet nourish as to a peaceful, federated West! War and brazen clamour and the yelling eagles of a conqueror!' That is what he said."

There was a silence, then Rand spoke in a curious voice, "Saul among the prophets! In the future, let us have less of Ludwell Cary."

COMPANY TO SUPPER 207

"Lewis, why did Colonel Burr come here to-night?"

Rand turned from the fire and began to pace the room, head bent and hand at mouth, thinking rapidly. His wife raised her hands, still wrapped in the silver scarf, to her heart, and waited. As he passed for the third time the tall harp, he drew his hand heavily across the strings. The room vibrated to the sound. Rand came back to the hearth, took the armchair in which Cary had sat, and drew it closer to the glowing embers. "Come," he said. "Come, Jacqueline, let us look at the pictures in the fire."

She knelt beside him on the braided rug. "Show me true pictures! Home in Virginia, and honourable life, and noble service, and my King a King indeed, and this Colonel Burr gone like a shadow and an ugly dream! — that is the picture I want to see."

For a moment there was silence before the white ash and the dying heart of the wood, then Rand with the tongs squared a flaky bed and drew from top to bottom a jagged line. "This," he said, "is the great artery; this is the Mississippi River." He drew another line. "Here to the southwest is Mexico, and that is a country for great dreams. There the plantain and the orange grow and there are silver and gold — and the warm gulf is on this side, and the South Sea far, far away, and down here is South America. The Aztecs lived in Mexico, and Cortez conquered them. He burned his ships so that he and his Spaniards might not retreat. Here is the land west of the Mississippi, unknown and far away. There are grassy plains that seem to roll into the sun, and there are great herds of game, and warlike Indians, and beyond the range of any vision there are vast mountains white with snow. Gold, too, may be there. It is a country enormous, grandiose, rich, and silent, — a desert waiting dumbly for the strong man's tread." He turned a little and drew another line. "To this side, away, away to the east, here where you and I are sitting, watching, watching, here are the Old Thirteen, — the Thirteen that the English took from the Indians, that the children of the English took from England. It is the law of us all, Jacqueline, the law of the Three Kingdoms: the battle is to the strong and the race to the swift. The Old Thirteen are stable; let them rest! Together they make a great country, and they will be greater yet. But here is the Ohio — la belle Rivière, the Frenchmen call it. And beyond and below the Ohio, through all the gigantic valley of a river so great that it seems a fable, south to New Orleans, and westward to the undiscovered lies the country that is to be! And Napoleon, in order that he may brandish over England one thunderbolt the more, sells it for a song! — and we buy it for a song — and not one man in fifty guesses that we have bought the song of the future! The man who bought it knows its value — but Mr. Jefferson cares only for Doric lays. He'll not have the Phrygian. He dreams of cotton and olives, of flocks and herds, rock salt and peaceful mines, and the manors of the Golden Age, — all gathered, tended, worked, administered by farmers, school-teachers, and philosophers! The ploughshare (improved) and the pruning-hook, a pulpit for Dr. Priestley, and a statue of Tom Paine, a glass house where the study of the mastodon may lead to a knowledge of man, slavery abolished, and war abhorred, the lion and the lamb to lie down together and Rousseau to come true — all the old mirage — perfectibility in plain sight! That is his dream, and it is a noble one. There is no room in it for the wicked man. In the mean time he proposes to govern this land of milk and honey, this bought-and-paid-for Paradise, very much as an eastern Despot might govern a conquered province. The inconsistencies of man must disconcert even the Thinker up in the skies. Well — it happens that the West and this great new city of ours, there at the mouth of the river, with her levees and her ships, her merchants, priests, and lawyers, do not want government by a satrap. They want an Imperial City and a Cæsar of their own. Throughout the length and breadth of this vast territory there is deep dissatisfaction — within and without, for Spain is yet arrogant upon its borders. The Floridas — Mexico — fret and fever everywhere! It is so before all changes, Jacqueline. The very wind sighs uneasily. Then one comes, bolder than the rest, sees and takes his advantage. So empires and great names are made."

"So good names are lost!" she cried. "It is not thus that you spoke one October evening on our way from Albemarle!"

Rand dropped the iron from his hand. "That was a year and a half ago, and all things move with rapidity. A man's mind changes. That evening! — I was in Utopia. And yet, if we reigned, — if we two reigned, Jacqueline, — we might reign like that. We might make a kingdom wise and great."

"And Mr. Jefferson, and all that you owe to him? And your letter to him every month with all the public news?"

"That was before this winter," he answered. "We have almost ceased to write. I am not like James Madison or James Monroe. I cannot follow always. Mr. Jefferson is a great man — but it is hungry dwelling in the shadow of another."

"Better dwell in the shadow forever," cried Jacqueline, with passion, "than to reign with faithlessness in the sun!"

"I am not faithless —"

"So Benedict Arnold thought! Oh, Lewis!"

"You speak," said Rand slowly, "too much like the Churchills and the Carys."

In the silence that followed, Jacqueline rose and stood over against him, the scarf trailing from her hand and the amethysts rising and falling with her laboured breathing. He glanced at her and then went on: "Burr leaves Richmond to-morrow. He does not go West till summer, and all his schemes may come to naught. What he does or does not do will depend on many things, chiefly on whether or not we go to war with Spain. I am not going West with him — not yet. I have let him talk. I have brought him and Adam Gaudylock together; I have put a little money in this land purchase of his upon the Washita, and I have given him some advice. That is all there is of rebellion, treason, and sedition, — all the cock-a-hoop story! Ludwell Cary may keep his own breath to cool his own porridge. And you, Jacqueline, you who married *me*, you have not a soul to be frighted with big words! You and I shall walk side by side."

"Shall we?" she said. "That will depend. I'll not walk with you over the dead — dead faith, dead hope, dead honour!"

"I shall not ask you to," he answered. "You are not yourself. You are using words without thought. It is the cold, the lateness, and this dying fire — Ludwell Cary's arrogance as well. Dead faith, hope, honour! — is this your trust, your faith?"

"Lewis, Lewis!"

He rose, crossed the shadowy space between them, and took her hands. "Don't fear — don't fear! We two will always love. Jacqueline, there is that within me that will not rest, that cries for power, and that overrides obstacles! See what I have overridden since the days beneath the apple tree! I am not idly dreaming. Conditions such as exist to-day will not arise again. Upon this continent it is the time of times for the bold — the wisely bold. This that beckons is no mirage in the West; it is palpable fact. Say that I follow Burr — follow! overtake and pass him! He has a tarnished name and fifty years, — a supple rapier but a shrunken arm. He's

COMPANY TO SUPPER

daring; but I can be that and more. He plans; I can achieve. I am no dreamer and no braggart when I say that in the West I can play the Corsican. What can I do here? Become, perhaps, Governor of Virginia; wait until Mr. Jefferson is dead, and Mr. Madison is dead, and Mr. Monroe is dead, and then, if the world is yet Republican, become President? The governorship I do not want; the presidency is but a chance, and half a lifetime off! But this — this, Jacqueline, is real and at hand. Say that I go, say that I gain a throne where you and I may sit and rule, wise and great and sovereign, holding kingdoms for our children —"

"Oh!" exclaimed Jacqueline.

Rand drew her to him. "Don't fear — don't fear! The child will come — we want him so!"

"Promise me," she cried, — "promise me that you will see Colonel Burr no more, write to him no more! Promise me that you will put all this away, forever, forever! Oh, Lewis, give me your word!"

"I will do nothing rash," he said. "We will go back to Roselands, — we will watch and wait awhile. Burr himself does not go West until the summer. Ere then I will persuade you. That first July evening, under the mimosa at the gate, even then this thing was vaguely, vaguely in my mind."

"Was it?" she cried. "Oh me, oh me!"

"You are wearied," he said, "chilled and trembling. I wish that Ludwell Cary had aired his views elsewhere to-night! Put it all from your mind and come to rest —"

"Lewis, if ever you loved me — if ever you said that you would give me proof —"

"You know that I love you."

"Then, as I gave up friends and home for you, give up this thing for me! No, no, I'll not cease to beg" — She slipped from his arm to her knees. "Lewis, Lewis, this is not the road — this is not the way to freedom, goodness, happiness. Promise me! Oh, Lewis, if ever you loved me, promise me!"

From Rand's house on Shockoe Hill Ludwell Cary walked quickly homeward to the Eagle, where he and his brother lodged. As he walked he thought at first, hotly and bitterly enough, of Lewis Rand and painfully of himself, but at length the solemnity of the white night and the high glitter of the stars made him impatient of his own mood. He looked at the stars, and at the ivory and black of the tall trees, and his mind calmed itself and turned to think of Jacqueline.

In the Eagle's best bedroom, before a blazing fire and a bottle of port, he found Fairfax Cary deep in a winged chair and a volume of Fielding. "Well, Fair?" he said, with his arm upon the mantel-shelf and his booted foot upon the fender.

The younger Cary closed his book and hospitably poured wine for his brother. "Were you at the Amblers'?" he asked. "It's a night for one's own fireside. I went to the Mayos', but the fair Maria is out of town. On the way I stopped at Bowler's Tavern to see his man about that filly we were talking of, and I had a glass with old Bowler himself. He let out a piece of news. Who d' ye think is in town and under Bowler's roof? — Aaron Burr!"

There was a silence, then Cary said quietly, "Are n't you mistaken, Fair?"

"Not in the least," answered the other. "He came in a sloop from Baltimore yesterday. It is not known that he's in town; he does not want it known. He's keeping quiet, — perhaps he has another duel on his conscience. I don't believe old Bowler knew he had let the cat out. Burr leaves to-morrow. He was out visiting to-night."

"How do you know that?" Cary demanded, with sudden sharpness.

COMPANY TO SUPPER

"Bowler's best bedroom in darkness — no special preparations for supper — Burr's man idling in the kitchen — mine host taking no care to speak low, — in short, the wedding guest was roaming. I wonder where he was!"

The elder Cary raised and drained the glass of wine. He knew where Aaron Burr had supped and passed the evening, and a coldness that was not of the night crept upon him. As for Lewis Rand, he cared not what he did nor why he did it, but for Jacqueline Churchill. This had been the client from the country! All the time she was keeping it secret that Burr was there. She had turned pale. No wonder! — the faithful wife!

"Take care, that glass is thin — you'll break it!" warned the younger Cary, but the glass had snapped in the elder's fingers.

"Pshaw!" said Cary; "too frail for use! I'm off to bed, Fair. That bill comes up to-morrow, and it means a bitter fight. Good-night, — and I say, Fair, hold your tongue about Aaron Burr. Good-night!"

In his room he put out the candle, parted the window curtains, and looked upon Orion, icily splendid in the midnight sky. "What is there that is steadfast?" he thought. "Does she love him so?" He stood for a long time looking out into the night. He thought of that evening at Fontenoy when he had come in from the sultry and thunderous air and had found Rand seated in the drawing-room and Jacqueline at her harp, singing To Althea, —

> "Minds innocent and quiet take
> That for a hermitage."

The words and the vision of Fontenoy that night were yet with him when at last he turned from the window and threw himself upon the bed, where he finally fell asleep with his arm flung up and across his eyes.

CHAPTER XVI

AT LYNCH'S

RAND, walking hastily through the hall of the Capitol, came out into the portico. Before him, between the great pillars, the landscape showed in glittering silver, in the brown of leafless trees and the hard green of pine and fir. The hill fell steep and white to the houses at its base and to the trampled street. In the still and crystal air the river made itself plainly heard. Across, on the Chesterfield side, the woods formed a long smudge of umber against the blue of the afternoon sky.

There were people here in the open air as there had been in the corridor, a number of men talking loudly, or excitedly whispering, or in silence rolling triumph beneath the tongue, or digesting defeat. Rand's progress, here as there, brought a change. The loud talking fell, the whisperers turned, the silent found their voices, and there arose a humming note of recognition and tribute. Rand had carried the Albemarle Resolutions, and that with a high hand. He moved through the crowd, acknowledging with a bend of his head this or that man's salute, frankly smiling upon good friends, and finely unconscious of all enemies, until at the head of the broad steps he came upon Adam Gaudylock seated with his gun beside him, smoking reflectively in the face of the Albemarle Resolutions and the general excitement. At Rand's glance he rose, took up the gun, and slid the pipe into his beaded pouch. The two descended the steps together.

"I am going to Lynch's," said Rand. "The stage will soon be in and I want the news. Well?"

AT LYNCH'S

"He's off," answered Gaudylock. "Chaise to Fredericksburg at six this morning. Pitch dark and no one stirring, and he as chipper, fresh, and pleased as a squirrel with a nut! Pshaw! a Creek pappoose could read his trail! He's from New England anyway. I want a Virginian out there!"

They walked on down the white hillside. The hunter, tawny and light of tread, scarce older to the eye, for all his wanderings, than the man beside him, glanced aslant with his sea-blue eyes. "When are you coming, Lewis?"

"Never, I think," said Rand abruptly; then after a moment's silent walking, "They should better clean these paths of snow. Mocket says a brig came in yesterday from the Indies; — attacks on Neutral Trade and great storms at sea. I've a pipe of Madeira on the ocean that I hope will not go astray. I wish that some time you would send me by a wagon coming east antlers of elk for the hall at Roselands."

"Why, certainly!" quoth Gaudylock. "And so you are going to settle down like every other country gentleman, — safe and snug, winter and summer, fenced in by tobacco and looking after negroes? I'll send you the skin of a grizzly, too."

"Thank you," replied Rand; then presently, "I dreamed last night — when at last I got to sleep — of my father. Do you remember how he used to stride along with his black hair and his open shirt and his big stick in his hand? I used to think that stick a part of him — just his arm made long and heavy. I tried once to burn it when he was asleep. Ugh!"

"I dreamed," said Gaudylock imperturbably, "of a Shawnee girl who once wanted me to stay in her father's lodge. 'It is winter in the forest,' quoth she, 'and the wolves begin to howl. All your talk of places where the river runs through flowers and the pale faces build great villages is the talk of singing birds! Stay by the fire, Golden-tongue!' and I stayed — in the dream.

> "When you see a partridge
> Scurrying through the grass,
> Fit an arrow to the bow,
> For a man will pass!

Heigho!"

"I am already," retorted Rand, "at the place where the river runs through flowers and the pale faces have built villages. Who will say that I did not cross the forest? — I was years in crossing it! Here is Lynch's."

The coffee house on Main Street was the resort of lawyers, politicians, and strangers in town, and towards dusk, when the stage and post-rider were in, a crowded and noisy place. It was yet early when Rand and Gaudylock entered, and neither the mail-bag, nor many habitués of the place had arrived. The room was quiet and not over brightly lit by the declining sun and the flare of a great, crackling fire. There were a number of tables and a few shadowy figures sipping chocolate, wine, or punch. Rand led the way to a corner table, and, sitting down with his back to the room, beckoned a negro and ordered wine. "I am tired, voice and mind," he said to Gaudylock, "and I know you well enough to neglect you. Let us sit still till the papers come."

He drank his wine and, with his elbow on the table, rested his forehead upon his hand and closed his eyes. Adam emptied his glass, then, leaning back in his corner, surveyed the room. Two men came and seated themselves at a neighbouring table. They were talking in lowered voices, but Gaudylock's ears were exceedingly keen. "A great speech!" said one. "As great as Mr. Henry ever made. Do you remember old Gideon Rand?"

The other shrugged. "Yes; and I remember old Stephen

AT LYNCH'S

Rand, Gideon's father — a pirate of a man, sullen, cruel, and revengeful! A black stock!"

"The Waynes were not angels either — save by comparison," quoth the first. "All the same it was a great speech."

"I grant you that," said the other. "Black stock or not, we'll see him Governor of Virginia. Curious, is n't it?"

They became aware of their neighbours, glanced uneasily at each other, raised their eyebrows, and changed to a distant table. Rand made no sign of having heard. He put out his hand to the Burgundy, filled his glass, and drank it slowly, then closed his eyes again. A figure, half buried in the settle by the fire, folded a month-old journal and, rising, displayed in the light from the hickory logs the faded silk stockings, the velvet short-clothes, brocaded coat, and curled wig of M. Achille Pincornet, who taught dancing each winter in Richmond, as in summer he taught it in Albemarle. Mr. Pincornet, snuff-box and handkerchief in hand, looked around him, saw the two at the corner table, and crossed to them. "Mr. Rand, I make you my compliments. I was in the gallery. Ah, eloquence, eloquence! — substance persuasively put! Minerva with the air of Venus! I, too, was eloquent in my day! Pray honour me!"

Rand touched the extended snuff-box with his fingers, muttered an absent word or two, and again sank into revery. Mr. Pincornet, with an affable, "Ah, hunter!" to Gaudylock, passed on to greet an entering compatriot, the good Abbé Dubois.

Rand sat still, his head propped upon one hand, the fingers of the other moving upon the board before him, half aimlessly, half deliberately, as though he wrote in a dream. Opposite him rested Adam, placid as an eastern god. The room began to fill and the murmur of voices to deepen. "The Red Deer is late," affirmed some one. "Damned heavy roads!"

"Then they've sent on a rider!" cried another. "Here's Lynch's man with the bag!"

It being the custom to address letters, papers, and pamphlets to gentlemen at "Lynch's Coffee House," there was now a general movement of interest and expectation. A negro carrying a pair of saddle-bags advanced, obsequious and smiling, to a high desk at one side of the room and placed thereon the news from the outer world. The genial Mr. Lynch, proprietor of the establishment, took his place behind the desk with due solemnity, and a score of lawyers, merchants, and planters left tobacco, wine, julep, and toddy to press around his temporary throne. Every day at this hour Lynch mounted this height, and he dearly loved the transient importance. Now he solemnly unfastened the bags, drew out a great handful of matter, looked it over, amid laughing clamour, with pursed lips and one raised, deprecating hand, then in a cheerful, wheezing voice began to call out names, — "Major Du Val — Major Baker — Mr. Allan — Mr. Munford — Mr. Chavallie — Colonel Harvie — Major Gibbon — Dr. Foushee — Mr. Warrington — Major Willis — Mr. Wickham — Mr. Rand —"

There was a moment's check while Lynch craned his neck. "Mr. Rand's not here, I believe?"

"Lewis Rand, — no!" quoth Mr. Wickham. "What should he do in a mere coffee house with mere earthly newspapers? He's walking somewhere in a laurel garden in the cool of the evening."

Rand's voice came out of the depths of the room that was now just light enough to see the written word. "I am here, Mr. Lynch." He rose and came forward. "Good-afternoon, gentlemen — good-afternoon, Mr. Wickham!"

"Did you hear?" asked Wickham coolly. "Well, it is a laurel garden, you know! Mr. Lynch, let's have candles —"

"Yes, sir," said Mr. Lynch. "Colonel Ambler — Mr. Carrington — Mr. Rutherfoord — Mr. Page — Mr. Cary — Mr. Fairfax Cary —"

"They are coming later," said a voice.

"Thank you, Mr. Mason — Mr. Carter — Mr. Call — Mr. Cabell — the Abbé Dubois —"

The list went on. Candles were lighted on every table and on the mantel-shelf, though outside the windows the west was yet red. Two negroes brought and tossed into the cavernous fireplace a mighty backlog of hickory. The sound of the fire mingled with the rustle of large thin sheets of paper, the crisp turning of Auroras, National Intelligencers, Alexandria Expositors, Gazettes of the United States, excited journals of an excited time, with softly uttered interjections and running comment, and with now and then a high, clear statement of fact or rumour. At home, the hour's burning question was that of English and Spanish depredation at sea, attack upon neutral ships, confiscation and impressment of American sailors. In Washington, the resolutions of Gregg and Nicholson were under consideration, and all things looked toward the Embargo of a year later. Abroad, the sign in the skies was still Napoleon — Napoleon — Napoleon! Now, at Lynch's, as the crowd increased and the first absorbed perusal of script and print gave way to exchange of news and heated discussion, the room began to ring with voices. Broken sentences, words, and talismanic phrases danced as thick as motes in a sunbeam. "Non-Importation. . . . Gregg. . . . Too wholesale. . . . Nicholson. . . . Silk, window-glass. . . . Napoleon. . . . Brass, playing-cards, books, prints, beer, and ale. . . . Napoleon. . . . The Essex of Salem, the Enoch and Rowena. . . . Texas — the seizure of Texas. Two millions for the Floridas. . . . The Death of Pitt. . . . Napoleon — Austerlitz. . . . 'Decius' in the Enquirer — that's John

Randolph of Roanoke. . . . 'Aurelius'—that letter of 'Aurelius'—"

Rand, at the corner table, had moved his chair so as to face the room. Letters and papers were spread before him; he had broken the seal of a thin blue sheet and drawn a candle close to the fine, neat, and pointed writing. The letter interested him, and he apparently took no heed of the rapid and disjointed speech around him. But the word "Aurelius" brought a sudden, darting glance, a movement of the lower lip, and a stiffening of the shoulders. Gaudylock, who sat and smoked, supremely indifferent to the display of newspapers, marked the flicker of emotion. "He sees a snake in the grass," he thought lazily. "Who's 'Aurelius'?"

Rand turned the thin blue page, snuffed the candle, and fell again to his reading. Right and left the talk continued. "Glass, tin. . . . The Albemarle Resolutions. Great speech. He's over there. . . . All this talk about Aaron Burr. . . . Austerlitz — twenty thousand Russians. . . . Westwood the coiner got clean away on a brig for Martinique. One villain the less here, one the more in Martinique. Martinique! that's where the Empress Josephine comes from—"

"My faith!" said Adam. "It's worse than the mocking-birds in June!"

The doors opened and the two Carys entered the coffee room. Rand lifted his eyes for a moment, then let them fall to the third sheet of his letter. Mr. Lynch bustled forward. "Ha, Mr. Cary, your letters are waiting! Mr. Fairfax Cary, — your servant, sir! — Eli, wine for Mr. Cary — *the* Madeira. Christopher, more wood to the fire! The night is falling cold."

"Very cold, Mr. Lynch," said Ludwell Cary. "Colonel Ambler — Mr. Wickham, we meet again!" — and his brother, "We never have such cold in Albemarle, Mr. Lynch!

AT LYNCH'S

Ha, your fire is good, and your wine's good, and your company's good. There's a table by the fire, Ludwell."

They moved to it, exchanging greetings, as they went, with half the room, sat down, drank each a glass of wine, and fell to their letters, careless of the surrounding war of words. The elder's mail was heavy, — letters from London, from New York, from Philadelphia, one from his overseer at Greenwood, others from clients, colleagues, and strangers, — all the varied correspondence of the lawyer, the planter, and the man of the world. Fairfax Cary's letters were fewer in number, but one was gilt-edged, curiously folded, and superscribed in a strong and delicate hand. "Miss Dandridge seals with a dove and an olive branch?" murmured the elder brother. "Lucky Fair! What's the frown for?"

"Olive branch?" quoth the other. "She should seal with a nettle! Listen to this: 'Mr. Hunter has been some time with us at Fontenoy. Mr. Carter spent his Christmas here — he dances extremely well. Mr. Page gives us now and then the pleasure of his company. He turns the leaves of my music for me. Mr. Lee and I are reading Sir Charles Grandison together. I see Mr. Nelson at Saint Anne's.' Saint Anne! Saint Griselda! Her letters are enough to make a man renounce the world, the flesh, and the devil, and turn Trappist —"

"I wish the room would turn Trappist," said the other. "I am tired of talk. I would like to be somewhere in the woods to-night — quiet. We won't stay long here. There has been contention enough to-day."

The younger leaned forward. "Lewis Rand is over there — three tables back."

"I know. I saw him when we came in. Read your letters and we will be gone."

The minutes passed. Outside Lynch's the western red

faded, and the still, winter night came quickly on. Within, fire and candles burned bright, but to not a few of Mr. Lynch's patrons the flames danced unsteadily. It was an age of hard drinking; the day had been an exciting one, and Lynch's wine or punch or apple toddy but the last of many potations. The assemblage was assuredly not drunken, but neither was it, at this hour and after the emotional wear and tear of the past hours, quite sane or less than hectic. Its mood was edged. Now, in the quarter of an hour before the general start for home and supper, foreign and federal affairs gave way to first-hand matters and a review of the day that was closing. It had been a field day. The city of Richmond was strongly Federal, the General Assembly mainly Republican. At Lynch's this evening were members, Federalist and Republican, of the two Houses, with citizens, planters, visitors enough of either principle. When the general talk turned upon the Albemarle Resolutions and the morning's proceedings in the House of Delegates, it was as though an invisible grindstone had put upon the moment a finer edge.

Lewis Rand, sweeping his letters and papers together, had nodded to Adam and moved from his table to that of a pillar of the Republican party, with whom he was now in attentive discourse. Apparently he gave no heed to the voices around him, though he might have heard his own name, seeing that wherever the talk now turned it came at last upon his speech of that morning. Presently, "Mr. Rand!" called some one from across the room.

Rand turned. "Mr. Harrison?"

"Mr. Rand, there's a dispute here. Just what did you mean by — " and there followed a quotation from the morning's speech.

Rand moistened his lips with wine, turned more fully in his chair, and answered in a sentence of such pith as to bring applause from those of his party who heard. In a moment there was another query, then a third; he was presently committed to a short and vigorous exposition and defence of the point in question. The entire room became attentive. Then, as he paused, the strident voice of a noted and irascible man proclaimed, "That's not democracy and not Jefferson — that doctrine, Mr. Rand. Veil her as you please in gauze and tinsel, you've got conquest by the hand. You may not think it, but you're preaching — what's the word that 'Aurelius' used? — 'Buonapartism.'"

A Federalist of light weight who had arrived at quarrelsomeness and an empty bottle put in a sudden oar. "'Buonapartism' equals Ambition, and both begin with an R." He looked pointedly at Rand.

"My name begins with an R, sir," said Rand.

"Pshaw! so does mine!" exclaimed the man at the table with him. "Let him alone, Rand. He does n't know what he is saying."

Rand turned to the first speaker. "'Buonapartism,'— that's a word that's as ample as Charity, but I hardly think, sir, that it covers this case. It's a very vague word. But writers to the Gazette are apt to be more fluent than accurate."

"I should n't call it vague," cried his opponent. "It's a damned good word, and so I'd tell 'Aurelius,' if I knew who he was."

"It was n't random firing in that letter," said a voice from another quarter of the room. "I don't much care to know the gunner, but I'd mightily like to know who was aimed at. It was a damned definite thing, that letter. 'Buonapartism — the will to mount — sacrifice of obligations — Genius prostituted to Ambition — sin against light — a man's betrayal of his highest self and his own belief — the mind's incurable blindness — I, I am above all law — to take rich gifts and hold the gods in contempt — Dædalus wings'" — The speaker paused to fill his glass. "Yes, I should powerfully like to know at whom 'Aurelius' was aiming."

"At no one, I think," said Rand coolly. "He made a scarecrow of his own, and then was frightened by it. His chain-shot raked a man of straw, — and so would I tell 'Aurelius,' if I knew who he was."

As he spoke, he moved to face the fire. He had not raised his voice, but he had given it carrying quality. Cary raised his eyes, and laid down the paper he had in his hand. A genial, down-river planter and magistrate entered the conversation. "Well, I for one don't hold with all this latter-day hiding behind names out of Roman history! Brutus and Cato and Helvidius, Decius and Aurelius, and all the rest of them! Is a man ashamed of his English name?"

"Or afraid?" said Rand, then bit his lip. He had not meant to carry things so far, but the pent-up anger had its way at last. His mind was weary and tense, irritable from two sleepless nights and from futile decisions, and he inherited a tendency to black and sudden rage. It was true he had walked through life with a black dog at his heels. Sometimes he turned, closed with, throttled, and flung off his pursuer; sometimes he left him far behind; more than once he had seen him mastered and done with, dead by the wayside, had drawn free breath, and had gone on with a victor's brow. Then, when all the fields were smiling, came at a bound the dark shape, leaped at the throat, and hung there. It was so this evening at Lynch's. He strove with his passion, but he was aware of a wish to strive no longer, to let the black dog have his way.

There was a laugh for the speaker before him. "You see, sir," cried a noted lawyer, "Brutus and Cato, Helvidius,

AT LYNCH'S

Decius, and Aurelius, and all the noble Romans died before duelling came in! 'Sir, the editor of the — ahem! — newspaper, I take exception to this statement in your pages.' 'Sir, I refer you to Junius Brutus. Answer, Roman!' Never a sound from Limbo! — 'Sir, Decius has grossly misrepresented. Where shall I send my challenge?' 'To Hades, no less! Not the least use in knocking up John Randolph of Roanoke.' — 'Sir, I am at odds with Aurelius. Pray favour me with the gentleman's address.' 'Sir, he left no name. You see, he lived so long ago!'"

Amid the laugh that followed, Cary turned a smiling face upon the speaker. "*I* will answer, Mr. Wickham, for Aurelius. Do you really want to challenge me?" He slightly changed his position so as to confront Rand's table. "In this instance, Mr. Rand, I am certain there was no fear."

His speech, heard of all, wrought in various ways. Mocket the day before had not exaggerated the general interest in the letter signed "Aurelius." Now at Lynch's there arose a small tumult of surprise, acclaim, enthusiasm, and dissent. His friends broke into triumph, his political enemies — he had few others — strove for a deeper frown and a growling note. The only indifferent in Lynch's was Adam Gaudylock, who smoked tranquilly on, not having read the letter in question nor being concerned with Roman history. Lewis Rand sat in silence with compressed lips, bodily there in the lit coffee room, but the inner man far away on the mind's dark plains, struggling with the fiend that dogged him. Fairfax Cary's cheek glowed and his eyes shone. He looked at his brother, then poured a glass of wine and raised it to his lips. "Wait, Fairfax! We'll all drink with you!" cried a neighbour. "Gentlemen and Federalists, glasses! — Ludwell Cary, and may he live to hear his children's children read 'Aurelius'!"

The Federalists drank the toast with acclaim, while the Republicans with equal ostentation did no such thing. Mr. Pincornet in his corner, hearing the words "Gentlemen" and "Cary," drank with gusto his very thin wine, and Adam drank because he had always liked the Carys and certainly had no grudge against "Aurelius," whoever he might be.

In the first lull of sound the man at the table with Lewis Rand spoke in a loud, harsh, but agreeable voice. "Well, Mr. Cary, the staunchest of Republicans, though he can't drink that toast, need not deny praise to a masterpiece of words. Words, sir, not facts. What I want to know is at whom — not at what, at *whom* — you were firing? I thought once that Aaron Burr was your mark. But he's too light metal — a mere buccaneer! That broadside of yours would predicate a general foe — and I'm damned if I would n't like to know his name!"

"We would all like to know his name," said Rand. "And when we know it, I for one would like to hear Mr. Cary's proofs of faithlessness to obligations."

In the hush of expectation which fell upon the room the eyes of the two men met. In Rand's there was something cold and gleaming, something that was not his father's nor his grandfather's, but his own, deadly but markedly courageous. Cary's look was more masked, grave, and collected, with the merest quiver of the upper lip. In the mind of each the curtain strangely lifted, not upon Richmond or Fontenoy or the Court House at Charlottesville, but upon a long past day and the Albemarle woods and two boys gathering nuts together. This lasted but an instant, then Cary spoke. "In that letter, Judge Roane, 'Aurelius' had no thought of Aaron Burr. I doubt if in writing he meant to give to any image recognizable face and form. I think that, very largely, he believed himself but personifying the powers of evil and the tendencies thereto inherent in the Democrat-Republican as in all human doctrine. If he builded better than he knew, if he held the mirror up, if, in short, there's any whom the cap fits" — He paused a moment, then said sternly, "Let the wearer, whoever he may be, look to his steps!" and turned to face Rand. "Seeing there is no name to divulge, there are of course no proofs of faithlessness." He rose. "It is growing late, gentlemen, and I, for one, am committed to Mrs. Ambler's party. Who goes towards the Eagle?"

There was a movement throughout the coffee room. It was full dark, home beckoned, and a number besides Cary were pledged to the evening's entertainment. From every table men were rising, gathering up their papers, when Rand's voice, harsh, raised, and thick with passion, jarred the room. "I hold, Mr. Cary, that not even to please his fine imagination is a gentleman justified in publicly weaving caps of so particular a description!"

Cary turned sharply. "Not even when he weaves it for a man of straw? — your own expression, Mr. Rand."

"Even men of straw," answered the other thickly, "find sometimes a defender. By God, I'll not endure it!"

"All this," said Cary scornfully, — "all this for the usual, the familiar, the expected Federalist criticism of Republican precept and practice! What, specifically, is it, Mr. Rand, that you'll not endure?"

"I'll endure," replied Rand, in a strained, monotonous, and menacing voice, "no taunt from you."

As he spoke, he threw himself forward. "Have a care, sir!" cried Cary, and flung out his arm. He had seen, and the men around had seen, the intention of the blow. It was not struck. Amid the commotion that arose, Rand suddenly, and with an effort so violent and so directed that it had scarcely been in the scope of any other there, checked himself upon the precipice's verge, stood rigid, and strove with white lips for self-command. His inmost, his highest man had no desire to feel or to exhibit ungoverned rage, but there was a legion against him — and the black and furious dog. The coffee house was in a ferment. "Gentlemen — gentlemen! — What's the quarrel, Rand? — Ludwell Cary, I'm at your service! — Bills and bows! bills and bows! — or is it coffee and pistols?" Fairfax Cary had sprung to his brother's side. Adam Gaudylock, annihilating in some mysterious fashion the distance between the corner table and the group in the light of the fire, was visible over Rand's shoulder. Mr. Pincornet, chin in air and with his hand where once a sword had been, tiptoed upon the fringe of the crowd. The clamour went on. "Is it a challenge? — was a blow struck? — Mr. Cary, command me! — Mr. Rand —"

Cary and Rand, standing opposed, three feet of bare floor between them, looked fixedly at each other. Both were pale, both breathing heavily, but for both the unthinking moment had passed. Reflection had come and was standing there between them. To Rand it wore more faces than one, but to Cary it was steadily a form in white with amethysts about the neck. There had been — it was well, it was best — no blow struck, no lie given. Cary drew a long breath, shook himself slightly like a swimmer who has breasted a formidable wave, and broke into a laugh. "No affront and no challenge, gentlemen! That is so, is it not, Mr. Rand?"

If there was an instant's sombre hesitation, it was no more. "Yes, that is so," said Rand. "After all, men should be more stable. There is no quarrel, gentlemen."

He bowed ceremoniously to Cary, who returned the salute. Each moved from where he had stood, and the tide at Lynch's came between them. There was some questioning, some excited speech, some natural disappointment at matters

AT LYNCH'S

going no further. It was not clearly understood what offence had been given or what taken, but many felt aggrieved by the check on the threshold of a likely affair. However, it was, they could concede, the business of the two principals, each of whom could afford to ignore any seeming reflection upon his unreadiness to pick up the glove — if a glove had been thrown. As the assemblage broke up and flowed homeward, the most pertinent comment, perhaps, was that of the down-river planter: "If 't was just a breeze, and all over, why did n't they shake hands? Gad! when I was young and we fell out and made up over the wine, we went roaring home arm over shoulder! Your manners are too cold. A bow is nothing — one can bow to a villain! Men of honour, when the quarrel's over, should shake hands!"

"Precisely," said his companion, who chanced to be Mr. Wickham. "They are men of honour; they did n't shake hands. *Ergo* the quarrel's not over! — Here we are at the Eagle."

CHAPTER XVII

FAIRFAX AND UNITY

"BAH!" exclaimed Major Churchill. "Long ago Hamilton said the last word on the subject. Aaron Burr's sole political principle is to *mount*. The Gazette says he has started West — gone, I'll swear, to light the fuse."

"Then I hope the mine will blow up under him," said Fairfax Cary. "Can you tell me, sir, if Miss Dandridge is at home?"

The Major looked over the top of his Gazette. "Miss Dandridge is sitting beneath the catalpa tree." The other made a movement towards the door. "Mr. Page is with her. He is reading aloud — Eloïsa to Abelard, or some such impassioned stuff. Don't apologize! I have no objection to expletives."

The younger Cary laid down his hat, took a chair with great deliberation, and flecked his boot with his riding-whip. "The catalpa shall be sacred for me. Eloïsa to Abelard! Is it a long poem, sir?"

"It is longer than its author was. Sentimental rubbish!"

Major Edward folded the Gazette with his one hand, laid it on the library table, and leaned back in his leather chair. "It is not my opinion that Unity cares for Mr. Page. She cares for what many men and an occasional woman have cared for — liberty."

"I would give her liberty."

"She may possibly prefer it," said the Major dryly, "first hand."

The young man laughed ruefully. "So little liberty as she

has left me! I am bound hand and foot to her chariot wheels. There's nothing I would n't do for her, short of hearing Page read aloud."

"You 'll win in the end, I think. And I hope you may. Unity Dandridge is wilful, but she is a fine woman."

"The finest in the world — the most beautiful — the most sparkling — the most loyal —"

"You 'll not find her lacking in spirit. She will speak her mind, will Miss Dandridge! The Carys, fortunately, have a certain fine obstinacy of their own. It is a saving grace."

The other laughed. "I never heard that the Churchills lacked it, sir. Anyhow, I mean to marry Miss Dandridge. I 've told her and the world my intention, and they may count upon my carrying it out. If she only knew how lonely it is at Greenwood! Breakfast, dinner, and supper — Ludwell at the head of the table and I at the foot, and a company of ghosts in between —"

"Ludwell may yet marry."

Fairfax Cary shook his head. "No. He 'll never marry. If the Carys are obstinate, sir, they are also constant."

Major Churchill rose, turned to the bookshelves, and drew forth a volume. "Is he not over that?" he asked harshly.

"No, he is not. He 'll never be over it. And they say matches are made in heaven!"

"Bah! They are made on earth, and cracked hearts can be mended like any other cracked ware. 'A little crudded milk, fantastical puff-paste,' with a woman's name — and it has power to turn the sunshine black! Let him play the man and put her out of mind!"

"He does play the man," answered the other, with spirit. "He neither sulks nor shirks. It remains that there was but one woman in the world for him, and that she is at Roselands with Lewis Rand."

The Major's book fell with a crash to the floor. He stooped quickly and recovered it before the younger man could give him service. "I shall run Mustapha on the sixteenth at Staunton against Carter's York," he said, in a shaking voice. "Have you seen that Barbary mare Dick has gotten over from England?"

"No," answered the young man. "I'll take a look at the stables before I go. What is your book, sir?"

"It is" — said the Major. "I'm damned if I know what it is!" and he looked at the volume in his hand. "Paul and Virginia — faugh!" He threw the book down and stalked to the window. Fairfax Cary sat in silence, one booted knee over the other, an arm upon the back of his chair, and the riding-whip depending from his hand. The Major turned. "They have laid down Pope, and Mr. Page is making his adieux! Humph! I can remember a day when the poem was considered vastly moving. I would advise you to strike while the iron is hot."

"Sometimes I think it will take an earthquake to move her toward me," said the other. "I'll give Page three minutes in which to clear out, and then I'll try again. It would amuse you, sir, to know how many times I have tried. If to have an object in life is praiseworthy, I am much to be lauded!"

"You have always evinced a fine determination," admitted the Major. "Well, life must have an object, fair or foul. With it, cark and care; without it, ditchwater! This way disappointment; that, fungi on a log. Vanity in either direction, but a man of honour must prefer the rack to the stocks."

Fairfax Cary looked at his watch. "Page's time is up. I'll go pursue my object, sir."

The pursuit took him over the greensward to the bench built around the great catalpa. The heat of the day was broken and the evening shadows lay upon the grass. Mr.

Page was gone. Unity sat beneath the catalpa, elbow on knee and chin in hand, studying a dandelion at her feet. The poetical works of Mr. Alexander Pope lay at a distance, face down. The sky between the broad catalpa leaves was very blue, and a long ray of sunshine sifted through to gild the tendrils of Miss Dandridge's hair and to slide in brightness down her flowery gown. She glanced at the young man striding towards her from the house, then again admired the dandelion.

Fairfax Cary stooped, picked up Pope, and regarded the open pages with disfavour. "And at home he probably reads only The Complete Farrier — on Sundays maybe the Gentleman's Magazine or The Book of Dreams!"

"Who?" asked Unity.

"My rival. If he read Greek, he would yet be my rival and an ignorant fellow."

"He does read Greek," said Miss Dandridge severely, "and 'ignorant fellow' is the last thing that could be applied to him. Did you ride over from Greenwood to be scornful?"

"I rode over to be as meek as Moses and as patient as Job —"

"They were never my favourites in Scripture."

"Nor mine." He closed the book, swung his arm, and Pope crashed into a lilac bush. "There," he said, "goes meekness, patience, and the eighteenth century. This is the nineteenth. Time is no endless draught, no bottomless cup. Waste of life is the cankered rose. You know that you treat me badly."

"Do I? — I did not mean to."

"You do. Now you've got to say to me, 'I love you and I'll marry you,' or 'I love you not and I'm going to marry some one else.' If it's the first, I'll be the happiest man on earth; if the second, I'll go far away and try to forget."

"Won't you sit down?"

"You have kept me standing in spirit these three years Standing! — kneeling! Now, will you or won't you?"

"I do not care in the least for Mr. Page. He is merely an agreeable acquaintance."

"And Mr. Dabney?"

"The same. He entertains me —"

"Mr. Lee — Mr. Minor — Ned Hunter —"

"What applies to one applies to all."

"I am glad to hear it. All merely agreeable acquaintances. And Mr. Fairfax Cary? He is, perhaps, in the same category?"

"Perhaps. Oh, what a beautiful butterfly! — there, on that trumpet flower! I think it is a Tawny Emperor."

"I see," said the young man. "Excuse me a moment while I frighten him away." He gravely shook the trumpet vine, and the light splendour spread its wings and sailed to a securer realm. "Now that the Emperor is gone perhaps you will pay attention. Am *I* merely an agreeable acquaintance?"

"Oh — agreeable!" murmured Miss Dandridge.

"I am not trying to be agreeable. I am looking for the truth. Am I, then, merely an acquaintance?"

Unity sighed. "Why not say 'friend'?"

"'Friend' is good as far as it goes. It does not go far enough."

"Yes, it does," said Miss Dandridge. "It goes further than all your less sober travellers.

"Love me little, love me long.

You want such violent things!"

"I want you. Is it, then, only a poor, pale friendship?"

"Why call it poor and pale? Friendship can be rosy-cheeked as well as — as other things. Look how the grass is burned — and all the locusts are singing of the heat!"

"It is beneath you to trifle so. If this is all, it is poor and pale, and the sooner it dies, the better! Unity, I'm waiting for your *coup de grâce*."

"I'm tired," said Unity. "You hurt me, and I'm tired."

"I never heard you say that before. Look at me! the tears are in your eyes."

"Everybody cries over Eloïsa to Abelard.

> "O death all-eloquent! you only prove
> What dust we dote on, when 't is man we love!

Where are you going?"

"Home first, then — I don't know where. Good-bye."

"Don't go."

"I'm afraid the book in the lilac bush is spoiled. If you'll allow me, I'll send you another copy."

"Please don't go."

"The tears are on your cheeks. It is a moving poem.

> "Oh, may we never love as those have loved!

This is the third and last good-bye. Good-bye."

The younger Cary turned and resolutely walked away. Miss Dandridge rose and followed him. He did not turn his head, and the thick turf could not echo her light footfall. He walked firmly, with the port of a man who hears a distant drum beat to action. Miss Dandridge admired the attitude through her tears. He walked rapidly and the sweep of greensward between them widened. It was no great distance to the driveway and the white pillars of the house. Uncle Dick and Uncle Edward, Deb, the servants, any one, might be looking out of the windows. For one moment Unity stopped short as Atalanta when she saw the golden apple, then she began to run. She touched her goal within ten feet of the house, and he stood still and looked at the hand upon his arm. "Oh!" she panted. "Don't go! I — I — I —"

"I — ?"

"I love you. Oh!"

If any window saw, it was discreet and never told, remembering perhaps a youth of its own. The embrace was not prolonged beyond a minute. Unity, red and beautiful, released herself, looked about her like a startled dryad, and made again for the catalpa. Fairfax Cary followed, and they took that portion of the circular bench which had between it and the house the giant bole of the tree. Before them dipped the shady hollow, filled with the rustling of leaves, cool and retired as its parent forest.

"Oh, yes, yes; it's true, gospel true!" cried Unity. "But I'll not be married for a long, long year!"

"A year! You're going to be cruel again."

"No, no, I'm not cruel! I never was. 'T was all your imagination. When I marry, I'll be married hard and fast, hand and foot, wind and rain, sleet and snow, June and December, forever and a day, world without end, amen! holidays and all! I may live forever, and I'll be married all that time. I want just one little year to say good-bye to Unity Dandridge in."

"We'll take her to Greenwood with us."

"No, no. We'll bury her in the flower garden the day before. Just one year — please!"

"Oh, Unity, when you say 'please'!"

"This is August. I'll marry you twelve little months from now — please!"

"A thousand things may happen —"

"They won't — they won't. Don't you love Unity Dandridge? Then let her live a little longer!"

"Kiss me —"

Unity did as she was bid. The sunlight left the hollow, but stayed bright upon the hills beyond. It was August, but in a treetop somewhere a solitary bird was singing. Nearer the earth the crickets and cicadas began their evening concert, a shrill drumming in the warm, still air. There was a scent of dry grass, a feeling of summer at its full. Dewy freshness, tender green, mist of bloom, and a thousand songs were far away, and yet upon the bench beneath the catalpa there was spring.

"The sun is setting," said Unity at last. "Let us go speak to Uncle Dick."

"He'll be glad, I think. May I stay to supper? I want to hear Unity Dandridge sing afterwards."

"Yes, Uncle Dick will be glad — he and Uncle Edward will be very glad. I don't believe that Unity Dandridge will want to sing to-night. She'll be thinking of that grave in the flower garden."

"No! She shall think of the sunrise at Greenwood — sunrise and splendid roses and the million harps of heaven playing!"

"Oh!" cried Unity, "the sunrise at Greenwood should have been for your brother!"

"Yes, for him and your cousin. Blind fate! He is worth a thousand of me, and he sits lonely there in his house — and I am here!"

"There's no pure joy."

"When I tell him to-night, he will feel but pure joy for me — not one thought of self, of the sunrise he might have watched at Greenwood! Oh, Justice and her balances! There goes the last rim of the sun."

"I'll sing to you what you will — and you may stay as long as you like — and I'll love you all my life. Oh! Now let's go find Uncle Dick."

Uncle Dick was easily found, being in fact upon the porch in his especial chair, with the dogs around him, and in his hand a silver goblet of mint and apple brandy. "Hey! What, what!" he cried, "has the jade said Yes at last?

Where's Edward? Edward, Edward! Kiss me, you minx! Fair, I wish that my dear friend, your father, were alive. Well, well, patience does it, and the Lord knows, Unity, he's been patient! Oh, you black-eyed piece, you need a bit and bridle! Here's Edward! Edward, the shrew's tamed at last! Such a wedding as Fontenoy will have!"

Four hours later, when supper was over, and Aunt Nancy in the "chamber" had been visited by the affianced pair, and all matters had been discussed, and Unity at the harpsichord had sung without protest a number of very sentimental songs, and Deb had gone unwillingly to bed, and first one uncle and then the other had thoughtfully faded from the drawing-room, and good-night, when it came to be said in the moonlit porch, took ten minutes to say, and the boy who brought around the visitor's horse had caught with a grin and a "Thank 'e, sah!" the whirling silver dollar, and Major Edward's voice had sounded from the hall door behind Unity, "Good-night, Fair; bring Ludwell with you to-morrow night," and Unity had echoed softly, "Yes, bring Ludwell," and the last wave of the hand had been given, Fairfax Cary cantered down the driveway and through the lower gates. Out upon the red highway he put his horse to the gallop, and rode with his bared head high to the wind and the stars of night.

At Greenwood there was but one light burning. He saw it half a mile from the house, lost it, then caught it again, crowning like a star the low hilltop. Bending from the saddle, he opened the gate, passed through, and rode on beneath the oaks to the house door. The light shone from the library. When a negro had taken his horse, the younger Cary entered to find his brother sitting before a mass of books and papers, wine on the table, and a favourite dog asleep upon the hearth. "You are late," said the elder, looking up with a smile. "Fontenoy, of course?"

"Fontenoy, of course. Ludwell, I've won!"

The elder brother pushed back his chair, rose, and, going to the younger, put both hands upon his shoulders. "Fair, I'm glad! I told you that you would. She's the loveliest black-eyed lady — and as for you, you deserve your fortune! *Monsieur mon frère*, I make you my congratulations!"

"What a blaze of light you've got in here! All the way home my horse's hoofs were saying, *Unity Cary — Unity Cary.*"

Ludwell laughed. "You're drunk with joy. The room is not brightly lit. Sit down and tell me all about it."

"'T was underneath the catalpa tree. We quarrelled —"

"As usual."

"Page had been there, reading aloud, — reading Eloïsa to Abelard."

"Oh!"

"We quarrelled. I said good-bye forever, and walked away. She came after me over the grass. Ludwell, to hold the woman that you love in your arms, close, close —"

"I can guess 't was bliss. And then?"

"Heaven still — only quieter. We went back to the bench under the catalpa."

"Happy tree! And I never thought it a poetic growth — the flowers are so sticky! Now Unity shall plant one at Greenwood."

"'Unity'! Is n't it sweet to say just 'Unity'?"

The other laughed again. "I think you are a very satisfactory lover! And when's the marriage, Fair?"

"Not for a whole year — she won't marry me for a whole year to come!"

"Why, that's too long," said the elder kindly. "What reason?"

"Time to say farewell. Once she's married, she will never see Unity Dandridge again!"

Both laughed, but there was much tenderness in their laughter. "Oh, she's individual!" said Ludwell. "Even when you add the Cary, she'll be Unity Dandridge still. A year! Perhaps she may relent."

"I've given my word not to ask her."

"Ah! — well, a year's not so long, Fair. She's a lovely witch — she'll charm the hours away. This time next year how gay we'll make the old house!"

The younger paced the room. "I can't go to bed. Michaelmas — Christmas — St. Valentine's — Easter — the Fourth — then August again. Twelve months!"

"You'll ride to Fontenoy in the morning."

"That's true — and you'll ride with me. The last thing that she said was that I was to bring you. Ludwell, I want to say that not even Unity, though I love her so much, could ever make me love you an iota the less. You know that, don't you?"

"Yes, I know, Fair," said the other from the great chair. "We are friends as well as brothers. I'm as glad for your happiness as if it were my own, and I'll ride with you to Fontenoy to kiss my new sister. You've both chosen wisely, and it's a great day for Greenwood! Stop that striding here and there like an ecstatic lion! Sit down and tell me all about it again. The wine's good, and I'll light more candles. There!"

"You're the best fellow in the world, Ludwell," said the younger gratefully. "She had on a gown with little flowers all over a yellowy ground, and there was a curl that came down on her white neck — and when I had gone away forever and then felt her hand upon my arm, it was like a swordstroke opening Paradise. It isn't really late, is it? I could talk till dawn!"

CHAPTER XVIII

THE GREEN DOOR

THE coach of Mrs. Jane Selden entered Charlottesville at nine in the morning, and did not turn homeward again until the afternoon stood at four. The intermediate hours were diligently used by the small and withered lady in plum-coloured silk and straw bonnet, scarf of striped, apple-green gauze, and turkey-feather fan. She came to town but once in three months, and made of each visit a field day. Every store was called at, for buying must be done for herself and her plantation to last until Christmas-tide. Lutestring, calico, chintz and prunella, linsey and osnaburg; gilt-edged paper, sticks of wax, and fine black ink; drugs of sorts, bohea, spice, and china were bought and bestowed in brown paper parcels in corners of a vehicle ample as Cinderella's pumpkin coach, while Jamaica sugar and Java coffee, old rum, molasses, salt and vinegar, hardware, kitchen things, needs of the quarter, and all heavy matters were left to be called for by her wagon next day. Shopping over, she took dinner with an ancient friend, and afterwards called upon the doctor and the minister. The post-office came next in order, and then the blacksmith, for one of her four sleepy coach horses had cast a shoe. The fault remedied, she looked at her watch. "Half-past three. Stop at the green door, Gabriel."

Coach and four made a wide turn, swung drowsily down the main street, and drew up before a one-story brick building with a green door and a black lettered sign above, "Lewis Rand, Attorney-at-Law."

Mrs. Selden, putting her head out of the window, directed a small negro, lounging near, to raise the knocker below the sign; but before she could be obeyed, the door opened and Rand himself came quickly down the steps. "Come, come!" he said; "I knew it was your day in town, and I was wondering if you were going by without a word."

"Don't I always stop? A habit is a habit. We are all miserable sinners, and the world can't get on without lawyers. I want to ask you how I'm to keep old Tom Carfax off my land. There is no one with you?"

"No one. Mocket has ridden over to North Garden, and I've just dismissed a deputation from Milton." As he spoke, he opened the coach door and assisted his old friend to alight.

Together they went into the office, which was a cool little place, with a climbing rose at the windows, a bare floor, and a dim fragrance of law-books. The shade was grateful after the August heat and glare. Mrs. Selden, seated in a capacious wooden chair, wielded her turkey fan and looked about her at the crowded book-shelves, the mass of papers held down on desk and deal table by pieces of iron ore, the land maps on the wall, the corner ledger and high stool, the cupboard whose opened door disclosed bottles and glasses, and the blush roses just without the two small windows. "I like the law," she remarked. "There's a deal of villainy in it, no doubt, but that's a complaint to which all ways of making a living are liable. Even a shoemaker may be a villain. How does it feel to be a great lawyer, Lewis?"

He smiled. "Am I a great one?"

"You should know best, but it's what men call you. What was your deputation from Milton? About the governorship?"

"Yes."

"What did you say?"

"I thanked them for the honour they did me, and told them that I had declined the nomination."

"You have declined it! Why?"

He smiled again. "You used to preach contentment when I was a boy and you heard me rage out against my father. Well — shall I not rest content with being a great lawyer?"

His old neighbour regarded him keenly above her turkey-feather fan. "Lewis Rand, Lewis Rand," she said at last, "I wish I knew your end."

He laughed. "Do you mean my aim in life, or my last hour?"

"The one," said his visitor sharply, "will be according to the other. We all wander through a wood into some curious place at last. You're the kind of person one thinks of as coming into a stranger place than common. Have you heard the news about Unity Dandridge and Fairfax Cary?"

"Yes. She was at Roselands yesterday."

"It's good news. Unity Dandridge needs a master, and there's been no woman at Greenwood this weary while. Ludwell Cary will never marry."

"I see nothing to prevent his marrying."

Mrs. Selden suspended the waving of her fan. "He won't. Don't dislike him so, Lewis. It shows in your forehead."

"Is it so plain as that?" asked Rand. "Well, I do dislike him."

"Enmities are born with us, I suppose," said his visitor oughtfully. "I remember a man whom, without reason, ated. Had I been a man, I would have made it my study quarrel with him — to force him into a duel — to make y with him secretly if need be! I would n't have stopped murder. And it was all a mistake, as I found when he was ad and I did n't have to walk the same earth with him any more. It's a curious world, is the heart of man. And so you won't be Governor of Virginia?"

"Not now — some later day, perhaps. You see it takes all my time to be a great lawyer!"

"You don't deceive me," said Mrs. Selden, with great dryness. "But good or bad, your reason's your own, and I'll not ask you to satisfy an old woman's curiosity. In my day it was something to be Governor of Virginia."

She waved her fan more vigorously than before, and the wind from it blew a paper from the table beside her. She was birdlike in her movements, and before Rand could stoop, she had caught the sheet. "Rows and rows of figures!" she exclaimed. "Is it a sum you're doing?"

He nodded, taking it from her. "Yes; a giant of a sum," he answered easily, and put the paper in his pocket. "Now what is old Carfax doing on your land?"

The consultation over, Mrs. Selden left the office and was handed by Rand into the pumpkin coach. When he had closed the door, he yet stood beside the lowered glass, his arm, sleeved in fine green cloth, laid along its rim, his strong face, clear cut and dark, smiling in upon his old friend. In his mind was the long and dreary stretch of his boyhood when she and Adam Gaudylock were the only beings towards whom he had a friendly thought. He was one of those men whose minds still hold communion with all the selves that they have left behind. Each in its day had been a throbbing, vital thing, and though at times he found the past obtrusive and wished to throw it off, he could never utterly so. There was for him no Lethe. But if he tasted the disa vantages of so compound a self, to others the array enrich the man, making him vibrant of all that had been as w as all that was. It put them, too, to speculation as to h great an army he would gather ere the end, and as to the n ture of the last recruit. The visitor from the Three-Notched Road looked at him now with her keen old eyes and laid her mittened hand upon his arm. "Be a good man, Lewis Rand! Be a great one if you will, but be good. That comes first."

Rand touched her withered hand with his lips. "It is women who are good. And you'll not come to town again until nearly Christmas! I'll ride over before then, and I'll settle Carfax for you. You are going home now?"

"Vinie Mocket is cutting watermelon rind for me. I'll stop there first and then I'll go home! Give my love to Jacqueline. I heard at the Swan that Mr. Jefferson is at Monticello. Is that true?"

"Yes, it is true."

"Humph!" said Mrs. Selden. "Then you'll be at Monticello all hours. I wish you'd ask him for a seedling of that new peach tree."

"I shall not be there all hours," said Rand, "but I'll manage to get the seedling for you. Good-bye, good-bye!"

The coach and four lumbered on down the dusty Main Street. Mrs. Selden, sitting opposite her brown paper bundles, waved her fan and looked out on the parching trees and the straggling, vine-embowered houses. For half an hour there had been a thought at the back of her head, and now it suddenly opened wings. Those strangely arranged lines of figures on that paper which had fluttered to the floor, they formed no sum that Lewis Rand was working! The paper that they covered was not a stray leaf; it had been folded like a letter. There was, she remembered, a piece of wax upon it. It was a day when men of mark often wrote to each other in cipher — there was nothing strange in Lewis Rand so corresponding with whom he chose. Most probably it was a letter from the President — though that could hardly be, seeing that the President was at Monticello! Mrs. Selden looked out of the window towards that low, green mountain which was now rising before her, and frowningly tried to remember some gossamer of speech which had been blown to her upon the Three-Notched Road. A quarrel between Rand and the President? — pshaw! it could hardly have been that! She had a sudden memory of Rand's face ere he grew to manhood, of the ardent eyes and the involuntary gesture of reverence which he used when he spoke of Mr. Jefferson. He could not even speak of him without a certain trembling of the voice. Any one could see the change in him since then, but it was hardly to be believed that the old feeling did not abide at the bottom of the well! Mrs. Selden was annoyed. The letter might have been from Mr. Madison, or Mr. Monroe, or Albert Gallatin, or John Randolph, — though John Randolph, too, had quarrelled with the President, — or Spencer Roane, or almost any great Democrat-Republican. It was no business of hers whom it was from. A colour crept into her withered cheek, and she tapped her black silk shoe upon the floor of the coach. "Yes; a giant of a sum," Lewis had said with great easiness, and then had put the paper out of sight. Why had he not been frank? He might have said to an old friend, "That's a cipher, — you see men will be riddlers still!" and then have laid away the letter as securely as he pleased! Mrs. Selden hated deceit in anything, great or small, and hated to find flaws in folk of whom she was fond. It was a trifle truly, but Lewis Rand had meant to give her a false impression, and that when he knew as well as she how she detested falsity! As for his reasons for concealment, — let him keep his reasons! She angrily told herself that Jane Selden had no desire to pry into a politician's secrets. But he should have said that the letter was a letter! With which conclusion, the coach having

THE GREEN DOOR

drawn up before Vinie Mocket's door, Mrs. Selden dismissed the matter from her mind, and, descending, was met by Vinie herself at the gate.

"I've got the sweetmeats all cut, Mrs. Selden! Grapes and baskets, and hearts with arrows through them, and vases of roses. I never did any prettier. Won't you come in, ma'am? There's water just drawn from the well."

"Then I'll have a glass, and I'll just look at the sweetmeats. It is late and I must be going home. Vinie, why don't you have your gate mended?"

"It always was broken," said Vinie. "I'm always meaning to have it mended. Will you sit on the porch, ma'am? It's cooler than inside."

The short path was lined with zinnias and with prince's feather and the porch covered with a shady grapevine. Vinie brought a pitcher beaded with cool well water, and then a salver spread with fanciful shapes cut from the delicate green rind of melon and ready for preserving. Mrs. Selden drank the well water and approved Vinie's skill; then, "Your brother's gone to North Garden," she said abruptly. "Mr. Rand's affairs must keep him busy."

"Yeth, ma'am. Tom comes and goes," said Vinie wistfully. "I wish he'd be Governor of Virginia."

"Who? Tom?"

The girl laughed. "La, no, ma'am! Mr. Rand." The tone conveyed, pleasantly enough, both the grotesque impossibility of Mr. Tom Mocket aspiring to such a post, and the eminent suitability of its lying in the fortunes of Lewis Rand. Vinie, shy and pink and faintly pretty in her shell calico, leaned against the wooden railing beneath the grapevine, and appealed to her visitor: "I'm always after Tom to make him say he'll run. Tom can do a great deal with him — he always could. I reckon all his friends want him to take the nomination. But Tom says he has a bigger thing in mind —"

"Who? Tom?"

"No, ma'am. Mr. Rand. I forgot! Tom said I was n't to tell that to any one." Vinie looked distressed. "Won't you have another glass of water, ma'am? The drouth this year is something awful — all the corn burned up and the tobacco failing. Tom will be back soon from North Garden. Yeth, ma'am, he works right hard for Mr. Rand. The last time he was here he said that whether he ended in a palace or a dungeon, he'd remember Tom somewhere towards the last. Yeth, ma'am, it was a funny thing to say, but he was always mighty fond of Tom."

"Does he come here often?"

"Right often, — when there's work to be done at night, or when he wants to meet some one at a quieter place than the office. He's always known he could use this house as he pleased," Vinie ended simply. "Tom and I would go barefoot over fire for Mr. Rand."

"Well, my dear, I hope he won't ask you to," said her visitor, with dryness. She rose. "I've a long drive before me, so I'll not sit longer. Who's that — I left my glasses in the coach — who's that speaking to Gabriel?"

"It's Mr. Gaudylock."

"Gaudylock! He's not been in Albemarle for a year! When did he come back?"

"Just the other day, ma'am." A smile crept over Vinie's face. "He brought me a comb like the Spanish women wear. He's a mighty kind man — Mr. Gaudylock."

The hunter and Mrs. Selden met at the broken gate. "I am glad to see you back, Adam," she said. "You're a rolling stone, but all the same we're fond of you in Albemarle."

"I'm surely fond of Albemarle, ma'am," answered Adam.

"When I've rolled long and far enough and the moss is ready to gather on me, I reckon I'll roll back to a hillside in the old county. I'm sorry to see the drouth so bad. We've had a power of rain over the mountains."

"Not long since, I had a letter from a kinsman of mine in Louisiana, and he spoke of you. He said that up and down the rivers you were known, that the villages made it a holiday when you came to one, and that in the forest your name was like Robin Hood's."

"Robin Hood? Who's he?" demanded Adam; then, "Oh, you mean the man in the poetry book. I reckon he never saw the Mississippi in flood, and his forest would have laid on the palm of your hand. Yes, I'm known out there." He gave his mellow laugh. "A letter of introduction from Adam Gaudylock is a pretty good letter, whether it's to the captain of an ark, or a Creek sachem, or a Natchitoches settler, or a soldier at Fort Stoddert. Let me help you in, ma'am."

He handed her to her seat with the sure lightness and the woodsman's grace which was part of his charm, then gave her order to Gabriel. The coach turned and went back through the Main Street, and so on, in the yellow afternoon, to the Three-Notched Road. As she passed again the green door, Mrs. Selden looked out, but the door was fast and the shutters closed behind the blush roses. "He must have gone home early," she said to herself, and all the way along the Three-Notched Road she thought of Lewis Rand and his career.

Rand had not gone home, but was walking down the street towards the Eagle and the post-office. Presently the stage would be in, and he carried a letter the posting of which he did not care to entrust to another. He walked lightly and firmly, in the glow before sunset, and as he approached the post-office steps he met, full face, coming from the other end of the town, Colonel Richard and Major Edward Churchill and Fairfax Cary. They were afoot, having left their horses at the Swan while they waited for the incoming stage. The post-office had a high white porch, and on this were gathered a number of planters and townsfolk, while others lounged below on the trodden grass beneath three warped mulberries. All these, suspending conversation, watched the encounter.

Rand lifted his hat, and Fairfax Cary answered the salute with cold punctilio, but the two Churchills, the one with a red, the other with a stony countenance, ignored their nephew-in-law. The four reached together the post-office steps, a somewhat long and wide flight, but not broad enough to accommodate a blood feud. Rand made no attempt at speech, conciliatory or otherwise, but with a slight gesture of courtesy stood aside for the two elder men to pass and precede him. The smile upon his lip was half bitter, half philosophic, and as they passed, he regarded them aslant but freely. The burly, heated figure of the Colonel was trembling with anger, while Major Edward, striving for indifference, achieved only a wonderful, grey hauteur. They had been talking of the drouth, and they talked on while they went by Rand, but their voices sounded hollow like drums in a desert. They took as little outward notice of the living man whose fate entwined with theirs as if he had been a bleached bone upon the desert sands. They went on and, upon the porch above, mingled with a group of friends and neighbours.

Rand put himself in motion, and he and Fairfax Cary mounted step for step. The elder man looked aside at his companion of the moment, slender and vigorous, boyishly handsome in his dark riding-dress. He harboured no enmity towards the younger Cary, and for Unity he had only admiration and affection. His mind was full of recesses, and in one of them there hovered on bright wings a desire for the esteem of these two. In his day-dreams he steadily conferred upon them benefits, and in day-dreams he saw their feeling for him turn from prejudice to respect and fondness. Now, after a moment's hesitation, he spoke. "*I* have no quarrel, Mr. Cary, with a happiness that all the county is glad of. Miss Dandridge and my wife are the fondest friends. May I offer you my congratulations?"

He had ceased to move forward, and the other paused with him. The younger Cary was thinking, "Now if I were Ludwell, I'd accept this with simplicity, since, damn him, in this the man's sincere." He looked at the toe of his boot, swallowed hard, and then faced Rand with a sudden, transfiguring brightness of mien. "I thank you, Mr. Rand. Miss Dandridge is an angel, and I'm the happiest of men. Will you tell Mrs. Rand so, with my best regards?" He hesitated a moment, then went on: "No sign of rain! This weather is calamitous! I hope that Roselands has not suffered as Greenwood has done?"

"But it has," said Rand, with a smile. "The corn is all burned, and the entire state will make but little tobacco this year. Miss Dandridge is better than an angel; she's a very noble woman — I wish you both long life and happiness!"

They said no more, but mounted the remaining steps to the level above. Fairfax Cary joined the two Churchills and their friends, while Rand, after a just perceptible hesitation, entered the small room where the postmaster was filling, with great leisureliness, the leather mail-bag. Besides himself there was no other there; even the window gave not upon the porch, but on a quiet, tangled garden. He took the letter from his breast pocket and stood looking at it. The postmaster, after the first word of greeting, went on with his work, whistling softly as he handled the stiffly folded, wax-splashed missives of the time. The wind was in the west, and the fitful air came in from the withered garden and breathed upon Rand's forehead. He stood for perhaps five minutes looking at the letter, then with a curious and characteristic gesture of decision he walked to the high counter and with his own hand dropped it into the mail-bag, then waited to see it covered by the drift from the postmaster's fingers. "Don't the world move, sir?" said the latter worthy. "It has n't been so long since there was n't any mail for the West anyhow, and now look at this bag! Kentucky, and this new Tennessee, and Mississippi, and Louisiana, and the Lord knows what besides! Letters coming thick and fast to Mr. Jefferson, and letters going out from every one who has a dollar or an acre or a son or brother in those God-forsaken parts where Adam Gaudylock says they don't speak English and you walk uphill to the river! I like things snug, Mr. Rand, and this country's too big and this mail's too heavy. You have correspondents out there yourself, sir."

"Yes," answered Rand, with indifference. "As you say, Mr. Smock, all the world writes letters nowadays. Certainly it is natural that from all over the West men should write to Mr. Jefferson."

"Natural or not, they do it," quoth Mr. Smock doggedly. "I thought I heard the stage horn?"

Rand looked at his watch. "Not yet. It lacks some minutes of its time," he said, and, leaning on the counter, waited until he saw the mail-bag filled and securely fastened. Lounging there, he took occasion to ask after the health of Mr. Smock's wife, and to commiserate the burnt garden without the window. If the expression of interest was calculated, the interest itself was genuine enough. A shrewd observer might have said that in dealing with the voters of his county Rand exhibited a fine fusion of the subtle politician with the well-wishing neighbour. The facts that he was quite simply and sincerely sorry for the postmaster's ailing wife, and that he had the yeoman's love for fresh and springing green instead of withered leaf and stalk, in no wise militated against that other fact that it was his cue to conciliate, as far as might be, the minds of men. He almost never neglected his cue; when he did so, it was because uncontrollable passion had intervened. Now the postmaster, too, shook his head over the ruined garden, entered with particularity into the doctor's last report, and by the time that Rand, with a nod of farewell, left the room, had voted him into the Governor's chair, or any other seat of honour to which he might aspire. "Brains, brains!" thought Mr. Smock. "And a plain man despite his fine marriage! If there were more like him, the country would be safer than it is to-day. There is the horn!"

The stage with its four horses and flapping leather hanging, its heated, red-coated driver and guard, and its dusty passengers swung into town with great cracking of a whip and blowing of a horn, drew up at the post-office just long enough to deliver a plethoric mail-bag, and then rolled on in a pillar of dust to the Eagle. The crowd about the post-office increased, men gathering on the steps as well as upon the porch above and on the parched turf beneath the mulberries. There was a principle of division. The Federalists, who were in the minority, held one end of the porch; the more prominent Republicans the other, while the steps were free to both, and the space below was given over to a rabble almost entirely Republican. Rand, with several associates, lawyers or planters, stood near the head of the steps;—all waited for the sorting and distribution of the mail. The sun was low over the Ragged Mountains, and after the breathless heat of the day, a wind had arisen that refreshed like wine.

Rand, his back to the light, and paying grave attention to a colleague's low-voiced exposition of a point in law, did not at first observe a movement of the throng, coupled with the utterance of a well-known name, but presently, as though an unseen hand had tapped him on the shoulder, he turned abruptly, and looked with all the rest. Mr. Jefferson was coming up the street, riding slowly on a big, black horse and followed by a negro groom. The tall, spare form sat very upright, the reins loosely held in the sinewy hand. Above the lawn neckcloth the face, sanguine in complexion and with deep-set eyes, looking smilingly from side to side of the village street. He came on to the post-office amid a buzz of voices, and the more prominent men of his party started down the steps to greet him. The few Federalists stiffly held their places, but they, too, as he rode up, lifted their hats to their ancient neighbour and the country's Chief Magistrate. A dozen hands were ready to help him dismount, but he shook his head with a smile. "Thank you, gentlemen, but I will keep my seat. I have but ridden down to get my mail. — Mr. Coles, if you will be so good! — It is a pity, is it not, to see this drouth? There has been nothing like it these fifty years. — Mr. Holliday, I have news of Meriwether Lewis. He has seen the Pacific.

> "Tiphysque novos
> Detegat orbes; nec sit terris
> Ultima Thule.

Mr. Massie, I want some apples from Spring Valley for my guest, the Abbé Correa. — Mr. Cocke, my Merinos are prospering despite the burned pastures."

Mr. Coles came down the steps with a great handful of

THE GREEN DOOR

letters and newspapers. The President took them from him, and, without running them over, deposited all together in a small cotton bag which hung from his saddle-bow. This done, he raised his head and let his glance travel from one end to the other of the porch above him. Of the men standing there many were his bitter political enemies, but also they were his old neighbours, lovers, like himself, of Albemarle and Virginia, and once, in the old days when all were English, as in the later time when all were patriots, his friends and comrades. He bowed to them, and they returned his salute, not genially, but with the respect due to his fame and office. His eye travelled on. "Mr. Rand, may I have a word with you?"

Rand left the pillar against which he had leaned and came down the steps to the waiting horseman. He moved neither fast nor slow, but yet with proper alacrity, and his dark face was imperturbable. The fact of some disagreement, some misunderstanding between Mr. Jefferson and the man who had entered the public arena as his protégé, had been for some time in the air of Albemarle. What it was, and whether great or small, Albemarle was not prepared to say. There was a chill in the air, it thought, but the cloud might well prove the merest passing mist, if, indeed, Rumour was not entirely mistaken, and the coolness a misapprehension. The President's voice had been quiet and friendly, and Rand himself moved with a most care-free aspect. He was of those who draw observation, and all eyes followed him down the steps. He crossed the yard or two of turf to the black horse, and stood beside the rider. "You wished me, sir?"

"I wish to know if you will be so good as to come to Monticello to-night? After nine the house will be quiet."

"Certainly I will come, sir."

"I will look for you then." He bowed slightly and gathered

up his reins. Rand stood back, and with a "Good-afternoon to you all, gentlemen," the President wheeled his horse and rode down the street towards his mountain home. The crowd about the post-office received its mail and melted away to town house and country house, to supper at both, and to a review, cheerful or acrimonious, of the events of the day, including the fact that, as far as appearances went, Lewis Rand was yet the President's staff and confidant. The Churchills and Fairfax Cary rode away together. In passing, the latter just bent his head to Rand, but Colonel Dick and Major Edward sat like adamant. Rand took the letters doled out to him by Mr. Smock, glanced at the superscriptions, and put them in his pocket, then walked to the Eagle and spoke to the hostler there, and finally, as the big red ball of the sun dipped behind the mountains, betook himself to Tom Mocket's small house on the edge of town.

He found Vinie on the porch. "Is Adam here?" he asked. She nodded. "That's well," he said. "I want a talk with him — a long talk. And, Vinie, can you give me a bit of supper? I won't go home until late to-night; — I have sent my wife word. Tell Adam, will you? that I am here, and let us have the porch to ourselves."

CHAPTER XIX

MONTICELLO AGAIN

THE night was hot and dark when Rand, riding Selim, left the town and took the Monticello road. He forded the creek, and the horse, scrambling up the farther side, struck fire from the loose stones. Farther on, the way grew steep, and the heavy shadow of the overhanging trees made yet more oppressive the breathless night. The stars could hardly be seen between the branches, but from the ground to the leafy roof the fireflies sparkled restlessly. Rand thought, as he rode, of the future and the present, but not of the past. It was so old and familiar, this road, that he might well feel the eyes of the past fixed upon him from every bush and tree; but if he felt the gaze, he set his will and would not return it. For some time he climbed through the thick darkness, shot with those small and wandering fires, but at last he came upon the higher levels and saw below him the wide and dark plain. In the east there was heat lightning. Here on the mountain-top the air blew, and a man was free from the dust of the valley. He drew a long breath, checked Selim for a moment, and, sitting there, looked out over the vast expanse; but the eyes of the past grew troublesome, and he hurried on. It was striking nine when a negro opened the house gate for him and, following him to the portico, took the horse from which he dismounted. Light streamed from the open door, and from the library windows. Except for a glimmer in the Abbé Correa's room, the rest of the house was in darkness. If Mrs. Randolph and her daughters were there, they had retired. He heard no voices. In the hot and sulphurous night the pillared, silent house with its open portal provoked a sensation of strangeness. Rand crossed the portico and paused at the door. Time had been when he would have made no pause, but, familiar to the house and assured of his welcome, would have passed through the wide hall to the library and his waiting friend and mentor. Now he laid his hand upon the knocker, but before it could sound, a door halfway down the hall opened, and there appeared the tall figure of the President. He stood for a moment, framed in the doorway, gazing at his visitor, and there was in his regard a curious thoughtfulness, an old regret, and — or so Rand thought — a faint hostility. The look lasted but a moment; he raised his hand, and, with a movement that was both a gesture of welcome and an invitation to follow him, turned and entered the passage which led to the library. Rand moved in silence through the hall, where Indian curiosities, horns of elk, and prehistoric relics were arranged above the marble heads of Buonaparte and Alexander the First, Franklin and Voltaire, and down the narrow passage to the room that had been almost chief of all his sacred places. It was now somewhat dimly lit, with every window wide to the night. Jefferson, sitting beside the table in his particular great chair, motioned the younger man to a seat across from him, evidently placed in anticipation of his coming. Rand took the chair, but as he did so, he slightly moved the candles upon the table so that they did not illumine, as they had been placed to illumine, his face and figure. It was he who began the conversation, and he wasted no time upon preliminaries. The night was in his blood, and he was weary of half measures. This storm had long been brewing: let it break and be over with; better the open lightning than the sullen storing up of unpaid scores, unemptied vials of wrath! There were matters of quarrel:

well, let the quarrel come! The supreme matter, unknown and undreamed of by the philosopher opposite him, would sleep secure beneath the uproar over little things. He craved the open quarrel. It would be easier after the storm. The air would be cleared, though by forces that were dire, and he could go more easily through the forest when he had laid the trees low. It was better to hurry over the bared plain towards the shining goal than to stumble and be deterred amid these snares of old memories, habits, affections, and gratitudes. The past — the past was man's enemy. He was committed to the future, and in order to serve that strong master there was work — disagreeable work — to be done in the present. Ingratitude! — that, too, was but a word, though a long one. He was willing to deceive himself, and so ideas and images came at his bidding, but they hung his path with false lights, and they served, not him, but his inward foe.

He spoke abruptly. "That Militia Bill, — the matter did not approve itself to my reason, and so I could not push it through. I understood, of course, at the time that you were vexed —"

"I should not say that 'vexed' was the word. I was surprised. You will do me the justice to acknowledge that I cheerfully accepted the explanation which you gave me. You are fully aware that I, of all men, would be the last to deny your right — any man's right — of private judgment. All this was last winter, and might have been buried out of sight."

"I have heard that a letter of mine in the Enquirer gave you umbrage. It was my opinion that the country's honour demanded less milk and water, less supineness in our dealings with England, and I expressed my opinion —"

"The country's honour! That expression of your opinion

placed you among the critics of the administration, and that at an hour when every friend was needed. It came without warning, and if it was meant to wound me, it succeeded."

Rand moved restlessly. "It was not," he said sombrely; "it was not meant to wound you, sir. Let me, once for all, sitting in this room amid the shades of so many past kindnesses, utterly disavow any personal feeling toward you other than respect and gratitude. It was apparent to me that the letter must be written, but I take God to witness that I regretted the necessity."

"The regret," answered the other, "will doubtless, in the sight of the Power you invoke, justify the performance. Well, the nine days' wonder of the letter is long over! A man in public life cannot live sixty years without suffering and forgiving many a similar stab. The letter was in February. Afterwards —"

"I ceased to write to you. Through all the years in which I had written, we had been in perfect accord. Now I saw the rift between us, and that it would widen, and I threw no futile bridges."

"You are frank. I have indeed letters from you, written in this room" — There was upon the table an orderly litter of books and papers. From a packet of the latter Jefferson drew a letter, unfolded it, and, stretching out his long arm, laid it on the table before his visitor. "There is one," he said, "written not three years ago, on the evening of the day when you were elected to the General Assembly. I shall ask you to do me the favour to read it through."

Rand took the letter and ran his dark eye down the sheets. As he read, the blood stained his cheek, brow, and throat, and presently, with a violent movement, he rose and, crossing the room to a window, stood there with his face to the night.

The clock had ticked three minutes before he turned and, coming back to the table, dropped the letter upon its polished surface. "You have your revenge," he said. "Yes, I was like that — and less than three years ago. I remember that night very well, and had a spirit whispered to me then that this night would come, I would have told the spirit that he lied! And it has come. Let us pass to the next count in the indictment."

"The Albemarle Resolutions —"

"I carried them."

"I wished them carried, but I should rather have seen them lost than that in your speech — a speech that resounded far and wide — you should have put the face you did upon matters! You knew my sentiments and convictions; until I read that speech, I thought they were your own. The Albemarle Resolutions! I have heard it said that your zeal for the Albemarle Resolutions was largely fanned by the fact that your personal enemy was chief among your opponents!"

"May I ask who said that?"

"You may ask, but I shall not answer. We are now at late February."

"The Assembly adjourned. I returned to Albemarle."

"You took first a journey to Philadelphia."

"Yes. Is there treason in that?"

"That," said Jefferson, with calmness, "is a word not yet of my using."

Rand leaned forward. "Yet?" he repeated, with emphasis.

There fell a silence in the room. After a moment of sitting quietly, his hands held lightly on the arm of his chair, Mr. Jefferson rose and began to pace the floor. The action was unusual; in all personal intercourse his command of himself was remarkable. An inveterate cheerful composure, a still sunniness, a readiness to settle all jars of the universe in an extremely short time and without stirring from his chair, were characteristics with which Rand was too familiar not to feel a frowning wonder at the pacing figure and the troubled footfall. He was a man bold to hardihood, and well assured of a covered trail, so assured that his brain rejected with vehemence the thought that darted through it. To Mr. Jefferson the word that he had audaciously used could have no significance. Treason! Traitor! Aaron Burr and his Jack-o'-Lantern ambitions, indeed, had long been looked upon with suspicion, vague and ill-directed, now slumbering and now idly alert. In this very room — in this very room the man had been talked of, discussed, analysed, and puffed away by the two who now held it with their estranged and troubled souls. Burr was gone; this August night he was floating down the Ohio toward New Orleans and the promised blow. Had some fool or knave or sickly conscience among the motley that was conspiring with him turned coward or been bought? It was possible. Burr might be betrayed, but hardly Lewis Rand. That was a guarded maze to which Mr. Jefferson could have no clue.

Jefferson came back to the table and the great chair. "You were, of course, as free as any man to travel to Philadelphia or where you would. I heard that you were upon such a journey, and I felt a certitude that you would also visit Washington. Had you done this, I should have received you with the old confidence and affection. I should have listened to the explanation I felt assured you would wish to make. At that time it was my belief that there needed but one long conversation between us to remove misapprehension, to convince you of your error, and to recall you to your allegiance. Do not mistake me. I craved no more than was human, no more than was justified by our relations in the past — your allegiance to me. But I wished to see you devoutly true to the principles you professed, to the Republican Idea, and to all that you, no less than I, had once included in that term. I looked for you in Washington, and I looked in vain."

"You make it hard for me," said Rand, with lowered eyes. "I had no explanation to give."

"When you neither came nor wrote, I assumed as much. It was in April that you returned to Albemarle. Since then I have myself been twice in the county."

"We have met —"

"But never alone. Had you forgotten the Monticello road? After the Three-Notched Road, I should have thought it best known to you."

"I have not forgotten it, sir. But I might doubt my welcome here."

"You might well doubt it," answered the other sternly. "But had there been humility in your heart — ay, or common remembrance! — that doubt would not have kept you back. When I saw at last that you would not come, I —"

He paused, took from the table a book and turned its leaves, then closed and laid it down again. "I whistled you down the wind," he said.

There was a silence, then, far away in the hot night, a dog howled. The hall clock struck the hour. Rand drew his breath sharply and turned in his chair. "And you brought me here to-night to tell me so?"

"I will answer that presently. In these three years you have made yourself a great name in Virginia; and now your party — It is still your party?"

"It is still my party."

"Your party wishes to make you Governor. You have

travelled fast and far since the days when you walked with your father! Yesterday I was astounded to hear that you had refused the nomination."

"Why should you be 'astounded'?"

"Because I hold you for a most ambitious man, and this is the plain, the apparent step in your fortunes. At what goal are you aiming?"

"I did not want the governorship, sir."

"Then you want a greater thing. What it is — what it is" — With a sudden movement he rested his elbow on the table and regarded Rand from under the shelter of his hand. "And so," he said at last, in an altered voice, — "and so you will not be Governor. Well, it is an honourable post. This is late August, and in November you return to Richmond —"

"I go first across the mountains to examine a tract of land I have bought."

"Indeed? When do you go?"

"I have not altogether decided."

"Will you take Mrs. Rand with you?"

"I think so. Yes."

"It is," said Mr. Jefferson, "a rough journey and a wild country for a lady."

As he spoke he rose, and, going to a small table, poured for himself a little wine in a glass and drank it slowly, then, putting the glass gently down, passed to a long window and stood, as Rand had stood before him, looking out into the night. When he turned, the expression of his face had again changed. "It is growing late," he said. "In two days I return to Washington. The world will have grown older ere we meet again. Who knows? We may never meet again. This night we may be parting forever. You ask me if I brought you here to tell you that I acquiesced in this quarrel of your making, shook you from my thoughts, and bade you an eternal farewell. That is as may be. Even now — even now the nature of our parting is in your hands!"

Rand also had risen. "In this room, what can I say? Your kindness to me has been very great. My God, sir, I should be stock or stone not to feel abashed! And yet — and yet — Will you have it at last? You ask discipleship — you must have about you tame and obedient spirits — a Saint James the Greater and a Saint James the Less to hearken to your words and spread them far and wide, and all the attentive band to wait upon your wisdom! Free! We are tremendously free, but you must still be Lord and Master! Well, say that I rebel —"

"I see that you have done so," said Jefferson, with irony. "*I* am not your Lord and Master."

"I would not, if I could, have shunned this interview to-night. For long we have felt this strain, and now the sharp break is over. I shall sleep the better for it."

"I am glad, sir, that you view it so."

"For years I have worn your livery and trudged your road, — that fair, wide country road with bleating sheep and farmer folk, all going to markets dull as death! I've swincked and sweated for you on that road. Now I'll tread my own, though I come at last to the gates of Tartarus! My service is done, sir; I'm out of livery."

"Your road!" exclaimed the other. "Where does it lie, and who are your fellow travellers? John Randolph of Roanoke and the new Republicans? or monarchism and the Federalists? Or have I the honour, to-night, to entertain a Virginian Cæsar? — perhaps even a Buonaparte?" His voice changed. "Have you reflected, sir, that there is some danger in so free an expression of your mind?"

"I have reflected," answered Rand, "that there is no danger

so intolerable as the chafing of a half-acknowledged bond. The clock is striking again. I owe you much, sir. I thank you for it. While I served you, I served faithfully. It is over now. I look you in the face and tell you this, and so I give you warning that I am free. Henceforth I act as my free will directs."

"Act, then!" said the other. "Act, and find a weight upon your genius heavier than all behests of duty, friendship, faith, and loyalty rolled in one! Single out from all humanity one man alone, and that yourself, surround him with a monstrous observance, sacrifice before him every living thing that shall cross his path, crown him with gold, and banish from his court every idea that will not play the sycophant! Seat him, a chained king, high in some red star! — and still, like a wandering wind, large and candid thought, straying some day past your gloomy windows, shall look within and say, 'See this slave to himself chained upon his burning throne!' When at last you hear the voice, try to break away."

He left the window and, crossing to the mantel, pulled the bell-rope. Old Burwell appeared at the door. "Mr. Rand's horse, Burwell," directed the master, in a cheerful voice, then, when the negro was gone, spoke on without change of tone. "The night has altered while we talked. There is a great bank of cloud in the west, and I think the drouth is broken. You will reach Roselands, however, before the rain comes down. Pray present my respectful salutations to Mrs. Rand."

"You are very good," said Rand. "My wife"— He hesitated, then, "I would have you aware that my wife's hand would keep me in that same country road I spoke of, among those same green fields and peaceful, blameless folk! Her star is not like mine—"

"I esteem her the more highly for it," answered the other. "I hear your horse upon the gravel — Selim, still, is it not?

A pleasant ride to you home through this fresher air! Good-night — and good-bye."

"I am not the monster I appear to you," said Rand. "A man may go through life and never encounter the irresistible current. When he does — I am as little superstitious as you, but I tell you I am borne on! All the men and women whose blood is in my veins hurry me on, and there is behind me a tide of circumstance. For all past kindnesses I thank you, sir. I admire you much, reverence you no little, and bid you a long farewell."

He walked to the door, then, turning, swept the room with one slow look. "I was fifteen," he said, "the day I first came here. There was a glass of lilies on the table. Good-night, sir, — and good-bye."

Without, the night was indeed cooler, with a sighing wind, and in the west a thickening wrack of clouds. It was very dark. The restless and multitudinous flicker of the fireflies but emphasized the shadow, and the stars seemed few and dim. It was near midnight, and the wide landscape below the mountain lay in darkness, save for one distant knoll where lights were burning. That was Fontenoy, and Rand, looking toward it with knitted brows, wondered why the house was so brightly lighted at such an hour. In another moment the road descended, the heavy trees shut out the view of the valley, and with very much indeed upon his mind, he thought no more of Fontenoy. It was utterly necessary to him to find a remedy for the sting, keen and intolerable, which he bore with him from Monticello. He felt the poison as he rode, and his mind searched, in passion and in haste, for the sovereign antidote. He found it and applied it, and the rankling pain grew less. Now more than ever was it necessary to go on. Now more than ever he must commit himself without reserve to the strong current. When it had borne him to a fair and far country, to kingship, sway, empire, and vast renown, then would this night be justified!

He left the mountain, and, riding rapidly, soon found himself upon the road to Roselands. It was also the Greenwood road. Between the two plantations lay a deep wood, and as he emerged from this, he saw before him in the dim starlight a horseman, coming towards him from Roselands. "Is that you, Mocket?" he called.

The other drew rein. "It is Ludwell Cary. Good-evening, Mr. Rand. I have just left Roselands."

"Indeed?" exclaimed Rand. "May I ask—"

"I came from Fontenoy at the request of Colonel Churchill. Mrs. Churchill fell suddenly very ill to-night. They think she will not last many hours, and she asks continually for her niece. Colonel Churchill sent me to beg Mrs. Rand to come without delay to Fontenoy. I have delivered my message, and she but waits your return to Roselands—"

"I will hurry on," said Rand. "Be so good as to tell Colonel Churchill that Joab will bring her in the chaise—Mammy Chloe with her. I am sorry for your news. Accept, too, our thanks for the trouble to which you have put yourself—"

"It is nothing," answered Cary. "My brother and I chanced to be at Fontenoy. Mrs. Rand is much distressed, and I'll detain you no longer—"

He bowed, touched his horse, and rode into the wood. Rand turned in his saddle and looked after him for a long moment, then shook his reins, broke into a gallop, and passed presently through the Roselands gates and up the dark drive to the stone steps and open door. Jacqueline met him on the threshold. She was trembling, but not weeping; there was even a wistful fire and passion in her dark eyes and a rose-leaf colour in her cheeks. "Did you meet him?" she said.

"Did he tell you? I am all ready. He says that Aunt Nancy thinks that it is years ago, and that I'm Jacqueline Churchill still. I thought you would never, never come"— She turned and threw herself into his arms. "Oh, Lewis, we are going to Fontenoy!"

CHAPTER XX

THE NINETEENTH OF FEBRUARY

"THAT'S true," quoth Gaudylock. "It's the cracked pitcher that goes oftenest to the well, and a delicate lady that's lain a-dying on her bed this twenty year may live to see you and me and the blacksmith buried! There never was a Churchill that I did n't like, and I'm certainly glad she's better this morning. If you're going to Greenwood, I'll bear you company for a bit. I'm bound for Roselands myself."

Ludwell Cary dismounted and, with his bridle across his arm, walked beside the hunter. "Albemarle has not seen you for a long while," he said pleasantly. "The county is fond of you, and glad to have you home again."

"So a lady told me the other day!" answered Adam. "It has been a year since I was in Albemarle, — but I saw you, sir, last winter in Richmond."

"Last winter? I don't recall —"

"At Lynch's Coffee House. The twentieth of February. The day the Albemarle Resolutions were passed."

"Ah!" breathed Cary. The two walked on, now in sun, now in shade, upon the quiet road. The drouth was broken. There had been a torrential rain, then two days of sunshine. A cool wind now stirred the treetops; the mountains drew closer in the crystal air, and the washed fields renewed their green. So bright and sunny was the morning that the late summer wore the air of spring. Cary stood still beside a log, huge and mossy, that lay beside the road. "Let us rest here a moment," he said, and, taking his seat, began to draw in the dust before him with the butt of his whip. "I do not remember seeing you that day. I did not know that you were in Richmond."

"I was there," answered Adam cheerfully, "on business." He took an acorn from the ground and balanced it upon a brown forefinger. "It's a handsome place — Lynch's — and, my faith, one sees the best of company! I was there with Lewis Rand."

"Ah!"

The sound was sharp, and long like an indrawn breath. Adam, who could read the tones of a man's voice, glanced aside and remembered the quarrel. "Thin ice there, and crackling twigs!" he thought. "Look where you set your moccasin, Golden-Tongue!" Aloud he said, "You and your brother came in out of the snow, and read your letters by the fire. It had fallen thick the day before."

"Yes, I remember. A heavy fall all day, but at night it cleared."

"Yes," went on the other blithely. "I was at Lewis Rand's on Shockoe Hill, and when I walked home, the stars were shining. What's the matter, sir?"

"Nothing. Why?"

"I thought," quoth Adam, "that some varmint had stung you." He looked thoughtfully at the acorn. "You are a schollard, Mr. Cary. Is the whole oak, root, branch, and seed, in the acorn — bound to come out just that way?"

"So they say," answered Cary. "And in the invisible acorn of that oak a second tree, and that second holds a third, and the third a fourth, and so on through the magic forest. Consequences to the thousandth generation. You were saying that you were at Mr. Rand's the night of the nineteenth of February."

"Was I?" asked Adam, with coolness. "Oh, yes! I went

over to talk with him about a buffalo skin and some antlers of elk that he wanted for Roselands — and the stars were shining when I came away." To himself he said, "Now why did he start like that a moment back? It wasn't because the snow had stopped and the stars were shining. Where was *he* that night?"

Cary drew a circle in the dust with the handle of his whip. "You were at Lynch's with Mr. Rand the next afternoon. And immediately after that you returned to the West?"

Adam nodded. The acorn was yet poised upon his finger, but his keen blue eyes were for the other's face and form, bent over the drawing in the dusty road. "Ay, West I went," he said cheerfully. "I'm just a born wanderer! I can't any more stay in one town than a bird can stay on one bush."

"A born wanderer," said Cary pleasantly, "is almost always a born good fellow. How long this time will be your stay in Albemarle?"

"Why, that's as may be," answered Adam, with vagueness. "I'm mighty fond of this country in the fall of the year, and I've a hankering for an old-time Christmas at home — But, my faith; wanderers never know when the fit will take them! It may be to-morrow, and it may be next year."

"You and Mr. Rand are old friends?"

"You may say that," exclaimed the hunter. "There's a connection somewhere between the Gaudylocks and the Rands, and I knew Gideon better than most men. As for Lewis, I reckon there was a time when I was almost his only friend. I've stood between him and many a beating, and 't was I that taught him to shoot. A fine place he's making out of Roselands!"

"Yes," agreed Cary, with a quick sigh; "a beautiful place. The West is in a ferment just now, is it not? One hears much talk of dissatisfaction."

"Why, all that sort of thing is told me when I come home," said Adam. "The Indians call such idle speech talk of singing birds. My faith, I think all the singing birds in the Mississippi Territory have flown East! In the West we don't listen to them. That's a fine mare you're riding, sir! You should see the wild horses start up from the prairie grass."

"That would be worth seeing. Have you ever, in your wanderings, come across Aaron Burr?"

Adam regarded the other side of the acorn. "Aaron Burr! Why, I wouldn't say that I mayn't have seen him somewhere. A man who traps and trades, and hunts and fishes, up and down a thousand miles of the Mississippi River is bound to come across a mort of men. But 't would be by accident. He's a gentleman and a talker, and he was the Vice-President. I reckon he runs with the Governor and the General and the gentleman-planter and the New Orleans ladies." Adam laughed genially. "I know a red lip or two in New Orleans myself, but they're not ladies! and I drink with the soldiers, but not with the General. What's your interest, sir, in Aaron Burr?"

"The common interest," said Cary, rising. "When you quit Albemarle this time, you quit it alone?"

Gaudylock tossed aside the acorn. "That is my fortune," he answered coolly.

Cary swung himself into his saddle. "The woods, I see, teach but half the Spartan learning. We'll part here, I think, unless you'll come by Greenwood?"

"Thank you kindly, sir, but I've a bit of a woodsman's job to look after at Roselands. What was the Spartan learning?"

"You are going," replied the other, "to the house of a gentleman who knows the classics. Ask him. Good-day!"

"Good-day," said Adam somewhat abruptly, and with

a thoughtful face watched the other ride away. "He has been listening," thought the hunter, "to singing birds. Now when, and where, and to how loud a singing? The nineteenth of February — and the snowstorm — and the stars shining as I walked home from Shockoe Hill. He did n't know that I was in Richmond! Then, was he on Burr's trail? Humph! Where *was* Mr. Ludwell Cary the night of the nineteenth of February?" Adam took up his gun and coonskin cap. "I 'll see if Lewis can make that light," he said, and turned his face to Roselands.

Ludwell Cary rode to Greenwood, dismounted, and, going into the library, took from the drawer of his desk a letter, opened it, and ran it over. "As to your enquiries," said the letter, "Swartwout and Bollman are believed to be in New Orleans, Ogden in Kentucky, and Aaron Burr himself at a Mr. Harman Blennerhassett's on the Ohio. Rumour has it that Burr's daughter and her son are travelling to meet him. It says, moreover, that a number of gentlemen in the East are winding up their affairs preparatory to leaving for the West. One and all look more innocent than lambs, but they dream at night of señoritas, besieged cities, and the mines of Montezuma! There's a report to-day that Burr is levying troops. That's war. If these men go, they'll not return."

Cary laid down the letter. "If these men go, they'll not return. Is Lewis Rand so fixed in Albemarle?"

He moved from the desk to an old chess table and, sitting down, began to move the pieces this way and that. "The nineteenth of February — the nineteenth of February." He saw again a firelit room, and heard the tapping of maple boughs against a window. There she sat in her dress of festive white, listening to a denunciation of Aaron Burr and those concerned with him — and all the time the man beneath her roof! Cary sighed impatiently and moved another piece. Adam

Gaudylock, who had let slip that he had been there as well — and then had been careful to let slip no other fact of value, except, indeed, the fact that he was thus careful! Cary covered his lips with his hand and sat staring at the board. The problem, then, was to construct from the hunter's character the hunter's part. A keen trader, scout, and enthusiast of the West, known to and knowing the men of those parts, and able to bend the undercurrents — a delighter in danger, with a boy's zest for intrigue, risk, and daring — an uncomplex mind, little troubled by theories of political obligation, political faith and unfaith, loyalty to government or its reverse — a being born to adventure, but to adventure under guidance, skilled and gay subaltern to some graver, abler leader — that, he thought, would be Adam Gaudylock. An old, old friend of Lewis Rand's — "There's a connection somewhere between the Gaudylocks and the Rands."

Cary put out his hand and moved a piece with suddenness. "Granted the connection," he said aloud. His eye gleamed. "That night Rand agreed with Burr. Gaudylock would have been there to give information; probably, seeing that he went West immediately afterwards, to receive instructions. But he is an asset of Lewis Rand's, not of Burr's."

His hand touched the piece again. "An asset of Lewis Rand's — Rand and Burr — Rand and Burr. What was it that they plotted that night while she talked to me of the new song she had learned? An expedition against Mexico, an attack upon the dominions of the King of Spain with whom we are at peace? Or a revolution in the country west of the Ohio? The one's a misdemeanour; the other's treason." He moved a rook. "Most like 't was both — the first to mask the second. The boldest, simplest, most comprehensive stroke; there, there would show the mind of Lewis Rand!"

He rose and paced the long, cool room, then came back to the chess table. "They parted. Burr to the North, as I found the next morning; this trader, as he says, back to the West; Lewis Rand quiet in Richmond, quiet here in Albemarle. Quiet! That speech of his — those letters in the Enquirer. How long has he been breaking with Mr. Jefferson? That journey, too, to Philadelphia — whom did he see there? Swartwout, Bollman, perhaps Burr himself? Home he comes to Albemarle and begins improving Roselands. Cases too, in court, and a queue of waiting clients, and Richmond to return to in November. Granted there's a strange emigration West; but Lewis Rand — Lewis Rand's as fixed in Virginia as are the Churchills and the Carys!"

He slowly lifted and as slowly moved a queen. "And what other course, from time out of mind, does the disloyal pursue? A mask — all a mask. He, too, is for the West. He goes to join Burr; goes, if his fate stands true, to supplant Burr. Matters draw to a point, and he has little time to spare! Say that he goes"— A movement of his arm, involuntary and sharp, jarred the table and disarranged the board. "Will he go alone?"

Cary rose and walked the floor. "I must know — I must know." He paused at a western window, and with unseeing eyes gazed into the blue distance. "Were he Ludwell Cary, would he fare forth on his adventure alone? Perhaps. Being Lewis Rand, will he go without her, leave her behind? A thousand times, no! Even now this daughter of Burr's is hurrying by day and by night over rough and over smooth, to join her father; how much more, then, shall lover go with lover, the faithful wife with the all-conquering husband! She shall be there to buckle on our armour, to heal us with her kiss when the long day's work is over!" He bent his brow upon his arm. "O God, O God!"

From the hall without there sounded a clear whistle, and Fairfax Cary appeared in the library door. "Are you there, Ludwell? It's all dark in here after the sun outside. I am going to town."

The elder brother left the window. "Wait a little, Fair. I want to talk to you. Do you remember the night of the nineteenth of February?"

"Yes," said the other. "It had been snowing, and then it cleared brilliantly. I went to the Mayos, and I stopped by Bowler's Tavern. It was the night that Aaron Burr slept in Richmond. I told you, you know, that he was supping out."

"Yes. With Lewis Rand."

There was a silence, then, "So!" exclaimed Fairfax Cary, with a long whistle.

"You are not surprised?"

"No. It explains."

"Yes," assented the other sombrely, "it explains. Fair, I want to find out when Adam Gaudylock goes West."

"Gaudylock!" cried the other; then after a moment, "Well, I'm not surprised at that, either. I can tell you now when he's going. In two weeks' time."

"How do you know?"

"Unity sent a message about some work or other to Tom Mocket's sister Vinie. I gave the message, and the girl fell to talking about Adam. She was wearing a Spanish comb which he had brought her. I told her 't was pretty, and she said 'Yes: 'twas from New Orleans, and if Miss Unity would like one, Mr. Adam was going there again in two weeks.'"

"Two weeks!" brooded the other. "Fair, would you not say from every appearance that Lewis Rand is as fixed in Albemarle and in Virginia as you or I or any honest man? He improves Roselands; he has an important case coming on; it is supposed that in November he will return to Richmond. I happen to know that he has retaken the house on Shockoe Hill." He moved restlessly. "Why should I dream that he is preparing a moonlight flitting? dream that I see him in the gold southwest, treading his appointed road, triumphant there as here? A moonlight flitting! When he goes, he'll go by day — walk forth in bronze and purple, unconcerned and confident, high and bold as any Cæsar! From what egg did he spring that he can play the traitor and the parricide — and yet, and yet the rose bend to his hand? Does it look, Fair, as though he were in marching order?"

The other considered. "Do you believe that he is going West to join Burr?"

"I do. And yet this week he is defending a case in court, and there are others coming on. He is busy, too, at Roselands, and he has taken the Richmond house. I am, perhaps, a suspicious, envious, and vindictive fool."

"Roselands and the Richmond house might be a mask. He refused the nomination for Governor."

Ludwell Cary started violently. "I had forgotten that! You have it, Fair. He would do that — he would refuse the nomination. Lewis Rand, Lewis Rand!"

"Have you any proof that he is conspiring with Burr?"

"None that I could advance — none. I have an inward certainty, that is all. Nor can I — nor can I, Fair, even speak of such a suspicion. You see that?"

"Yes, I see that."

"I repented last winter of having written that letter signed 'Aurelius.' I *knew* nothing, and it seemed beneath me to have made that guesswork public. That he was my enemy should have made me careful, but I was under strong feeling, and I wrote. He has neither forgotten nor forgiven. Denounce him now as a conspirator against his party and his country?

That is impossible. Impossible from lack of proof, and impossible to me were proofs as thick as blackberries! But if I can help it, he shall not leave Virginia."

"Is it your opinion that he would take her with him?"

"Yes, it is."

"Would she go?"

Cary rose, moved to the window, and stood there a moment in silence. When, presently, he came back to the table, his face was pale, but lifted, controlled, and quiet. There was a saying in the county, — "The high look of the Carys." He wore it now, the high look of the Carys. "Yes, Fair, she would go with him."

There was a silence, then the younger spoke. "She is at Fontenoy. Mrs. Churchill may linger long, and her niece is always with her. Rand could not take his wife away."

"It's a check to his plans, no doubt," said the other wearily. "He's frowning over it now. He'll wait as long as may be. He would sin, but he would not sin meanly. In his conception of himself a greatness, even in transgression, must clothe all that he does. He'll wait, gravely and decently, even though to wait is his heavy risk." He made a gesture with his hand. "Do I not know him, know him well? Sometimes I think that for three years I've had no other study!"

"You should have let me challenge him that first election day," said Fairfax Cary gloomily. "If we had met and I had put a bullet through him, then all this coil would have been spared. What do you propose to do now?"

"At the moment I am going to Fontenoy."

"I would speak, I think, to Major Edward."

"Yes: that was in my mind. If there is any right, it lies with the men of her family. Fair, on the nineteenth of February *I* was at Lewis Rand's!"

"Ah!" exclaimed his brother.

"I was admitted, as I have since come to see, by mistake, and against orders. I found her alone in her drawing-room, and we sat by the dying fire and we talked of this very thing, this very plot, this very Aaron Burr — yes, and of the part a stronger than Burr might play in the West and in Mexico! She told me that her husband was busy that night — excused him because he was engaged with a client from the country. A client from the country! and I, who would have taken her word against an angel's, I sat there and wondered why she was distrait and pale! She was pale because there was danger, she was absent because she was contriving how she might soonest rid the house of one who was not wanted there that night! She was dressed in gauze and gems; she had supped with Aaron Burr —"

"I see — I see!"

"When at last I perceived, though I could not guess the reason, that she wished to be alone, I bade her good-night, and she watched me — oh, carefully! — through the hall and past the other doors and out of the house. I came home through the starlight and over the snow to the Eagle. I found you there by the fire, and you told me that Aaron Burr was in Richmond. Then, then, Fair, I *knew*. I knew with whom Lewis Rand was engaged, I knew who was the client from the country! The next morning I made my inquiries. Burr had gone at dawn, muffled and secret and swift — one man to see him off. That man, I learned to-day, was Adam Gaudylock. He, too, was at Rand's the night before. A triumvirate, was it not? Well, she knew, she knew — and women, too, have dreamed of crowns!"

He rose. "I'm going to ride to Fontenoy. You can bear me witness that I've kept away since her return. Now I shall keep away no longer. I will speak to Major Edward. Her family may draw a circle out of which she may not step."

"There's been," said the other, "no true reconciliation. She's only at Fontenoy because the Churchills could not refuse a dying woman. They speak to her as to a stranger to whom, as gentlemen, they must needs be courteous. And she's proud, too. Unity says they are far apart."

"I know. But though the Churchill men are stubborn, they are Virginians and they are patriots. This touches their honour and the honour of their house. If Rand plots at all, he's plotting treason. How much does she know, how little does she not know? God knows, not I! But they may make a circle she cannot overstep — no, not for all the magician's piping!" He rested his forehead upon his clasped hands. "Fair, Fair, she was my Destiny! Why did he come like a shape of night, with the power of night? And now he draws her, too, into the shadow. He's treading a road beset — and they are one flesh; she travels with him. Oh, despair!"

"Have out a warrant against him."

"What proofs? and what disgrace if proved! No, Fair, no."

"Then let me challenge him."

The other smiled. "Should it come to that, I will be the challenger! I am your senior there. Don't forget it, Fair." He rose from the table. "Do you remember that first day we rode to Fontenoy when I came home from England? The place was all in sunshine, all fine gold. She was standing on the porch beside Major Edward; she lifted her hand and shaded her eyes with a fan — there was a flower in her hair. Three years! I am worn with those three years." For a moment he rested his hand on the other's shoulder. "Fair, Fair, you know happy love — may you never know unhappy love! I am going now to Fontenoy. Is there a message for Unity?"

CHAPTER XXI

THE CEDAR WOOD

JACQUELINE closed the door of her aunt's chamber softly behind her, passed through the Fontenoy hall, and came out upon the wide porch. There, in the peace of the September afternoon, she found Unity alone with the Lay of the Last Minstrel. "Aunt Nancy is asleep," she said. "I left Mammy Chloe beside her. Unity, I think she's better."

"So the doctor said this morning."

"I think she's beginning to remember. She looks strangely at me."

"If she does remember, she'll want you still!"

Jacqueline shook her head. "I think not. How lovely it is, this afternoon! The asters are all in bloom in the garden, and the gum tree is turning red." She threw a gauze scarf over her head. "I am going down to the old gate by the narrow road."

"I wish," said Unity, "that I had the ordering of the universe for just one hour! Then Christians would become Christian, and you wouldn't have to meet your husband outside the gates of home."

The other laughed a little. "Oh, Unity, Christians won't be Christian, and even as it is, 't is sweet to be at home! Until you go away to Greenwood, you'll not know how dear was Fontenoy! To hear the poplars rustling and to smell the box again— Is it not strange that I should have a light heart when they look so cold upon me?"

"I have hopes of Uncle Dick, but Uncle Edward"— Unity shook her head. "I don't understand Uncle Edward."

"I do," answered Jacqueline, "and I love him most. I'll go now and leave you to the Last Minstrel. Does Fairfax Cary come to-night?"

"He may —"

Jacqueline laughed. "'He may.' Yes, indeed, I think he may! Oh, Unity, smell the roses, and look at the light upon the mountains! Good-bye! I'm for Lewis now."

She passed down the steps and through the garden toward the cedar wood which led to the old gate on the narrow road. Unity heard her singing as she went. The voice died in the distance. A door opened, Uncle Edward's step was heard in the hall, and his voice, harsh and strange, came out to his niece upon the porch: "Unity, I want you in the library a moment."

Jacqueline kept her tryst with Rand under the great oak that stood without the old gate, on land that was not the Churchills'. It was their custom to walk a little way into the wood that lay hard by, but this afternoon the narrow road, grass-grown and seldom used, was all their own. They sat upon the wayside, beneath the tree, and Selim grazed beside them. There was her full report of all that concerned them both, and there was what he chose to tell her. They talked of Fontenoy, and then of Roselands — talked freely and with clasped hands. Her head rested on his shoulder; they sat in deep accord, bathed by the golden light of the afternoon; sometimes they were silent for minutes at a time, while the light grew fairer on the hills. When an hour had passed they rose and kissed, and he watched her across the road and through the gate into the circle of Fontenoy. She turned, and waited to see him mount Selim and ride away. He spoke from the saddle, "At the same hour to-morrow," and she answered, "The same hour." Her hands were clasped upon the topmost bar of the gate. He wheeled Selim, crossed the road, half swung himself from the saddle, and pressed his lips upon them. "Come home soon!" he said, and she answered, "Soon."

When the bend of the road had hidden horse and rider, she left the gate and began her return to the house. Her path lay through a field, through the cedar wood, and through the flower garden. In the field beside a runlet grew masses of purple ironweed. She broke a stately piece, half as tall as herself, and with it in her hand left the autumn-coloured field and entered the little wood where the cedars grew dark and close, with the bare, red earth beneath. At the end of the aisle of trees could be seen the bright-hued garden and a fraction of blue heaven. Holding the branch of ironweed before her, Jacqueline passed through the wood toward the light of sky and flowers, and came at the edge of the open space upon a large old tree, twisted like one of those which Dante saw. As she stepped beneath the dark and spreading boughs a man, leaving the sunlit flower garden for the shadow of the cedars, met her face to face. "You!" he cried, and stopped short.

The branch of ironweed dropped from her hand. "I did not know that you were at Fontenoy. I have not seen you this long while — except for that moment the other night. Is it not — is it not the loveliest day?"

"I came from the library into the flower garden and on to this wood because I wished to think, to be alone, to gain composure before I returned to the house — and you front me like a spectre in the dimness! Once before, I entered this wood from the flower garden and it was dark, dark as it is to-day, though the weather was June. Nor do I, either, count the other night when I came to Roselands as Colonel Churchill's messenger. It has been long, indeed, since we truly met."

THE CEDAR WOOD

"You are not well, Mr. Cary!"

"I am — I am," said Cary. "Give me a moment."

He rested his arm against the red trunk of the cedar and covered his eyes with his hand. Jacqueline stood, looking not at him but at the coloured round of garden. Her heart was fluttering, she knew not why. The moment that he asked went by and, dropping his arm, he turned upon her a face that he had not yet schooled to calmness.

"The evening of the nineteenth of February," he said. "That was the last time we really met. Do you remember?"

"Yes, I remember. It was the day of the deep snow."

Cary regarded her mutely; then, "Yes, that was the important thing. We all remember it because of the snow. You were learning a new song that you promised to sing to me when I came again. But I never heard it — I never came again."

"I know. Why was that?"

"Do you ask?" he cried, and there was pain and anger in his voice. "I thought it not of you."

The crimson surged over Jacqueline's face and throat. She bent toward him impetuously, with a quick motion of her hands. "Ah, forgive me!" she cried. "I know — I know. I was told of the quarrel next day in the coffee house. I — I was more sorry than I can say. I understood. You could not, after that, come again to the house. Oh, more than almost anything, I wish that you and Lewis were friends! It is wrong to try to make you think that that evening does not live in my memory. It does — it does!"

"I am willing to believe as much," he returned, with a strange dryness. "I know that you remember that evening, but I hardly think it altogether on my account —"

The colour faded from her cheek. "On whose, then? My husband's?"

"And your guest's."

"You were my guest."

"Oh," cried Cary, "I'll not have it! You shall not so perjure yourself! He has taken much from me; if your truth is his as well, then indeed he has taken all! I know, I know who was the guest that night, the man with whom you supped, the 'client from the country.'"

She gazed at him with large eyes, her hand upon her heart, then, with an inarticulate word or two, she moved to the gnarled and protruding roots of the cedar and took her seat there facing his troubled figure and indignant eyes. "Who was the guest, — the client from the country?"

"Aaron Burr."

She drew a difficult breath. "How long have you known?"

"Since that night. No — do not be distressed! I learned it not from you, — you kept faithful guard. But when I left you, within the hour I knew it."

"And — and if he were there, what harm?"

Cary regarded her in silence; then, "The letter that I read you that night from your uncle, from one of the heads of your house, from a patriot and a man of stainless honour, that letter was, I think, sufficiently explicit! There was the harm. But Major Churchill's opinion, too, is perhaps forgot."

"No," cried Jacqueline, "no; you do not understand! Listen to me!" She rose, drawing herself to her full height, the red again in her cheek, her eyes dark and bright. "I am going to tell you the truth of this matter. Are you not my friend, whose opinion I value for me and mine? You are a true and honourable gentleman — I speak with no fear that what I say will ever pass beyond this wood! Uncle Edward's letter! You think that what was said in Uncle Edward's letter — ay, and what you, too, said in comment — was already known to me that night! Well, it was **not**.

THE CEDAR WOOD

Oh, it is true that Colonel Burr had supped with us, and it is also true that I was most heartily sorry for it! At table, while he talked, I saw only that green field so far away, and General Hamilton bleeding to his death, — yes, and I thought, 'Oh me, what would they say to me at Fontenoy?' But I knew no worse of Colonel Burr than that one deed, and I bore myself toward him as any woman must toward her husband's guest! I am telling you all. He was Lewis's guest, Lewis's correspondent, and this was an arranged meeting. I knew that and I knew no more. After supper they talked together, and I sat alone by the fire in the empty drawing-room. I was bidden — yes, I will tell you this! — I was bidden to keep all visitors out, since it must not be known that Colonel Burr was then in Richmond! You came, and by mistake you were admitted. I was lonely at heart and hungry for news from home, I let you stay, and you read to me what my uncle had to say of the man who was at that instant beneath my roof, engaged in talk with my husband! You read, and then you, too, took up the tale! 'Traitor — treason. . . . A man whom, had you the power, you would arrest at once. . . . False to his honour, false to his country. . . . Traitor and maker of traitors. . . . And where is your husband to-night?' Well, I did not choose to tell you where was my husband that night — and, since I was frightened, and cold at heart, and knew not what to say, and — and was frightened, I *lied* to you! But as for that which I now see that you have thought of me — you are much mistaken there! Until you read me Uncle Edward's letter, I did not know what men said of Aaron Burr!"

"I wronged you," said Cary, with emotion. "I doubted you, and I have been most wretched in the doubting. Forgive me!"

"You wronged me, yes!" she cried. "But am I the only

one you've wronged? Oh, I see, I see what since that night you have thought of Lewis! It was the next day that you quarrelled in the coffee house! Oh, all these months, have you been mistrusting Lewis Rand, believing him concerned with that man, suspecting him of — of — of *treason?* There, too, you are mistaken. Listen!"

She came closer to him, all colour, light, and fire against the dark cedars. "I am going to tell you. You are generous, open-minded, candid, fair — you will understand, and you will know him better, and you and he may yet be friends! I have that at heart — you would hardly believe how much I have that at heart. Have you been dreaming of Lewis Rand as the aider and abetter of Colonel Burr's designs, whatever they may be! as a conspirator with him against the peace of the country, against Virginia, against the Republic? You have, you have, — I read it in your face! Well, you are wrong. Oh, I will tell you the clean truth! He was tempted — he saw below him the kingdoms of the earth — and oh, remember that around him are not the friendly arms, the old things, the counsel of the past, the watchword in the blood, the voice that cries to you or to my uncles and so surely points to you the road! I will tell the whole truth. I will not say that his mind sees always by the light by which we rest. He has come another way and through another world. How should he think our thoughts, see just with our eyes? He has come through night and hurrying clouds; his way has been steep, and there are stains upon his nature. I that love him will not deny them! He was tempted as Ludwell Cary would not have been. Oh, perhaps if I had not been there, he would have made his compact. But I was there! and I besought him — and that night he swore to me —"

Cary threw out his arm with a cry. "Stop, stop! I take God to witness that I never thought of this!"

THE CEDAR WOOD

She went on, unheeding. "He swore to me that whatever in that world of his he had thought of Aaron Burr and of his projects, however keenly he had seen the dazzling fortune that lay in that western country, yet, as I had left my world for his, so would he leave that night, in this, his world for mine! And he did so — he did so that night before the dawn!"

She raised her hand to her eyes and dashed away the bright drops. "You have done an injustice. All this time you have thought him what that night you called Aaron Burr. I know not where Colonel Burr is now, but since the night of the nineteenth of February, he and my husband have had no dealings."

"My God!" said Cary, in a low voice; then, "This is all your assurance?"

"All?" she echoed proudly. "It is enough."

He turned away and, walking to the edge of the wood, stood there, striving for some measure of self-command. His hands opened and shut. Lewis Rand was a perjured traitor, and it only remained to tell Jacqueline as much.

The garden swam before his eyes, then the mist passed and he saw with distinctness. There was a path before him that led away between walls of box to the green and flowery heart of the place, and at the heart was a summer-house. He saw it all again. There was the morning in June, there was the blowing rose, there was the sudden vision — Rand and Jacqueline, hand in hand, with mingled breath! It was into this path that he had turned — it was to this wood that he had stumbled, leaving them there. He felt again the icy shock, the death and wormwood in his soul. They had had the gold, they had loved and embraced while, with his face to the earth, he had lain there beneath that tree where now she stood. Well, Time's globe was turning — there were shadows now for the lovers' country! Their land, too, would have its night; perhaps an endless night. He entertained the fierce, triumphant thought, but not for long. He had loved Jacqueline Churchill truly, and her happiness was more to him than his own. When, presently, he reached the consideration of her in that darkened country, moving forever over ash and cinder beneath an empty, leaden heaven, he found the contemplation intolerable. A tenderness crept into his heart, divine enough as things go in the heart of man. The summer-house mocked him still, and the image of Rand walked with armed foot through every chamber of his brain, but he wished no worse for Jacqueline than unending light and love. After the first red moment, it was not possible to him to put out one lamp, to break one flower, in her paradise. It hung like a garden in Babylon over the dust and sorrow of the common way, over the gulf of broken gods and rent illusions. To jar that rainbow tenure by the raising of his voice, to bring that phantom bliss whirling down to the trodden street, lay not within the quality of the man. He closed his eyes and fought with the memory of that June morning when he and Colonel Churchill had come upon the summer-house; fought with that and with a hundred memories besides, then looked again, and quietly, at the autumn place, bright with late flowers and breathed over by the haunting fragrance of the box. Another moment and he turned back to the wood and the great tree.

Jacqueline sat beneath the cedar, the branch of ironweed again within her hand. She had found it natural that Ludwell Cary should turn away. It was not easy to struggle against a misconception, to re-marshal facts and revise judgments — often it was hard. She waited quietly, fingering the tufts of purple bloom, her eyes upon the clear sky between the cedar boughs. When at last she heard his step and looked up, it was with an exquisite kindness in her large, dark eyes. "It was a natural mistake," she said. "Do not think that I blame you. It is hard to believe in good when we think we see evil."

"I am thankful," he answered, "that you are back in your shrine. Forgive me my error."

She looked at him fixedly. "But concerning Lewis — there, too, was error. Why should you continue enemies?"

There was a silence, then Cary spoke, sadly and bitterly. "You must leave me that. There are men who are born to be antagonists. When that is so, they find each other out over half the world, and circumstance may be trusted to square for them a battle-ground. Mr. Rand and I, I fear, will still be enemies."

"Then what I have told you makes no difference —"

"You are mistaken there. What you have told me shall have its weight."

"Why, then," cried Jacqueline, "you cannot judge him as you have been judging throughout a spring and summer! You are just and generous — will you not try to be friends? Ere this men have left off being foes, and many and many a battlefield is now thick with wild flowers. I should be happy if you and Lewis would clasp hands."

Her voice was persuasion's own, and there was a tremulous smile upon her red lips, and a soft light in her dark eyes. "There is a thing that I have long divined," she said, "and that is the strange regard for what you think and what you are that exists deep, deep down in his mind. It lies so deep that he is mainly ignorant that it is there. He thinks that you and he are all inimical. But it is there like an ancient treasure far down in the ocean depths, far below the surface storm. There is in him a preoccupation with you. Often and often, when questions of right and wrong arise, I know that his thought descends to that secret place where he keeps an image of you! I know that he interrogates that image, 'Is it thus or so that you would do?' And if, at times, scornfully or sullenly or with indifference, he does the opposite to what the image says, yet none the less at the next decision will his thought fly to that same judgment bar! It is an attraction that he fights against, a habit of the mind that he would break if he could — but it is there — indeed, indeed it is there! It is despotic — I do not think that he can escape. Ah, if you and he were friends, you would be friends indeed!" She looked at him pleadingly, with her hand outstretched.

Cary shook his head. "You are mistaken," he said harshly. "I am conscious of no place where my spirit and that of Mr. Rand may touch. I cannot explain; we are enemies: you must let us fight it out."

"Does it so much matter that you are Federalist and he Republican?"

"It matters very little."

"Or that you are a Cary, with all that that means, while he is Lewis Rand from the Three-Notched Road?"

"That matters not at all."

"Or that you are rival lawyers? Or that in politics he has defeated you? Or — Oh, my friend, now *I* am dealing unjustly! Forgive me — forgive me and make friends!"

"Would he," asked Cary sombrely — "would he agree? I think not. I am sure not. I think rather that he cherishes this enmity, feeds it, and fans it. Our lines in life have crossed, and now there is no force can lay them parallel. The sun is sinking, and I must see Major Edward again."

She rose from her seat beneath the cedar. "I'll hope on," she said. "Some day, if we live long enough, all clouds will break. Time withstands even the stony heart."

"Do you think," he demanded, "that mine is a stony

heart? Well, be it so, since this is a game of misunderstanding! I will say this. If I could come, the next nineteenth of February, to your house on Shockoe Hill, and find him there, and find you happy with him there, then, then I think I would clasp hands —"

"Ah," she cried, "do not wait until February! We shall be there on Shockoe Hill in November."

He stooped and lifted her branch of ironweed. "You are sure?"

"Why, yes," she answered. "The house has been retaken. We go to Richmond as soon as Lewis comes back from over the mountains."

"From —"

"He has bought land in the western part of the state. He is going on a journey soon to examine it."

' Toward the Ohio?"

"Yes; toward the Ohio. How did you know?"

"And you — you will not go with him?"

"He has talked of my going. But I cannot now that my aunt is ill."

"Perhaps he will wait?"

"Yes; he says that he will. How pale you are! I am sure you are not well?"

They had stepped from out the wood into the light of the garden. She looked at him with concern, but he dismissed her question with a gesture of his hand and a laugh that sounded strangely in her ears. "It is," he said, "the fading light. Are you going in now?"

"Not yet. Daphne is ill at the quarter, and I'll walk down to her cabin first. Do you stay to supper?"

"No, not to-night. But I wish to see Major Edward again. If you'll allow me, I will go on to the library."

"Certainly," answered Jacqueline, and, when he had kissed

her hand and said good-bye, watched him across the flower garden and up the steps that led to the glass doors. He passed into the room, out of her sight, but she still stood there among the asters and the box. His look was strange, she thought, and her hand had been crushed, rather than held, to his lips. She drew her scarf about her; the September evening was falling chill. The sunset light struck full upon the glass doors. She wondered why, for the second time in an afternoon, Ludwell Cary wished to see Uncle Edward, there in the library. Only once or twice, in the fortnight that she had been at Fontenoy, had she entered the library, and it was the room of all others that she loved. She thought now of the old green chair and of her father's portrait, and of every loved and dreamed-of detail, and she felt shut out in the dusk and chill. A sensation of strangeness crept over her. She thought, "If I were dead and trying to make the living hear, I should feel this way. And they would not even try to hear; they would shut the door and keep me out, all alone in the dark."

She stood for a full minute staring at the panes and the red reflected glare of the sun, then drew the scarf closer over her head, and took the path that led to the quarter.

CHAPTER XXII

MAJOR EDWARD

RAND rose from the supper-table and led the way into the dim, high-ceilinged room that served him as study and library. "Bring the candles," he said over his shoulder, and Tom Mocket obediently took up the heavy candelabra. With the clustered lights illuminating freckled face and sandy hair, he followed his chief. "Don't you want me to start the fire?" he asked. "These October nights are mortal cold."

"Yes," answered Rand. "Put a light to it and make the room bright. Fire is like a woman's presence."

As he spoke, he walked to the windows and drew the curtains, then took from his desk a number of papers and began to lay them in an orderly row upon the table in the middle of the room. "Mrs. Churchill is quite out of danger. My wife returns to Roselands to-morrow."

"That's fortunate," quoth Mocket, on his knees before the great fireplace. "You always did cut things mighty close, Lewis, and I must say you are cutting this one close! Adam, he goes along from day to day laughing and singing, with a face as smooth as an egg, but I'll warrant he's watching the sun, the clock, and the hourglass!"

"I know — I know," said Rand. "The sun is travelling, and the clock is striking, and the sands are running. This was a cursed check, this illness at Fontenoy. But for it I should be now upon the Ohio." He left the table and began to pace the room, his hands clasped behind him. "Two weeks from here to this island — then eight weeks for that twelve hundred miles of river, and to gather men from New Madrid and Baton Rouge and Bayou Pierre. October, November, December. Say New Orleans by the New Year. There will be some seizing there, — the banks, the shipping. If the army joins us, all will be well. But there, Tom, there! there is the 'if' in this project!"

"But you are sure of General Wilkinson!"

Rand paused to take a letter from his pocket. "Burr is. I have this to-day from him in cipher. Listen!" He unfolded the paper, brought it into the firelight, and began to read in a clear, low voice. "'Burr has written to Wilkinson in substance as follows: Funds are obtained and operations commenced. The eastern detachment will rendezvous on the Ohio the first of November. Everything internal and external favours our views. The naval protection of England is secured. Final orders are given to my friends and followers. It will be a host of choice spirits. Burr proceeds westward never to return. With him go his daughter and grandson. Our project, my dear friend, is brought to a point so long desired. Burr guarantees the result with his life and honour, with the lives and honour and fortune of hundreds, the best blood of our country. Burr's plan of operation is to move down rapidly from the falls on the fifteenth of November, with the first five hundred or one thousand men, in light boats, now constructing for that purpose, to be at Natchez between the fifth and fifteenth of December, there to meet Wilkinson, there to determine whether it will be expedient in the first instance to seize on, or pass by, Baton Rouge. The people of the country to which we are going are prepared to receive us; their agents, now with Burr, say that if we will protect their religion, and will not subject them to a foreign power, then in three weeks all will be settled. The gods invite us to glory and fortune; it remains to be seen whether we deserve the boon.'"

Rand ceased to read and refolded the paper. "So Colonel Burr, with more to the same effect. If he writes thus to General Wilkinson, he is undoubtedly very sure of that gentleman and of the army which he commands. I am not of as confident a temper, and I am sure of no one save Lewis Rand."

The other blew the flames beneath the pine knots. "There's Gaudylock."

"I except Gaudylock."

Tom rose from the brick hearth and dusted his knees. "And there's me."

Rand smiled down upon his old lieutenant. "Ah, yes, there's you, Tom, — you and Vinie! Well, if we are fortunate, you shall come to me in the spring. By then we'll know if we are conquerors and founders of empire, or if we're simply to be hanged as traitors. If the fairer lot is ours, you shall have your island, my good old Panza!"

"And if it's the other?" demanded Tom, with a wry face.

Rand gave his characteristic short laugh. "It shall not be the other. The hemp is not planted that shall trouble us. There are no more astrologers now that we are grown wise, — and still a man trusts in his star! I trust in mine. Well, next week you'll open the office as usual, and to all that come you'll state that I've gone, between courts, to look at a purchase of land in Wood County. I'll bring that forgery case to an end day after to-morrow, and by Monday Adam and I will be out of Albemarle."

Mocket drew a long breath. "Monday! That's soon, but the sooner, I reckon, the better. Sometimes just any delay is fatal. For all his singing, I know that Adam is anxious — and he's weatherwise, is Adam! There's something in the air. The papers have begun to talk, and everywhere you turn there's the same damned curiosity about Aaron Burr and

New Orleans and Mexico and the Washita lands! Moreover, when a man's as quiet as Mr. Jefferson is just now, I suspect that man. Best to get quite out of reach of a countermine. You've gone too far not to go a deal farther."

"Just so," agreed the other. "Many and many a league farther. Now, this paper of directions. I'll go over it carefully with you, and then I'll burn it. First, as to Roselands, the stock, and the servants. Joab and Isham go with us, starting on horseback an hour behind the chaise."

"You take no maid for Mrs. Rand?"

"It cannot be managed. When we reach this island, I can doubtless purchase a woman from Mr. Blennerhassett."

"Mrs. Rand does not know yet, does she, Lewis?"

"She does not know. She will not know until we are over the mountains and return is impossible." He turned from the fire, walked the room again, and spoke on as to himself. "When I tell her, there will be my first battle, and the one battle that I dread! But I'll win it, — I'll win because I *must* win. She will suffer at first, but I will make her forget, — I will love her so that I will make her forget. If all goes well and greatness is in our horoscope, she shall yet be friends with the crown upon her brow! Yes, and gracious friends with all that she has left behind, and with her Virginian kindred! When all's won, and all's at peace, and the clash and marvel an old tale, then shall her sister and her cousin visit her."

He paused at the fireplace and stirred the logs with his foot. "But that's a vision of the morrow. Between now and then, and here and there, it never fails that there's an ambushed road." He stood a moment, staring at the leaping flames, then returned to the table. "Back to business, Tom! When Roselands is sold —"

"Do you know," suggested Tom, "I've been thinking

that, now he is going to be married, a purchaser might be found in Fairfax Cary."

"Fairfax Cary!" exclaimed the other, and drummed upon the table. "No; they will not want it, those two. Poor old Tom! your intuitions are not very fine, are they?"

"Well, I just thought he might," said the underling. "But he may live on at Greenwood with Ludwell Cary."

Rand struck his foot against the floor. "Don't let us speak that name to-night! I am weary of it. It haunts me like a bell — *Ludwell Cary! Ludwell Cary!* And why it should haunt me, and why the thought of him always, for one moment, palsies my will and my arm, I know no more than you! When I shake the dust of this county from my feet, it shall go hard but I will shake this obsession from my soul! Somewhere, when this world was but a fiery cloud, all the particles of our being were whirled into collision. Well, enough of that! Whoever purchases Roselands, it will not be a Cary. What's the matter now?"

"There's a horse coming up the drive."

Rand dropped the paper in his hand and sat listening. "Unlucky! I wanted no visitor to-night. It may be but a messenger. Ring the bell, will you, for Joab."

The horse came on and stopped before the great doorstone. There was the sound of some one dismounting, Joab speaking, and then the voice of the horseman. Rand started violently. "Are we awake?" he said, rising. "That is Major Churchill's voice."

Joab appeared at the door. "Marse Lewis, Marse Edward Churchill say kin he trouble you fer a few minutes' conversation? He say he lak ter see you alone —"

"One moment, Joab," said the master, gathering the papers from the table as he spoke. "Tom, you'll go back to the dining-room and wait for me there. No; not by that door

— there's no use in his meeting you. What imaginable thing has brought him here?" He replaced the papers in a drawer, closed and locked it, looked up to see that Mocket was gone, and spoke to the negro. "Show Major Churchill in here."

The Major entered, dry, withered, his empty sleeve pinned to the front of his riding-coat. "Mr. Rand, good-evening. Ha, a cheerful fire against a frosty night! I come in out of the cold to a blaze like that, sir, and straightway, by a trick of the mind that never fails, I am back at Valley Forge!"

Rand looked at him keenly. "Permit me to hope, sir, that there is nothing wrong at Fontenoy? My wife is well?"

"Fontenoy is much as usual, sir," answered his visitor, "and my niece is very well. It is natural that my appearance here should cause surprise."

Rand pushed forward a great chair. "Yes, I am surprised," he said, with a smile. "Very much surprised. But since you bring no bad news, I am also glad. Won't you sit, sir? You are welcome to Roselands."

Major Edward took the edge of the chair, and held out his long, thin fingers to the blaze. "Yes; Valley Forge," he repeated, with his dry deliberation. "Valley Forge — and starving soldiers moaning through the icy night! Washington rarely slept; he sat there in his tent, planning, planning, in the cold, by the dim light. There was a war — and there were brave men — and there was a patriot soul!"

"I learn from Jacqueline that Colonel Churchill and you too, sir, have shown her for some days past much kindness, tenderness, and consideration. She has been made happy thereby."

"My niece has never been other than dear to me, sir," said the Major, and still warmed his hand. "I believe, Mr. Rand, that your father fought bravely in the war?"

"He did his part, sir. He was a scout with General

Campbell and, I have heard, fought like a berserker at King's Mountain."

"If he did his part," the Major replied, "he did well, and is to be reckoned among the *patres patriæ*. It is a good inheritance to derive from a patriot father."

"So I have read, sir," said Rand dryly.

There was a silence while the flames leaped and roared. The Major broke it. "You would take me, would you not, Mr. Rand, to be a man of my word?"

"I should, sir."

"It has been my reputation. The last time that I spoke to you —"

Rand smiled gravely. "That was two years and a half ago, and your speech was to the effect that never should you speak to me again. Well! opinion and will have their mutations. Men of their word, Major Churchill, know better than most how little worth are the words of men. However you come here to-night, pray believe that you are welcome, and that I would gladly be friends."

Major Edward drew a long breath, pushed back his chair somewhat from the warmth of the fire, and from under shaggy brows regarded his nephew-in-law with the eyes of an old eagle, sombre and fierce. "Be so good, then, as to conceive that I come with an olive branch."

"It is difficult," said Rand, after a pause and with a smile, "to conceive that, but if it be true, sir, then hail to the olive! This feud was not of my seeking." He leaned forward from his chair and held out his hand. "Ever since the days of the blue room and that deep draught of Fontenoy kindness, a light has dwelt for me over the place. Will you not shake hands, sir?"

The other made an irresolute movement, then drew back. "Let us wait a little," he exclaimed harshly. "Perhaps I will, sir, in the end, perhaps I will! It is in the hope that eventually we will strike hands that I sit here. But such signs of amity come with better grace at the battle's end —" He paused and glared at the fire.

"There is, then, to be a battle?"

The Major swung around from the red light of the logs. "Mr. Rand, we — my brother Dick and I — propose a lasting peace between the two houses, between Fontenoy and Roselands. My brother Henry, sir, the father of — of your wife, sir, was as near to us in love as in blood, and the honour, safety, and peace of mind of his daughter are very much our concern! You will say that by perseverance in this long estrangement we have ignored the last of these. Perhaps, sir, perhaps! Old men are obstinate, and their wounds do not heal like those of youth. Enough of that! We — my brother Dick and I — are prepared to let bygones be bygones. We have cudgelled our brains — I mean, we have talked matters over. We are prepared, Mr. Rand, to meet you halfway —"

"Thank you," said Rand. "On what specific proposition?"

Major Edward rose, took a short turn in the room, and came back to his chair. "Mr. Rand, in the matter of the nomination for Governor, is it too late to recall your refusal? I think not, sir. Your party has named no other candidate. As a Federalist, I know, sir, but little of that party's inner working, but I am told that you would sweep the state. Far be it from me to say that I wish to see a Democrat-Republican Governor of Virginia! I do not. But since the gentleman for whom I myself, sir, shall vote, is undoubtedly destined to defeat, we — my brother Dick and I — consider that that post may as well be filled by you, sir, as by any other of your Jacobinical party. No one doubts your ability — you are diabolically able! But, sir, I would bury this arm where a damned cutthroat barber surgeon buried the other before I would cry on to such a post any man who did not enter the race with heart and hands washed clean of all but honour, plain intents, and loyalty! In the past he may have been tempted — he may have listened to the charmer, charming never so wisely — there is in man an iron capacity for going wrong. He may have done this, planned that — I know not; we all err. It is not too late; he may yet put behind him all this —"

"I do not think that I understand," said Rand. "All what, sir?"

The Major faced around from the fire with a jerk. "All this. I am explicit, sir. All this."

"Ah!" answered Rand. "I am dull, I suppose. All this. Well, sir?"

"I should," continued the Major, with emphasis, "regard the acceptance of the nomination as proof positive of the laying aside of all conflicting ideas, uneasy dreams, and fallacious reasoning, of all intents and purposes that might war with a sober and honourable discharge of exalted public duties. They are exalted, sir, and they may be so highly discharged, so ably and so loftily, as to infinitely dignify the office that has already great traditions. A Governor of Virginia may be the theme, sir, of many a far distant panegyric —"

Again he rose and stalked across the room, then, returning to the hearth, stood before Rand, his high, thin features somewhat flushed and his deep old eyes alight. "Mr. Rand, it would be idle to deny to you that I have had for you both dislike and mistrust. You may, if you choose, even strengthen these terms and say that I have regarded you with hatred and contempt. I am a man of strong feelings, sir, and you outraged them — you outraged them! Well, I am prepared to bury all that. Become a great Governor of Virginia, serve your land truly, according to the lights vouchsafed to a Republican, and, though we may not vote for you, sir, yet we — my brother Dick and I — we will watch your career with interest — yes, damn me, sir! with interest, pride, and affection!" He broke off to stare moodily into the fire and, with his foot, to thrust farther in a burning log.

"An olive branch!" exclaimed Rand, smiling. "This is a whole grove of olives! I am sorry about the governorship—"

"I have made enquiries," interrupted the other harshly. "You have but to signify your change of mind to your committee, and your name is up. The governorship — the governorship is not all! It is but a step from Richmond to Washington. There's field enough for even a towering ambition." He looked around him. "And Roselands. This place has always had a charm. In the old days it was famed for hospitality — for hospitality and for the beauty of its women."

"In neither respect, sir, has it lost its reputation."

Major Edward made a gesture of acquiescence. "I dare say not, sir, I dare say not. I am told that Republicans flock here. And Jacqueline is a beautiful woman. Well, sir, why should not pilgrimages be made to Roselands as to Monticello? You have begun to improve it. Continue, and make the place a Garden of Eden, a Farm of Cincinnatus, a — a — what you will! Dick thinks that you may not be in funds to plant and build as you desire. If that is so, sir, either he or I might with ease accommodate you — " He paused.

"I take your offer as it is meant," said Rand, "and thank you both. But my affairs are in order, and I am not straitened for money."

The Major made a courteous gesture. "It was but a supposition. Well, Mr. Rand, why not? Why not make the picture real that we are painting? Eminent in public affairs — eminent in the law — ay, there, sir, I will praise you unreservedly. You are a great lawyer — worshipped by your party and in the line of succession to its highest gift, fixed in your state and county and happy in your home, rounding out your life with all that makes life worthy to be lived, —

"Honour, love, obedience, troops of friends.

Is not the picture fair enough, sir? There is in it no mirage, no Fata Morgana, no marsh fire. You are a man of great abilities, with ample power to direct those inner forces to outward ends that shall truly gild your name. Truly, sir, not falsely. Gold, not pinchbeck. Clear glory of duty highly done, not a cloudy fame whose wings are drenched with blood and tears. Come, sir, come — make an old man happy!" He dragged his chair nearer to Rand and held out his hand.

"I cannot accept the nomination for Governor, sir," said Rand. "There are various considerations which put it out of the question. I cannot go into these with you. You must take it from me that it is impossible."

The Major drew back. "That is final, sir?"

"That is final."

There was a silence. Rand sat, chin in hand, thoughtfully regarding his visitor. Major Churchill, erect, rigid, grey, and arid, stared before him as though indeed he saw only snowy plains, fallen men, and a forlorn hope. At last he spoke in a dry and difficult voice. "You persevere in your intention of returning to Richmond and to your house on Shockoe Hill in November?"

"It is my plan, sir, to go to Richmond in November."

"Immediately upon your return from over the mountains?"

Rand shot a glance at his interlocutor. "Immediately."

"These lands that you are going to see, sir — they are not as far as the Washita?"

"No; they are not as far as the Washita." Rand sat upright and let his hand fall heavily upon the arm of his chair. "That is a curious question, Major Churchill."

"Do you find it so?" asked the Major grimly. "*I* should, were it asked of me — so damned strange a question that it would not pass without challenge! But then, I am not declining governorships nor travelling West."

Rand rose from his chair. "Major Churchill" — He stopped short, bit his lip, and walked away to the window. There he drew the curtain slightly aside and stood with brow pressed against a pane, gazing out into the frosty darkness. A half moon just lifted the wide landscape out of shadow, and from the interlacing boughs of trees the coloured leaves were falling. Rand looked at the distant mountains, but the eye of his mind travelled farther yet and saw all the country beyond, all the land of the To Be, all the giant valley of the Mississippi, all the rolling, endless plains, all Mexico with snowy peaks and mines of gold. The apparition did not come dazzlingly. He was no visionary. He weighed and measured and reckoned carefully with his host. But there, beyond the mountains, lay no small part of the habitable world, — and the race of conquerors had not died with Alexander or Cæsar, Cortez or Pizarro! Witness Marengo and Austerlitz and that throne at Fontainebleau! He dropped the curtain from his hand and turned to the firelit room and to the tense grey figure on the hearth. "Major Churchill, if, softened by Jacqueline's presence there at Fontenoy, you came to-night to Roselands with the simple purpose of making friends with the man she loves, then, sir, that man would be a heartless churl indeed if he were not touched and gratified, and did not accept with eagerness such an overture. But, sir, but! There is more, I think, in your visit to-night than meets the eye. You demand that I shall become my party's candidate for the governorship. I answer it is not now possible. You insist that I shall busy myself with improvements here at Roselands, and to that end you offer to reinforce my purse. I answer that Roselands does very well, and that I am not in need of money. You preach to me patriotism and refer to General Washington; you speak poetically of gold *versus* pinchbeck, and true glory *versus* fame with drenched wings; you ask me certain questions in a voice that has hardly the ring of friendship — and last but not least you wish to know if a parcel of land that I have bought over the mountains is situate upon the Washita! The Washita, Major Churchill, is on the far side of the Mississippi, in Spanish Territory. May I ask, sir, before I withdraw my welcome to Roselands, by what right you are entitled to put such a question to me, and what is, indeed, the purport of your visit here to-night?"

Major Edward Churchill rose, stark and grey, with narrowed eyes and deliberating, pointing hand. "You are a villain, sir; yes, sir, a damned, skilled, heart-breaking villain! Bold! yes, you are bold — bold as others of your tribe of whom the mythologies tell! Arrogant as Lucifer, you are more wretched than the slave in your fields! You might have been upon the side of light; you have chosen darkness. It will swallow you up, and I, for one, shall say, 'The night hath its own.' You have chosen wrongly where you might have chosen rightly, and you have not done so in blind passion but in cold blood, fully and freely, under whatever monstrous light it is by which you think you walk! I have warned you of the gulf, and I have warned in vain. So be it! But do not think, sir, do not think that you will be allowed to drag with you, down into the darkness, the woman whom you have married! I wish that my niece had died before she saw your face! Do you know what she thinks you, sir? She thinks you a lover so devoted that at her pleading you put forever from you a gilded lure; a gentleman so absolutely of your word that for her to doubt it would be the blackest treason; a statesman and a patriot who will yet nobly serve Virginia and the country! God knows what she does n't think you — the misguided child! She's happy to-night, at Fontenoy, because she's coming home to you to-morrow. That I should have lived to say such a thing of Henry Churchill's daughter! When I rode away to-night, she was singing." He burst into spasmodic and grating laughter. "It was that song of Lovelace's! By God, sir, she must have had you in mind.

> "I could not love thee, dear, so much,
> Loved I not honour more.

Yes, by God, she was thinking of you! Ha ha, ha ha!"

"You are an old man," said Rand. "It is well for you that you are. I wish to know who is responsible for these conjectures, suspicions, charges — whatever term you choose, sir, for all are alike indifferent to me — which brought you here to-night? Who, sir, is the principal in this affair? You are an old man, and you are my wife's kinsman; doubly are you behind cover; but who, who, Major Churchill, set you on to speak of towering ambition and blood-drenched wings and broken vows and deceived innocence, and all the rest of this night's farrago? Who, I say — who?"

"Ask on, sir," answered the Major grimly. "There is no law against asking, as there is none to compel an answer. Sir, I am about to remove myself from a house that I shall not trouble again, and I have but three words to say before I bid you good-night. I warn you not to proceed with your Luciferian schemes, whatever they may be, sir, whatever they may be! I warn you that it is ill travelling over the mountains at this season of the year, and I solemnly protest to you that my niece shall not travel with you!"

"And who," asked Rand calmly, — "and who will prevent that?"

"Sir," answered the other, "a grain of sand or a blade of grass, if rightly placed." He shook his long forefinger at the younger man. "You have been fortunate for a long turn in the game, Lewis Rand, and you have grown to think the revolving earth but a pin-wheel for your turning. You will awake some day, and since there is that in you which charity might call perverted greatness, I think that you will suffer when you awake. In which hope, sir, I take my leave. Mr. Rand, I have the honour to bid you a very good-night."

The master of Roselands rang the bell. "Good-night, Major Churchill. I am sorry that we part no better friends, and I regret that you will not tell me what gatherer up of rumour and discoverer of mares' nests was at the pains to procure me the honour of this visit. I might hazard a guess — but no matter. Joab, Major Churchill's horse. Good-night, sir."

He bowed formally. Major Churchill stood for a moment looking straight before him with a somewhat glassy stare, then, "Good-night, Mr. Rand," he said, in a voice like a wind through November reeds, made a bow as low and as studied as that with which he had once honoured Rand in the Fontenoy drawing-room, turned with martial precision, and stalked from the room.

Lewis Rand stood long upon the hearth, staring down into the fire. He heard Major Edward's horse go down the drive and out upon the highroad with a swiftness that spoke of a rider in a passion. The sound of hoofs died away, and he still stood looking into the red hollows, but at last with a short and angry laugh he turned away and opened the door which led to the dining-room. "Are you still there, Tom? Come in, man! The accusing angel has gone."

Tom appeared, and the two went back to the great table in the centre of the room. Rand unlocked the drawer and took out the papers in the perusal of which they had been interrupted. Mocket snuffed the candles and tossed another log of hickory upon the fire. "It falls in with what Gaudylock suspected," said Rand's measured voice behind him, "and it all dates back to the nineteenth of February. When he left the house that night, he must have known —"

"Of whom are you talking?" asked Tom at the fire. "Major Edward?"

"No, not Major Edward. And now he is using his knowledge. She told me to-day that he was often at Fontenoy. Too often, too often, Ludwell Cary!"

"Now, after stopping my mouth, you have spoken his name yourself!" remarked Tom. "You and he are over against each other in that case to-morrow, are n't you?"

"In every case we are over against each other," said the other abruptly. "And we shall be so until Judgment Day. Come, man, come! we have all these to go through with before cockcrow."

CHAPTER XXIII

A CHALLENGE

THE Charlottesville Robbery Case was one of no great importance save to those directly concerned. It had to do with a forged note, a robbery by night, and an absconding trusted clerk of a company of British Merchants. When the case came up for trial on this October day, the Court House was well filled indeed, but rather on account of the lawyers engaged than because of the matter's intrinsic interest. The British Merchants had retained Mr. Ludwell Cary. The side of the prisoner, mentioning that fact in a pitiful scrawl addressed to the law office of Messrs. Rand and Mocket, found to its somewhat pathetic surprise that Mr. Rand himself would take the case and oppose Mr. Cary.

The two had fought it with a determination apparent to every bystander, and now, on the last day of the trial, the counsel for the prosecution rose to sum up his case. He was listened to with attention, and his speech was effective. The theme was the individual who, after forgery and embezzlement, had taken French leave, quitting a post of trust and credit for regions where he hoped to enjoy his ill-gotten gains in peace and quietness. The regions had proved inhospitable, and a sheriff had escorted the unlucky adventurer with that which was not his own back to the spot whence he had started. His transgression was now to be traced from the moment — day or night, or sunrise or sunset; what mattered the moment? — when the thought passed through his brain, "Why should I plod on like other men?"

"'Passed through,' did I say? — nay, it tarried; at first

like a visitor who will one day take his leave, then a cherished inmate, and at last lord and master of every crevice of that petty mansion! It *dwelled* there, and day by day it fed itself with remembered examples. 'There was Tom, over on the Eastern Shore, grew tired, too, of working for his employers, — and he robbed the till one night, and got off on a sloop to the Havana, and now they say he has a pirate ship of his very own! And Dick. Dick got tired, too, in a tan-yard in Alexandria, and when his master sent him on a mission to Washington, he took his foot in his hand and went farther. He had his expenses in his pocket, so why not? He's prospering now in a bigger and gayer town than Alexandria! And Harry. Harry was more trusted than them all, but he, too, got tired — in a warehouse at Rocket's — of plod, plod, plod! serve, serve, serve! So he forged a name, and took the gold that lay beneath his hand, tore up his indentures, and fled in the night-time — over the hills and far away! He's a rich man now, somewhere near the sunset, rich and great, with clerks of his own. He had the advantage of education, had Harry! Examples! Examples thick as hops! What's Buonaparte himself but a poor Corsican lieutenant that stole an empire? I'll be bold, too. I'll steal, and then I'll steal away!'

"So scullion soul to pliant body. His thought is father to his deed, and there is the usual resemblance between son and parent. What matters it that he has lived in his employer's house, and has found him no Egyptian taskmaster, but a benefactor, lavish of favours? What matters it that he has in charge things of trust and moment which, by miscarrying, will work distress to many? What matters it that others are about him, engaged in this same drudgery of doing one's duty, to whom, should he succeed in villainy as he trusts to do, his example will remain, a wrecker's light to entice the

A CHALLENGE

storm-tossed upon a rocky shore? What matters it, — I am told, gentlemen, that the prisoner has a good and industrious sister, — what matters it that rarely, rarely, is there ill-doing without, somewhere in the shadowed background, some bruised and broken heart? What does it matter that he betrays his trust, breaks his oath, blackens his name, slurs his friends, and recruits the army, wan and sinister, of all the fallen since time began? To him, apparently, it matters less than a drifting leaf in the wind of this October day. He remembers all that he should forget, and forgets all that should be remembered. There pass by him in long parade Tom and Dick and Harry and others of their ilk. He sees them, and he sees little else. It is a host of choice spirits, and they have banners flying. His courage mounts. Brave emulation! noble rivalry! He, too, will be bold; he, too, will join their regiment! For him, too, the spoils of opportunity and a daughter of the game! He feels the summer in the air, and all Brummagem rises upon his horizon. Farewell to patient drudgery and the slow playing over of the tune of life! He's for a brisker air, he's for 'Over the hills and far away.'

"His little plans are laid. I say 'little,' gentlemen, advisedly, for in all this there is no greatness. We speak of a self-seeker here, and all the ends of such an one are small, and he himself has not attained the full stature of a man. The ambitious soul before us! By stealth he practises until he can sign his employer's name, more lifelike almost than life! By stealth he gains impressions of the keys. By stealth he eyes the only wealth that his mole mind can value! By stealth he makes his preparations, and by stealth he cons the miles and the post-houses between him and the country to which he means to carry himself and his stolen goods! He is assiduous at his desk; his employers nod approval, praise him for a lad of parts, and hold him up for emulation. In his brain one air continues, — 'Over the hills and far away.'

"The day approaches. The forgery is done, the accustomed hand slips easily in and out of the golden drawer, and all the roads are got by heart. We have the loan of a horse — before another dawn we will be gone. O Fortune of great thieves, stand pat! and kindly tune run on! 'Over the hills and far away.'

"We have been told by the worthy gentlemen, his employers, that so trustworthy did they consider the prisoner at the bar, so able in their affairs and assiduous in their service, that this very day it was in their minds to increase his pay and to raise him quite above his fellow clerks to an honourable post indeed. He did not give them time, gentlemen, he did not give them time! The hour is here, the notes are sewn within the lining of our well-brushed riding-coat, the master key is in our itching palm! We'll lurk until midnight, then in the dark room we will unlock the drawer. If we are heard, softly as we step in the silence of the night — if a watchman come — the worse for the watchman! We carry pistols, and the butt of one against his forehead will do the work. For we are bold, gentlemen, we are as bold as Cæsar or Buonaparte! We won't be stopped — we won't! We're for 'Over the hills and far away.'"

The counsel for the prisoner addressed the Judge. "Your Honour, no watchman, dead or alive, being among the witnesses, and there being no capable proof of what were or were not my client's thoughts upon the night in question, I indignantly protest —"

The objection was sustained. The interruption over, the attorney for the British Merchants went evenly on. "We have Mr. Rand's word for it that the prisoner had no thought of the watchman, and no intention of using, even in case of

A CHALLENGE

need, the weapons with which it has been proved he was provided. Mr. Rand must know. As a rule, gentlemen bearing arms about their persons may be considered the potential users of said arms, whether the antiquated rapier or the modern pistol — but then, I bethink me, we are not speaking of men of honour. We are speaking of a small criminal in a small way, and Mr. Rand assures us that his thoughts matched his estate — they were humble, they were creeping. Headstrong, proud, and bold are words too swelling for this low and narrow case. To wear a weapon with intent to use is one thing, to buckle it on as a mere trivial, harmless, modish ornament and gewgaw is quite another! We have Mr. Rand's word for it that it was so worn. Gentlemen, the prisoner, armed, indeed, as has been proved, was absolutely innocent of even the remotest intent to use under any provocation beneath high heaven the pistols — oiled, primed, and duelling type — with which, by chance or for the merest whim of ornament, he had decked his person upon this eventful night. Mr. Rand tells us so, and doubtless he knows whereof he speaks.

"So armed and so harmless, gentlemen, the prisoner, having committed forgery, does now his second crime — the pitiful robbery. The key that he has forged with care is true to him, the gold lies at his mercy, underneath his hand; he lifts it up, the shining thing; he bears it away. The hour has struck, the deed is done; irrevocable, it takes its place upon the inexpugnable record. He has stolen, and there is no power in heaven or earth to change that little fact. We are grown squeamish in these modern days, and no longer brand a thief with heated iron. No letter will appear, seared on his shoulder or his hand, but is he less the thief for that? He himself has done the branding, and Eternity cannot wear out the mark. He goes. With his stolen gold he steals away. It is night. There are only the stars to watch his flight, and he cares not for the stars — they never tell. Have they not, time out of mind, stood the friend of all gentlemen of the road? He quits the house that has seen his crime; he leaves dull and honest men asleep; he bestows no parting glance upon the dim, familiar ways. His native land is naught — he's for green fields and pastures new — he's for Tom and Dick and Harry, and all their goodly company — he's for 'Over the hills and far away.'"

The counsel for the prosecution finished his speech. The judge summed up the case, the jury retired, and very shortly returned with the expected verdict of Guilty. The chalk-white and shaking prisoner stood up, was sentenced and removed, and, the business of the day being over, the court adjourned.

Good-naturedly, laughing and talking after the morning's restraint, the crowd, gentle and simple, from the lower part of the room, was in the course of jostling toward the door, when there came a sudden check coupled with exclamations from those nearest the bar, and with a general turning of heads and bodies in that direction.

The lawyer for the prosecution and the lawyer for the defence stood opposed, a yard of court-room floor between them, and around them a ring of excited friends and acquaintances. There had been high voices, but now a silence fell, and the throng held its breath in cheerful expectation of the bursting of a long predicted storm.

"This," said Cary's clear and even voice, not raised, but smoothly distinct, — "this is a challenge, sir. I take it rightly, Mr. Rand?"

"You take it rightly, Mr. Cary. I shall presently send a friend to wait upon you."

"He will find me, sir, at the Swan. As the challenged party,

A CHALLENGE

it is my prerogative to name hour and place. You shall shortly be advised of both."

"I am going to my office, sir, where I will await your messenger. You cannot name an hour too soon, a place too near for me."

"Of that I am aware, Mr. Rand. I will make no delay that I conceive to be unnecessary. I am, sir, your very humble servant."

"I am yours, Mr. Cary."

The two bowed profoundly and parted company, making their several ways through the throng to the Swan and to the office with the green door. With them went their immediate friends and backers. The crowd of spectators, talking loud or talking low, conjecturing, explaining, and laying down the law, jesting, disputing, hotly partisan, and on the whole very agreeably excited, finally got itself out of the Court House and the Court-House yard, and the autumn stillness settled down upon the place.

At Roselands, in the late afternoon, Jacqueline came out upon the doorstone and sat there, listening for Selim's hoofs upon the road. The weather was Indian summer, balmy, mild, and blue with haze. On the great ring of grass before the stone yellow beech leaves were lying thick, and the grey limbs of the gigantic, solitary tree rose bare against the blue. Jacqueline sat with her chin in her hand, watching the mountains, more visible now that the leaves were gone. She saw the cleft through which ran the western road, and she thought with pleasure of the days before her. She loved the journeys to Richmond, and this one would be more beautiful, and new. They would be gone ten days, perhaps, — ten days of slow, bright travel through sumptuous woods, of talk close and dear. She was exquisitely happy as she sat there with her eyes upon the Blue Ridge. The last fortnight of her stay at Fontenoy had been almost a blissful time. Her uncles changed, and no longer passed her with averted eyes, or, when they spoke, used so cold a ceremony as to chill her heart. They grew almost natural, they seemed even tender of her. Uncle Dick had once again called her "My little Jack," though he groaned immediately afterwards and, getting up, looked out of the window, and Uncle Edward left the library door ajar. Jacqueline laid her head upon her arm and laughed. It was coming right — it was coming right! — and next year they would all dance at Fontenoy with light hearts, at Unity's wedding. It had begun to come right the evening of the day that she had met Ludwell Cary in the cedar wood. She wondered, slightly, at that coincidence, and then she fell again to dreaming.

Lewis was coming; he had passed through the gate — and she started up. He rode on to the back of the house, left his horse there, and, striding through the hall and down the three stone steps, joined her where she stood upon the greensward, among the fallen leaves. "Good-evening to you!" she said, touched his shoulder with her hand, and raised her face to his. He drew her to him, kissed her with fierce passion, and let her go, then walked to the beech tree and stood with his back to the house, staring at the long wall of the mountains, dark now against a pale gold sky. She followed him. "Lewis! what is the matter?"

He answered without turning, "We are not going, quite yet awhile, over the mountains. Man proposes, and Ludwell Cary disposes. Well! we will stay merrily at home. But he shall pay the score!"

"What do you mean?"

"Two weeks! What may not happen over there in two weeks? And I bound here, hard and fast, hand and foot! By what? — by the plaything code of a plaything honour! Now,

A CHALLENGE

if he were any other man under the canopy, I would not stay! The question is, is it imaginable that all this was of set purpose?"

"Lewis, what is the matter?"

Rand turned. "The matter, child? The matter is that you may unpack, and that we will give a dinner party! We do not travel to-morrow; no, nor the next day, nor the next! I have to await a gentleman's leisure."

She hung upon his arm. "Lewis, Lewis, what is it? You are trembling —"

He laughed. "Do you think it is with fear?"

"Don't, don't!" she cried. "Don't be so angry — don't look so black! I am afraid of you. What is it, dearest, dearest?"

"Wait," he said harshly. "Wait, Jacqueline, a moment."

He put her abruptly from him, walked to the doorstone, and, sitting down, bowed his face upon his hands. For some moments he remained thus, while she stood under the beech tree, her hand upon her heart, watching him. At last he lifted his head, rose, and came back to her. "To-day, in the court room, I challenged Ludwell Cary. He has named, as is his right, time and place of our meeting. The time, something more than two weeks from to-day; the place, five miles from Richmond. I confess that I was taken by surprise. I had expected to-morrow morning and the wood beyond the race-course. If I thought — what, by all the gods, I do think! — that he had dared — that he had done this deliberately, with intent to keep me here, I — Jacqueline! why, Jacqueline!"

"I'm — I'm not going to swoon," said Jacqueline, with difficulty. "Air, that is all — let me sit down a moment on the grass. A duel — you and Ludwell Cary."

"I and Ludwell Cary." Rand uttered his short laugh.

"How steadily have we been coming just to this! I think I knew it long ago. I have in me so much of the ancient Roman that I prize him, now that we are at grips, and think him a fair enemy. If I did not hate him, I would love him. But it is the first, and I'll not forgive this pretty trap he's laid! What does he think will come after these two weeks he has me shackled? Does he think that he can always keep me here? — or only until — until it is too late to go?" He struck his hand against the beech tree. "Well, well, mine enemy, we will try conclusions."

Jacqueline rose from the grass, came to him, and laid her head upon his breast. "Lewis, is there no way out with honour? Must it be? He is my friend and you my husband whom I love. Will you face each other there like — like General Hamilton and Aaron Burr? Oh, break, my heart!"

Rand kissed her. "There is no way out. He means me to stay, and I will do it — for this while, Cary, for this while! Look, Jacqueline; the sun is setting over the road we should have gone! I have been a fool. Six weeks ago should have seen us far, far upon that shining track! Now the world is spinning from me, the glory rolling under, and I feel the dark. Adam is right; once started on this trail, I should have gone like the strong arrow's flight. I knew the warriors were behind me, and yet I idled, — waited first to break with my old chief, — as if my going would not have done that work, as short, as clean! — and waited last because of a sick woman's whim! If I had not let you go to Fontenoy, we might to-day have heard the rushing of a mightier river than the Rivanna yonder! Delay, delay, where haste itself should have felt the spur!"

"If I had not gone to Fontenoy," cried Jacqueline, "my aunt might have died with her last wish ungratified! If I had not gone, oh, what would they not have thought of me, most rightly, most justly! Now we are almost friends again, — the thing I've prayed for, longed for, wept for, since that June! Was this not worth the waiting? There is something here that I do not understand. Why should you so greatly care to see these lands? Say that there is some money lost and some vexation — what does that count against this nearing home — this making friends?" She struck her hands together. "And yet — and yet if we had gone, there would not have been this day, this quarrel, and this challenge! There would not be this day to come, when I shall hear what, from now till then I'll dream I hear! O Christ, I heard them then, the pistol shots! Why did we not go, Lewis, days ago?"

"Now you are weeping," said Rand, "and that will ease your heart. Could I have helped it, I would not have told you of this quarrel. You could not, however, have failed to hear; it was a public thing, and the town is buzzing with it. See, Jacqueline, I am no longer passionate. The dog is down. The mistake, if mistake it was, is made; we are not over the mountains; we are here in Albemarle, at Roselands, underneath the beech tree. I was never one to weep for spilt milk. This way is stopped, and this moment foreclosed. Well, there are other moments and other ways! The sun is down and the night falls dark and cold. Come, dry your eyes!"

"That is soon done. The thorn is in my heart."

"I will draw it out," he answered. "I'll draw it out with love. Don't think that Ludwell Cary can hurt me; it's not within his kingdom. Do not grieve that men are enemies; smile and say, 'It will be so a few years longer!' I am glad with all my heart that you are friends again with all at Fontenoy. As for this journey, I stayed for you, Jacqueline. It was needful for me to go, but I stayed that you might part friends with your kindred. Remember it one day."

"Why," she cried, — "why did you not go without me? You would not have been long gone, and I should have waited your return there at Fontenoy! Then this day and this quarrel would not have come! Ludwell Cary and you to meet — O God!"

"I did not wish to go without you. You do not understand — but trust me, Jacqueline; trust me, trust me!" He took her in his arms. "Come, now! It is twilight, and there's a dreariness in these fallen leaves. Come indoors to the fire and the light, and the books and the harp. Deb arrived to-day, did she not?"

"Yes; she is somewhere with Miranda. They have been playing dolls with the last flowers."

He stopped a moment as they were moving over the grassy ring. "Flower dolls! They were playing flower dolls that morning in June when I came down from the blue room and out into the garden. There they sat, on the red earth in the little cedar wood, with their bright ladies. Deb told me all their names. She told me more than that — she told me you were reading in the arbour. Jacqueline, are you sorry that I found you there?"

"No, I am not sorry; I am glad. You could make me wretched, but you could not make me repentant. Oh, Lewis! I shall hear those shots to-night —"

"No, you will not — I shall read you to sleep. Why, if you were a soldier's wife, would you hear all the bullets flying? There, the last red has faded, and I hear the children's voices! Come in; come in out of the dark."

CHAPTER XXIV

THE DUEL

IT was nine o'clock of a November morning when a coach, driven out from Richmond, passed a country tavern and a blacksmith's shop, and, turning from the main road, went jolting through a stubble-field down to the steep and grassy bank of the James. It was a morning fine and clear, with the hoar frost yet upon the ground. The trees, of which there were many, were bare, saving the oaks, which yet held a rusty crimson. In the fields the crows were cawing, and beyond the network of branch and bough the river flashed and murmured among its multitude of islets. The place was solitary, screened from the highroad by a rise of land, and fitted for a lovers' meeting or for other concerns of secrecy.

The coach drew up beneath a spreading oak with the mistletoe clustering in the dull red upper branches. Three men stepped out, — Lewis Rand, the gentleman acting as his second, and a good physician. "We are first on the field," said Rand, looking at his watch. "It is early yet. Pompey, drive a hundred yards down the bank — as far as those bushes yonder — and wait until you are called. Ha! there could be no better spot, Mr. Jones!"

"I've seen no better in my experience, sir," answered Skelton Jones. "When I was last out, we had the worst of fare! — starveling locust wood — damned poor makeshift at gentlemanly privacy — stuck between a schoolhouse and a church! But this is good; this is nonpareil! Fine, brisk, frosty weather, too! I hate to fight on a muggy, leaden, dispirited day, weeping like a widow! It's as crisp as mint, this morning — hey, Doctor?"

"I find," said the doctor, in a preoccupied tone, "that I've left my best probe at home. However, no matter — I've one I can use."

"I hear wheels," remarked Rand. "He is on the hour."

A chaise mounted the knoll of furrowed land and came down to the grassy level and the waiting figures. It stopped, and Ludwell Cary and his brother got out. "Drive over there where the coach is standing," directed the latter, and chaise and negro driver rolled away. The elder Cary walked forward, paused within a few feet of his antagonist, and the two bowed ceremoniously.

"I trust that I have not kept you waiting, Mr. Rand."

"Not in the least, Mr. Cary. The hour has but struck."

Fairfax Cary strode up, and the salutations became general. Skelton Jones looked briskly at his watch. "With your leave, gentlemen, we'll to formalities. The Washington stage has just gone by, and we will all wish to get back for the mail. Mr. Fairfax Cary, shall we walk a little to one side? You have, I see, the case of pistols. Dr. McClurg, if you will kindly station yourself beneath yonder oak —"

The seconds stepped aside for their conference, and the doctor retreated to the indicated oak. Lewis Rand and Ludwell Cary exchanged a comment or two upon the weather, then fell silent. The one presently sat down upon the root of a tree, and, drawing out a pocket-book, began to look over certain memoranda; the other walked near the river and stood gazing across its falls and eddies and innumerable fairy islands to the misty blue of the farther woods. The seconds returned and proceeded to measure the distance — ten paces, after which they loaded the pistols. Skelton Jones advanced, the ends of two strips of paper showing from his closed hand.

"Gentlemen, you will draw for choice of position. The longest strip carries the advantage. Thank you. Mr. Cary, Fortune favours you! We are ready now, I think."

The two laid aside their riding-coats. Cary walked across the leaf-strewn lists and, turning, stood with his back to the sun. Rand took the opposite place. The seconds presented the loaded pistols. As Cary took his from his brother, their hands touched — that of the younger was marble cold. Skelton Jones crossed to his principal's right, and Fairfax Cary moved also to his proper place. There was a minute's pause while the sun shone and the leaves drifted down, then, "Are you ready, gentlemen?" cried Rand's second.

The principals answered in the affirmative. Fairfax Cary gave the word, *"Present!"* The two raised their weapons, and Skelton Jones began to count "One — two — three! Fire!" Rand fired. Cary swayed slightly, recovered himself, and stood firm. Fairfax Cary took the count. "One — two — three! Fire!" The elder Cary slowly turned the muzzle of his pistol from his waiting antagonist, and fired into the air.

The report echoed from the winding river-banks. For an appreciable moment, until it died away, the participants in the meeting stood motionless, then the seconds bestirred themselves and ran forward.

"But a single shot, each, gentlemen — that was agreed upon!" cried the one, and the other, "Ludwell, you are wounded! Where is it? Dr. McClurg! Dr. McClurg!"

"It is nothing, Fair, — through the shoulder." Cary waved him aside and turned a face, pale but composed, upon Lewis Rand, who now stood before him. Rand's hue was dark red, his features working. "Why," he demanded hoarsely, — "why did you not fire upon me?" The agitation, marked as it was, ceased or was controlled even as he spoke. The colour faded, the brow lost its corrugations, and the voice its thickness. Before his antagonist could reply, he spoke again. "It was yours, of course, to do what you pleased with. I sincerely trust that your wound is not deep. I have regretted the necessity — I profess myself entirely satisfied."

"That is well," answered Cary, "and I thank you, Mr. Rand. The wound is utterly of no consequence."

"Here is Dr. McClurg," said Rand. "I will wait yonder to hear that confirmed."

He walked to the river-bank and stood, as Cary had stood a little earlier, gazing over the falls and eddies and fairy islands to the blue woods on the farther shore. Under the oak which he had left, the doctor looked and handled, with a pursed lip, a keen eye, and a final "Humph!" of relief. "High and clean through and just a little splintered. You'll wear your arm in a sling for a while, Mr. Cary! Mr. Fairfax Cary, you're too white by half! There's a brandy flask in yonder case. Mr. Jones, the wound is slight."

"Why, that's good hearing!" cried Skelton Jones. "Mr. Cary must return to town in the coach, with Mr. Fairfax Cary and with you, Doctor. Mr. Rand and I will take the chaise. My profound regard, and my compliments, Mr. Cary! Mr. Fairfax Cary, may I have the pleasure of acting with you again! Doctor, good-morning. Now, Mr. Rand."

Rand turned from his contemplation of the river, advanced toward the group beneath the oak, and bowed with formality to Cary, who, arresting the doctor's ministrations, returned the salute in kind. The chaise, beckoned to by Mr. Jones, came up; there was a slight and final exchange of courtesies, and the two Republicans entered the vehicle and were driven away.

"Give them five minutes' start, Fair," ordered Cary. "Then call the coach; I want to get back to town for the Washington mail."

"You'll get back to town and get to bed!" stormed the other. "'Fire in the air,' quotha! *I* could have brought down a kite from the blue! You might, at least, have broken a wing for him!"

"Oh, I might, I might," said the other wearily. "But I did n't. I never liked this work of breaking wings. Now, Doctor, that is a bandage fit for a king! Call the coach, Fair. This much of the business is over."

The chaise carrying Lewis Rand and his companion traversed with rapidity the miles to Richmond. The road was fair, and the day bright and cool. The meeting by the river had occupied hardly an hour; the world of the country was yet at its morning stirring, and filled with cheerful sound. Above the fields the sky showed steel blue; the creepers upon the rail-fencing still displayed, here and there, five crimson fingers, and wayside cedars patched with shadow the pale ribbon of the road. Rand kept silence, and his late second, at first inclined to talkativeness, soon fell under the infection and stared blankly at the fence corners. A notorious duellist, he may have been busy with dramas of the past. Rand's thought was for the future.

They came into Main Street and drove to Rand's office. "We'll dismiss the chaise here," said the latter. "I have a few directions to give, and then I'm for the post-office and the Eagle."

"I will precede you there," answered the other. "Allow me, sir, before we part, to express the gratification I have felt in serving, to the best of my poor abilities, a gentleman of whom the party expects so much —"

' Rather allow me, sir, to express my gratitude —" and so on through the stilted compliment of the day. Assurances from both sides over at last, and the chaise discharged, the one walked briskly down the unpaved street toward the Eagle, and the other entered quietly the bare and business-like room from whose window, last February, he had fed the snow-birds. The room was not vacant. Before the table, with his arms upon it, and his head upon his arms, sat Mocket. At the sound of the closing door he started up, stared at Rand, then fell back with a gasp of relief, and the water in his eyes.

"Lewis? Thank the Lord!"

"It's Lewis," said the other. "My good old fellow, did you think only to see my ghost? Well, the comedy is over."

"Lord! it's been a long hour!" breathed his associate. "What did you do to him, Lewis?"

"He has a ball through his shoulder. It is not serious. I don't want to talk about it, Tom." Rand spoke abruptly, and, walking to his desk, sat down, drew a piece of paper toward him, and dipped a quill into the ink-well. "Is Young Isham there? He is to take this note to the house, to Mrs. Rand."

Mocket went to find Young Isham. Rand, alone in the room, wrote in his strong, plain hand: —

JACQUELINE: — We met an hour ago. He is slightly wounded — through the shoulder. I tell you truth, it is in no wise dangerous. I am unhurt.

The hand travelling across the sheet of paper paused, and Rand sat for a moment motionless, looking straight before him; then, with an indrawn breath, he dipped the quill again into the ink and wrote on, —

He fired into the air.

Thine,   LEWIS.

He sanded the paper, folded and sealed it, sat for a moment longer, leaning back in his heavy chair, then rose and himself gave the missive to Young Isham, with orders to make no

THE DUEL

tarrying between the office and the house on Shockoe Hill. Rand's slaves had for him a dog-like affection combined with a dog-like fear of his eye in anger. The boy went at once, and the master returned to the waiting Tom. "The Washington stage is in," he said. "I am going now to the Eagle, and you had best come with me. Then back here, and to work! Where is that man from the Bienville at Norfolk?"

"He's waiting at the Indian Queen. I can get him here in ten minutes. This morning's Argus says that the Bienville of New Orleans sails on Saturday — valuable cargo and no passengers."

"Ah," said Rand; "the Argus's eyes are heavy."

"A half-breed hunter was here this morning. He says that, ten days ago, crossing the Endless Mountains with his face to the east, he met the great hunter they call Golden-Tongue walking very fast, with his face to the west. Learning that he was on his way to Richmond, Golden-Tongue gave him this to be delivered in silence to you." Mocket took from the table a feather and held it out to the other.

"A blackbird feather," exclaimed Rand, turning it over in his hand. "That would mean — that would mean — 'It is the fall of the leaf. The bird has flown south. Follow all the migratory tribe! follow while the air is yet open to you, or stay behind with the sick and the old and the faint of heart and the fighters against instinct! Winter comes. It is time to make haste.'" He laid the feather down with a smile. "That's Adam. Well, Adam, we will see how swift the Bienville can fly! I may yet be first at New Orleans. Wilkinson and I to welcome Burr and all the motley in his river-boats with a salvo from the city already ours. Ha! that's a silvery dream, Tom, and an eagle's pinion for Adam's blackbird quill!" He laughed and took up his hat. "Let's down the street first, and then you may find the man from the Bienville. There's a long day's work before us, and to-night" — He drew a quick breath. "To-night I have a task that is not slight. Come away! It's striking twelve."

The two closed the office and went out into the sunny street. "Where are all the people?" exclaimed Mocket. "It's as still as Sunday."

A boy at a shop door, hearing the remark, raised a piping voice. "Everybody's down at the Eagle and the post-office, sir. I heard them say there's big news. Maybe the President's dead!"

The distance to the Eagle was but short. Rand walked so rapidly that his companion had difficulty to keep beside him, and walked in silence, cutting short every attempt of Tom's to speak. They came within sight of the tavern. The long lower porch seemed crowded, the street in front filled with people. There were horsemen, a coach and a chaise or two, a rapid shifting of brown, green, blue, and plum-coloured coats, a gleam here and there of a woman's dress. A bugle sounded, and there issued from Governor Street first a roll of drums and a shouted order, and then a company in blue and white with tall, nodding plumes.

"There are the Blues!" cried Tom. "My land! What is the fuss about?"

They were now upon the edge of the throng, which suddenly fell from excited talking to a breathless attention. A tall man of commanding presence and ringing voice had mounted a chair, set at the top of the steps to the Eagle porch, and unfolded a paper. Rand touched upon the shoulder the man before him. "Mr. Ritchie, I have just come in from the country, and have heard nothing. What, sir, is the matter?"

"Treason, sir!" answered the editor of the Enquirer. "Treason. An attempt to disrupt the Republic! A blow in the face of Washington and Henry and Franklin, of the sacred dead and the patriot living! The lie direct to the Constitution! Apollyon stretching himself, sir; but, by gad! Apollyon foiled! Listen, and you will hear. Foushee's reading the Proclamation for the second time."

"Ah," said Rand, in a curious voice. "A Proclamation. From —"

"From the President. Evil hasn't prospered, and though we can't hang Apollyon, we can hang Aaron Burr. Listen now."

The reader's voice was sonorous, and his text came fully to all the crowd in the Richmond street.

"*Whereas information has been received that sundry persons, citizens of the United States or resident within the same, are conspiring and confederating together to begin and set on foot, provide and prepare, the means of a military expedition or enterprise against the Dominions of Spain, against which nation war has not been declared by the constitutional authorities of the United States; that for this purpose they are fitting out and arming vessels in the western waters of the United States, collecting provisions, arms, military stores, and other means; are deceiving and seducing honest men and well-meaning citizens under various pretences to engage in their criminal enterprises; are organising, officering, and arming themselves for the same, contrary to the laws in such cases made and provided, — I have therefore thought it fit to issue this my proclamation, warning and enjoining all faithful citizens who have been led to participate in the said unlawful enterprise without due knowledge or consideration to withdraw from the same without delay, and commanding all persons whatsoever engaged or concerned in the same to cease all farther proceedings therein as they will answer the contrary at their peril, and will incur prosecution with all the rigours of the law. And I hereby enjoin and require all officers, civil or military, of the United States, or of any of the States or Territories, and especially all Governors, and other executive authorities, all judges, justices, and other officers of the peace, all military officers of the militia, to be vigilant, each within his respective department and according to his functions, in searching out and bringing to condign punishment all persons engaged or concerned in such enterprise, and in seizing and detaining, subject to the disposition of the law, all vessels, arms, military stores, or other means provided or providing for the same, and in general preventing the carrying on such expedition or enterprise by all the lawful means within their power. And I require all good and faithful citizens and others within the United States to be aiding and assisting herein, and especially in the discovery, apprehension, and bringing to justice of all such offenders, and the giving information against them to the proper authorities.*

"*In testimony whereof I have caused the seal of the United States to be affixed to these presents, and have signed the same with my hand. Given at the City of Washington on the twenty-seventh day of November, 1806, and of the sovereignty and Independence of the United States the thirty-first.*

THOMAS JEFFERSON."

"That is n't all," said Mr. Ritchie in Rand's ear. "The plot was not only against Spain — it looked to the separation of the West from the East, with the Alleghanies for the wall between. General Wilkinson is the hero. It seems that Burr thought to implicate him and secure the army. Wilkinson sent Burr's letters in cipher to the President. The Government has had knowledge from various sources, and while he was thought to be dozing last summer, Mr. Jefferson was as wide awake as you or I. The militia are out in Wood County, and

Burr will be taken somewhere upon the Ohio. Wilkinson has put New Orleans under martial law. Informer or no, he's now more loyal than loyalty itself. The Bienville is to be searched at Norfolk for a consignment of arms. They say Eaton's implicated, and Alston, Bollman, Swartwout, and this man Blennerhassett. Truxtun's name is mentioned, and it's said that Decatur was applied to. Andrew Jackson, too, has been friendly with Burr. Well, we'll see what we will see! Treason and traitor are ugly words, Mr. Rand."

"They are so considered, Mr. Ritchie," said Rand, with calmness. "Thanks for your courtesy, and good-morning!"

He bowed and made his way, not unaccosted, through the crowd to the Eagle porch. There was much excitement. The Governor was speaking from the head of the steps. Below him planters, merchants, lawyers, and politicians were now listening eagerly, now commenting *sotto voce*, while beyond them the nondescript population swayed and exclaimed. To one side were massed the tall plumes of the Blues. Rand saw, near these, Fairfax Cary's handsome face, not pale as it had been between nine and ten o'clock, but alert, flushed, and — or so Rand interpreted its light and energy — triumphant. He went on into the house, ordered and drank a small quantity of brandy, and when he came back upon the porch was met by those near him with a cry of "Speech! Speech!" The Governor's periods were at an end, and John Randolph of Roanoke held the impromptu tribune. Rand's eloquence, if not as impassioned and mordant, was as overwhelming, and his reasoning of a closer texture. Those around him loudly claimed him for the next to address the crowd, which now numbered a great part of the free men of Richmond. He shook off the detaining hands and, with a gesture of refusal to one and all, made his escape by a side step into the miscellany of the street, and finally out of the throng, and, by a détour, back to the deserted square where stood his office. He had lost sight of Mocket, but as he put his key into the door, the other came panting up, and the two entered the bare, sunshine-flooded room together. Rand locked the door and, without a look at his trembling subaltern, proceeded to take from his desk paper after paper, some in neatly tied packets, some in single sheets, until a crisp white heap lay on the wood beneath his hand. "Light a fire," he said over his shoulder. "There's absolutely nothing, is there, in that desk of yours?"

"Nothing. For the Lord's sake, Lewis, is this the end of everything?"

"Everything is a large word. It is the end of this." He pushed a table closer to the fireplace and transferred to it his armful of papers. "Strike a light, will you? Here goes every line that can incriminate. If Burr did as he was told, and burned two letters of mine, there'll not be a word when I finish here." He tore a paper across and tossed it into the flame. "Tom, Tom, don't look so woe-begone! Life is long, and now and then a battle will be lost. A battle — a campaign, a war! But given the fighter, all wars will not be lost. Somewhere, there awaits Victory, hard-won, but laurel-crowned!" He tore and burned another paper. "This fat's in the fire, this chance has gone by, this road's barricaded, and we must across country to another! Well, I shall make it serve, the smooth, green, country road that jog-trots to market! What is man but a Mercenary, a Swiss, to die before whatever door will give him moderate pay? I would have had a kingdom an I could. I would have ruled, ay, by God, and ruled well! The great wheel will not have it so. Down, then, that action! and up this. The King is dead: long live the King! — *alias* the Law, Respectability, Virginia, and the Union!" He tossed in a double handful.

"All those!" said Tom dully. "I hate to see them burn."

"They might have burned this morning," answered the other. "I gave you orders to burn them if I fell, the moment you heard it."

"But you did not fall."

"No. He fired into the air." Rand tore the paper in his hand across and across. "He had me in his trap. That was why — that was why he spared to fire! Oh, I could take this check from the hand of Fortune, or the hand of Malice, or the hand of Treachery, or the hand of Policy, but, but" — he crushed the torn paper in his hands, then flung it from him with a violent and sinister gesture — "to take it from the hand of Ludwell Cary — that requires more than my philosophy is prepared to give! Let him look to himself!" He thrust in another bundle, and held down with an ashen stick the mass of curling leaves.

CHAPTER XXV

OLD SAINT JOHN'S

THE distance was so great from the more populous part of the town to Saint John's on Church Hill, and the road thereto so steep, in hot weather dusty, in wet deep in mud, that it had become the Richmond custom to worship within the Capitol, in the Hall of the House of Delegates. But during this August of the year 1807 the habit was foregone. It was the month in which Aaron Burr, arrested in Alabama in January, brought to Richmond in the early spring, and, since the finding of a true bill, confined in the penitentiary without the town, was to be tried for his life on the charge of high treason. Early and late, during the week, every apartment of the Capitol was in requisition, and though the building itself was closed on Sunday, the Capitol Square remained, a place of rendezvous, noise, heat, confusion, and dispute. There was in the town a multitude of strangers, with a range from legal, political, military, and naval heights, through a rolling country of frontiersmen, to a level of Ohio boatmen, servants, and nondescript. Many were witnesses subpœnaed by the Government, others had been called by Burr, and yet others brought upon the scene by varied interests, or by the sheer, compelling curiosity which the trial evoked. One and all were loudly and fiercely partisan. The lesser sort and ruder fry congregated in numbers beneath the trees about the Capitol, and it was thought with propriety that during this month church-going ladies would prefer to attend Saint John's. Here, therefore, on a Sunday in mid-

August, the Reverend John Buchanan preached to a large and noteworthy assemblage.

The day was hot, but the chestnut trees and sycamores gave a grateful shade, and large white clouds in a brilliant blue threw now and then a transient screen between sun and earth. The broad and murmuring river and the far stretch of woodland upon the Chesterfield side gave, too, a sensation of space and coolness. Faint airs carried the smell of midsummer flowers, and bees droned around the flat tombstones sunk in honeysuckle. The congregation gathered slowly, the masculine portion of it lingering, as was the custom, in the wide old churchyard until the second tinkling of the bell should call them indoors. They had thus the double advantage of talk and observation of the Progress of Women. These traversed the path to the church door like a drift of blossoms in the summer air, saluted on either hand by the lowest of bows, the most gallant lifting of bell-shaped hats. Whatever might be said of the men's dress, from the fair top-boot to the yards of lawn that swathed the throat, that of the weaker sex, in the days of the Empire, was admirably fitted for August weather. Above pale, thin stuffs, girdled beneath the breast and falling straight and narrow to the instep, rose bare white neck and arms, while each charming face looked forth from an umbrageous bonnet of fine straw. Bonnet and large fan appeared the only ample articles of attire; even the gloves were but mitts. By ones and twos, or in larger knots, the wearers of this slender finery entered Saint John's with sedateness, took their seats in the dim old pews, and waited in the warm, fragrant, whisper-filled air for the ringing of the second bell and the entrance of the men. After church, custom would still reign, and all alike would linger, laugh, and talk beneath the trees, while the coaches drew up slowly and the grooms brought the saddle-horses from the rack, and those who meant to walk gathered courage for the dusty venture.

Jacqueline Rand and Unity Dandridge, the one in her customary white, the other in a blue that marvellously set off dark hair, dark eyes, and brilliant bloom, entered Saint John's together and passed up the aisle to a seat halfway between door and pulpit. By some miscalculation of Unity's they were very early, a fact which presently brought a whispered ejaculation of annoyance from Miss Dandridge. "I love a flutter when I come in and the knowledge that I've turned every head — and here we've entered an empty church! Heigho! Nothing to do for half an hour."

"Read your prayer book," suggested Jacqueline. "Oh! does it open just there as easily as all that?"

"It always did open just there," answered Miss Dandridge. "It's something in the binding. Heigho! 'Love, honour, and obey.' *Obey!*"

"Your entrance," said her cousin, "was not entirely unseen, and here comes one whose head is certainly turned."

"Is it?" asked Unity, and hastily closed the prayer book as Fairfax Cary entered the pew behind them.

Jacqueline turned and greeted the young man with a smile. There was now between Greenwood and Roselands, between the house on Shockoe Hill and the quarters of the Carys at the Swan, a profound breach, an almost utter division. Lewis Rand and Ludwell Cary were private as well as political enemies, and all men knew as much. There had been no attempt on the part of either to conceal the fact of the duel in November. Their world of town and country surmised and conjectured, volubly or silently, according to company, drew its conclusions, and chose its colours. The conclusions were largely false, for it occurred to no one — at least outside of Fontenoy — to connect the quarrel and the duel with the President's proclamation and the Burr conspiracy. During the past winter Cary had been much in Albemarle, little in Richmond, and the encounters of the two had not been frequent. In the spring, however, matters had brought him to the city, and in the fever and excitement of the ensuing summer he and Rand were often thrown into company. When this was the case, they spoke with a bare and cold civility, and left each other's neighbourhood as soon as circumstances permitted. Cary came, of course, no more to the house on Shockoe Hill. Jacqueline, remaining in town through the summer because her husband remained, saw him now and again in some public place or gathering. He bowed low and she inclined her head, but they did not speak. Her heart was hot and pained. She had pleaded that afternoon in the cedar wood for his better understanding of Lewis, and to what purpose? — an open quarrel and a duel! She did not want to speak; she wanted to forget him.

But for Fairfax Cary, friend and shadow though he was of the elder brother, her feeling was different. He was a man to be liked for himself, and he loved and was to marry Unity. He adopted his brother's quarrel: he and Lewis barely spoke, and that despite the fact that Lewis had for him a strange half-grim, half-vexed admiration; he came no more than the elder Cary to the house on Shockoe; but when they met abroad, Jacqueline was sure of some greeting, half gay, half stiff, some talk of Fontenoy, some exchange of sentiment upon one topic dear to each, some chivalrous compliment to herself. He made a gallant and devoted lover, and Jacqueline could not but applaud Unity's choice and feel for him an almost unmixed kindness.

Because of the trial, which drew friends, kindred, and acquaintances to Richmond, the marriage, which was to have been celebrated in August, had been postponed to September.

Unity came to town for a month and stayed with her cousin. Her lover would not enter Lewis Rand's house, nor did she ask him to do so. Her kindred in Richmond were numerous, and they might and did meet in a score of Federalist mansions, at various places of entertainment, and, as now, at church.

He answered Jacqueline's welcome and Miss Dandridge's bright blush and brief "How d' ye do?" with the not-too-profound bow, the subdued and deprecatory smile, and the comparative absence of compliment that church demanded, then, seating himself, leaned forward with his arm upon the back of their pew and entered into low-toned conversation.

"They were early." — "Yes: too early!" — "So much the better, for now they could see all the famous folk enter. Army, Navy, Law, and Letters are all coming to church. To-morrow is the indictment."

"Ah!" murmured Jacqueline; and Unity, "They say he held a levee at the Penitentiary yesterday. Personally, I prefer a surly traitor to one who is so affable, smiling, and witty."

"I also," agreed her lover. "But Colonel Burr is no Grand Seigneur of a traitor out of the dismal romances that you read! He meant no harm — not he! His ideas of *meum* and *tuum* may be vague, but when all's said, he's the most courteous gentleman and a boon companion! I think that we are well-nigh the only Federalists in town who have not forgotten that this man slew Hamilton, and who keep the fact in mind that, defend him as they please, his counsel cannot say, 'He loved his country and wished no other empire!' After the indictment to-morrow, Hay will speak and the Government begin to call its witnesses. Who is this coming in — the lady with Mrs. Carrington? Look! It's Burr's daughter — it's Mrs. Alston!"

"She's a brave woman," said Unity. "One can't but honour such spirit, courage, and loyalty. She's dressed as if it were a gala day!"

"If you'll let me pass," whispered Jacqueline, "I will speak to her. We met at the Amblers' the other night. There's an anxious heart behind that fine fire!"

She rose and, slipping past Unity, moved up the aisle to the Carrington pew. The two left behind looked after the gliding white figure in silence. Unity sighed. "To me Lewis Rand's like a giant, and she's like his captive. And yet — and yet there's much that's likeable in the giant, and I can perfectly well see how the captive might adore him!"

"I can't," retorted the other. "I'll grant his ability, but there's a little worm at the heart! Even his genius will one day turn against him; it is the tree too tall that falls the soonest. He's not coming here to-day?"

"No. He's out of town. All the Republican papers are wondering why the President did not include him among the counsel for the Government."

"I dare say," said the younger Cary grimly. "Well, that would have been an entertainment worth hearing, that speech for the prosecution!"

"Don't let's talk of him any more. I feel a traitor to Jacqueline when I do. How slow the people are in coming!"

"They may stay away as long as they please," murmured her lover. "I like a quiet time for worship before all the fuss and flutter. You should always wear blue, Unity."

"You told me yesterday that I should always wear pink. At last, here enters a man!"

"It is Winfield Scott, just up from Williamsburgh. He doesn't like the law and will go into the army. Here are all the Randolphs and the beautiful Mrs. Peyton!"

Unity moved to let Jacqueline reënter the pew. The

church was beginning to fill, and the whispering and noise of fluttering fans increased. All the windows were open to the breeze, and the soft scents and sounds and colours, the dimness within the church, and the August skies and waving trees without, combined to give a drowsy, mellow, and enchanted air to old Saint John's and to the gathering people.

"The choir have come into the gallery," said Fairfax Cary. "I hear the scrape of Fitzwhyllson's viol."

"The quiet is over and here comes the world," answered Jacqueline. "Who is that with Mr. Wickham — the tall, lean man?"

"It is the Governor of Tennessee and a fire-eater for Burr — Andrew Jackson by name. The third man is Luther Martin."

"He may be learned in the law," murmured Unity, "but I would like to know the University that taught him dress. See, Jacqueline, Charlotte Foushee has the newest bonnet yet!"

"That is Commodore Truxtun coming in with Edmund Randolph. He looks a seaman, every inch of him! Who is the young gentleman in blue?"

"Oh, that," replied Unity, "is Mr. Washington Irving of New York. He has just returned from the Grand Tour, and he writes most beautifully. He has sent me an acrostic for my keepsake that — that —"

"That I could not have written had I tried till doomsday," finished Fairfax Cary. "Do you like acrostics, Mrs. Rand?"

Jacqueline smiled. "No, nor keepsakes either. Unity and I both like strong prose and books with meanings. Her *façons de parler* are many."

"Well, anyhow," said Miss Dandridge, "I like Mr. Washington Irving. He does n't only write acrostics; he writes prose as well. Here is the Chief Justice."

"The second bell is ringing. We'll have all the churchyard now. Here comes the Tenth Legion — Hay, Wirt, and McRae! Mark Wirt bow to Martin!"

"Will General Wilkinson be here?"

"Speak of — one that's often named in church — and see the waving of his red cockfeather! This is the General now. Ahem! he looks what he is."

"And the other with the sash?"

"Eaton. They are both tarred with the same brush! Here, coming toward us, is one of very different make! You met him yesterday, did you not? Ha! Captain Decatur, allow me to give you anchorage!"

As he spoke, he held open the pew door. Captain Stephen Decatur smiled, bowed, and entered, and was presently greeting with a manly, frank, and engaging manner the beautiful Mrs. Rand and the equally lovely Miss Dandridge, to both of whom he had been presented at an evening entertainment. The church was now filled and the bell ceased ringing. From the gallery came the deeper growl of the bass viol and the preliminary breath of a flute. A moment more and the minister walked up the aisle and, mounting the tall old pulpit, invoked a blessing, then gave out in a fine mellow voice with a strong Scotch accent: —

> "The spacious firmament on high,
> With all the blue, ethereal sky
> And spangled heavens, a shining frame,
> Their great Original proclaim."

The choir in the gallery, viol, flute, and voices, took up the strain, and the congregation beneath following in their turn, there arose and floated through the windows a veritable pæan, so sweet and loud that the boatmen on the river heard.

On went the service until the sermon was reached, and on went the sermon from "firstly" to "eighteenthly and last, my brethren." The sermon was upon Charity, and included no allusion to the topic of the day uppermost in men's minds, for this minister never evinced any party spirit, and thought politics not his province. The discourse ended, the plate was carried and the benediction given, whereupon, after a decorous pause, the congregation streamed forth to the green and warm churchyard.

Here it broke into groups, flowery bright on the part of the women, gallant and gay enough on the side of the attending gentlemen. The broad path was like the unfolding of a figured ribbon, and the sward on either hand like sprinkled taffeta. The sky between the large white clouds showed bluer than blue, and the leaves of the sycamores trembled in a small, refreshing breeze. The birds were silent, but the insect world filled with its light voice the space between all other sounds. Outside the gate coaches and horses waited. There was no hurry; the ribbon unrolled but slowly, and the blossomy knots upon the taffeta as leisurely shifted position.

Theodosia Alston and Jacqueline came out of church together, in a cluster of Carringtons and Amblers. Besides her affianced, Unity had for company Captain Decatur, Mr. Irving, and Mr. Scott. The throng, pressing between, separated the cousins. Aaron Burr's daughter, though she talked and laughed with spirit and vivacity, was so evidently anxious to be away that the friend with whom she had come made haste down the path to their waiting coach. Jacqueline, meaning to tarry but a moment beside the woman for whom all, of whatever party, had only admiration and sympathy, found herself drawn along the path to the gate. The Carrington coach rolled away, and she was left almost alone in the sunny lower end of the churchyard.

The ribbon was unrolling toward her, and she waited, glad of the moment's quiet. She saw Unity's forget-me-not blue, and Charlotte Foushee's bonnet, piquant and immense, and Mrs. Randolph's lilac lutestring, and all the blue and green and wine-coloured coats of the men moving toward her as in a summer dream, gay midges in a giant shaft of sunlight. A great bee droned past her to the honeysuckle upon the wall against which she leaned. She watched the furred creature, barred and golden, and thought suddenly of the bees about the mimosa on the Three-Notched Road.

A middle-aged gentleman, of a responsible and benevolent cast of countenance, came up to her. "A very good day to you, my dear Mrs. Rand!"

"And to you, Colonel Nicholas."

"You are of my mind. You do not care to dilly-dally after church. 'T is as bad as a London rout, where you move an inch an hour. Well, there are men here to-day who have made some stir in the world! Do you go to-morrow to the Capitol?"

"Yes. My cousin and I have seats with Mrs. Wickham."

"It will not be such a trial as was Warren Hastings's. Yet it will have its value both to the eye and the ear. If it were possible, I would have there every young boy in town. Is Mr. Rand at home?"

"No. He is in Williamsburgh for several days."

The gentleman hesitated. "Vexatious! I have something for his own hand, and I myself go out of town after to-morrow. It may be important —"

"Cannot I give it to him?"

"It is a small packet, or letter, from the President. He sent it to me by a private messenger, with a note asking me to do him the friendly service to place it directly in Mr. Rand's hand. I have it with me, as I thought I might meet Mr. Rand here."

"He will hardly return before Wednesday. When he comes, I will give him the letter with pleasure."

The other took from his pocket a thick letter, strongly sealed, and addressed in Jefferson's fine, precise hand. "I must be away from Richmond for a week or more, and the matter may be important. I can conceive no reason why, so that it be put directly into Mr. Rand's hand, one agent should be better than another. I'll confide it to you, Mrs. Rand."

"I will do as the President directs, Colonel Nicholas, and will give it to my husband the moment he returns."

She put out her hand, and he laid the packet in it. Hanging from her arm by a rose-coloured ribbon was a small bag of old brocade. This she opened, and slipped into the silken depths the President's somewhat heavy missive. "He shall have it on Wednesday," she said.

The dispersing congregation touched and claimed them. Mr. Wirt and Commodore Truxtun bore off her companion, and she herself, after a moment of gay talk with all the Randolphs, rejoined Unity and her court. Fairfax Cary called their coach, and Captain Decatur and Mr. Irving and Mr. Scott saw them in, and still talked at the lowered windows until Big Isham on the box, with a loud crack of his whip, put the greys in motion.

The coach went slowly down the hill. Unity yawned and waved her fan. "I like Captain Decatur. Think of sailing into a tropic harbour and destroying the Philadelphia on a day like this! Lend me your fan; it is larger than mine. What have you in your bag?"

"My prayer book, and something that Colonel Nicholas gave me for Lewis. I could think only of Theodosia Alston, and of how long to-night will be to her!"

OLD SAINT JOHN'S

"She believes that he will be acquitted."

"She does not know, and pictures of what we fear are dreadful! Knowledge is like death sometimes, but not to know is like frightened dying! Oh, warm, warm! I shall be glad when it is all over and we leave Richmond for the mountains and the streams again, and for your wedding, dearest heart!"

"Oh, my wedding!" said Unity. "My wedding's like a dream. I don't believe I'm going to have any wedding!"

CHAPTER XXVI

THE TRIAL OF AARON BURR

AT an early hour the crowd in the Hall of the House of Delegates was very great, and as it drew toward the time when the principals in the drama would appear, the press of the people and the heat of the August day grew well-nigh intolerable. In the gallery were many women, and their diaphanous gowns and the incessant flutter of their fans imparted to this portion of the Hall a pale illusion of comfort. In the hall below, men stood upon the window-sills, choked the entrances, crowded the corridors without. Not only was there a throng where something might be heard and seen, but the portico of the Capitol had its numbers, and the green surrounding slopes a concourse avid of what news the birds might bring. Within and without, the heat was extreme, even for August in Tidewater Virginia; an atmosphere sultry and boding, tense with the feeling of an approaching storm.

In the gallery, beside Unity and Mrs. Wickham, around her women of Federalist families who were loath to believe any one guilty who was prosecuted, or persecuted, by the present Government, and women of Republican houses who asserted, while they waved their fans, that, being guilty, Aaron Burr must be, should be, would be hanged! sat Jacqueline Rand, and wondered somewhat at her weakness in coming there that day. It had been, perhaps, in the last analysis, a painful curiosity, a vague desire to see the place, the men, all the circumstance and environment, with which her husband — she thanked God with every breath — had no connection! He might have had here his part, she knew tremulously; it might have been his rôle to stand here beside Aaron Burr, and, with a passionately humble and grateful heart, she nursed the memory of that winter night when he had sworn to her that from that hour he and this enterprise should be strangers.

There had been days and weeks of preliminaries to the actual trial for high treason, but she had not before been in this hall. All her delicacy shrank from the thought of sitting here beside her husband, conscious of his consciousness that she knew all that might have been, and saw in fancy more prisoners at the bar than one. No man would like that. He had come often to the Capitol during the days of skirmishing prior to the general engagement; had he not done so, it would have been at once remarked. She expressed no desire to accompany him, nor did he ever ask her to do so. She was aware of the general surprise that he had no place among the Government counsel. Whether or not such place had been offered to him, pressed upon him, she did not know, but she thought it possible that this was the case. If so, he had refused as was right. Acceptance, she knew, would have been impossible.

All through these months there had been between them a silent pact, a covenant to avoid all superfluous mention of the topic which met them on every hand, from every mouth, in every letter or printed sheet. Rand was much occupied with important cases, much in demand in various portions of the state, much away from home. She was not a woman to demand as her right entrance into every chamber of another's soul. Her own had its hushed rooms, its reticences, its altars built to solitude; she was aware that beyond, below, above the fair chamber where he entertained her were other spaces in her husband's nature. Into some she looked as through open door and clear windows, but others were closed to her, and she was both too proud and too pure of thought to search for keys that had not been offered her.

She knew that her husband had not meant to be absent from Richmond that day. An unexpected turn in the case he was conducting had compelled his presence in Williamsburgh, and on the other hand, in Richmond, the labour of finding an impartial jury had been brought to a sudden end by Burr's *coup de main* in refusing to challenge and calmly accepting as prejudiced a twelve as perhaps, in the United States of America, ever decided whether a man should live or die. The move had hastened the day when the Government was to begin its cannonade.

Lewis was yet in Williamsburgh. Had he been present in this hall, watching events with his fellow lawyers, fellow politicians, fellow countrymen, who knew nothing of one snowy night a year ago last February, his wife, for both their sakes, would have remained away. As it was, she had been persuaded. Unity would not for much have missed the spectacle, friends had been pressing, and at last her own painful interest prevailed. She was here now, and she sat as in a waking dream, her hands idle, her eyes, wide and dark, steadily fixed upon the scene below. She saw, leaning against a window, Ludwell Cary, and, the centre of a cluster of men in hunting-shirts, Adam Gaudylock.

The Capitol clock struck twelve. As the last stroke died upon the feverish air, the Chief Justice entered the Hall and took the Speaker's chair. Beside him was Cyrus Griffin, the District Judge. Hay, the District Attorney, with his associates William Wirt and Alexander McRae, now appeared, and immediately afterward the imposing array of the prisoner's counsel, a phalanx which included no less than four sometime Attorneys-General and two subalterns of note.

These took the seats reserved for them; the marshal and his deputies pressed the people back, and the jury entered and filled the jury box. Below and near them sat a medley of witnesses — important folk, and folk whom only this trial made important.

A loud murmur was now heard from without; the marshal's men, red and perspiring, cleared a thread-like path, and the prisoner, accompanied by his son-in-law, entered the Hall. He was dressed in black, with carefully powdered hair. Quiet, cool, smiling, and collected, he was brought to the bar, when, having taken his place, bowed to the judges, and greeted his counsel, he turned slightly and surveyed with his composed face and his extremely keen black eyes the throng that with intentness looked on him in turn. It was by no means their first encounter of eyes. The preliminaries of that famous trial had been many and prolonged. From the prisoner's arrival in April under military escort to the present moment, through the first arraignment at that bar, the assembling of the Grand Jury, the tedious waiting for Wilkinson's long-deferred arrival from New Orleans, the matter of the subpœna to the President with which the country rang, the adjournment from June to August, the victory gained by the defence in the exclusion of Wilkinson's evidence, and the clamour of the two camps into which the city was divided, — through all this had been manifest the prisoner's deliberate purpose and attempt to make every fibre of a personality ingratiating beyond that of most, tell in its own behalf. He had able advocates, but none more able than Aaron Burr. His day and time was, on the whole, a time astonishingly fluid and naïve, and he impressed it.

There was in this moment, therefore, no novelty of encounter between him and the stare of the opposing throng. He was not seeing them, nor they him, for the first time. Yet the situation had its high intensity. This day was the beginning of the actual trial, and only the day which brought the verdict could outweigh it in importance. This was the lighting of the lamp that was to search out mysteries; this was the bending of the bow; this was the first rung of the ladder which might lead — where? As John Marshall's voice was heard from the bench and the prisoner turned from his steadfast contemplation of the throng, a psychic wave overflowed and lifted all the great assembly. This was spectacle, this was drama! The oldest of all the first principles stirred under the stimulus, and with savage naturalness sucked in the sense of pageant.

The court was opened. Counsel on both sides brought forward and disposed of a minor point or two, then, amid a silence so great that the twittering of the martins outside the windows seemed importunate and shrill, proclamation was made, the prisoner stood up, and the indictment was read.

"*The grand inquest of the United States of America for the Virginia District upon their oath do present that Aaron Burr, late of the city of New York, and State of New York, attorney-at-law, being an inhabitant of and residing within the United States, and under the protection of the laws of the United States, and owing allegiance and fidelity to the same United States, not having the fear of God before his eyes, nor weighing the duty of his said allegiance, but being moved and seduced by the instigation of the Devil, wickedly devising and intending the peace and tranquillity of the said United States to disturb, and to stir, move, and excite insurrection, rebellion, and war against the said United States, on the tenth day of December, in the year of Christ one thousand, eight hundred and six, at a certain place called and known by the name of Blennerhassett's Island, in the county of Wood and District of Virginia aforesaid, and within the jurisdiction of this court, with force and arms, unlawfully, falsely, maliciously, and traitorously did compass, imagine, and intend to raise and levy war, insurrection, and rebellion against the said United States —"*

And so on through much thunderous repetition to the final, —

"*And the said Aaron Burr with the said persons as aforesaid traitorously assembled and armed and arranged in manner aforesaid, most wickedly, maliciously, and traitorously did ordain, prepare, and levy war against the said United States, and further to fulfil and carry into effect the said traitorous compassings, imaginings, and intentions of him the said Aaron Burr, and to carry on the war thus levied as aforesaid against the United States, the said Aaron Burr with the multitude last mentioned, at the island aforesaid, in the said county of Wood within the Virginia District aforesaid, and within the jurisdiction of this court, did array themselves in a warlike manner, with guns and other weapons, offensive and defensive, and did proceed from the said island down the river Ohio in the county aforesaid, within the Virginia District, and within the jurisdiction of this court, on the said eleventh day of December, in the year one thousand, eight hundred and six aforesaid, with the wicked and traitorous intention to descend the said river and the river Mississippi, and by force and arms traitorously to take possession of the city commonly called New Orleans, in the territory of Orleans, belonging to the United States, contrary to the duty of their said allegiance and fidelity, against the Constitution, peace, and dignity of the United States and against the form of the Act of Congress of the United States in such case made and provided.*"

The clerk ceased to read. When the last sonorous word had died upon the air, the audience yet sat or stood in silence, bent a little forward, in the attitude of listeners. This lasted an appreciable moment, then the tension snapped. Marshall moved slightly in his great chair, Judge Griffin coughed, a rustling sound and a deep breath ran through the Hall. The prisoner, who had faced with the most perfect composure the indictment's long thunder, now slightly inclined his head to the Judges and took his seat. His counsel, ostentatiously easy and smiling, gathered about him, and the District Attorney rose to open for the Government in a lengthy and able speech.

In the gallery, among the fluttering fans, Jacqueline asked herself if her rising and quitting the place would disturb those about her. She was in the very front, beside the gallery rail, there was a great crowd behind, she must stay it out. She bit her lip, forced back emotion, strove with resolution to conquer the too visionary aspect of all things before her. It had been foolish, she knew now, to come. She had not dreamed with what strong and feverish grasp such a scene could take prisoner the imagination. She saw too plainly much that was not there; she brought other figures into the Hall; abstractions and realities, they thronged the place. The place itself widened until to her inner sense it was as wide as her world and her life. Fontenoy was there and the house on the Three-Notched Road; Roselands, and much besides. For all the heat, and the fluttering of the fans, and the roll of declamation from the District Attorney, who was now upon the definition of treason, one night in February was there as well, the night that had seen so much imperilled, the night that had seen, thank God! the cloud go by. Of all the images that thronged upon her, creating a strange tumult of the soul, darkening her eyes and driving the faint colour from her cheek, the image of that evening was the most insistent. It was, perhaps, aided by her fancy that in that cool survey of the Hall in which the prisoner indulged himself, his eyes, keen and darting as a snake's, had rested for a moment upon her face. She could have said that there was in them a curious light of recognition, even a cool amusement, a sarcasm, — the very memory of the look made for her a trouble vague, but deep! Had he, too, given a thought to that evening, to the man whom he did not secure, and to the woman with whom he had talked of black lace and Spanish songs? She wondered. But why should Colonel Burr be amused, and why sarcastic? She abandoned the enquiry and listened to the heavy lumbering up of Government cannon. "Courts of Great Britain — Foster's Crown Laws — Demaree and Purchase — Vaughan — Lord George Gordon — Throgmorton — United States *vs.* Fries — Opinion of Judge Chase — Of Judge Iredell — Overt Act — Overt Act proven — Arms, array and treasonable purpose; here is bellum levatum if not bellum percussum — Treason and traitors, not potential but actual — their discovery and their punishment —"

On boomed the guns of the prosecution. Jacqueline listened, fascinated for a time, but the words at last grew to hurt her so that, could she have done so unobserved, she would have stopped her ears with her hands. The feverish interest of the scene still held her in its grasp, but the words were cruel and struck upon her heart. She could not free herself from the brooding thought of how poignant, how burning, how deadly poisonous they had been to her, had all things been different and she forced to sit in this place hearing them launched against another than Aaron Burr, there, there at that bar! She unlocked her hands, drew a long and tremulous breath, and, leaning a little forward, tried not to listen, and to lose herself in watching the throng below. Her eyes fell, at once, upon Ludwell Cary.

He was standing where she had before marked him, beside a window almost opposite, his arm upon the sill, his attention closely given to the District Attorney, who was now eulogising that great patriot, General James Wilkinson. Now, while Jacqueline looked, he turned his head. It was as though she had called and he had been ready with his answer.

Painfully raised in feeling and driven out of habitual citadels, tense and fevered, subtly touched by the storm in the air, she found in the moment no sense of self-consciousness, no question and no movement of aversion. She and Cary looked at each other long and fully, and with something of an old understanding; on her part a softening of pardon for the quarrel and the duel, on his a light and compassion that she could not clearly understand. She knew that he read her thoughts, but if he, too, was remembering that evening long ago in February, he must also remember that Lewis Rand gave up, that snowy night, definitely and forever, the fevered ambitions, the too-high imaginings, the conqueror's thirst for power; gave them up, and turned from the charmer into the path of right! There came into her heart a longing that Ludwell Cary should see the matter truly. He should have done so that afternoon in the cedar wood; where was the black mote that kept the vision out? She was suddenly aware — and it came to her with a dizzying strangeness — that there was in her own soul that reference of matters to the bar of Cary's idea, thought, and judgment which, that day in the cedar wood, she had told him existed in that of her husband. Were she and Lewis grown so much alike? or had her own soul always recognised, deferred to, rested upon, something in the inmost nature of the man into whose eyes she looked across this thronged and fevered space — something of rare equanimity, dispassionate yet tender, calm, high, impartial, and ideal? She did not know; she had not thought of it before. Her eyes dilated. Suddenly she saw the drawing-room at Fontenoy, green and gold and cool, with the portraits on the wall, — Edmund Churchill, who fought with King Charles; Henry his son, who fled to Virginia and founded the family there; a second Edmund, aide-de-camp to Marlborough; two Governors of Virginia and a President of the Council; the Lely and the Kneller — both Churchill women; and the fair face and form of Grandaunt Jacqueline for whom she was named. She smelled the roses in the bowls, and she saw herself singing at her harp. It was a night in June, the night of the great thunderstorm. Lewis Rand had come down from the blue room, and Ludwell Cary entered from the darkness of the storm.

> "Stone walls do not a prison make,
> Nor iron bars a cage;
> Minds innocent and quiet take
> That for a hermitage."

Unity's hand touched her. "Jacqueline, are you tired? Would you like to go away?"

The spell broke. Jacqueline was most tired, and she would very much have liked to go away, but a glance at her cousin and at the lady with whom they had come determined the question. That to both it was as good as a play, colour and animation proclaimed, and Jacqueline had not the heart to ring the curtain down. She shook her head and smiled. "We'll stay it out."

Her companion leaned back, relieved, and she was left to herself again. She knew that Cary's eyes were still upon her, but she would not turn her own that way. She made herself look at the judges upon the bench, the District Attorney, the opposing lawyers, even the prisoner. It was the heat and the thunder in the air that made her so tense and yet so tremulous. Every nerve to-day was like a harpstring tightly drawn where every wandering air must touch it. All this would soon be over — then home and quiet! The day was growing old; even now Mr. Hay was addressing the jury with an impressiveness that announced the closing periods of a speech. When he was done, would not the court adjourn until to-morrow? It was said the trial might last two weeks. Mr. Hay sat down, but alas! before the applause and stir had ceased, Mr. Wickham was upon his feet.

Mr. Wirt followed Mr. Wickham, and was followed in turn by Luther Martin. The firing was heavy. Boom, boom! went the guns of the Government, quick and withering came the fire from the defence. If advantage of position was with the first, the last showed the higher generalship. The duel was sharp, and it was followed by the spectators with strained interest. The Chief Justice on the bench and the prisoner at the bar, attentive though they both were, alone of almost all concerned seemed to watch the struggle calmly. It drew toward late afternoon. Luther Martin, still upon the Overt Act, after an ironic compliment or two to the Government counsel, and a statement that George Washington, the great and the good, might with a like innocency of intents have found himself in a like position with Colonel Burr, withdrew his guns for the night. The prosecution, after a glare of indignation, announced that on the morrow it would begin examination of witnesses; the Chief Justice said a few weighty words, and the court was adjourned.

Out to the air, the grass and the trees, the gleam of the distant James, and a tremendous and fantastic show of clouds, piled along the horizon and flushed by the declining sun, streamed the crowd. Excited and voluble, lavish of opinions that had been pent up for hours, and drinking in greedily the fresher air, it made no haste to quit the Capitol portico or the Capitol Square. There were friends and acquaintances to greet, noted people to speak to, or to hear and see others speak to, the lawyers to congratulate and the judges to bow to — and last but not least, there was the prisoner to mark enter, with the marshal, a plain coach and drive away to the house opposite the Swan, to which he had been removed from his rooms in the Penitentiary.

The women who had observed the first day of the great trial from the gallery made, of course, no such tarrying. They left the building and the square at once, and the men of their families present saw them into their carriages, or, if the distance home was not great, watched them walk away in little groups with a servant or two behind them.

At the head of the Capitol steps Jacqueline and Unity found Fairfax Cary awaiting them, and upon the grass below they were joined by Mr. Washington Irving. Mrs. Wickham was with them, Mrs. Carrington, Mrs. Ambler, and Miss Mayo. All the women lived within a short distance of one another, and all, escorted by the two gentlemen, would walk the little way across Capitol and Broad to Marshall Street. Unity was to take supper with Mrs. Carrington and to spend the night with Mrs. Ambler, and she would not go home first, unless — She looked at Jacqueline. "Did the fireworks frighten you, honey? Would you rather that I stayed with you?"

Jacqueline laughed. "The fireworks were alarming, were n't they, Mrs. Wickham? No, no; go with Mrs. Carrington, Unity. To-night I'm going to write to Deb and read a novel." They were now opposite the Chief Justice's house, and as she spoke, she paused and made a slight curtsy to the elder ladies. "Our ways part here."

"I will walk with you to your door," said Fairfax Cary.

She shook her head. "No, do not. I am almost there." Then, as his intention still held, she continued in a lower voice, "I had rather be alone. Obey me, please."

The small discussion ended in the group of ladies and their two escorts giving Jacqueline Rand her way, and with laughing good-byes keeping to their course down the street that was now bathed in the glow of sunset. She watched them for a moment, then turned her face toward her own house. The distance was short, and she traversed it lightly and rapidly, glad to be alone, glad to feel upon her brow the sunset wind, and glad at the prospect of her solitary evening. She was conscious of a strong revulsion of feeling. The sights and the sounds of the past hours were still in mind, but all the air had changed, and was no longer fevered and boding. She had thought too much and made too much, she told herself, of that vague and dark "It might have been." It was not; thank God, it was not! And Lewis, there in Williamsburgh, walking now, perhaps, down Duke of Gloucester Street, or sitting in the Apollo room at the Raleigh, — would she have had Lewis read her mind that day? Generous! had she been generous — or just? The colour flowed over her face and throat. "Neither just nor generous!" she cried to herself, in a passion of relief. "I'll go no more to that place!"

She reached her own gate, entered between the two box bushes, and mounted the steps to the honeysuckle-covered porch. The door before her was open, and the hall, wide and cool, with the tall clock and the long sofa, the portraits on the wall and a great bowl of stock and gillyflower, brought to her senses a blissful feeling of home, of fixedness and peace.

Mammy Chloe came from the back of the house, and in her mistress's chamber took from her her straw bonnet, gauze scarf, and filmy gloves, then brought her slippers of morocco and a thin, flowered house-dress, narrow and fine as an infant's robe.

"Has Joab gone to the post-office?" asked Jacqueline.

"Yaas 'm. De Williamsbu'gh stage done come, fer I heah de horn more 'n an hour ago. Dar Joab now!"

Mammy Chloe put down the blue china ewer, left the room,

and returned with a letter in her hand. "Dar, now! Marse Lewis ain' neber gwine fergit you! Ef de sun shine, or ef hit don' shine, heah come de letter jes' de same!"

Jacqueline took the letter from her. "Yes, Mammy, yes," she said, with a sweet and tremulous laugh. "He's a good master, is n't he?"

"Lawd knows I ain' neber had a better," assented Mammy Chloe. "He powerful stric' to mek you min', is Marse Lewis, but he ain' de kin' what licks he lips ober de fac' dat you is a-mindin'! I ain' gwine say, honey, an' I neber is gwine say, dat he's wuth what de Churchills is wuth, but I's ready to survigerate dat he's got he own wuth. An' ef hit's enough fer you, chile, hit's enough fer yo' ole mammy. Read yo' letter while I puts on yo' slippers."

Jacqueline broke the seal and read: —

JACQUELINE: — I am kept here for an uncertain time — worse luck, dear heart! Do not send what letters may have come for me, as I may leave sooner than I think for, and so would pass them on the road. Open any from the court in Winchester, where I have a case pending — if the matter seems pressing, take a copy, and send copy or original to me by to-morrow's stage. I am expecting a letter from Washington — an important one, outlining the Embargo measures. I looked for it before I left Richmond. If it has arrived, open it, dear heart, and glance through it to see if there be any message or enquiry which I should have at once. It is very hot, very dusty, very tiresome in the court room. I will leave Tom Mocket here to wind things up, and will get home as soon as I can. Then, as soon as the hurly-burly's over, we'll go to Roselands for a little while — to the calm, the peace, bright days and white nights! While I write here in the Apollo, you are at church in Saint John's. Shall I say, "Pray for me, sweet saint?" You'll do that without my asking. So I'll say instead, "Think of me, dear wife, and love me still."

        Thine,   Lewis.

 Jacqueline stood up in her faintly coloured gown, all rich light and rose bloom. From her dressing-table she took her keys, and, opening her mother's desk of rosewood and mother-of-pearl, lifted from it several letters and the packet which Colonel Nicholas had given her the day before. With these in her hands she left her chamber and went into the drawing-room. "Bring the candles," she said over her shoulder to Mammy Chloe. "It is growing too dark to see to read."

CHAPTER XXVII

THE LETTER

THE windows were open to the dusky rose of the west, and their long curtains stirred in the hot and fitful breeze. Jacqueline, waiting for the lights, pushed the heavy hair from her forehead and panted a little with the oppression of the night. Young Isham entered with the candles, and Mammy Chloe brought her upon a salver a cup of coffee and a roll. She ate and drank, then sent her old nurse away. The candles, under their tall glass shades, were upon the centre table, and beside them lay the letters she was to read. Her husband's own letter was slipped beneath the ribbon that confined her dress, and lay against her heart.

It was so hot and dull a night that she stood for a while at a window, leaning a little out, trying to fancy that there was rain in the fantastic mass of clouds that rose on either side of the evening star. The smell of the box at the gate was strong. She thought of Fontenoy, of Major Edward, and of Deb. A grey moth touched her; she looked once again at the bright star between the clouds, then, turning back into the room, drew a chair to the table and, sitting down, took into her lap the papers that lay beside the candles.

There had come a letter in the stage from Winchester. She opened it. "Could Mr. Rand arrive by such a day? The case was important — the interests large — the fee large, too. Could he come just as soon as the jury, the press, and Mr. Jefferson hanged Aaron Burr? An early reply —"

Jacqueline rose, brought writing-materials from the escritoire to the table, and copied rapidly, in her clear, Italian hand, the Winchester letter, then laid it to one side to be folded with her own to Lewis for to-morrow's stage to Williamsburgh. The next letter was, she knew, from Albemarle, and not important. She laid it aside. The third she opened; it was from a gentleman in Westmoreland who wished in a certain litigation "the services, sir, of the foremost lawyer in the state." Jacqueline smiled and laid it with the Albemarle letter. The matter might wait until the foremost lawyer's return. There were now two letters, and neither was from Washington. One was indeed about matters political, a tirade from a party leader on Rand's folly in declining, last year, the nomination for Governor, but it contained nothing to demand his instant attention. The other, which had come by boat from Norfolk, seemed of no consequence.

Jacqueline put both aside, and took into her hand the packet given her by Colonel Nicholas. She sat for a moment, looking at the superscription. "A letter from Washington," Lewis said, "outlining the Embargo measures. Open and glance through it to see if there be any message I should have at once." She thought no otherwise than that this was the letter in question. Mr. Jefferson was, she knew, upon the defensive in regard to these measures, and she was glad to believe that he had fallen into an ancient habit and was willing, as of old, to expatiate upon his policy to Lewis Rand.

She broke the red seals and unfolded the paper. It proved to be a letter covering a letter. She let fall the folded, inner missive, drew a candle nearer, and read in Jefferson's small, formal, and very clear hand: —

I have the honour to restore to you the letter which you will find enclosed. If you ask how it came into my hands, I have but to say that, in times of crisis and peril, rules of conduct, on the part of a government as of an individual, have somewhat to bow to necessity. Enough that it did come into my hands — last autumn. Judge if I have used it against you! It is now returned to you because I no longer conceive it necessary to hold it. I might have burned it; I prefer that you shall do so.

I have but a word to add to our conversation of last August at Monticello. I am a man of strong affections. Your youth and all the eager service you did me in those years, and the great hopes I had for you, endeared you to me. These things are present in my mind. Were they not so, you would have heard from me in other wise! Were they not so, that which I now enclose should not travel back to the writer's hand; it should remain, distinct and black, upon your Country's records, for your children's children to read with burning cheeks! I spare you, but you are of course aware that the affection of which I spoke is dead, dead as the trust with which I regarded you, or as the pride with which I dwelt upon your future! Reread and destroy that which I place in your hand.

THOMAS JEFFERSON.

Jacqueline laid down the large, blue, crackling sheet, and took from the floor beside her, where it had fallen, the President's enclosure. Hand and eye moved mechanically; she neither thought nor feared. Her judgment was in suspension, and she was unconscious of herself or of her act. The seals upon this second letter were broken. She unfolded it. On the outside it was addressed in a hand that, had she thought, she would have recognised for Tom Mocket's, to an undistinguished person at Marietta upon the Ohio; within, the writing was her husband's and the address was to Aaron Burr. The date was last August, the subject-matter the disruption of the Republic and the conquest of Mexico, and the detail of plans included the arrangement by which Rand was to leave Albemarle, ostensibly to examine a purchase of land beyond the mountains. He would leave, however, not to return. Once out of the country, he with his wife would press on rapidly to the Ohio, to Blennerhassett's island.

The summer night deepened, hot and languorous, with a sweep of moths to the candle flames, with vagrant odours of flowering vines and vagrant sounds of distant laughter, voices, footsteps down the long street. Jacqueline sat very still, the letter in her lap. The curtains at the window moved in the fitful air. Through the open doors from the kitchen in the yard behind the house came the strumming of a banjo, then Joab's deep bass: —

>"Go down, go down, Moses,
> Tell Pharaoh let us go!
> Go down, go down, Moses,
> King Pharaoh, let us go!"

There was a wave of honeysuckle, too faint and deadly sweet. A party of men, boatmen or waggoners, went by, and as they passed, broke into rough laughter.

Jacqueline rose, letting fall the letter. With her hand to her forehead she stood for a minute, then moved haltingly to the window. Her eyes were blank; she wanted air, she knew, and for the moment she knew little else. She was whelmed in deep waters, and all horizons were one. When she reached the casement, she could only cling to the sill, raise her eyes to the stars, and find nothing there to help her understand. There was in them neither calm nor sublimity; they swung and danced like insensate fireflies. The honeysuckle was too strong — and she must tell Joab she did not wish to hear his banjo to-night. The men who had passed were still laughing.

She put her hand again to her forehead, then presently withdrew it and looked over her shoulder at the paper lying upon the floor beside the table. By degrees the vagueness and the absence of sensation vanished. She had had her moments of merciful deadening, of indifference to pain; they were past, and torment now began.

Perhaps half an hour went by. She rose from the sofa upon which she had thrown herself, face down, pressed her hands to her temples, then, moving to the table, wrote there a word or two, folded and addressed the paper, and rang the bell. Young Isham appeared and she gave him the note, bidding him, in a voice that by an effort she made natural, to hasten upon his errand. When he was gone, she stooped and gathered from the floor the fallen letters — the President's and Lewis Rand's — and laid them in a drawer. The touch seemed to burn her, for she moaned a little. She wandered for a moment uncertainly, here and there in the room, then, returning to the sofa, fell upon her knees beside it, stretched out her arms along the silk, and laid her head upon them. "O God! O God!" she said, but made no other prayer.

The minutes passed. There was a step, the sound of the gate-latch, and a hand upon the knocker. She rose from her knees, and was standing by the table when, in another moment, the drawing-room door opened to admit Ludwell Cary. He came forward.

"You sent for me" — He paused, stepped back, and looked at her fully and gravely. "Something has happened. Tell me what it is."

"You know. You have known all the time. You knew last summer in the cedar wood!" Her voice broke; she raised her arms above her head, then let them fall with a cry. "You knew — you knew!"

"How have you come to know? No, don't tell me!"

"I am mad, I think. A letter came that told me. I see now how the world must look to madmen. It is a curious place where we are all strangers — and yet we think it is our safe home."

As she turned from him, she reeled. There was a great chair near, beside the window. Cary caught her by both hands, forced her to sit down, and drew the curtains apart so that the air of night came fully in. The quiet street was now deserted; the maple boughs, too, screened the place. "Look!" he said. "Look how brightly Venus shines! All the immense rack of clouds that we had at sunset has vanished. The box smells like the garden at Fontenoy, where, I make no doubt, Deb and Major Edward are walking up and down, counting the stars. Yes, I knew, that afternoon in the cedar wood — but not for happiness itself would I have robbed you of that faith, that confidence —"

She leaned forward in the great chair, her hands clasped upon its arms, her dark eyes wide upon the night without the window. "I sent for you because I wished you to tell me all. I wanted truth as I wanted air! I want it now. That day we met in the cedar wood — you and Uncle Edward talked together." She drew a difficult breath. "It was then that they — Uncle Dick and Uncle Edward — began to treat me as though — as though I had never left home! It was then — "

"They feared," said Cary gently, "for your happiness."

"I returned to Roselands, and in three days we were to travel across the mountains. Then at sunset, underneath the beech tree" — She sat for a moment perfectly still, then turned in her chair and spoke in a clear voice. "That was why you forced him to challenge you, and that was why you named a distant time and place? The truth, please."

"That was why."

She rose from the chair and leaned, panting, against the window-frame. "Was there no other way —"

"It seemed the simplest way," he answered quietly. "There was no harm done, and it answered my purpose." He paused, then went on. "My purpose was to detain Mr. Rand from so rash and so fatal a step until it was too late for him to take it."

She turned from the window. "You are generous," she said, in a stifled voice. "I ask your pardon for my hard thoughts of you. Oh, for a storm and a wind to blow! It is too hot, too heavy a night. I never wish to smell the honeysuckle again."

He followed her back to the light of the candles. "Listen to me for a moment. I do not think that you know — I am not sure that I know — the iron strength of the laws that rule an ambitious nature. Ambition becomes an atmosphere; the man whose temperament and self-training enure him to it breathes it at last as though it were his native air. It becomes that — an inner and personal clime, the source and spring of countless actions, great and small. The light, too, is refracted, and the great background of life is not seen quite truly. It is, I think, an enchanted air, into which a man drifts upon a river of dreams and imaginations — and how hard to reascend, against the current!" He paused, stood a moment with downcast eyes, measuring the table with his hand, then drew a quick breath and spoke on. "Given his parentage and descent, his unhappy and hardly-treated boyhood, the visions, the rebellions, the longings with which he must have walked the hot and rank tobacco-fields; given the upward struggle of his youth, so determined and so successful; given the courage, the hardihood, the wide outlook of a man who has neither inherited nor been granted, but has himself hewn out and built up his holding in life; given genius and sense of power, will, perseverance, and the fatal knowledge that all events and all currents habitually bend to his hand,

— given all this and opportunity" — He raised his head and met her eyes. "It is not strange and it is not monstrous that Mr. Rand should have involved himself, to a greater or less degree, in this attempt upon the West. God is my witness, I would not have you think it strange and monstrous! Ambition is, perhaps, the most human of all qualities. Many and many an ambitious man has been loved, loved passionately, loved deservedly! — many a conqueror, many a one of those who failed to conquer and who were called by an ugly name! Love does not love the ambition; it loves that which is love-worthy below the iron grating and the tracery of false gold! As the world goes, Lewis Rand and I are enemies; but I could swear to you to-night that I see, that I have always seen, a greatness in him! I believe it to be distorted and darkened, but the quality of it is greatness. Were I he" — He paused for a moment, then continued, with dignity. "Were I he, I would say to the lady who, for love, had given me her hand in wedlock, — 'Love me still. My land is one of storm and darkness, of rude wastes and frowning strongholds whence sometimes issue robber bands. But it is not a petty land, and side by side with all that is wrong runs not a little that is heroic and right! Love me still and help me there, even though — even though I am forsworn to you!'"

"I would not have you think," she said clearly, — "I would not have you even lightly dream, that his country is not my country! I love him!"

"I know that you do."

"There is no place so dark that I would not wait for him there as for the dawn. There is no flood I would not cross to him; there is no deep pit in which I would not seek him, were he fallen there! He has done wrong, and I am unhappy for it. But never think, never dream, that, though I see the dark and broken ground, I would leave that country, or am less than wholly loyal to its King!"

"I have neither thought nor dreamed it."

"When I — when I learned this thing, it shook me so! My brain whirled, and then I thought of you and called to you."

"There is no service to which you could call me that I would not thankfully render. I am your friend and your people's friend. There is one thing more I should like to say to you. Do not fear for him. There is no reason to believe that this will ever be discovered. The lips of those who know are sealed."

"Who knows?"

"On our side your uncles, my brother and I, — and your cousin, I think, guesses. The President, also, is aware —"

She reddened deeply. "I know," she said, in a stifled voice. "The President, too, is generous —"

"On his — on Mr. Rand's side, certain men whom we need not name. That he has secured their silence, events have proved, and I take it for granted that he has been careful to recall and to destroy any writing that might incriminate. He is, I think, quite safe."

She turned from him and, sitting down by the table, laid her head upon her arms. He regarded her for a moment with compassion and understanding, chivalrous and deep, then, moving to the window, stood there with his face to the evening star. At last she spoke in a broken and tremulous voice "Mr. Cary —"

He came to her side. "It is a peaceful night, still and bright. You will sleep, will you not? Leave all this to Time and to the power of steadfast love! You may yet see in this land the grandeur of the dawn."

"I know that I shall," she answered. "And when I see it,

I shall think reverently of you. It was like you to come, like you to help me so. Now, good-night!"

She took his hand, and before he could prevent her, raised it to her lips. "No,— let me! You are generous and you are noble. I acknowledge it from my heart. Good-night— good-bye!"

He showed for a moment his pent emotion, then strove with and conquered it. "I will go. Your cousin is from home, and you are alone to-night. Would you prefer that she should return?"

"No. I had rather be alone."

He took the hand that she gave him, kissed it, and said good-night. When he was gone and his step had died from the street, she stood for some moments as he had left her, then, with a sobbing breath, turned to the table and took the letters from the drawer.

CHAPTER XXVIII

RAND AND MOCKET

TOM MOCKET, returning to Richmond twenty-four hours after his friend and patron, found it too late that evening to see Lewis and to report the happy winding up of all matters in Williamsburgh. The next morning he was at the office betimes, but though he waited long, no Lewis appeared. At last Tom sent a boy to the house on Shockoe, who returned with the statement that Mr. Rand was gone to the Capitol. "Then I'll go too," thought Tom. "I've got nerve as well as he!"

It was the fourth day of the actual trial, and interest was at white heat. Tom whistled to himself as he crossed the Capitol Square where men blocked the paths or, on the grass beneath the trees, recounted, disputed, and prophesied. When he reached the building, it was with much difficulty that he effected an entrance, and with more that he at last edged himself into the Hall of the House of Delegates. Sturdy perseverance and an acquaintance with a doorkeeper, however, can accomplish much, and these finally placed Mocket where, by dint of balancing himself upon an advantageous ledge of masonry, he had a fair view of both participants and spectators.

General William Eaton was being examined. The throng sat or stood silently attentive, swayed forward as by a wind. Marshall upon the bench, long and loose-jointed, with a quiet, plain face, was listening with intentness; the opposing counsel sat alert, gathered for the pounce; the prisoner, with a contemptuous smile, regarded the witness, who indeed cut but a poor figure. The District Attorney's voice, deliberate and full, asked a question, and General Eaton proceeded to give in detail Colonel Burr's expression of treasonable intentions.

Mocket, who had at first looked and listened with a thumping heart and a strong feeling that, visible to all, the letter T might be somewhere sewn or branded upon his own person, by degrees grew bolder. There was n't any letter there, that was certain, and a slight sense of personal danger might even become a welcome sauce to such a great affair as this! His fright vanished, and his ferret eyes began to rove.

There was Adam Gaudylock, still with his musket. It was a day when men habitually journeyed with pistols in their holsters or a dirk somewhere about them, but Adam carried that musket merely because he loved it — like a dog or a woman! Tawny and blue-eyed, light and lithe, indifferent and pleased to see the show, the hunter listened to General Eaton and laughed behind his hand to a fellow woodsman. "My certie, he's trained!" thought Tom. "It's not much they'll get from him!"

His eyes left Adam and travelled in search of Lewis Rand, finding him at last where he sat at no great distance from the group of central importance. His face was turned in Mocket's direction, and the light from a high window fell upon it. "He does n't see me," thought Tom to himself. "Who's he looking at like that?"

The witness's voice, raised by suggestion of counsel to a higher note, came athwart Mocket's speculations. "I listened to Colonel Burr's mode of indemnity; and as I had by this time begun to suspect that the military expedition he had on foot was unlawful, I permitted him to believe myself resigned to his influence, that I might understand the extent and motive of his arrangements. Colonel Burr now laid open his project of revolutionizing the territory west of the Alleghany; establishing an independent empire there; New Orleans to be the capital, and he himself to be the chief; organizing a military force on the waters of the Mississippi, and carrying conquest to Mexico—"

On went Eaton's disclosures, punctuated by heated objections from Wickham and Luther Martin, and once or twice by a scornful question from Burr himself. It was damning testimony, and the throng hung breathless on the various voices. Mocket listened also, but listened with his eyes upon his chief, and when there arose some interruption and dispute over technicalities, his freed mind proceeded to deal with Rand's change of aspect. It occurred to him to wonder if the light which showed it to him could be falling through a veil of storm cloud, but when he glanced at the high window, there was only the blue August heaven. What, then, gave Lewis so dark a look? "The black dog he talks of has got him sure," thought Tom. "What's happened to anger him like that?"

The voice of the witness again made itself heard. "Colonel Burr stated that he had secured to his interests and attached to his person the most distinguished citizens of Tennessee, Kentucky, and the territory of Orleans; that the army of the United States would act with him; that it would be reinforced by ten or twelve thousand men from the above states and territories, and that he had powerful agents in the Spanish territory. He proposed to give me a distinguished command in his army; I understood him to say the second in command. I asked him who would command in chief. He said, General Wilkinson. I said that General Wilkinson would act as lieutenant to no man in existence. 'You are in error,' said Mr. Burr. 'Wilkinson will act as lieutenant to me—'"

Mocket moved with care along the ledge until he had

brought within his view another portion of the Hall. "That look of his is n't fixed on nothing! Now we'll see." He stood on tiptoe, craned his neck, and surveyed the crowded floor. "Humph!" he remarked at last. "I might have known without looking. If I were Ludwell Cary—"

The counsel for the prisoner and the prisoner himself were subjecting the witness to a riddling fire of cross-questions. Mocket, on his coign of vantage, was caught again by the more apparent drama, and looked and listened greedily. Eaton at last retired, much damaged, and Commodore Truxtun was sworn. This was a man of different calibre, and from side to side of the long room occurred a subtle intensification of respect, interest, and attention. On went the examination, this time favourable, on the whole, to Burr. "The prisoner frequently, in conversation with me, mentioned the subject of speculations in western lands, opening a canal and building a bridge. Colonel Burr also said to me that the government was weak, and that he wished me to get the navy of the United States out of my head; that it would dwindle to nothing; and that he had something to propose to me that was both honourable and profitable; but I considered this nothing more than an interest in his land speculations—"

The August heat was maddening. Now and then a puff of wind entered from the parched out-of-doors, but it hardly refreshed. The flutter of the women's fans in the gallery made a far away and ineffectual sound. "All his conversations respecting military and naval subjects and the Mexican expedition," went on Truxtun's voice, "were in event of a war with Spain. I told him my opinion was, there would be no war, but he was sanguine of it. He said that after the Mexican expedition he intended to provide a formidable navy; that he meant to establish an independent government and give liberty to an enslaved world. I declined his propositions to me because the President was not privy to the project. He asked me the best mode of attacking the Havana, Carthagena, and La Vera Cruz—"

The day wore on. Truxtun was released, and the Attorney for the United States called Blennerhassett's servants to prove the array at the island and the embarkment upon the Ohio. They did their best with a deal of verbiage, of "Colonel Burr said" and "Mr. Blennerhassett said," and with no little bewilderment under cross-examination. "Yes, sir; I'm telling you, sir. Mr. Blennerhassett allowed that Colonel Burr and he and a few friends had bought eight hundred thousand acres of land, and they wanted young men to settle it. He said he would give any young man who would go down the river one hundred acres of land, plenty of grog and victuals while going down the river, and three months' provision after they got to the end; every young man must have his rifle and blanket. When I got home, I began to think, and I asked him what kind of seed we should carry with us. He said we did not want any, the people had seeds where we were going—"

"Of what occupation were you upon the island?" demanded Mr. Wirt.

"A gardener, sir. And then Mr. Blennerhassett said to me, 'I'll tell you what, Peter, we're going to take Mexico, one of the finest and richest places in the world!' He said that Colonel Burr would be King of Mexico, and that Mrs. Alston, daughter of Colonel Burr, was to be the Queen of Mexico whenever Colonel Burr died. He said that Colonel Burr had made fortunes for many in his time, but none for himself, and now he was going to make something for himself. He said that he had a great many friends in the Spanish territory; that the Spaniards, like the French, had got dissatisfied with their government, and wanted to *swap* it.

He told me that the British also were friends in this piece of business. I told him that the people had got it into their heads that Colonel Burr wanted to divide the Union. He sent me to Mason County with a letter, but I was n't to deliver it until I had the promise that it should be burned before me as soon as 't was read, for, says he, it contains high treason."

"Gad!" thought Mocket to himself, "I 'm glad that some one else's letters are burned as well! If I were as cool as Aaron Burr looks —"

Mr. McRae questioned the witness: "Well, who went off this December night?"

"Mr. Blennerhassett, sir, and the whole of the party."

"At what time of the night?"

"About one o'clock."

"Did all that came down to the island go away?"

"All but one, who was sick."

"Had they any guns?"

"Some of them had. Some of the people went a-shooting; but I do not know how many there were."

"What kind of guns; rifles or muskets?"

"I can't tell whether rifles or muskets. I saw no pistols but what belonged to Mr. Blennerhassett himself."

"Was there any powder or lead?"

"They had powder and they had lead. I saw some powder in a long, small barrel like a churn. Some of the men were engaged in running bullets."

"What induced them to leave the island at that hour of the night?"

"Because they were informed that the Kenawha militia were coming down."

The cross-examination of this witness and some desultory firing by the opposed counsel ended the day's proceedings.

The court adjourned, and the crowd streamed forth to the open air. Mocket, among the first to leave the hall, waited for his chief beside the outer doors. Townspeople, country neighbours, and strangers poured by, and he spoke to this one or to that. A group of Federalists approached; among them Ludwell Cary. They were talking, and as they passed Mocket heard the words, "When I return to Albemarle next week — " They went on down the steps; others streamed by, and presently Rand appeared. His lieutenant joined him, and together they left the Capitol and struck down the parched slopes to Governor Street.

"Things are all right at Williamsburgh," ventured Mocket, finding the silence oppressive. "I got in too late to see you last night. Were you at the Capitol yesterday also?"

"Yes."

"A man told me they had Adam on the stand. They got nothing from him?"

"Nothing."

"I've the papers all straight for the Winchester case. What do you want me to do —"

"I want you to be silent."

The other glanced aslant, with a lift of his brows and a twist of his lip. "That's a black rage," he thought; "Gideon and old Stephen and the Lord knows who beside all speaking together!"

They left Governor Street and presently arrived in silence before Rand's office. Mocket unlocked the door and they went in together. The senior partner dragged a chair before the empty fireplace and, sitting down, stared at the discoloured bricks as though he saw vistas through the wall. Tom worked among the papers on his desk, moving his fingers noiselessly, and now and then glancing over his shoulder. The clock on the wall ticked loudly.

Rand spoke at last. His voice had a curious suppressed tone, and upon his forehead, between the eyes, was displayed the horseshoe frown of extreme anger. Mocket had seen it earlier in the day, and it was now distinct as a brand. "I am not going," he said, "to take the Winchester case. This damned business here will soon be over. I shall wait to hear the verdict, and then I'm going to Albemarle."

"What d'ye think the verdict will be?"

"They'll acquit him. Barring Wirt, he has all the talent on his side. I'll leave you here to clear up things."

"Does Mrs. Rand wait here for you?"

"No. She leaves Richmond with Miss Dandridge to-morrow."

Tom took out his knife and began to whittle, an occupation that in him denoted sustained mental exertion. The other sat on before the empty fireplace, the mark upon his forehead, his hand twitching where it lay upon the arm of his chair. The clock ticked loudly; the sun, now low in the heavens, sent its gold shafts through the window; outside, the locusts shrilled in a dusty sycamore. Rand rose and, going to the cupboard, took from it a bottle and a glass, poured out brandy for himself, and drank it. In an age of hard drinking he was accounted puritanically abstemious. Mocket, glancing after him, knew that the draught meant disturbance so deep that the organism needed, rather than craved, the strength within the glass. Rand came back to the fireplace.

"Do you remember when, in November, I burned here, or thought I burned here, all papers, all letters —"

"Do I?" asked Mocket, with emphasis. "There's nothing happened to make me forget."

"A man cannot weave a net so fine that some minnow will not slip through and become leviathan! It escaped and has grown. Well, that too was in the nature of things." He took the ash-stick from the corner of the hearth and handled it as though he were again holding down burning papers. "So things are all right at Williamsburgh? I had a happy home-coming."

"You always have that," said Tom simply. "You've had a wonderful fortune, and more there than anywhere. I'm always telling Vinie — "

"Vinie!" answered the other. "Vinie would always blindly worship on. The sun might darken and go out, but where's the odds since she would never know it! Faith like a dog's or a child's or Vinie's — there's comfort there! But the awakened mind, and Judgment side by side upon the throne with Love — Oh, there's verjuice in the world!" He broke into harsh laughter.

"I wish I knew what ailed you," thought Mocket. "I'll try another tack." He stopped whittling and turned from his desk. "Coming out of the Capitol, I heard Ludwell Cary say that he goes next week to Albemarle."

"It is indifferent to me," replied the other, "whether he goes or stays." His hands closed upon the ash-stick until his nails were white. Suddenly he spoke without apparent relevance. "He is one of those men who are summoned in time of trouble — when the mind is tossed and the heart is wavering. They always answer — they come down the street at night, between the box bushes, up the steps beneath the honeysuckle — on such an errand they would not fear the lion's den! They are magnanimous, they are generous, they are out of our old life, they can tell us what we ought to do!" He struck the ash-stick violently against the hearth. "Honeysuckle and box and the quiet of the night, and 'Yes, I knew, I knew. 'T was thus and so, and I would counsel you — ' Oh, world's end and hell-fire! forgiveness itself grows worthless on such terms!"

He threw the stick from him, rose abruptly, and walked to the window.

"The clouds pile up, but they do not break, and the heat and fever of this August air grow intolerable. To abstract the mind — to abstract the mind" — He stood listening to the locusts and all the indefinable hum of the downward-drawing afternoon, then turned to Tom. "Give me those Winchester papers. Now what, exactly, did you do in Williamsburgh?"

CHAPTER XXIX

THE RIVER ROAD

THE days of speeches, for the Government and for Aaron Burr, — Hay, Wirt, and McRae against Edmund Randolph, Wickham, Botts, Lee, and Luther Martin, — went crackling by with bursts of heavy artillery and with running fire of musketry. It was a day of orators, and eloquence was spilled like water. At last the case rested. The Chief Justice summed up, exhaustively, with extraordinary ability, and with all the impartiality humanly possible to a Federalist Chief Justice dealing with a Republican prosecution. The jury, as is known, brought in a Scotch verdict, whereupon the prisoner was immediately upon his feet with a vehement protest. Finally the "Not proven" was expunged from the record, and Aaron Burr stood "Acquitted." The famous trial for treason was over.

As, throughout the summer, all roads led to Richmond, now, in the fierce heat and dust of early autumn, there was an exodus which left the town extremely dull after all the stir and fascination of the Government's proceedings. Burr, indeed, discharged for treason, was still held in bail to answer for the misdemeanor, judges and lawyers were still occupied, and many witnesses yet detained. But the result of the matter was a foregone conclusion. Here, too, there would be a "Not proven," with a demand on the part of the accused for a "Not guilty," and a final direction by the judges to the jury to return a verdict in the usual form. The trial of a man for a misdemeanor in levying war with Spain — a misdemeanor which, if proved, could entail only imprisonment — was an infinitely less affair than a prosecution for high treason, with the penalty of an ignominious death suspended like a sword of Damocles. The little world in Richmond felt the subsidence of excitement, realized how warm and dusty was the town, and began to think of its plantations and of country business. Witnesses and visitors of note took the homeward road. The Swan, the Eagle, the Bell, the Indian Queen, crowded all the summer, saw their patrons depart by stage, by boat, in coach and chaise, and on horseback. Many private houses were closed, and the quiet of the doldrums fell upon the place.

Jacqueline and Unity had been ten days in Albemarle. The two Carys, a servant behind them with their portmanteaus, rode away from the Swan on the first day of September. It was understood between the brothers that they were to make all haste to Greenwood. But there were houses on the way where kinsmen and friends might be trusted to do what they could to detain the two. Both were anxious to be at home — Fairfax the more eager, as was natural. The marriage was set for the middle of the month. As they rode out of town he had begun with, "I'll see her in four days," and the next morning, passing through the gates of the plantation where they had slept, he had irrelevantly remarked, " Now it is but three." The elder brother laughed and wished him Houssain's carpet.

Throughout the day they rode as rapidly as the heat permitted, but when at dusk they were captured by a kinsman with a charming wife and a bevy of pretty daughters, it was evident that they would not resume the road at dawn. It was noon, indeed, before they unclasped all these tendrils and pursued their journey, and at sunset another plantation put out a detaining hand. Fairfax Cary swore with impatience.

The other laughed again, but when, late next morning, they got away with a message called to them from the porch, "You'll be at Elm Tree this afternoon. Tell Cousin William —" he looked kindly at his junior's vexed face and proposed a division of forces.

"We can't neglect Elm Tree, and then there's Cherry Hill and Malplaquet still before us. Why shouldn't you just speak to them at Elm Tree, then ride on to the inn at Deer Lick and sleep there to-night? You could start with the first light, ride around Cherry Hill, and give Malplaquet the slip. I'll make your excuses everywhere. It's hard if a man can't be forgiven something — when he's on the eve of marrying Unity Dandridge! You'll be at Greenwood to-morrow night, and I dare say they'll ask you to breakfast at Fontenoy. Come, there's a solution!"

"You're the best fellow! And what will you do?"

"I'll sleep to-night at Elm Tree and ride soberly on to-morrow, take dinner at Cherry Hill, and sleep again at Malplaquet. They'll all be disappointed at not seeing the prospective bridegroom, but I'll make them understand that a man in love can't travel like a tortoise! I'll ride from Malplaquet by the river road and be at home that afternoon. You had better take Eli with you."

They rode together to Elm Tree, and parted under these conditions.

Lewis Rand left Richmond on the third of September. He travelled rapidly. There were no kinsmen to detain him on the road, and while he had hot partisans and was not without friends, there was not within him the Virginian instinct to loiter among these last, finding the flower in the moment, and resolutely putting off the morrow. His quest was for the morrow.

He rode now in the hot September weather, by field and

forest, hill and dale and stream, and rested only when he would spare the horses. Young Isham was with him; Joab had been sent on with Jacqueline. When night fell, he drew rein at the nearest house. If he knew the people, well; if he did not know them, well still; on both sides acquaintance would be enlarged. Hospitality was a Virginian virtue; no one ever dreamed of being unwelcome because he was a stranger. In the morning, after thanks and proffers of all possible service, he took the road again. It was his purpose to make the journey, despite the heat, in three days.

The last night upon the road he spent at a small tavern hard by an important crossroads. It was twilight when he dismounted, the fireflies thick in the oak scrub and up and down the pale roads, a crescent moon in the sky, and from somewhere the sound of wind in the pine-tops. Young Isham and the hostler took away the horses, and Rand, mounting the steps to the porch, found lounging there the inn's usual half-dozen haphazard guests. To most of these he was known by sight, to all by name, and as, with a "Good-evening, gentlemen!" he passed into the low, whitewashed main room, he left behind him more animation than he had found. When, a little later, he went into the supper-room, he discovered at table, making heavy inroads upon the bacon and waffles, an old acquaintance — Mr. Ned Hunter.

"Mr. Hunter, good-evening."

"Hey — what — the Devil! Good-evening to you, Mr. Rand. So, after all, your party, sir, did n't hang Colonel Burr!"

The two ate supper with the long table between them, and with no great amiability of feeling in presence. The Republican was the first to end the meal, and the Federalist answered his short bow with an even more abbreviated salute. Rand went out into the porch, where there were now only one or two lounging figures, and sat down at the head of the steps. Mr. Hunter came presently, too, into the air, and leaned against the railing, whistling to the dogs in the yard.

"You are going on in the morning, Mr. Rand?"

"Yes. At dawn."

"You'll be in Charlottesville, then, by two o'clock. Earlier, if you take the river road."

"I shall take the river road."

"It is broken riding, but it is the quickest way. Well, I won't be many hours behind you! My humble regards, if you please, to Mrs. Rand. There's nothing now at Fontenoy but wedding talk. I am sure I hope Miss Dandridge may be happy! Here, Di! here, Rover! here, Vixen!"

Rand arose. "I've had a long day and I make an early start. Good-night to you, gentlemen!"

When, in the morning, Young Isham came to his door with the first light, the boy found his master already up and partly dressed. Rand stood by the window looking out at the pink sky. "A bad night, Young Isham," he said, without turning. "Sleep's a commodity that has somehow run short with me. Are the horses ready?"

"Yaas, marster."

"Have you had your breakfast?"

"Yaas, marster."

"Help me here, then, and let's away. Roselands by one!"

Young Isham held the gilt-buttoned waistcoat, then took from the dresser the extravagant neckcloth of the period, and wound it with care around his master's throat. Rand knotted the muslin in front, put on his green riding-coat, and took from the dresser his watch and seals. "Bah! there's a chill in these September dawns! Close the portmanteau. Where did you put the holsters?"

"Dar dey is, sah, under yo' han'."

The boy, on his knees, worked at the straps of the portmanteau. Rand, waiting for him to finish, drew out a pistol from its leather case, looked it over and replaced it, then did the same with its fellow. "Are you done?" he said at last. "Bring everything and come on. I'll swallow a cup of coffee and then we'll be gone. We should pass Malplaquet by nine."

They rode away from the half-awakened inn. A mist was over the fields, and when they presently came to a stretch of forest, the leaves on either hand were wet. The grey filled arcades and hollows, and the note of the birds was as yet sleepy and without joyousness. They left the woods and, mounting a hill, saw from its summit the sun rise in splendour, then dipped again into fields where from moment to moment the gold encroached. They rode rapidly in the freshness of the morning, by wood and field and stream, so rapidly that it was hardly nine when they passed a brick house with pillars set on a hill-top in a grove of oaks. Rand looked at it fixedly as he rode by. Malplaquet was a Cary place, and it had an air of Greenwood.

Three miles further on, sunk in elder and pokeberry and shaded by a ragged willow, there appeared a wayside forge. The blacksmith was at work, and the clink, clink of iron made a cheerful sound. Rand drew rein. "Good-morning, Jack Forrest. Have a look, will you, at this shoe of Selim's."

The smith stooped and looked. "I'll give him a new one in a twinkling, Mr. Rand! From Richmond, sir?"

"Yes; from Richmond."

"Burr got off, didn't he? If the jury'd been from this county, we'd have hanged him sure! Splitting the country into kindling wood, and stirring up a yellow jacket's nest of Spaniards, and corrupting honest men! If they won't hang him, then tar and feathers, say I! Soh, Selim! You've been riding hard, sir."

"Yes. I wanted to be at home."

" 'T is mortal weather. When September's hot, it lays over July. We'll have a storm this afternoon, I'm thinking. There's a deal of travel despite the heat, and I'm not complaining of business. Mr. Cary of Greenwood is just ahead of you. There, sir, that's done!"

The smith arose, patted Selim on the shoulder, and stood back. "You've got a fine horse, Mr. Rand, and that's certain. By Meteor, ain't he, out of Fatima?"

"Yes. Which of the Carys did you say —"

"Ludwell Cary. He came from Malplaquet and rode by an hour ago. The other passed yesterday —"

"Did Mr. Cary say which road he would take at the ford?"

"No, he did n't. The main road, though, I reckon. The river road's bad just now, and he seemed to have time before him. Thankee, Mr. Rand, and good-day to you!"

Followed by Young Isham, Rand travelled on by the dusty road, between the parching elder and ironweed, blackberry and love vine. There was dust upon the wayside cedars, and the many locust trees let fall their small yellow leaves. As the sun mounted the heat increased, and with it the interminable, monotonous, and trying *zirr, zirr*, of the underworld on blade and bush. He rode with a dark face, and with lines of anger between his brows. It had come to him like a chance spark to a mine that Ludwell Cary was not at Greenwood, was yet upon the road before him. He knew day and hour when the other had left Richmond, and there had been more than time to make his journey.

Before him, on the lower ground, a belt of high and deep woods proclaimed a watercourse, and he presently arrived beside a shrunken stream. Here was a mill, and the miller and a man or two were apparent in the doorway. The ford lay a hundred yards beyond, and on the far side of the stream the river road and the main road branched. Travellers paused as a matter of course to give and take the time of day, and now the miller, dusty and white, came out into the road. "Morning, morning, Mr. Rand! From Richmond, sir? So we could n't hang Aaron Burr, after all. Well, he ought to have been, that's all I've got to say!"

"Give me a gourd of water, will you, Bates? This dust is choking."

"'T is that, sir. But we'll have a storm before the day is over. There's a deal of travel just now. Mr. Cary of Greenwood passed a short while ago."

A negro brought a dripping gourd. Rand put it to his lips and drank the cool water. "Which road," he asked, as he gave back the gourd, — "which road did Mr. Cary take? The main road or the river road?"

The miller looked over his shoulder. "Jim and Bob and Shirley, which road did Mr. Cary take?"

"I did n't notice."

"Reckon he took the main road, Bates."

"I was n't looking, but you could hear his horse's hoofs, and that would n't have been so on the river road."

"'T wuz de main road, sah."

Rand and Young Isham went on, down by the mill and along the bank to the clear, brown, shallow ford, crossed, and paused beneath a guide-post upon the crest of the further bank. The trees hid the mill. Before them stretched the main road, to the right dipped between fern and under arching boughs the narrow, broken river road. "If he went this way," said Rand slowly, "I'll go that. Young Isham —"

"Yaas, marster."

"The mare's spent. No need to give her this rough travelling. Take the main road and take it slowly. Let her walk,

THE RIVER ROAD

and when you reach Red Fields, stop and have her fed. I'll go and go fast by the river road."

Master and slave parted, the latter keeping to the sunny thoroughfare, the former plunging into the narrow, heavily shaded track that ran through ravine and over ridge, now beside the water and now in close woods of birch and hemlock. The road was bad, but Selim and his master bent to it grimly, with no nice avoidance of rut or stone or sunken place. To the horse there was before him food and rest, to the man his home. They took at the same pace the much of rough and the little of smooth, and the miles fell behind them. The sun was high, but there were threatening masses of clouds, with now and then a distant roll of thunder. The road was solitary, little used at any time, and to-day as lonely a woodland way as might well be conceived.

Rand rode with closed lips, and with the mark between his brows. Passion was having its way with him, such passion as had lived with him, now drowsing, now fiercely awake, in the days at Richmond between his return from Williamsburgh and the close of the trial. He saw Roselands and Jacqueline beneath the beech tree, but he also saw, and that with more distinctness, the face and form of the man who rode toward Greenwood. He longed for Jacqueline, but he had not forgiven her. He knew that he would when he saw her face — would forgive her with a cry for the waste of the hot, revengeful days, the sleepless nights, since they had parted. Her face swam before him, between the hemlock boughs, but he was not ready yet to forgive, not yet, not until he got to Roselands and she met him with her wistful eyes! He was not a fool; the Absolute within him knew where lay the need for forgiveness, but it was deeply overlaid with human pride and wrath. He was at the old, old trick of anger with another when the fault was all his own. As for Ludwell Cary —

His hand closed with force upon the bridle and his eyes narrowed. "From the first, from that day upon the Justice's Bench, from that day when we gathered nuts together, I must have hated. Now it is warp and woof, warp and woof!" He touched Selim with the spur. "If there were truly a heaven and truly a hell, and I, in flames myself, saw him in Abraham's bosom, not to escape from that torment would I call to him, 'Once we were neighbours, once it seemed that we might have been friends — come down, come down and help me, Cary!'"

He laughed, a harsh sound that came back from the rock above him. By no means always, far from even often, a hardened or an evil man, to-day the stream of thought was stirred and sullied from every black pool and weedy depth, and there came floating up folly, waste, and sin. His reason slept. Had he, by some Inquisitor not to be disobeyed, been suddenly obliged to give why and wherefore for his hatred, the trained intellect must have agreed with the questioner. "These causes fail of sufficiency." That was true, but the truth was sophistry. He dealt now with the fact that he hated, and in his mind, as he rode at speed along the river road, he did not even review the past which had given birth to this present. He hated, and his hand closed upon the rein within it as though there was there, in addition, another thread.

A hemlock bough brushed violently against his face. He struck it aside, and, coming to the rocky top of a little rise, checked Selim for a moment of the fresher air. It came like a sigh from the darkening clouds. Rand looked out over field and forest to the massed horizon, then shook the reins, and Selim picked his way down the ridge to a woodland bottom through which flowed a stream. Rand heard the ripple of the water. A jutting boulder, crowned by a mountain ash, hid the road before him; he turned it and saw the stream, some yards away, flowing over mossed rocks and beneath a dark fringe of laurel. He saw more than the stream, for a horseman had paused upon the little rocky strand, and, hearing hoofs behind him, had partly turned his own steed. Rand's hand dragged at the bridle-rein and Selim stood still.

For a moment the two men, so suddenly confronted, sat their horses and stared at each other. Between them was a narrow rocky space, about Rand a heavy frame of leaves, behind Cary the clear flowing stream. Above the treetops the mounting clouds were dark, but the sun rode hot and high in a round of unflecked azure. The silence held for a heart-beat, then Rand spoke thickly: "So you, too, took the river road?"

"Yes. It is rough but short. When did you leave Richmond?"

"As soon as I could. You would have been better pleased, would you not, had I never left it? In your opinion, I should be in durance there, laid by the heels with Aaron Burr!"

"You are not yourself, Mr. Rand."

"Do not push innocence upon the board! When did it begin, your deep interest in my concerns? Before the world was made, I think, for always we have been at odds. But this — this especial matter, Ludwell Cary, this began with the letter which you wrote and signed 'Aurelius'!"

"A letter that told the truth, Mr. Rand."

"That is as may be. Telling the truth is at times an occupation full of danger."

"Is it?"

"The nineteenth of February — ah, I have you there! Was it not — was it not a pleasant employment for a snowy night to sit by the fire and learn news of an enemy — news the more piquant for the lips that gave it!"

"You are speaking, sir, both madly and falsely!"

They pressed their horses more closely together. Cary was pale with anger, but upon Rand's face was a curious darkness. Men had seen Gideon look so, and in old Stephen Rand the peculiarity had been marked. When he spoke, it was in a voice that matched his aspect. "Last October in the Charlottesville court room — even that insult was not insult merely, but a trap as well! It is to be acknowledged that yours was the master mind. I walked into your trap."

"That which I did is not to be called a trap. Your ambition enmeshed you then, as your passion blinds you now."

Rand's voice darkened and fell. "Who gave you — who gave you the right of inquisition? What has your soul or your way of thinking to do with mine? You are not my keeper. I would not take salvation at your hands — by God, no! Why should the thought of you lie at the bottom of each day? It shall not lie at the bottom of this one! I do not know where first we met, but now we 'll part. You have laid your finger here and you have laid it there, now take your hand away!"

"Do you well, and I will," said Cary sternly.

The other drew a labouring breath. "Two weeks ago I was in Williamsburgh, in the Apollo, listening in the heat to idle talk — and you in Richmond, you came at her call! You came down the quiet street, and in between the box bushes, and up the steps under the honeysuckle. What did you say to her there in the dusk, by the window? You were a Cary — you were part and parcel of the loved past — you had all the shibboleths — you could comfort, commiserate, and counsel! Ha! I wish I might have heard. 'Aurelius' dealing with the forsworn and the absent! 'Here the blot, and there the stain, and yon a rent that's hard to mend. If there's salvation, I see it not at present.' So you resolved

CARY SAW AND FLUNG OUT HIS ARM, SWERVING HIS HORSE,
BUT TOO LATE

THE RIVER ROAD

all her doubts, and laid within her hand every link of a long chain. You have my thanks."

"I will not," said Cary, after a silence, — "I will not be moved by you now, and I will not talk with you now. You are beside yourself. I will say good-day to you, Mr. Rand, and in a less passionate hour I will tell you that you have judged me wrongly."

He gathered up his reins and slightly turned his horse. It had been wiser to break into violent speech, or even to deal the other a blow. As it was, the very restraint of his action was spark to gunpowder. Rand's hand fell to a holster, drew and raised a pistol. Cary saw and flung out his arm, swerving his horse, but too late. There was a flash and a report. The reins dropped from Cary's grasp; he sank forward upon his horse's neck, then, while the terrified animal reared and plunged, fell heavily to earth and lay beside the stream with a ball through his heart.

CHAPTER XXX

HOMEWARD

THE frightened birds rose in numbers from the forest trees. Cary's horse, with a snort of terror, reared and turned. Rand flung himself from Selim and dashed forward to the black's bridle, but he was too late. The horse clattered down the little strand, plunged into the flashing water, and in another moment reached the opposite bank and tore away along the river road.

The sound of hoofs died away. All sound seemed to die, that of the stream, of the birds, of the air in the trees. It was as still as the desert. Very quietly and subtly the outward world put itself in accord with the inward; never again would sky or earth, tree or leaf or crystal water, be what it was an hour ago. Life and the scenery of life had a new aspect.

The murderer moved to the side of the murdered, knelt stiffly, and laid his hand upon the heart. It, too, was still. Rand stood up. The pistol was yet in his clasp; he swung his arm above his head and hurled the weapon into the stream. A pace or two away was a smooth and rounded rock like a giant pebble. He sat down upon it, locked his hands, and looked about him. The sky was blue, the leaves were green, the sun shone hot, the water was at its ancient song — whence, then, came the noxious change, and what was the matter with the universe? Cary lay among the stones, with head thrown back and one arm stretched out as though the hand were pointing. The face was quiet, set in the icy beauty of death, and young. There came a roll of thunder. Rand looked at his clasped hands, opened them, and moved the right one slightly to and fro. There was blood upon his coat-sleeve — a great smear. He drew a sighing breath. He felt as a voyager might who awakened on a planet not his own and at midnight saw the faint star where once he lived. As yet the wonder numbed. The complete cessation of anger, too, was confusing. There was only the plane of existence, grey and featureless. This lasted some moments, then the lights began to play.

He rose from the stone and, going to the water's edge, knelt and tried to wash the blood from his sleeve, but without success. He stood up with a frown. The clouds were high above the treetops, though the sun yet shone. At a little distance Selim was quietly grazing, the birds had returned to their song, the squirrels to their play along the leafy boughs. Rand looked at his watch. "Twelve o'clock — twelve o'clock." Suddenly a thought struck him. "The pistol, with my name engraved on it —"

He had flung the weapon far into the water. The stream was hardly more than a wide brook, but its bed was broken, and above and below the little ford the water fell over ledges into small, deep pools. Where had the pistol fallen? If into one of these, he could not find it again. He had no time to sound them one by one. He moved along the bank, his keen eyes searching the water. The pistol was nowhere visible; it must have gone into midstream, into a pool below a cascade. If so, it might lie there, undiscovered, a thousand years. He stood irresolute. Could he have done so, he would have dragged the stream, but there was now no time to squander. Once more he made certain that it lay nowhere in clear water or near the shore, then abruptly left the search.

He stood in thought for another moment, then with deliberation moved to his victim's side and looked down upon him with a face almost as blank and still as the dead man's own.

Presently he spoke: "Good-bye, Cary." The sound of his own voice, strained and strange, hardly raised above a whisper and yet, in the silence of this new world, more loud than thunder, broke the spell. He uttered a strangled cry, dashed up the strand to the grazing horse, flung himself into the saddle, and applied the spur.

He and Selim did not cross the stream. His mind worked automatically, but it was a trained mind, and knew what the emergency demanded. He retraced the river road to a point beyond the rock and the mountain ash, and there left it. Once in the burned herbage under the trees, he looked back to the road. There was rock and there was black leaf-mould. If in the latter any hoof-prints showed confusedly, the coming storm held promise of a pelting and obliterating rain. He pushed into a thick-set wood, and began a desperate ride across country. It was necessary to strike the main road below Red Fields.

Their way was now dangerous enough, but he and Selim made no stay for that. They went at speed over stock and stone, between resinous pines, through sumach and sassafras. Lightnings were beginning to play, and the thunder to roll more loudly. The sunbeams were gone, the trees without motion, the air hot and laden. Horse and man panted on. Rand's mind made swift calculation. He had ordered Young Isham to walk the mare. For all that time had seemed to stop, there at the stream behind him, the minutes were no longer than other minutes, and there had passed of them no great number. He had ridden from the ford to the stream at speed, and now he was going as rapidly. He would presently reach the main road, and Young Isham would not have passed.

It fell as he had foreseen. One last burst through brush and vine and scrub and they reached the edge of the wood.

Before them through the trees he saw the main road. Rand checked the horse. "Stand a bit, Selim, while I play the scout."

Dismounting, he moved with caution through a mass of dogwood and laurel to the bank. At a distance beneath him lay the road, bare under the storm clouds. Above and below where he stood it was visible for some rods, and upon it appeared neither man nor beast. He went back to Selim, mounted, and together they made shift to descend the red bank. As, with a noise of breaking twigs and falling earth and stone, they reached the road, a man, hitherto hidden by the giant bole of the oak beneath which he had sat down to rest, rose and came round his tree to see what made the commotion. Between the cause and the investigator was perhaps fifty feet of road. Rand muttered an oath, then, with a characteristic cool resolve, rode up to M. Achille Pincornet and wished him good-day.

"Good-day, Mr. Rand," echoed the dancing master, and stared at the bank. "Parbleu, sir! Why did you come that way?"

"I left my servant a little way down the road and struck into the woods after a doe I started. I'll gallop back and meet him now. Are you for Charlottesville, Mr. Pincornet?"

"Not to-day, sir. I have a dancing class at Red Fields." Mr. Pincornet still stared. "I would say, sir, that the chase had been long and hard."

Rand laughed. "Am I so torn and breathless? No, no; it was short but rough — a few minutes and perhaps half a mile! Well, I will rejoin my negro and we'll make for town before the storm breaks."

"Wait here and your negro will come to you."

"Mahomet to the mountain? No; he is a sleepy-head, and I shall find him loitering. Good-day, good-day!"

With a wave of his hand he left the dancing master still staring and turned Selim's head to the east. He rode quickly, but no longer headlong, and he scanned with deliberation the long stretch of the main road. When at last he saw that which he sought, he backed his horse into the shadow of a great wayside walnut, drew rein, and awaited Young Isham's approach.

The boy and the mare came steadily on, moving at quickened speed under the lowering skies. Young Isham did not see his master until he was almost beneath the walnut tree; when he did so, he uttered a cry and well-nigh fell from the mare.

"Gawd-a-moughty, marster!"

Rand spoke without moving. "Get down, Young Isham, and come here."

The negro obeyed, though with shaking knees. "Lawd hab mercy, marster, whar you come f'om? I done lef' you at de ford."

"I'll speak to you of that presently. Whom have you passed on the road since you left the ford? How many people and what kind of people? Think now."

"I ain' pass skeerce a soul, sah. Eberybody skurryin' in f'om de storm. Jes' some niggahs wid mules, an' a passel ob chillern, an' a man I don' know. Dey ain' stop ter speak ter me, an I ain' stop ter speak ter dem."

Rand leaned from his saddle and laid the butt of his riding-whip upon the boy's shoulder. "Look at me, Young Isham."

"Yaas, marster."

"You did not leave me at the ford. We took the main road together, and we've been travelling together ever since, except that perhaps ten minutes ago I rode on ahead and waited for you beneath this tree." He raised the whip handle and brought it down heavily. "Look at me, Young Isham, — in the eyes."

The boy whimpered. "Yaas, marster."

"We crossed the ford at the mill."

"Yaas, marster."

"And we kept on together by the main road."

"We — Yaas, marster."

"We have travelled together all the way from Richmond, and we have travelled by the main road. Now say what I have said."

"Marster —"

"Say it!"

"Don', marster, don'! I'll say jes' what you say! We done cross de ford an' tek de main road —"

"Yes."

"An' we done keep de main road, jes' lak dis."

"That's enough. If you forget and say the wrong thing, Young Isham, —"

"Don', marster! Fer de Lawd's sake, don' look at me lak dat! I ain' gwine fergit, sah, — de Lawd Jesus know I ain'!"

Rand lifted the whip handle from his shoulder. "Mount, then, and come on. There's no good in idling here."

A few moments later they overtook and passed Mr. Pincornet, now briskly walking, kit under arm, toward his dancing class. They bowed in passing, and Rand, turning in his saddle, looked back at the figure in faded finery. "There's danger there," he thought. "Where isn't it now?" As he faced again toward Charlottesville, his glance fell upon Young Isham, and he saw that the boy was looking fixedly at his sleeve.

The master made no movement of avoidance. "The mare's going well enough," he said quietly. "We'll draw rein at Red Fields, and then hurry home. Use your whip and bring her on."

They paused at Red Fields, then went on to the edge of town. The forked lightnings were playing and the trees beginning to sway. "We'll stop a moment," Rand said over his shoulder, "at Mr. Mocket's."

Door and window of the small house where Tom and Vinie lived were shut against the storm. Tom was yet in Richmond, and Vinie was afraid of lightning. In the darkened atmosphere the zinnias and marigolds up and down the path struck a brave note of red and yellow. The grapevine on the porch was laden with purple bunches that the rising wind bade fair to break and scatter. Rand dismounted, with a gesture bidding the boy to await him, entered the broken gate, and, walking up the path between the marigolds, knocked upon the closed door.

There was a sound within as of some one rising hastily, an exclamation, and Vinie opened the door. "I knew 't was you! I just said to myself, 'That ith Mr. Rand's knock,' and it was! Wait, thir, and I'll make the room light."

She threw open the closed shutters. "I'm jutht afraid of lightning when I'm by myself. How are you, thir?"

"Very well. Vinie, I want a basin of warm water and soap."

"Yeth, thir. The kettle's on. I'll fix it in Tom's room."

In the bare little chamber Rand washed the blood from his coat-sleeve. It was not easy to do, but at last the cloth was clean. He came out of the room with the basin in his hands. Vinie, waiting in the little hall, started forward. "Open the back door," he said, "and let me throw this out." Vinie tried to take the basin. "I'll empty it, thir." Her eyes fell upon the water. "You've hurt yourself!"

"No," answered Rand. "I have not. It is nothing — a bit of a cut that I gave myself."

He pushed the door open and poured out the stained water upon the ground, then took fresh from a bucket standing by and rinsed the basin before he set it down upon the table. "Vinie —"

"Yeth, thir."

"I want a promise from you."

"Yeth, Mr. Rand."

"You've always been my good friend, ever since long ago when you came from the little house in Richmond to this little house in Charlottesville, and I was reading law with Mr. Henning. Why, I don't know what I should do without you and Tom!"

Vinie's eyes filled. "I could n't — Tom and me could n't — do without you, Mr. Rand. You're our best friend, and we'd die for you, and you know it. I'll promise you anything, and I'll keep my promise."

"I know that you will. It's nothing more than this. Vinie, I don't want it known that I stopped here to-day, and I want you to forget — look at me, Vinie."

"Yeth, thir."

"I want you to forget what I asked you for, and what I did in Tom's room."

"Yeth, thir," said Vinie, with large eyes. "And that you cut yourself?"

"That, too. Everything, Vinie, except that, coming along the main road, I stopped a moment at the gate to say how d'ye do, and to tell you that Tom would be at home in two or three days. That is all, and my coming into the house and the rest of it never was. Do you understand?"

"I won't say anything at all, thir."

"It's a promise?"

"Yeth, thir. I promise."

They went out into the porch together. "Ith n't there anything else?"

Rand, studying in silence the clouds and the whirling dust, had started down the step or two to the path between the marigolds. He paused. "I can't think of anything, Vinie"; then, after a moment, and very oddly, "Would you give me, once more, a cup of cool water?"

Vinie brought it in her hand. "You always thaid this water washed the dust off clean."

Rand drank, and gave back the cup. "Thank you. I'll go on now. How your vine has borne this year!"

"Yeth. I'm going to make some wine this week. Good-bye."

Her visitor passed through the little yard, between the vivid flowers. At the gate he turned his head. "Tom is really coming, Vinie, in two or three days."

"Yeth, thir," said Vinie. "I'll be mighty glad to see him."

Rand mounted, and he and Young Isham rode away. Vinie stood upon the porch and watched them as far as the turn in the road. A gust of hot wind blew against her, ruffling her calico dress and lifting light tendrils of hair from her forehead and neck. In the southwest the lightning flashed fiercely and there came a crash of thunder. Vinie uttered a startled cry, clapped her hands to her ears, and ran into the house.

Rand rode through a portion of the main street of Charlottesville. He kept the pace of a man who wishes to be at home before the rain falls, but his manner of going showed no undue haste and no trepidation. Faces at doors and windows, men gathered before the Eagle and the post-office, greeted him. He answered each salute in kind, and at the Eagle drew rein long enough to reply to the inevitable questions as to Richmond and the trial, and to agree that the rain was needed, since the main road, from Bates's Mill on, was nothing but a trough of dust.

"That's so," chimed in one. "If it was n't so rough, the river road would be pleasanter travelling. There's the first drop!"

Rand looked up at the clouds. "I'll gallop on, gentlemen. A rain is coming that will lay the dust."

Once upon the road to Roselands, neither horse nor mare was spared. Rand travelled at speed beneath an inky sky. At the turn to Greenwood he looked once toward the distant house, half hidden by mighty oaks. It was no more than once. He had a vision of a riderless horse, tearing away from a stream, through the woods, and he thought, "How soon?" He drew a difficult breath, and he put for a moment his hand before his eyes, then spurred Selim on, and in a little while came within sight of his own gates.

CHAPTER XXXI

HUSBAND AND WIFE

AS he rode up the drive, he saw Jacqueline waiting for him, a gleam of white upon the grey doorstone, beyond the wind-tossed beech. He dismounted, sent Young Isham around with the horses, and walked across the burned grass. She met him with outstretched arms, beneath the beech tree. "Lewis, Lewis!"

He held her to him, bent back her face, kissed her brow and eyes and mouth. There was a wild energy in clasp and touch. "You love me still?" he cried. "That's true — that's true, Jacqueline?"

"You know — you know it's true! I was born only to love you — and I thought that you would never come!"

The thunder crashed above them, and the advance of the rain was heard upon the beech leaves. "Come indoors — come out of the storm!" She drew his hand that she held to her and laid it on her bosom. "Oh, welcome home, my dear!"

They went together into the house and into their own chamber. The windows were dark with the now furious rain, but a light fire burned upon the hearth. Rand stood looking down upon it. His wife watched him, her arms resting upon the back of a great flowered chair. Suddenly she spoke. "Lewis, what is the matter?"

He half turned toward her. "I believed that you would see. And yet you were blind to that earlier course of mine."

"Something dreadful is the matter. Tell me at once."

After a moment he repeated sombrely, "'At once.' How

can I tell you at once? There are things that are slowly brought about by all time, and to show them as they truly are would require all time again. How can I tell you at all? My God!"

"I feel," she answered, "years older than I did two weeks ago. If there was something then to forgive, I have forgiven it. Our souls did not come together to share only the lit paths, the honey in the cup. Tell me, Lewis."

"It is black and bitter — there is no light, and it will kill the sweetness. If I could live with you and you never know it, I would try to do so — try to keep it secret from you as I did that lesser thing. I cannot — even now, without a word, you know in part."

"Tell me all — *that lesser thing.*"

Rand turned from the fire and, coming to the great chair against whose back she leaned, knelt in its flowered lap and bowed his forehead upon her hands. "I am glad," he said, in a voice so low that she bent to hear it, — "I am glad now that I have no son."

There was a silence while the rain dashed against the window-panes and the thunder rolled overhead; then Jacqueline pressed her cheek against his bowed head. "What have you done?" she whispered. "Tell me — oh, tell me!"

After a moment he told her. "I have killed a man."

"Killed — It was by accident!"

"No. It was not accident. I came upon him by accident — I'll claim no more than that. The black rage was there to blind me, make me deaf — mole and adder! But it was not accident, what I did. I'll not cheat you here, and I'll not cheat myself. The name of it is murder."

He felt her hands quiver beneath his forehead, and he put up his own and clasped her wrist. "Are you thinking, 'I should have left him in the tobacco-fields'? As for me,

I know that I ought never to have spoken to you there beneath the apple tree."

"Lewis, who was the man?"

He made no answer, and after a moment or two, numbed and grey, had passed, she needed none. The truth fell like a stroke from glowing iron. With a cry she dragged her hands from Rand's, left the chair, and, crossing the room, flung herself down beside the chintz-covered couch and cowered there with a hidden face. Rand arose and, walking to the window, stared at the veil of rain and the stabbing lightning. The clock ticked, a log upon the hearth parted with a soft sound, from the back of the house came faintly the homely cheer of the servants' voices. How deadly, how solemnly still, how wet and cold, was now a rocky strand upon the river road! He left the window and, coming to the couch, looked down upon the crouching figure of his wife. His brain was not numbed; it was pitilessly awake, and he suffered. The name of his star was Wormwood.

At last she stirred, lifted her head from her arm, and arose, moving stiffly and slowly as though she had grown old. Her face was drawn and colorless. She moved, mechanically, to the fire, laid fresh wood upon it, and, taking a small broom from the corner, made the hearth clean; then, returning, sat down upon the couch that was printed with bright roses and held out her hands. "Come," she said, in her low, musical voice. "Come, tell me —"

He sank upon his knees beside her and bowed his head upon her lap. "Jacqueline, Jacqueline! I rode away from Richmond, in black anger —"

He told her all, now speaking with a forced and hard deliberation, now with a broken and strangled voice, short words and short sentences — at the last, monosyllables.

When the tale was done, they stayed for a little, motionless.

HUSBAND AND WIFE

There was yet bright lightning with long peals of thunder, and the rain beat with passion against the panes. Jacqueline moistened her lips, tried to speak, at last found a broken and uncertain voice. "You left him — lying there?"

"The horse broke away — ran on through the wood. It will have been caught ere now, or it will make its way to Greenwood. Is Fairfax Cary at home?"

"He came last night. He was at Fontenoy this morning."

Rand stood up. "It is done, and all the rueing in the world will not make the breath alight again." With a gesture, singular and decided, he walked to the window and again looked out at the rain and lightning. "If I know — if I know Fairfax Cary — Has the horse been captured — and where? It may be known now, and it may not be known for hours." He stood, reviewing chances, and the shaken soul began to settle to its ancient base. At last he turned. "There's danger enough, but the struggle must be made. If you love me still, I'll find the heart to make it; ay, and to succeed!" Coming back to her, he took her in his arms. "You do love me? That is n't dead?"

"I love you, Lewis."

"Then, by God, I'll fight it out! Jacqueline, Jacqueline —"

She presently freed herself. "What are you going to do — what are you going to do now, Lewis?"

"I will tell you what I have done, and where the danger's greatest —"

"The danger?"

"The danger of discovery."

"Lewis — will you not tell them?"

"Tell them —"

"Is it not — oh, Lewis, is it not the only thing to do? Sin and suffering — yes, yes, the whole world sins and suffers! But oh, ignoble to sin and to reject the suffering!"

He stared at her incredulously. "Do you know, Jacqueline, — do you know what you are saying?"

"Will it be so hard?" she asked, and put out her arms to him. "It is right."

"Let me understand," he said. "When the mist cleared and I saw him lying there, I sat down upon a stone, and I said to myself, 'This is a strange land, and I am to eat the fruits thereof.' For a while I did not think of moving. You would have had me stay there as he stayed, watch there beside him until men came?"

She answered almost inaudibly, "It had been nobler."

"And then and there to have given myself up?"

"Lewis, if it was right — I would have said to God and the world and him, 'It is the least that I can do!'"

He stared at her. "By God, the *amende honorable!*"

There came blinding lightning, followed by thunder which seemed to shake the room. Rand crossed to the hearth and, with his booted foot upon the iron dogs, rested his arm upon the mantel-shelf and his head upon his hand. "I'll think of that awhile," he said harshly. "That means disgrace and may mean death."

He heard the drawing of her breath. There was a knock at the door followed by Mammy Chloe's voice. "De bread an' meat an' wine on de table, marster."

"Very well, Mammy, I'll come presently," the master answered; then, when she was gone, "This is the earth, Jacqueline. It was long while I sat there upon the stone and saw matters as they might be upon another plane, but that appearance passed. Because for those moments I saw its shape, I know the aspect that is before your eyes. But it is not reality that you see; it is an appearance, thin and unsubstantial as the mist upon the hills. Expiation, purgation, aided retribution, the criminal to spare Justice the search, and the offender against Society to turn and throw his weight into the proper scale! — that is a dream of the world as it may become. This is the present earth, — earth of the tobacco-fields, earth of the struggle, earth of the fight for standing-room! I have fought — and I have fought — I cannot cease to fight."

With his foot he pushed back the burning wood. "I did not kill him in self-defence. I killed him in anger. That is murder. Say, for argument, that it is confessed murder. I will tell you, as a lawyer, what that means. It means a full stop. Life stopped, work stopped, fame stopped — a period black as ink, and never to be erased! A stop deep as the grave and sharp as the hangman's drop, and the record that it closes empty, vile, read at the best with horror and pity, read at the worst with a glance aside at every man and woman whom the stained hand had ever touched! That is what would come if I followed this appearance." He struck the hand at which he looked against the mantel-shelf. "And if he says, 'Ay, Lewis Rand, it is so that I would do,' I will answer, 'Yes! being you! — but what, Ludwell Cary, had you lain in my cradle?'" His face worked and he turned from the mantel to the great chair. "Oh, *mother!*" he said beneath his breath.

Jacqueline came and knelt beside him. "Lewis, Lewis, is it all so dark?"

He touched her hair with his fingers. "Dark! I feel as though I were in a bare, light place. Underground, you know, but bare and flooded with light. Well, Jacqueline, well —"

She clung to him without speech, and he went on. "There is enough to create suspicion. We were travelling at the same hour, and it is known that we were opponents. The crossroads where I slept last night — there was nothing,

I think, said at the inn. Then the forge, and the mill. At the mill they will swear to telling me that he took the main road, and since they could not see the ford, they must suppose that I, too, went that way. The main road. There's the insistence. I kept to the main road. As for Young Isham, I can manage him. That old Frenchman is more difficult. Danger there — unless he holds his tongue. There's a witness indeed lying at the bottom of some pool below the strand, but the strand may sink into the sea before that witness is found! There is this and there is that, but they'll serve no warrant on the this and that the world can see. I have won more difficult cases."

"You propose," she cried, "to lie — and lie — and lie!"

After a moment he answered, with bitterness, "I am not unreasonable. I do not match white with black. The dyer's hand accepts the hue it works in. I'll not win rest, forgiveness, sleep! But, by God, I'll keep what men care for. I'll keep strength and reputation, name, and room to work a lever in! Ay, and I'll not endure the world to say, 'This was his friend, and that his lover; look how they are stained!' O God, O God!"

She put her arms around him. "There is no stain! I will forever love you. Love casts off soil as it casts out fear. Will you not come with me — and tell them?"

He sat for some minutes, still in her clasp, then, leaning forward, took her face in his hands and kissed her on the brow. "No!" he said, with finality.

Another moment and he arose. "I am hungry. I have not eaten since daybreak. As for sleep — I don't know when I slept. It is not only the darkness of the storm; it is growing late. I think that we will hear nothing to-night. We will sleep, and I need it." He moved to a table and took up the pair of holsters which, on entering, he had laid there

In a corner of the room stood a heavy chest of drawers. He placed the holsters in one of these, locked the drawer, and withdrew the key. "I'll think that out," he muttered, "just as soon as may be," then turned again to his wife. "I'll go now and get some meat and wine. Stay here by the fire, Jacqueline, and try to see that all this must be fought, and fought as I have said! Think of yourself, and think of Deb, Unity, your uncles — at last you will come to see that there is no other way."

He was gone. Jacqueline dragged herself from the chair to the hearth, sank down before the glowing logs, and saw at once a picture of the river road.

She had been lying throughout the night almost without motion, but toward three o'clock he was aware that she had left the bed. A moment, and he heard the tap of her slippers across the polished floor of the chamber, the hall, and the dining-room. She paused, he could tell, at the sideboard; when, presently, she slipped again into bed, she was trembling violently. He turned and put his arms about her. "I am so cold," she said. "It is cold indoors and out-of-doors."

"I have brought you misery," he answered, and then lay in silence.

They heard the clock ticking, and the sighing of the branches after the storm. For awhile she was quiet within his clasp, then the shuddering recommenced. He arose, put on his dressing-gown, and, going to the fireplace where the logs yet smouldered, threw on light wood and built a cheerful fire, then took her in his arms and carried her to the great chair of flowered chintz, set in the light of the dancing flames. "The wine will warm you. Look, too, what a fire I have made!"

She still shuddered, staring over her shoulder. "Draw

the blinds closer. There's a sound as of some one sighing."

"It is the wind in the beech leaves."

She put an arm across her eyes. "How long is he to lie there, stretched out upon the wet rocks, beside the stream? Oh, heartless!"

"The storm and darkness have made it long. He will be found this morning."

"He never was your enemy, Lewis. You thought him that, but he never was, he never was!"

"I want to tell you," he said, "that all rage is dead. I feel as though I had left anger far behind, and why there was in my mind so great venom and rancour I no longer know. Envy and jealousy, too, are gone. They have been struck out of life, and other things have come to take their place."

"Ay," she cried, "what other things! O God, O God!"

There was a long silence, while the wind sighed in the beech tree and the fire muttered on the hearth. Jacqueline sat in the flowered chair, her raised arms resting upon its back, her head buried in her arms. Rand, leaning against the mantel, gazed with sombre eyes at her strained and motionless form. As he stood there, his mind began to move through the galleries where she was painted. He saw her, a child, beneath the apple tree, and in her blue gown that day in the Fontenoy garden, and then again beneath the apple tree, a child no longer, but the woman whom he loved. He saw her face above him the afternoon they laid him in the blue room, and he saw her singing to her harp in the Fontenoy drawing-room, —

"The thirst that from the soul doth rise — "

He saw the next morning — the summer-house, the box, the mockingbird in the poplar tree, the Seven Sisters rose —

and then their marriage eve, and that fair first summer on the Three-Notched Road, and all the three years of their wedded life. The picture of her was everywhere, and not least in the house on Shockoe Hill. He saw her as she had been one snowy evening in February, and he saw her as she had looked the hour of his return from Williamsburgh — the pleading, the passion, and the beauty. And now — now —

The wind sighed again without the windows, and Jacqueline drew a shuddering breath. He spoke. "Jacqueline!"

She moved slightly. "Yes, Lewis."

"The night is quiet, after the storm. He lies at rest beside the stream. This morning he will be found, lifted tenderly, lamented, mourned. It is not a gruesome place. I remember trees and fluttering birds. He sleeps — he sleeps — like Duncan he sleeps well at last. Is he to be so pitied?"

She moaned, "Yes — but you also, you also! Oh, break, break!"

"Listen, Jacqueline. It lacks but an hour of dawn. When it is day, you may give me up. Rouse Joab and send for the sheriff and your uncles and for Fairfax Cary. I will dress and await them in the library. Indeed, you may do it now — there's no need to wait for dawn."

She rose from her chair and went the length of the room, resting at last, with raised arms and covered face, against the farthest window. He spoke on. "If all thought alike, Jacqueline, if all saw action and consequence with one vision — but we do not so, no, not on this earth! You and I are sundered there. Perhaps it is to my shame that it is so, — I cannot tell. What you asked for this afternoon, that confession, that decision, that accord with justice and acceptance of penalty, I cannot give freely and of conviction, Jacqueline. Why did you think I had that exaltation of mind? I have it not; no, nor one man in five hundred thousand! The man I — murdered — perhaps possessed it; indeed, I think that he did. But I — I do not own it, nor can I see matters with another's vision. I see a struggle to prevent disgrace and disaster, to retrieve and hold an endangered standing-room — a struggle determined and legitimate. I am capable of making it. But though I'll avow that another man's vision transcends mine, I'll dispute with him the power of loving! I love you with a passion as deep, strong, and abiding as if I, too, walked in that rarer air. I am of the earth and rooted in the earth, but I love you utterly. If you want this thing, I will give it to you. It was unmanly of me to say but now, 'You may do this, you may do that, and I will not lift a finger to prevent you.' I will not leave it to you, Jacqueline. I will awaken Joab and send him with a note to your uncles."

He moved toward the door, but before he could reach it his wife was before him, her weight thrown against him, her raised hands thrusting him back to the hearth. She shook her head, and her long hair shadowed her; she strove for utterance, but could find only a strangled "No — no"; then, still clinging to him, she slipped to her knees and so to her face, and lay there in a swoon in the red zone of the firelight.

CHAPTER XXXII

THE BROTHERS

AT Fontenoy the deluging rain and pitchy blackness of the night sufficiently warranted Colonel Dick's assertion that it was an evening for a sensible man to stay where he was, and that a bowl of punch and wedding-talk and Unity at the harpsichord were to be preferred to a progress to Greenwood through such a downpour and a foot of mud. Ludwell!— Ludwell would n't be there anyway. He was a man of sense and would be sleeping at Red Fields, if indeed he had ever left Malplaquet. Fairfax Cary was persuaded, and after a very happy evening in the drawing-room, went to bed and to sleep in the blue room.

Dressing, next morning, he gazed around him. The room was familiar to him, and he had a liking for it, from the mandarin on the screen to General Washington on the wall. The storm had passed away early in the night, and it was now a lovely morning, clear-washed, fresh, and fragrant. He looked out of the window toward the blue hills, and down into the garden where autumn flowers were in bloom, and as he dressed he hummed an air that Unity had sung.

> " Give me pleasure, give me pain,
> Give me wine of life again !
> Death is night without a morn,
> Give the rose and give the thorn."

Downstairs he found Miss Dandridge and Major Edward upon the wide porch. The wind had torn away a great bough from one of the poplars, and Colonel Dick and Deb upon the drive below were superintending its removal. Birds were singing, delicate airs astir. "It's going to be the divinest day!" said Unity, and led the way to the dining-room.

Breakfast went happily on with talk of politics, county affairs, and now and then from Colonel Dick a sly allusion to the approaching marriage. The meal was nearly over when old Cato, coming in from the hall, said something in a low voice to his master. Colonel Churchill pushed back his chair. "Excuse me a moment, Unity, my dear. There's a man wants to see me."

He left the room. Fairfax Cary and Major Edward continued a discussion of the latest Napoleonic victory; Unity played with her spoon and thought of her wedding-gown; Deb drank her glass of milk and planned a visit with Miranda to a blasted pine tree, lived in, all the quarter agreed, by a ha'nt that came out at night, like a ring of smoke out of a great black pipe!

Colonel Dick's figure appeared for an instant in the doorway. "Edward, come here a moment, will you?"

"A thousand hussars, and the thing went off like flaming tinder," finished Major Edward. He laid down his napkin and arose. "Excuse me, Unity. Very well, Dick," and left the room.

"Unity," enquired Deb. "Are there any ha'nts?"

"No, honey, no!"

"Just make believe?"

"Just make believe."

"Oh!" exclaimed Deb, and fell to wondering if the ha'nt would come out if only she and Miranda sat long enough before the tree. It might get hungry.

"Will you have another cup?" asked Unity of the guest, her hand upon the coffee-urn. "No? Then let us go and see what is the matter. They are not coming back."

"I want," whispered Fairfax Cary, as they left the table,

"to talk to you about — about two weeks from now. Don't you think it would be sweet and shady this morning, under the catalpa tree?"

He managed to touch her hand, and she turned her velvety eyes upon him with both laughter and moisture in their black depths. "I've chosen the place for Unity Dandridge's grave. Would you like to see it? It's underneath the flowering almond."

Fairfax Cary glanced behind him. The servants were out of the room; Deb was gathering crumbs for the birds. "Give me one kiss! If you knew how much I love you! The world's tuned to-day just to that."

"Such an old tune! The world has other things to think of and other airs than that!"

They went out into the hall. It was empty, but through the open doors voices sounded from the porch at the back of the house. Another moment and Major Edward appeared, stood still at the sight of Cary, then came on up the hall to meet the two. He looked intensely grey and meagre, and his thin lips twitched. "Fairfax," he said, — "Fairfax, look here —"

The other, who had been laughing, grew suddenly grave. "I have never heard you, sir, use a voice like that. Has anything happened?"

Major Edward made a little noise in his throat, then stiffened himself as if on parade. "There may have been an accident. It looks that way, Fair. It was Eli who came."

"Eli! What has happened at Greenwood? Ludwell's home?"

"Unity, my dear," said the Major, "let him come with me. Let's go into the library, Fair."

But Fairfax Cary was halfway down the hall. The Major hastened after him, and at the porch door laid a thin old hand upon the other's arm. "Fair, my boy, you are going to need all a man's courage. Think of Dick and me as of Fauquier Cary's — as of your father's — old, old friends. Come, now."

They found on the square porch at the back of the house, Colonel Churchill, the negro Eli, and a white man, roughly dressed. The first, seated on the steps, his elbows on his knees and his face in his hands, looked up with a gasp. "Fair, Fair —"

Cary spoke with steadiness. "What has brought you here, Eli? Mr. Ludwell came home last night?"

Eli, trembling violently, and of the ashen hue that a negro takes in terror, tried to answer, but at first there came only jabbered and meaningless words. He fell on his knees, and finally became coherent. "Marse Fair — Marse Fair — ain' I done lif' you bofe in dese ahms w'en you wuz jes' little fellers — he er lot de oldes' an' you nuttin' but er baby, toddlin' after him eberywhar he went! Ain' I done ride behin' you bofe dese yeahs an' yeahs? Oh, Gawd-a-moughty! O Lawd, hab mercy —"

Cary took him by the shoulder. "Eli, stop that crying out and tell me at once what is the matter! What has happened to Mr. Ludwell?"

"I'll tell you, Fair," answered the Major, in a shaking voice. "The negro can't do it. Ludwell did not come home last night, and this morning James Wilson, here, found Saladin —"

"Far up the river road, near my house," said the man upon the steps. "'T was just about daybreak. I didn't know, sir, whose horse he was, so I put him in my stable. Then my son and me and Joe White, a neighbour of mine, we set out down the river road."

"Oh, *my* young marster! Oh, *my* young marster!" wailed Eli. "De kindes' an' de bes'! Oh, Lawd hab mercy!"

"It was just dawn, sir, and we went down the road — we were on horseback — quite a good bit of miles. There was n't any sign until we came to where Indian Run crosses the road; but on the further side, where there's a strip of rocks, you know, sir —"

The speaker stopped short. "They found him there, Fair," finished Major Edward.

The young man turned squarely to the old. "Thank you, sir. You are the man for me. Was he — is he badly hurt?"

"There's nothing can ever hurt him more, my dear. It is you, and we with you, who must suffer now. They found him — they found him dead, Fair."

There was a silence; then, "Ludwell — Ludwell dead?" said Cary. "I don't believe you, Major Churchill."

He turned, walked to a bench that ran along the wall, and sat down. "Eli, get up from there and stop that camp-meeting wailing! Mr. Wilson, you perhaps do not yet know my brother's horse — black with a white star. Colonel Dick, they've got hold of the wrong end of some damned rigmarole or other —"

"I did n't know the horse, sir," replied Wilson, not without gentleness, "for I've been out of the county for a long time, and your brother used to ride a bay. But I knew your brother, sir."

"That's what I said, too, Fair," groaned Colonel Churchill from the steps. "I said it was all a damned mistake. But I was wrong. You listen to Edward. Edward, tell him all!"

"Yes, Dick. It is true, Fair, damnably, devilishly true. He had been dead for hours, Fair."

"Joe White's something of a doctor, sir," put in Wilson. "Joe said he would have been lying there since before the storm."

Fairfax Cary drew a gasping breath. "Lying there, suffering, through the storm and darkness? Thrown? Ill and fallen from his horse? Major Edward, don't play with me!" He started up. "Where is he now?"

"We left him there, sir, just as he was, with Joe White to guard him. My son, he undertook to rouse the nearest people. I happened to know, sir, that the sheriff was staying overnight near Red Fields, and I sent him there first. I told the coroner myself, and then I came as hard as I could ride to Greenwood, where I heard that you were here—"

"It was thought best not to move him at once, Fair. They are intelligent men, and they were right." The Major's hand closed around the other's wrist. "He did not suffer, Fair. He was not thrown. He was shot — shot through the heart!"

"And there, by God," came from the steps Colonel Dick's deep voice, "there, at least, there's something to be done! But oh, my poor boy, my poor boy!"

Unity came from the doorway, took her lover's hands, and pressed them to her lips. "Fair," she whispered, "Fair!"

He kissed her on the forehead. "There, dear! We won't sit under the catalpa tree this morning. Eli! get the horses."

"They have been ordered, Fair," said the Colonel. "We'll go together, you and Edward and I."

The little rocky strand above the stream upon the river road lay half in sun and half in shade. After the storm the air was crystal. Birds sang in the forest trees, and the stream laughed as it slid over ledges into deep pools. The sky was blue, the day brilliant, a cool wind rustled through the laurels, and the wet earth sent out odours of mould and trodden leaf. Perhaps a score of men and boys, engaged in excited talk and in as close a scrutiny of one quiet figure as a line which the sheriff had drawn would permit, turned at the sound of rapid hoofs and watched the Churchills and Fairfax Cary, with Wilson and Eli, come down to the stream.

"Back, all of you, men!" ordered the sheriff, in a low voice. "That is Mr. Fairfax Cary"; then turned to a spectator or two of importance: "Mr. Morris, Mr. Page — I hope you'll be so good as to meet them with me? This is a dreadful thing!"

The Fontenoy party splashed through Indian Run and dismounted. It was not an ungentle people, and the little strand, from the woods to the water, was now free from intruding figures. Only the sheriff, the coroner, and the two planters, old friends and neighbours, remained, and these joined the Churchills. Fairfax Cary walked alone to his brother's side and stood, looking down.

Ludwell Cary lay peacefully. One arm was outstretched, the head a little back, the face quiet, with nothing in it of wrath or fear or pain. The storm had not hurt him. There was little disarray. It was much as though he had thrown himself down there, beside the water, with a sigh for the pleasure of rest. The younger Cary waited motionless for the blood to come back to his heart and the mist before his eyes to clear. It cleared; he saw plainly his brother, guide, and friend, and with a cry he flung himself down and across the body.

The men at the water's edge turned away their faces. The rudest unit of the small throng beneath the trees put up a sudden hand and removed his cap, and his example was followed. It had been a known thing, the comradeship of these brothers, and there were few in the county more loved than the Carys.

Moments passed. The sheriff spoke in a low voice to Mr. Morris, whereupon the latter whispered to Colonel Churchill. "Edward," said the Colonel, "time's being lost. Had n't you better try to get him away?"

Major Edward moved along the bank to the two forms and stood in silence, gazing with twitching lips at the dead man's countenance, so impassive, cold, remote, alien now from all interests of this flesh, quite indifferent to love or to hate, supremely careless as to whether his story were ever told. The Major put his hand to his fierce old eagle eyes, and took it away wet with tears, slow, acrid, and difficult. He stooped and touched the living man. "Fair, — come, Fair!"

The other moved slightly, but did not offer to rise. Major Edward waited, then touched him again. "Fair, we want to mark closely how he lies, and then we want to take him to Greenwood. He has been here long, you know."

His words elicited only a low groan, but presently Cary lifted himself from the body, remained for a moment upon his knees, then rose to his feet. "Yes, to Greenwood," he said. "He lay here last night in the wind and rain, and I was warm and happy — I was asleep and dreaming! Why did I leave him at Elm Tree? If I had been with him—"

His face changed, startlingly. He stooped with rapidity, looked at and touched the dark stain upon the coat, straightened himself, and turned violently upon the Major and the little group which had now approached. "Who?" he demanded in a voice that rose to a hoarse cry. "Who?"

Colonel Churchill answered him. "We don't know, Fair, but by the living God, we'll find out!" and the sheriff, "We've no clue yet, sir, but if 't was plain murder — and it looks that way, for your brother was n't armed — then I reckon the man who did it will as soon find his ease in hell as in old Virginia!"

The farmer who had been first upon the ground spoke from the edge of the group. "I never heard a soul in this county say a hard word of Mr. Cary. I should n't ha' thought, barring politics, that he had an enemy."

"Ha!" said Major Edward, but not loudly.

The sheriff spoke again. "Mr. Fairfax Cary, we've got a kind of litter here, made of branches, and we'd best be going on. The sooner the law has its hand on this, the better. Shall we lift him now, sir?"

All were by this time gathered about the form on the earth, and the throng at the edge of the wood had also come nearer. Fairfax Cary, who had looked at each speaker in turn, now again bent his eyes upon his brother. That still figure, so fixed, so uncaring in the midst of harsh emotion, had apparently no accusation to make, was there only to state the all-inclusive fact, "I am in death, who, yesterday, could move and speak, could feel joy and grief, like you and these."

The little knot of men, who had been gazing at the dead as at the chief actor in a drama, began to look, instead, at Fairfax Cary, and to look the more steadily for their first glance. They saw a curious thing; they witnessed a transformation. Had he, like Proteus, slipped before their eyes into another shape, the vital change had hardly been more marked. He had been, even this morning, a young man, handsome and gallant, with a bright eye, a most happy manner, a charm and spirit wholly admirable. All Albemarle knew and liked him under that aspect. The men about him had seen grief and horror and rage, each exhibited strongly out of a strong nature. They now saw, from out of youth and the war of emotions, the man emerge. He came slowly but steadfastly, a man with a set purpose, which he was like to pursue through life. The growth of years took place almost at once, though not the growth that would have been but for this releasing stroke. Latencies in the backward and abysm of inheritance that would not have stirred under a less tremendous stimulus stirred under this, grew, and pushed aside the gay and even life that might have been. The growth was rapid and visible, as visible the sharp turn from every former shining goal to one which, an hour before, the runner had not seen. The men who watched him somewhat held their breath.

The change that was wrought was profound. The man who was stretched upon the earth looked now the younger of the two. He seemed also to have given something of the calmness of his state, for Fairfax Cary no longer grieved with voice or gesture or convulsion of feature. He was quiet, pale, and resolute, and he now spoke to the sheriff evenly enough. "Yes, Mr. Garrett, we'll take him home. Where is the litter?"

Four men brought it forward. Ludwell Cary was lifted by his brother and Colonel Churchill and laid reverently upon the stretcher of branches where the green leaves nodded above his quiet face. The little procession formed and, with the younger Cary walking beside the litter, crossed the shallow ford and moved slowly up the winding river road.

CHAPTER XXXIII

GREENWOOD

THE murder, by an unknown hand, of Ludwell Cary, shot through the heart, beside Indian Run, as he rode from Malplaquet to Greenwood, became the overwhelming topic of interest in Albemarle, and a chief subject far and wide throughout the great state. His kinsmen and connections were numerous, and he had himself been a man widely known, by many greatly liked, and by a few well loved. There arose from town and country a cry of grief and wrath, a great wave of sympathy for the one man left of all the Greenwood Carys, solitary now in the old brick house behind the line of oaks, and a loud demand for the speedy discovery and apprehension of the murderer. Indignation was high, the Court House and the Court House yard crowded on the morning of the inquest, the verdict brought in by the coroner's jury received by the county at large with incredulous disappointment. Death at the hands of a person unknown.

No evidence was produced in the court room which threw any clear light upon the commission of the deed, its motive, or its perpetrator. There were ample accounts of the capture of the horse, the finding of the body, its position, and the nature of the wound, — medical opinion in addition that death had been instantaneous, and probably received before the breaking of the storm. If there had been any telltale track or mark in the soil of the river road, the continued and beating rain had made the way impossible to read. Witnesses from Malplaquet told of Ludwell Cary's setting forth that morning, and Forrest, the blacksmith, vouched for his passing the forge, alone. Men from the mill at the ford swore to his pausing to answer their questions as to the trial of Aaron Burr, and to his riding on — by the main road. Here arose the confusion. They were certain that Mr. Cary had taken the main road. They thought so then, and they did not see yet how they were mistaken. They told the next man who came riding by that he had taken that road — the main road. It was not the next man, — boatmen and others had passed going up country, — but when Mr. Rand came up, they told him that Mr. Cary was on the road before him — the main road. Yes, sir, it was Mr. Rand and his negro boy, and he could speak for it that Mr. Cary was supposed to be riding to Greenwood by the usual road — the main road. The river road was after all very little shorter, and everybody knew that it was mortal bad.

Lewis Rand was called. He testified that he had left Richmond upon the third, having with him a negro boy known as Young Isham. The night of the sixth he had slept at the Cross Roads Tavern and gone on the next morning, passing Malplaquet about nine. His horse loosening a shoe, he stopped at Forrest's forge, and there learned from the smith that there was considerable travel, and that Mr. Cary of Greenwood had passed some time before. "You remember, Forrest? I asked you if Mr. Cary had mentioned which road he would take at the ford, and you answered that he had not, but that you supposed the main road — the other had been very bad all summer. Again, at the mill below the ford where I paused to ask for water, the miller, remarking on the travel home from Richmond, informed me that Mr. Cary had passed not long before. I asked him which road Mr. Cary had taken, the main road or the river road. He answered — or the men behind him answered, I cannot now remember which — 'The main road.'"

"Ay, that's what we said, and what we thought," interjected the miller.

"It was thus my impression, gained first at the forge," continued the witness, "that Mr. Cary was before me upon the main road. Until then, knowing him to have left Richmond several days before me, I had supposed him at Greenwood. I was not averse to a word with him on certain matters, and I rode rapidly, hoping to overtake him —"

"Upon the main road, sir?"

"The main road, of course. As I did not do so, I concluded that the approaching storm had caused him to hasten. It was very threatening, and the few that my boy and I passed were hurrying to shelter. At Red Fields I paused for a moment" — He looked toward a well-known planter, standing near. "Certainly, Mr. Rand," said the latter promptly. "We tried to make you stay out the storm, but you would be getting home."

"From Red Fields my boy and I rode on into town. I stopped at my partner's house to tell his sister when to expect him home from Richmond, and at the Eagle I drew rein for a moment and exchanged greetings with two or three gentlemen upon the porch. The rain was close at hand, and my boy and I pushed on to Roselands — where, next morning, a neighbour brought the news of this murder. I corroborate, sir, as I have been called to do, the statements of Mr. Forrest and Mr. Bates that it was the impression of all who greeted him as he passed that Mr. Cary was riding home by the usual road — the main road. I have nothing further to offer, sir."

"Thank you, Mr. Rand," said the coroner, and the witness left the stand.

He was followed by the keeper of a small ordinary upon the main road, halfway between the ford and Red Fields. "No, sir, Mr. Ludwell Cary did n't travel by the main road. I sat in my door with my glass and my pipe almost the whole day — until after the storm broke, anyhow. There was n't any custom — folk seemed to know it was going to rain like Noah's flood. There was hardly anybody on the road after about ten. Yes, I might have shut my eyes now and then, though I don't doze over my pipe and glass half as much as some people say I do. Anyhow, Mr. Ludwell Cary did n't ride that way — events prove that, don't they, sir? Yes, I remember well enough when Mr. Rand passed. I was n't dozing then, for the negro boy spoke to me, said there was going to be a big storm. It must have been after midday, Mr. Rand?"

"Yes, something after midday."

The witness knew, for he always had his glass at noon. He might have been dozing when the negro spoke to him, but he spoke plain enough. "'It's going to be an awful storm,' he said, and then I believe you said something, sir, though I don't remember what it was, and you both rode on. I was n't that sleepy that I could n't see straight. That's all that I know, Mr. Galt."

Two or three other witnesses were called, but they were of the main road, and the main road had nothing to show further than that it had been travelled upon by Lewis Rand and his negro boy. They had not seen Mr. Ludwell Cary since he rode to Richmond early in the summer. Yes, they were sure they had seen Mr. Rand and his negro boy — but the clouds were dark, and the dust blowing so that you had to hold your head down, and people were thinking of getting indoors. The boy was riding a mare with a white foot.

"I think we can leave the main road, gentlemen," declared the coroner. "Now the river road and the stream where this thing was done —"

Indian Run — where did Indian Run come from or lead to, and who might have been upon that lonely road, or lurking in the laurel and hemlock that clothed the banks of the stream? Three miles up the water was a camping-ground used by gypsies; at a greater distance down the stream a straggling settlement of poor whites, long looked at askance by the county. It might be that some wandering gypsy, some Ishmaelite with a grudge — The enquiry turned again to Fairfax Cary.

"When you went on, Mr. Cary, from Elm Tree, you too supposed that your brother would follow by the same road? You thought —"

"I did not think at all," answered Cary harshly. "I was lost in my own self and my own concerns. I was a selfish and heedless wretch, and I hurried away without a thought or care. What he told me I forgot at the time. But I have remembered it since. He told me that he would take the river road."

"And on your own way home you repeated that to no one?"

"To no one. I never spoke of him, I do not know that I ever thought of him from Elm Tree to Greenwood. Oh, my brother!"

A sigh like the wind over corn went through the room. The coroner bent forward. "Mr. Cary, can you think of any one who bore him ill-will — a runaway negro, perhaps, or some vagrant who might have been along that stream?"

"No. His slaves loved him. We had no runaways. I do not believe there is a man on Indian Run who would have touched him."

"Mr. Cary, had he any enemy?"

"He had one. He sits yonder. You have heard his testimony."

The court room murmured again. The old rivalry between Lewis Rand and Ludwell Cary, the antagonism of years, and the fact of a duel were sufficiently in men's minds — but what of it all? The duel was a year gone by; political animosities in Virginia might be, and often were, bitter enough, but they led no further than to such a meeting. The coroner looked disturbed. The murmur was followed by a curious hush; but if for an instant an idea was poised in the air of the court room, it did not descend, it was banished as preposterous. The moment's silence was broken by Lewis Rand. From his place at the side of the room he spoke with a grave simplicity and straightforwardness, characteristic and impressive, familiar to most there who had heard him before now, in this court room, on questions of life and death. "Everything is to be pardoned to Mr. Fairfax Cary's most natural grief. My testimony, sir, is as I gave it."

The coroner's voice broke in upon a deep murmur of assent. "I presume, Mr. Cary, that you bring no accusation against Mr. Rand?"

Fairfax Cary looked from under the hand with which, as he sat, he shaded his brow. "I have, here and now, no sufficient proof whereon to base accusation of any man. I will only say that I shall seek such proof."

A little longer, and the proceedings were over. The crowd dispersed, unsatisfied, hungry for further details and hazardous of solutions. The better class went home, but others hung long about the Court House yard, reading the notices pasted upon the Court House doors, the "WHEREAS upon the seventh day of September and on the river road where it is crossed by Indian Run" — commenting upon the rewards offered, relating this or that story of the Greenwood Carys, and recalling every murder in Albemarle since the Revolution. "Dole was shot down like that, three years ago, in North Garden — but then, Fitch was suspected from the first. Fitch had been heard to swear he'd do it, and they knew, too, it was his gun, and a child had seen him come and go. Lewis Rand was for the State. Don't you remember the speech he made? No; Tom Mocket made it, but Mr. Rand wrote it! Either way it hung Fitch. Curious, was n't it, that passage between Mr. Rand and Fairfax Cary? D' ye suppose he thought — d' ye suppose Fairfax Cary thought —"

"It is n't what a man thinks," stated a surly farmer. "It's what a man can prove."

"Well, he could n't prove that if he tried till doomsday!" cried another. "That's not Lewis Rand's trade!"

"You're right there, Jim," assented the group. "WHEREAS upon the seventh day of September and on the river road where it is crossed by Indian Run —"

Upon a September afternoon, clear and fair, full of the ripeness and strength of the year, the body of Ludwell Cary was given back to the earth. There was a service at Saint Anne's, after which, carried by faithful slaves and followed by high and low of the county, he was borne to the Cary burial-ground at Greenwood. It crowned a low hill at no great distance from the oaks about the house — a place of peace and quietness, with bird-haunted trees and a tangle of old flowers. Ludwell Cary was laid beside Fauquier Cary, the "Dust to dust" was spoken, and the grave filled in. All mourned who heard the falling earth, and the negroes wailed aloud, but Fairfax Cary stood like a rock. It was over. The throng melted away, leaving only the house servants, two or three old and privileged friends, and the living Cary. The last spoke to the first, thanked them, and sent them away; then, addressing himself to the two Churchills and the old minister, asked that he be left alone. They went, Major Edward turning at once, the others following more slowly. He watched them below the hill-top, then sat down beside the grave that was so raw and red for all the masking flowers.

At sunset Eli and Major Edward, grey and anxious, watching from the shadow of the oaks, saw him leave the burying-ground, look back once as he closed the gate, and come slowly down the hill. When he reached the house, and, after going to his own room, came down into the library, it was to find Major Churchill ensconced in an old chair by the western window, with a book in his hand. He looked up with eyes yet keen and dark beneath their shaggy brows. "If you'll allow me, Fair, I'll borrow this Hobbes of yours. It is printed larger than mine, and it has no damned annotation!"

Major Edward spent the night at Greenwood, and the two played chess until very late. The next morning, coming stiffly down at an early hour, he found no host. Fairfax Cary, he discovered on enquiry, had ordered his horse the night before, and as soon as it was light, had ridden off alone. Major Churchill passed the morning as best he might. He looked once from the windows toward the little graveyard on the hill, and thought of going there, then shook his head and pressed his lips together. He was old, and now, when he could, he evaded woe. The young had fibre and nerve to squander; brittle folk must walk lightly. The Major stared at the feathery trees that marked the place. The green became a blur; he stamped his foot upon the floor with violence, said something between his teeth, and turned from the window to a desolate contemplation of the backs of books.

It was after midday when Fairfax Cary returned. He came in, white and steady, apologized for his absence, and ordered dinner. The two ate little, hardly spoke, but drank their wine. As they passed out of the dining-room, the elder said, "You have been —"

"Yes. The river road."

They reëntered the library and, at Cary's suggestion, sat down again at the chess-table. They played one game, then fell idle, the young man staring straight before him at some invisible object, the elder watching him covertly but keenly.

"When," said the Major at last, — "when will you come with me, Fair, to Fontenoy?"

The other shook his head. "I do not know. Not now. I must not keep you here, sir."

"I have little to occupy me at home. You will tell me when I can do nothing for you here. You must remember, Fair, that Dick and Nancy and Unity and I and even little Deb want you, very heartily and lovingly want you, with us there. Unity —"

The young man took from his breast a folded note. "I have this from Unity. Read it. It is like her."

He unfolded it and gave it to the Major, who read the line it contained.

FAIRFAX, — I will marry you to-morrow if you wish. I know — I know it is lonely at Greenwood.   UNITY.

Major Churchill cleared his throat. "Yes, it is like her. And why not, Fair? Upon my soul, I do advise it! I advise it strongly. Not to-morrow, perhaps, but next day or the next. It can be quietly arranged — there could have been no wiser suggestion! Take her at her word, Fair."

Cary shook his head, thrust the note back in its place, and, rising with a quivering sigh, walked to the window. He stood there for some moments, his brow pressed to the pane, then returned to the table and, standing before the Major, spoke with harsh passion. "Is marriage, sir, a thing for me to think of now? No! not even marriage with Unity Dandridge. To marry now — to forget with all possible haste — to lie close and warm and happy and leave him there, cold, alone, and unavenged! No. I'll not do that. Wedding-bells, even slowly rung, would sound strangely, I think, to his ears. And as for that murderer, he might say when he heard them, 'Are the dead so soon forgot? Then up, heart! for this bridegroom will not trouble me.' Major Churchill, I will live alone at Greenwood until I have proof which will convince a judge and jury that my brother was not the only man who spurred from that ford by the river road! Lewis Rand may wind and double, but I'll scotch him yet, there by Indian Run! I'll transfix him there, there on that very strand, and call the world to see the man who murdered Ludwell Cary! When that's done, I'll rest, maybe, and think of happiness."

Major Churchill sat back in the deep old armchair and rested his head upon his hand. The hand was a trembling hand; the old soldier, grey and stark, with his pinned-up sleeve, looked suddenly a beaten soldier, conquered and fugitive. The young man saw the shaking hand. "You need no proof, sir," he said harshly. "I know that you know. You knew there beside the stream, the day we found him."

"Yes, Fair."

"And did you not know that I knew?"

"I have not been perfectly certain, but — yes, I believed you to know."

"I will not say that, knowing me, — for until now I have hardly known myself, — but knowing my father, sir, could you look for another course from his son? My brother's blood cries from the ground. There is no rest and no peace for me until his murderer pays!"

"Yes, Fair."

"I cannot tell you what my brother was to me. Brother of the flesh and of the spirit too — David — Jonathan. His friends mine and his enemies mine, his honour mine —"

"Yes, Fair. It was so I loved Henry Churchill."

The young man checked his speech, gazed at his guest a moment in silence, and turned away. The quiet held in the old room where bygone Carys looked from the walls, but at last the Major spoke with violence. "Don't think that I do not hate that man! Spare him, in himself, one iota of the penalty — not I! Cheat justice, see the law futile to protect an outraged people, stay the hangman's hand — am I one to will that? No man can accuse me of a forgiving spirit! I, too, loved your brother; I, too, believe in the blood debt! Ask me of this man himself, and I say, 'Right! Let him have it to the hilt — death and shame!' But — but —"

The Major's voice, high and shaking with passion, broke with a gasp. He had sat erect to speak, but now he sank back, and with his chin upon his hand looked again mere grey defeat.

Fairfax Cary turned from the window. "I am sorry," he said coldly and harshly. "In a lesser thing, Major Churchill, that consideration might stop me. It cannot do so, sir, in this."

"I am not asking that it should," answered the other. "I seldom ask too much of this humanity. You will do what you must, and what you will, and I shall comprehend your motive and your act. But I will stand clear of you, Fair. After to-day, you plan without my knowledge, and work without my aid!"

"If it must be so, sir."

"I have called myself," said Major Edward sombrely, "a Spartan and a Stoic. I believe in law and the payment of debts. I believe that a murderer should be tracked down and shown that civilization has no need of him. I loved your brother. And I sit here, a weak old man, and say, 'Not if it strikes through a woman's heart!' What a Stoic the Most High must be!"

"I think that I should know one thing, sir. Is it your belief that he has told your niece?"

The Major grew dark red, and straightened himself with a jerk. "Told my niece? Made her, sir, a confidante of his villainy, leagued her to aid him in cajoling the world? I think not, sir; I trust not! I would not believe even him so universal an enemy. If I thought that, sir, — but no! I have seen my niece Jacqueline twice since —" the Major spoke between his teeth — "since Mr. Rand's return from Richmond." He sat a moment in silence, then continued. "Her grief is deep, as is natural — do we not all grieve? But if I have skill to read a face, she carries in her heart no such black stone as that! Remember, please, that he told her nothing of his plot with Burr. You will oblige me by no longer indulging such an idea."

"Very well, sir. I know that Colonel Churchill has no suspicion. He contends that it was some gypsy demon — will not even have it that some poor white from about the still — says that no man in this county — Well! I, too, would have thought that once."

"My brother Dick has the innocence of a child. But others apparently suspect as little. You and I are alone there. And we have only the moral conviction, Fairfax. They were enemies, and they were in the same county on the same day. That is all you have to go upon. He has somehow made a coil that only the serpent himself can unwind."

"A man can but try, sir. I shall try. If you talk of an inner conviction, I have that conviction that I shall not try in vain."

Major Edward shaded his eyes with his hand. "God forbid that I should wish the murder of Ludwell Cary unavenged! But — but — shame and sorrow — and Henry Churchill's child" — He rose from his chair and stalked across the room. "I am tired of it all," he said, "tired of the world, life, death, pro and con, affections, hatreds, sweets that cloy, bitterness that does not nourish, the gash of events, and the salt with which memory rubs the wound! Man that is born of woman — Pah!" He straightened himself, flung up his grey head, and moved stiffly to a bookcase. "Where's Gascoigne's Steel Glasse? I know you've got a copy — Ludwell told me so."

"It is on the third shelf, the left side. Major Churchill, you understand that, for all that has been said, I must yet go my way?"

"Yes, Fair, I understand," said the other. "Do what you must — and God help us all!"

CHAPTER XXXIV

FAIRFAX CARY

THE December frost lay hard upon the ground, and a pale winter sky gleamed above and between bare limbs of trees. In Vinie Mocket's garden withered and bent stalk showed where had been zinnia and prince's feather, and the grapevine over the porch was but a mass of twisted stems. The sun shone bright, however, on this day, and as there was no wind, it was not hard to imagine it warm out-of-doors and the spring somewhere in keeping. It was the week before Christmas, and the season unwontedly mild.

Vinie, seated upon the doorstep in the sun, a grey shawl around her shoulders and her pink chin in her hand, stared at the Ragged Mountains and wondered when Tom was coming to dinner. A grey cat purred in the sun beside her. Smut the dog, lying in a patch of light upon the porch floor, broke out of a dream, got up, and wagged his tail.

"Who do you hear, Smut?" asked Vinie. "*I* think it ith Mr. Adam."

Adam came through the gate that had never been mended and up the little, sunny path. He had his gun, and in addition a great armful of holly and mistletoe, and he deposited all alike upon the porch floor. "A green Christmas we're having," he announced cheerfully, "so we might as well make it greener! I thought these would look pretty over your chimney glass."

"They'll be lovely," answered Vinie. "I just somehow didn't think of fixing things up this Christmas. I'll put them all around the parlour, Mr. Adam."

"I'll put them for you," said Adam. "This is n't mistletoe like you get in the big trees south, and it is n't holly such as grows down Williamsburgh way — but it's mistletoe and it's holly."

"Yeth," agreed Vinie listlessly. "I don't know which ith the prettier, the little white waxen berries or the red."

"I like the red," returned the hunter. "That in your hand — bright and quick as blood-drops."

"No," said Vinie, and let the spray drop to the floor. "Blood ith darker than that."

"Not if it's heart's blood — that's bright enough. What is the matter, little partridge?"

"Nothing," Vinie replied, with an effort. "I've been baking cake all morning, and I'm tired. I reckon you could n't have Christmas without baking and scrubbing and sweeping and dusting and making a whole lot of fuss about nothing — nothing at all." Her voice dragged away.

"You could n't have it without hanging up mistletoe and holly," quoth Adam. "I've been a month in these parts, and I've come around mighty often to see you and Tom. Why won't you tell me?"

Vinie turned upon him startled eyes. "Tell you?"

"Tell me what ails you. Why, you are n't any more like — Don't you remember that morning, a'most four years ago, when I found you sitting by the blackberry bushes on the Fontenoy road? Yes, you do. The blackberries were in bloom, and you had on a pink sunbonnet, and I broke you a lot of wild cherry for your very same parlour in there. You had been crying that day, too, — oh, I knew! — but you plucked up spirit and put the wild cherry all around the parlour. And now, look at you! — you are n't a partridge any longer, you're a dove without a mate. Well, why don't you cry, little dove?"

"I don't feel like crying," said Vinie. "There is n't anything the matter with me. I'm going to put the green stuff up, and Tom's got ever so many wax candles and two bottles of Madeira, and you'll come to supper —"

"I'll send you a brace of wild turkeys Christmas Eve. I'll shoot them over on Indian Run."

Vinie shrank back. "You look," exclaimed Adam, "as though you were on Indian Run, and I had turned my gun on you! Why did you go white and sick like that?"

He glanced at her again with keen, deep blue eyes. "Now the colour has come back. Were you frightened over there in those woods when you really were a bird? Indian Run! It is more than three months, is n't it, since Mr. Cary's death?"

"December," answered Vinie, in a fluttering voice, "December, November, October, and part of September — yeth, more than three months. Suppose we go now and put the holly up?"

"Let's stay here a little in the sun. The holly won't wither. I don't know a doorstep, East or West, that I like to sit on better than this. There's a variety of log cabins that I'm fond of, and maybe as many as four or five wigwams, but I'd like to grow old sitting in the sun before this little grey house! It is n't going to be long before the sap runs in the sugar trees and it's spring. Then all the pretty flowers will come up again and I'll help you draw cool water from the well. Don't you ever wear that Spanish comb I brought you?"

"I've got it put away. It's lovely."

"It ought n't to be put away. It ought to be stuck there, dark shell above your yellow hair. You'll wear it, won't you, Christmas Day?"

"Yeth, I'll wear it, Mr. Adam. Who's coming now, Smut?"

"He hears a horse. Wear the Spanish comb, and Tom shall brew us a bowl of punch, and we might get in some gay folk and a fiddle and have a dance. I'd like to stand up with you, little partridge."

Vinie put down her head and began to cry. "It's nothing, nothing! There is n't anything the matter! Don't think it, Mr. Adam. I jutht get tired and cold, and Christmas is n't like it used to be. Now I've stopped — and I'll dance with you with pleasure, Mr. Adam."

"That's right," said Adam. "Now, you dry your eyes, and we'll go into the parlour and I'll make a fire, and we'll put leaves and berries all around. Who is it coming by? Mr. Fairfax Cary."

"Yeth," answered Vinie. "He rides a black horse."

The hunter glanced at her again. "Little bird," he thought, "your voice did n't use to have so many notes." Aloud he said, "He's grown to look like his brother. I met him in the road the other day and we talked awhile. He's too stern and quiet, though. All the time we talked I was thinking of a Cherokee whom I once met following a war party that had killed his wife. Fairfax Cary had just the same air as that Indian — still, like an afternoon on a mountain-top. There's no clue yet as to who shot his brother."

Fairfax Cary, going by on Saladin, lifted his hat to the woman on the porch. "Yes, he's like that Cherokee," repeated Adam. "Where's he riding? — to Fontenoy, I reckon. Now, little partridge, let's go make the parlour look like Christmas."

Vinie rose, and the hunter gathered up the green stuff. She spoke again in the same fluttered voice. "Mr. Adam, do you think — do you think they'll ever find out —"

"Find out who shot Mr. Cary?" asked Gaudylock. "They may — there's no telling. Every day makes a trail like that more overgrown and hard to read. But if Fairfax Cary is truly like my Cherokee, I'd not care to be the murderer, even five years and a thousand miles from here and now. You may be sure the Cherokee got *his* man. Now you take the mistletoe and I'll take the holly, and we'll make a Christmas bower to dance in." He raised his great armful and went into the house singing, —

> "Once I was in old Kentucky,
> Christmas time, by all that's lucky!
> Bear meat, deer meat, coon and possum,
> Apple-jack we did allow some,
>   In Kentucky.
>
> "Roaring logs and whining fiddle,
> Up one side and down the middle!
> Two foot snow and ne'er a flower, —
> But Molly Darke she danced that hour,
>   In Kentucky!"

The hunter's surmise was correct. Fairfax Cary rode slowly on upon the old, familiar way to Fontenoy. All the hills were brown, winter earth and winter air despite the brightness of the sunshine. A blue stream rippled by, pine and cedar made silhouettes against a tranquil sky, and crows were cawing in a stubble-field. Cary rode slowly, plodding on with a thoughtful brow. The few whom he met greeted him respectfully, and he answered them readily enough, then pursued his way, again in a brown study. The Fontenoy gates were reached at last, and he was about to bend from his saddle and lift the heavy latch, when a slim black girl in a checked gown made a sudden appearance in the driveway upon the other side. "I'll open hit, sah! Don' you trouble. Dar now!"

The gate swung open, Cary rode through, and Deb appeared beside Miranda. "We've been walking a mile," she announced. "Down the drive and back again, through the hollow, round the garden, and up to the glass door — that's a mile. Are you going to stay to supper?"

Cary dismounted and walked beside her, his bridle over his arm. "I don't think so, Deb, — not to-night."

"I wish you would," said Deb wistfully. "You used to all the time, and you most never do now. And — and it's Christmas, and we aren't going to decorate, or have a party, or people staying!" Deb's chin trembled. "I don't like houses in mourning."

"Neither do I, Deb."

The colour streamed into his companion's small face. "I didn't mean — I didn't mean — I forgot! Oh, Mr. Fairfax, —"

"Dear Deb, don't mind. I wish you were going to have a Christmas as bright as bright! Won't there be any brightness for you?"

"Why, of course," answered Deb, with bravery. "I am going to have a lovely time. Uncle Dick says I can do what I please with the schoolroom, and Miranda and I and the quarter children — we're going to decorate. Unity's going to show us how, and Scipio's going to put up the wreaths. The quarter's to have its feast just the same, and I'm going to help Unity give out the presents. I expect it will be beautiful!"

The two walked on, Miranda following. Cary took the child's hand. "I expect it will be beautiful too, Deb. Sometimes ever so much brightness in just a little place makes up for the grey all around. Aren't you going to let me see the schoolroom?"

"Oh, would you like to?" cried Deb, brightening. "Certainly, Mr. Fairfax. Christmas is lovely, isn't it? Unity says that maybe she and I will slip down to the quarter and watch them dancing. I'm sure I don't want parties, nor people staying!"

Deb squeezed her companion's hand, and kept silence from the big elm to the lilac-bushes. Then she broke out. "But I don't understand — I don't understand at all —"

Cary, looking down upon her, saw her little pointed chin quiver again, and her brown eyes swim. "What don't you understand, poor little Deb?"

"I don't understand why I can't go to Roselands. I've always gone the day after every Christmas, and it is always like Christmas over again! And now Uncle Dick says, 'Stay at home, chicken, this year,' and Uncle Edward says he needs me to tell him stories, and Unity begged them at first to let me go, but when they wouldn't, she said that she couldn't beg them any more, and that she didn't think the world was going right anyhow." The tears ran over. "And Jacqueline," continued Deb, in a stifled little voice, — "Jacqueline wrote me a letter and said not to come this year if Uncle Dick and Uncle Edward wanted me at home. She told me I must always obey and love them — just as if I didn't anyhow. She said she loved me more than most anything, but I don't think that is loving me — to think I'd better not come to Roselands. She said I was most a woman, and so I am, — I'm more than twelve, — and that I was to love her always and know that she loved me. Of course I shall love Jacqueline always — but I wanted to go to Roselands." Deb felt in her pocket, found a tiny handkerchief, and applied it to her eyes. "It's not like Christmas not to go to Roselands the day after — and I think people are cruel."

"I wouldn't think that of your sister, Deb," said Cary, with gentleness. "Your sister isn't cruel. Don't cry."

"I'm not," answered Deb, and put carefully away a wet

ball of handkerchief. "I hope you'll like the schoolroom, Mr. Fairfax. It's all cedar and red berries, and Miranda's and my dolls are sitting in the four corners. It's lovely weather for Christmas — though I wanted it to snow."

Major Edward, seated at an old desk, going over old papers, looked up as Cary entered the library. A fire of hickory crackled and flamed on the hearth, making a light to play over the portrait of Henry Churchill and over the swords crossed beneath. An old hound named Watch slept under the table, the tall clock ticked loudly, and through the glass doors, beyond the leafless trees, showed the long wave of the Blue Ridge.

"Is it you, Fair?" demanded the Major. "Come in — come in! I am merely going over old letters. They can wait. The men who wrote them are all dead." He turned in his chair. "Have you just come in?"

"Yes, sir."

"Unity was here awhile ago. She went through the glass door — down to the quarter, I suppose."

"I will stay here for a while, sir, if I may. Don't let me disturb you. I will take a book."

"You do not disturb me," answered the Major. "I was reading a letter from Hamilton, written long ago — long ago."

"I met Deb in the driveway and we walked to the house together. Poor little maid! She is mightily distressed because she thinks there's a lack of Christmas cheer. I wish, sir, that she might have a merry Christmas."

"We'll do our best, Fair. Unity shall make it bright."

"The servants, too, — I give mine the usual feast at Greenwood, and I'm going down to the quarter for half an hour."

"The Carys make good masters. In that respect all here, too, goes on as usual. As for Deb, the child shall have the happiest day we can give her." He took from a drawer a small morocco case and opened it. "She'll have from Dick a horse and saddle, and I give her this." He held out the case, and Cary praised the small gold watch with D. C. marked in pearls. "The only thing," continued Major Edward wearily, "is that she cannot go to Roselands. She has cried her heart out over that."

"You declined the invitation for her?"

"Yes. I made Dick do so. She is growing into womanhood. It will not answer."

"Then, sir, Colonel Churchill must know —"

"He doesn't 'know,'" said the Major doggedly. "Nobody really knows. We may be all pursuing a spectre. I told Dick enough to make him see that Deb should not be brought into contact —"

There was a silence. Cary studied the fire, and Major Churchill unfolded deftly with his one hand a yellowing paper, glanced over it, and laid it in a separate drawer. "An order from General Washington — the André matter. Deb shall not visit Roselands again. Dick and I are not going to have both of Henry's children" — The Major's voice broke. "Pshaw! this damned weather gives a man a cold that Valley Forge itself couldn't give!" He unfolded another paper. "What's this? Benedict Arnold! Faugh!" Rising, he approached the fire and threw the letter in, then turned impatiently upon the younger man. "Well, Fairfax Cary?"

"Is it still," asked Cary slowly, "your opinion that she does not know?"

"She?"

"Mrs. Rand."

Major Edward dragged a chair to the corner of the hearth and sat heavily down. He bent forward, a brooding, melancholy figure, a thin old veteran, grey and scarred. The firelight showed strongly square jaw, hawk nose, and beetle brows. When he spoke, it was in a voice inexpressibly sombre. "I have seen my niece but three times since September. If you ask me now what you asked me then, I shall answer differently. I do not know — I do not know if she knows or not!"

"I think, sir, that I have a clue. The hour when he passed Red Fields —"

Major Churchill put up a shaking hand. "No, sir! Remember our bargain. I'll not hear it. I'll weigh no evidence on this subject. Enough for me to know in my heart of hearts that this man murdered Ludwell Cary, and that he dwells free at Roselands, blackening my niece — that he rides free to town — pleads his cases — does his work — ingratiates himself, and grows, grows in the esteem of his county and his state! That, I say, is enough, sir! If you have your clue, for God's sake don't impart it to me! I've told you I will not make nor meddle." Major Edward began to cough. "Open the window, will you? The room is damned hot. Well, sir, well?"

"I'll say no more, then, sir, as to that," Cary answered from the window. "I wish absolutely to respect your position. It will do no harm, however, to tell you that I am going to Richmond the day after Christmas."

"To Richmond! What are you going to Richmond for?"

"I want," replied the other, with restrained passion, — "I want to ride from Shockoe Hill at three o'clock in the afternoon, with my face to Roselands, and in my heart the knowledge that I have been foiled and thwarted in deep-laid and cherished schemes by the one whom, for no especially good reason, I have singled out of the world to be my enemy! I want to feel the black rage of the Rands in my heart. I want to sleep, the third night, at the Cross Roads Tavern, and I want to go on in the morning by Malplaquet. I want to learn at Forrest's forge that Ludwell Cary is on the road before me. Perhaps, by the time I reach the mill and cross the ford, I will remember what it was that I did next, and how I managed to be on two roads at once!"

He turned, and took up from a chair his hat and riding-whip. "'T is no easy feat," he said, with grimness, "to put one's self in the place of Lewis Rand. But then, other things are not easy either. I'll not grudge a little straining." He stood before the Major, holding out his hand — a handsome figure in his mourning dress, resolute, quiet, no longer breathing outward grief, ready even, when occasion demanded, to smile or to laugh, but essentially altered and fixed to one point. "I think, sir, I will look now for Unity. There is something I wish to say to her. Good-bye, sir. I shall not come again until after New Year."

Miss Dandridge, mounting the hill from the quarter, and sitting down to rest upon a great, sun-bathed stone beside the foot-path, heard a quick step and looked up to greet her betrothed. "It is so warm and bright," she said, "in this fence-corner that I feel as though summer were on the way. The stone is large — there's room for you, too, here in the sunshine."

He sat down beside her. "You have been making Christmas for the quarter?"

"I've been telling them that Christmas is to be bright. I have not seen you for a week."

He took her hand and pressed it to his lips. "Unity, I have been sitting there at home at Greenwood, thinking, thinking! Page came to see me, but I was such poor company that he did not tarry long. I rode here to-day to say something to you — Unity, don't you think you had better give me up?"

"No! I don't —"

"I do not think it is fair to you. I am not the man you knew — except in loving you I am not the man who sat with you beneath the catalpa. I am bereaved of the better part of me, and I see one object held up before me like a wand. I must reach that wand or all effort is fruitless, and there is no achievement and no harvest in my life. I may be years in reaching it. I love you dearly and deeply, but I am not given over to love. I am given over to reaching that wand. It has seemed to me, sitting there at Greenwood, it has seemed to me after Page's visit, that I should give you freedom —"

"It seems to me, sitting here upon this stone," answered Unity, "that I will not take it! And what under the sun Mr. Page's visit — I will wait until you are at leisure to love me as — as — as you loved me that day under the catalpa when you flung Eloïsa to Abelard into the rosebushes! Don't — don't! I like to cry a little."

"I have determined," he said, "to tell you what I am doing. You know that I seek to discover my brother's murderer, but you have not guessed that I know his name. It is Lewis Rand whom I pursue, and it is Lewis Rand whom I will convict of that deed on Indian Run!"

She gave a cry. "Lewis Rand! Fair, Fair, that's impossible!"

"Is it?" he asked sombrely. "Impossible to prove, perhaps, though I'm not prepared to grant that either, but true, Unity, true as many another black 'impossible' has been!"

"But — but — No one thinks — no one suspects. Fair, Fair! are you not mistaken?"

"No. Nor am I quite alone in my conviction. And one day the world that suspects nothing shall know."

There was a silence; then, "But Jacqueline," she whispered, with whitening lips. "Jacqueline" —

"She chose," he answered. "I cannot help it. She took her road and her companion."

"And you mean — you mean —"

"I mean to bring him to justice."

"To break her heart and ruin her life — to bring down wretchedness, misery, disgrace! Oh!" She caught her breath. "And Deb — and Uncle Dick and Uncle Edward — Fair, Fair, leave him alone!"

"You must not ask me that."

"But Ludwell would — Ludwell would have asked it! Oh, do you think he would have endured to bring woe like that upon her! Oh, Fair, Fair, —"

Cary sprang to his feet, walked away, and stood with his back to the great stone and his face toward Greenwood. He saw but one thing there, the graveyard on the hill beneath the leafless trees. When he came back to Unity, he looked as he had looked beside the dead, that day on Indian Run.

"We are alike, Ludwell and I," he said, "but we are not that much alike. I am little now but an avenger of blood. I shall be that until this draws to an end." He came closer and touched her shoulder with his hand. "Take me or leave me as I am, Unity. I shall not change, not even for you."

"But for tenderness," she cried, "for mercy, for consideration of an old house, for Jacqueline whom your brother loved as you love — as once you said you loved — me! For just pity, Fair!"

"On the other side," he answered, "is justice. Don't urge me, Unity. That is something your uncle has not done."

"Uncle Edward?"

"Yes."

There was a silence; then, "I see now," said Unity slowly. "I have n't understood. I thought — I did n't know what to think. Uncle Edward, too, — oh me! oh me! That is why

Deb is not to go to Roselands." She considered through blinding tears a little patch of sere grass. "But Jacqueline," she whispered, — "Jacqueline does not know?"

Cary looked at her. "Do you think that, Unity?"

Unity stared at the grass until the tears all dried. "She knows — she knows! That was a heart-breaking letter to Deb, and I could n't — I could n't understand it! She does not ask me there — does not seem to want to meet — I've hardly seen her since — since — And when we meet, she's strange — too gay at first for her, and then too still, with wide eyes she will not let me read. And she talks and talks — she talks now more than I do. She's not truly Jacqueline — she's acting a part. Oh, Jacqueline, Jacqueline!"

"Be very sure," he said, "that I have for her only pity, admiration, yes, and understanding!"

"But you intend — you intend —"

"To bring Lewis Rand to justice. Yes, I intend that."

From the quarter below them came the blowing of the afternoon horn. The short, bright winter day was waning, and though the sun yet dwelt upon the hill-top, the hollow at its base was filled with shadow. Unity rose from the stone. "I must go back to the house. I promised Deb I would read to her." She caught her breath. "It is the Arabian Nights — and he gave it to her, and she's always talking of him. Oh, all of us poor children! Oh, I used to think the world so sweet and gay!"

"What do you think," he said, "of the one who turns it bitter?"

She looked at him with pleading eyes. "Fair, Fair, will you not forego it — forego vengeance?"

"It is not vengeance," he answered. "It is something deeper than that. I don't think that I can explain. It seems to me that it is destiny and all that destiny rests upon." He drew her to him and kissed her twice. "Will you wait for me, wait on no other terms than these? If you will, God bless you! If it is a task beyond your strength, God bless you still. You will do right to give it up. Which, Unity, which? And if you wait for me, you must go no more to that man's house. If you wait for me, my brother is your brother."

"I will never give up Jacqueline!"

"I do not ask it. But you'll go no more to that house, speak no more to the man she most unhappily wedded. That is my right — if you wait for me."

She turned and threw herself into his arms. "Oh, Fair, if it is only he himself — if it is only that dark and wicked man — if you do not ask me to stop loving her, or writing to her, or seeing her when I can —"

"That is all — only to speak no more to that dark and wicked man."

"Then I'll wait — I'll wait till doomsday! Oh, the world! Oh, the thing called love! Don't — don't speak to me until I cry it out."

She wept for a while, then dried her eyes and tried to smile. "That's over. Let us go now and — and read the Arabian Nights. Oh me, oh me, if we are not merry here, what must Christmas be at Roselands!"

CHAPTER XXXV

THE IMAGE

THE murderer of Ludwell Cary unlocked the green door of the office in Charlottesville, entered, and opened the shutters of the small, square windows. Outside was a tangle of rose-stems, but no leaf or bloom. The January sunshine streamed palely in, whitening the deal floor and striking against a great land map on the wall. Upon the hearth had been thrown an armful of hickory and pine. Rand, kneeling, laid a fire, struck a spark into the tinder, and had speedily a leap and colour of pointed flames. He rose, opened his desk, drew papers out of pigeon-holes and laid them in order upon the wood, then pushed before it his accustomed chair. He did not take the latter; instead, after standing a moment with an indescribable air of weary uncertainty, he turned, went back to the firelit hearth, sat down, and, bending forward, hid his face in his hands.

A cricket began to chirp upon the hearth, then the branch of a sycamore, moved by the wind, struck violently against the low eaves of the house. Rand arose, put his hands to his temples, and moved away.

There were law-books on the shelves, and he took down one and fell to studying statutes that bore upon a case he had in court. He read for a time with a frown of attention, but by degrees all interest flagged. He turned a page, looked at it with vagueness, and turned no more. His chin fell upon his hand, and he sat staring at the patch of sunshine on the floor. It was like light on water — light on Indian Run.

Five minutes more and Mocket came in, soft and quick

upon his feet, sandy-haired and freckle-faced, with his quaint, twisted smile, and watery blue eye, that glanced aslant at his friend and partner. "Good-morning, Lewis."

"Good-morning, Tom."

Mocket stood by the fire, warming his hands. "If 't was a mild December, 't is cold enough now! The wind is icy, and it's blowing hard."

"Is it? I thought the air was still."

As he spoke, Rand arose, replaced the book on the shelf, sat down at his desk, and began to unfold papers. "Work!" he said presently, in a dull voice. "Work! That is the straw at which to catch! Perhaps one might make of it a raft to bear one's weight. I have known the day when in work I have forgotten hunger, thirst, weariness, calamity. I have worked at night and grudged an hour to sleep. What I have done, cannot I do again? But I would work better, Tom, if I could get some sleep."

"I am sorry you have bad nights," said Tom; "but if you slept as deep and innocent as a babe, you could n't do better work. That was a praising piece about you in the Enquirer."

"Nothing less than eulogy, Tom, nothing less! Well — get to work! Get to work!"

"I've brought the papers on this case that old Berry has been copying." Tom threw more wood on the fire, then moved to his own desk, dragging a chair after him. "By the way, I stopped at the Eagle for a dram to keep out the cold, and who should come riding by but Fairfax Cary —"

"Ah!" said Rand. "Is he home from Richmond?"

"I did n't know that he had been to Richmond."

"Yes. He went two weeks ago."

"I had n't observed it. Well, whenever he went, he's back again. As I say, I was coming down the steps, buttoning up my coat, and he drew rein — he was riding his brother's horse and he looked like his brother — and he says to me, says he, 'Mr. Mocket, —'"

Tom broke off, turned the papers in his hand, and uttered an exclamation of disgust. "Old Berry is getting to be too poor a copyist! You'll have to give this work somewhere else."

Rand spoke in his measured voice. "What did Fairfax Cary say, Tom?"

"Why, he did n't say much, and I 'm sure I did n't get any meaning out of what he did say! His words were, 'Mr. Mocket, I wish I could remember all that, on several occasions, I must have said to you.' Seeing," continued Tom, "that I have n't spoken to him more than a dozen times in my life, I should n't consider there would be much difficulty in that, and I told him as much. 'You 're mistaken,' he said. 'It is difficult. We all have bad memories. I 've been wondering, seeing that I have talked to you of so much, if I ever talked to you of that. On the whole, I don't think that I ever have. Cultivate your memory, Mr. Mocket. Mine is a damnably poor one.' And so," ended Tom, "he rode away and left me staring. I don't know whether his head is turned or not, but he looked strong enough for anything and all a Cary. If you know what he meant, it is more than I do. These reports are all straight enough now. Do you want to look over them?"

"No," said his partner, and stood up, moving back his chair with a grating sound. "I don't know why — I'm restless to-day." Walking across the room, he stopped before the map upon the wall, and stood there a long while in silence.

"How would it do, Tom," he asked at last, in a curiously remote and dreamy voice, — "how would it do to find two or three great white-covered waggons, store them with all a childless family would need, put to them teams sound and strong, procure a horse or two besides, a slave or two, a faithful dog, — then to take the long road — west — south — somewhere — anywhere — past the mountains and away, away" — His voice sank, then gathered strength and went on. "Flood and forest, low hills and endless plains, stillness and a measure of peace! Left behind the demon care, full before the eye the red, descending sun — at night the campfire, at dawn the start, and in between mere sleep without a dream! It is conceivable that, after much travel, in some hollow or by some spring, after long days and after sleep, one might stumble on new life." He struck the map with his hand. "Tom, sometimes I think that I will remove from Virginia to the West."

"You'd be a fool to do that now," answered Tom succinctly. "But you won't do it. I don't know what has been the matter with you this winter, but I reckon you still love power. Next year you'll be named for Governor of Virginia."

He fed the fire again, then, going to the window, looked down the street. "The wind has fallen."

"I am going," said Rand's voice behind him, "to ride down the Three-Notched Road. Mrs. Selden sends me word that old Carfax is annoying her again."

"Can't I go for you?"

"No. I do not mind the ride. Get the papers ready for court to-morrow."

Mocket helped him on with his heavy bottle-green riding-coat. "Lewis," spoke the scamp, with a queer note of affection and deprecation, "why don't you see Dr. Gilmer? You're growing thin, and do you know, you're haunted-looking! Tell him you cannot sleep, and make him give you bark or something. I couldn't carry on business without you, you know."

Rand looked at him with dark and sombre eyes. "Could n't

you, poor old Tom? Well, we'll keep it on awhile together. I don't want the doctor. Once, long ago, I might have doctored myself." He laughed. "Now there's no bark in Peru — no balm in Gilead. Well, what we cannot have, we must do without! Look out, will you, and see if Young Isham is there with Selim?"

The Three-Notched Road stretched red and stark between rusty cedars and gaunt trunks of locust trees. It was cold, and overhead the sun was fighting with the clouds. Rand went rapidly, his powerful horse taking the road with a long and easy stride. Few were abroad; the bare and frozen fields stretched on either hand to the hills, the hills rose to the mountains, grey and sullen in the changing light. That meadow, field, and hill had once been mantled with tender verdure, and would be so again, was hard to believe, the land lay so naked and so grim.

Mrs. Selden's small, red brick mansion appeared among the leafless trees. Rand checked Selim slightly, gazing at the place with the weary uncertainty he had before exhibited, then turned for the moment from the task, irksome now as were all tasks, and rode on past Mrs. Jane Selden's to the house in which he had lived with his father and mother, and had lived with Jacqueline.

The place had been rented out since that summer of 1804, but the tenant, failing to make payment, was gone, and for some months the house had been vacant. Rand and Selim moved slowly along the old, old familiar way. Every stick, every stone, every fence-corner was known to both. The man let his hand fall upon the brute's neck. "We're going home, Selim," he said. "We're going home."

It was not now the small, clean place, fresh with whitewash and bright with garden flowers, shone upon by the sun and sung about by birds, to which he had brought Jacqueline.

The tenant had been dull, and the place was fallen into disrepair. In the winter air and without a leaf or flower, it looked again as it had looked when he and Gideon lived there alone. He dismounted, fastened Selim to the fence, and entered by the gate beneath the mimosa tree.

That the mimosa had ever shown sensitive leaf and mist of rosy bloom ranked now among other impossibilities. He stood for a moment looking at it in silence, then walked up the narrow path, mounted the porch steps, and tried the door. It was locked, but with an effort of all his wasted strength he burst it open and so entered the house.

The rooms were unfurnished and forlorn. He went from one to another, pausing in each in the middle of the floor, and gazing around as if to replace in that empty square the objects of the past. This progress made, he looked for a place to rest, but there was neither chair nor bench. All was bare, unswept, and desolate. He went into the kitchen, for he remembered the old settle there upon the enormous hearth. That they could not have removed, it was too heavy. He found it, took off his riding-coat and made a pillow for his head, then lay down full length upon the time-darkened wood. He had lain so, often and often, a little boy, a larger boy, a long-limbed, brooding youth. It had been his refuge from the fields, though hardly a refuge from his father. Gideon had been always there, lounging in his chair on the other side of the hearth, black pipe in hand, heavy stick beside him, revolving in his slow-moving mind, there in the dusk after the day's work, tobacco — tobacco — tobacco — and how he should keep Lewis from learning. "It had been better if he had succeeded," said Rand aloud.

With Gideon still before his eyes he fell asleep. Grim as was that figure, there was in the vision of it a strange sense of protection. It was his father, and, giddy from want of sleep, he sank slowly into oblivion, much as before now he had travelled there in the other's presence,—travelled with a gloomy mind and a body sore from the latest beating. Now the mind was full of scorpions, and the body stood in deadly need of sleep. It took it with a strange reversion to long gone-by conditions. The thought of Gideon's stick, the feel of his heavy hand upon his shoulder, were with him as of yore. The difference was that the man was comforted by what had been the boy's leaden cross.

Exhausted as he was, he slept at first heavily, and without a dream. This state lasted for some time, but eventually the brain took up its work, and the visions that plagued him recommenced. He turned, flung out his arm, moaned once or twice, lay quiet, then presently gave a cry and started up, pale and trembling, the sweat upon his brow. He wiped it off, drew a long, shuddering breath, and sat staring.

The kitchen windows were small, and half darkened by their wooden shutters. While he slept, the day had rounded into an afternoon, with more of sunshine than the morning had contained. The gold entered the room uncertainly, dimly, filtering in by the small apertures and striking across to the cavernous fireplace.

Rand knew it was but a trick of the light touching here and there in mote-filled shafts,—a trick of the light aiding the vagaries of an overwrought brain. He put forth his arm and found that it was so—there was no chair there and no figure seated in the chair. It was a trick of the light and an effect of imagination, an imagination that was hounded, day by day, from depth to pinnacle, from pinnacle to depth, back and forth like a shuttlecock in giant hands. No chair was there and no seated figure. He sank back on the settle and found that he saw them both.

The first sick leap of the heart was past. What he saw, he

knew, was a mere effect of light and shadow and tragically heightened fancy: when he moved in a certain direction, the dim picture faded, broke into pieces, was gone; but lean far back in the settle, look out with eyes of one awakened from a maze of fearful dreams, and there it was again! He had no terror of it; what was it at last but the projection of a face and form with which his mind had long — had long been occupied? It had ousted the vision of his father; and that, too, was not strange, seeing that, day by day, the thought of the one — the one — the one had grown more and yet more insistent. "Cary," said Rand, in a hollow voice, "Cary!"

The light and shadow made no answer. Rand waited, gazing with some fixedness, and imagination at white heat saw the head, the face, the form, the quiet dress, the whole air of the man, the look within his eyes and the smile upon his lips. The figure sat at ease, as of old it had sat upon the Justice's Bench the day of the election, as it had sat beside the bed in the blue room at Fontenoy. Imagination laid Lewis Rand again in that room, showed him the mandarin screen, the sunny, happy morning, the pansies in the bowl. "If," he cried, — "if I had died then, I had not died a wicked man. Cary — Cary — Cary! I am in torment!"

There came no reply. Rand bowed his head. Without, in the afternoon sky, a cloud hid the sun. When the solitary man in the deserted house looked again, there were no shafts of light, no dark between to create illusion; all was even dusk, forbidding, grey, and cold. He rose from the settle and left the room and the house. Selim whinnied at the gate, and his master, coming swiftly down the path and out of the enclosure, unknotted the reins, mounted, and rode off at speed.

Rand's haste did not hold. Remorse does not necessarily break habit, and the habit of his lifetime was attention to detail, system in matters of business, scrupulous response to the call where he acknowledged the right. He drew rein at Mrs. Selden's, dismounted, and lifted the knocker.

Cousin Jane Selden herself met him in the hall. "Lewis! I'm as glad to see you as if you brought the south wind! Come in to the fire, and I'll ring for cake and wine. It is bitter weather even for January. All's well at Roselands?"

"All's well."

They entered the small parlour and sat down before the fire. "I saw Jacqueline," continued Mrs. Selden, "at church last Sunday. I thought her looking very badly — pale and absent. I know, Lewis Rand, that you love each other dearly. There has been no quarrel?"

"No quarrel."

"I don't know," quoth Mrs. Selden, "of which I'm most sensible when it's in the air — an east wind or something amiss. The wind's in the north to-day, but the latter's on my mind. What is wrong, Lewis?"

"My dear old friend, what should be wrong?"

"That is what I asked you."

"Then nothing," he replied, "nothing but the north wind. Now about Carfax —"

Advice given on the subject of all dealings with Carfax, the adviser rose to take his leave. Mrs. Selden removed her spectacles and laid them in her key-basket. It was a sign with her that she was about to speak her mind.

"Lewis," she said, "I was a good friend to you once."

"Do I not know that?" he answered. "The best friend a poor boy ever had."

"No, not quite that — except, perhaps, to help you a little with Jacqueline. Mr. Jefferson was the best friend a poor boy ever had."

Rand winced. "You say true. The best friend a boy could have. Give me another glass of wine, and then I'll go."

"A man like that during youth and a woman like Jacqueline for your manhood — you have had much to prop your life."

"Yes. Very much."

"Then," she said sharply, "don't let it fall. Grow upward, Lewis, like the vine that gave its strength to make this generous wine! If you don't, you'll disappoint your Maker, to say nothing of some poor earthly friends! Don't fall — don't run upon the earth like poison oak. You're meant for noble uses — to help your kind, and to rejoice the heart of the Maker of strong men. Don't you fail and fall, Lewis Rand!"

Rand paused before her. "How should I help my kind, now — now?"

His old friend looked at him a little wonderingly. "Do the simple right, my dear, whatever it is that you see before you."

"The simple right! And to rejoice the heart of my Maker — if I have one?"

"Do the right strongly and surely, Lewis."

"Whatever it is?"

"Whatever it is." Mrs. Jane Selden looked at him thoughtfully, her hands clasped upon her key-basket. "I'm only an old woman — just a camp-follower with an interest in the battle. I wish that you had had a friend of your own age — a man, and your equal in power and grasp. Gaudylock and Mocket and such — they're well enough, but you're high above them; you're a sort of Emperor to them. Could you but have had such a friend, Lewis — a man like the Carys —"

"For God's sake, don't!" cried Rand hoarsely. He poured out a glass of wine, looked at it, and pushed it away. "I will go now, for there is work waiting for me in town, and at home. Do as I tell you about Carfax. Good-bye, good-bye!"

Out upon the road, passing through a strip of pine and

withered scrub, he raised his hand, and for some moments covered his eyes. When he dropped it, he saw, in the strong purples of the winter evening, again that misty figure, riding this time, riding near him, not in the road, but apparent in the air against and between the tall trunks of pines. "Cary," he said again, "Cary!"

There was no response from the figure in the air. "Cary," cried Rand, "I would we had been friends!"

Selim reached the open country; the pines fell away, the form was gone. Rand touched his horse with the spur and rode fast between brown stubble-fields darkening to the hills and to the evening sky. "Friends," he repeated, "friends! That would be on terms of my doing the simple right — the simple right after the most complicated wrong! Terms! there are no terms."

Leaving the fields, he rode down to a stream, crossed it, and saw the shape against a pale space of evening sky. "Is it to be always thus?" he thought. "I would that I had never been born."

CHAPTER XXXVI

IN PURSUIT

JANUARY passed and February passed. Fairfax Cary, riding for the third time since the New Year from Malplaquet toward Greenwood, marked the blue March sky, the pale brown catkins by the brooks, and the white flowers of the bloodroot piercing the far-spread carpet of dead leaves. He rode rapidly, but he paused at Forrest's forge and at the mill below the ford. This also he had done before. Neither the smith nor the men at the mill knew the idea that brought him there, but they may have thought — if they thought at all — that he put strange questions. It was, moreover, matter of regret to them, and of much comment when he had passed, that Mr. Fairfax Cary had lost an old and well-liked way of making a man laugh whether he would or no. He did n't jest any more; he did n't smile and flash out something at them fit to make them hold their sides. He had aged ten years since September; he had the high look of the Carys, but he was even quieter than his brother had been — all the sparkle and play dashed out as by a violent hand. The smith and the men at the mill thought it a great pity, shook their heads as they looked after him, then fell again to work, or to mere happy lounging in the first spring airs.

The lonely horseman crossed the ford below the mill, drew rein beneath the guide-post, and halted there for some minutes, deep in thought. At last, with a shake of the head and an impatient sigh, he spoke to Saladin, and once again they took the main road. "It is the third time," thought the rider. "There is luck in the third time."

The quiet highroad, wide and sunny, seemed to mock him, and the torn white clouds sailing before the March wind might have been a beaten navy, carrying with it a wreck of hope. The gusty air brought a swirl of sere leaves across his path, and the dust rose chokingly. "Caw! caw!" sounded the crows from a nearby field. The dust fell, the wind passed, the road lay quiet and bright. "Never!" said Cary between his teeth. "I will never give up!"

Half an hour's riding, and he came in sight of a small ordinary, its low porch flush with the road, a tall gum tree standing sentinel at the back, and on the porch steps a figure which, on nearer approach, he recognized as that of the innkeeper. He rode up, dismounted, and fastened Saladin to the horse-rack, then walked up to and greeted a weight of drowsy flesh, centre to a cloud of tobacco smoke, and wedded for life to the squat bottle and deep glass adorning the step beside it.

"Good-morning, Mr. Cross."

The innkeeper stirred, removed his pipe, steadied himself by a hand upon the step, and turned a dull red face upon the speaker. "Morning, Mr. — Mr. Cary! Which way did you come, sir? I never heard you."

"I came up from the ford. You were asleep, I think."

Mr. Cross denied the imputation. "Not at this hour, sir, never at this hour — not at ten o'clock in the morning, sir! Later, maybe, when I've had my grog, I'll take my forty winks —"

"It is not ten o'clock. It is nearly twelve, Mr. Cross."

"Well, well!" returned Mr. Cross, whose face, blushing all the time, showed at no particular instant any particular discomfiture. "I must just have dropped off a bit. There's little business nowadays, and a man had better sleep than do worse! What'll you have, sir? I'll call my girl Sally to serve you."

"Nothing at the moment, Mr. Cross." Cary sat down upon the step beside the other. "I stopped here a month ago —"

"You did," answered the innkeeper. "You stopped in January, too, did n't you?"

"Yes. In January."

"I remember plain. You wanted to know this and you wanted to know that, but you certainly treated me handsome, sir, and I'm far from grudging you any information Joe Cross can give!"

"We will go back to the same subject," said Cary. "Any recompense in my power to make I should consider but your due, Mr. Cross, could you tell me — could you tell me what I want to know."

He had spoken at first guardedly, but at last with an irresistible burst of feeling. The innkeeper looked at him with dull wonder. "I'd do anything to oblige ye, Mr. Cary, I certainly would! But when we come to talking about the road, and who goes by, and who does n't go by, and about the seventh of September, and was n't I asleep and dreaming just before the big storm broke? — why, I say, sir, No! I don't think I was. 'Tween man and man, Mr. Cary, I don't mind telling your father's son, sir, that 't is possible I might ha' had a drop more than usual, and ha' been asleep earlier! But I was n't asleep when the negro spoke to me. 'Hit's gwine ter be an awful storm,' says he, just that way, just as if he were lonesome and frightened. His voice came to me as plain as my hand, and I know the mare he was riding. 'Hit's gwine ter be an awful storm,' says he —"

"The other — the other!" exclaimed Cary impatiently. "It is the other I would know of!"

"I told you before, and I tell you now," replied Mr. Cross, "that I don't seem somehow clearly to remember what the other said. I'll take my oath that he said something, for he's one that don't miss speaking to a voter when he finds him! It's just slipped my mind — things act sometimes as though there was a fog, — but I was n't drunk and I was n't asleep. No, sir! no more than I was just now when you come up and spoke to me — and it don't stand to reason, sir, that I could ha' seen two horses instead of one!"

Cary, sitting moodily attentive, chin in hand, and his eyes upon the sunny road, started violently. "Two horses instead of one," he repeated, with a catch of the breath. In a moment he was upon his feet, and the innkeeper, had he looked up and had he been less blear-eyed and dull, might have seen an approach to the old Fairfax Cary — colour in cheek and light in eye.

"I am your debtor, Mr. Cross. That's it — that's precisely it! You heard it asserted by all around you that he had gone by, and your keen mind arrived at the same conclusion. You saw and heard — in a fog — the negro boy, and later on your strong imagination provided him with a companion. Just that — you thought you saw two where there was but one! I'm your servant, Mr. Cross, your very humble, very obliged servant!"

He drew out his purse, abstracted from it all the gold it contained, and gently slid the pieces into the hand which happened to rest upon the steps in an apt position for their reception. "A trifle of drink-money, Mr. Cross! If I might suggest a toast, I would have you drink to the next Governor of Virginia! Good-day, Mr. Cross, good-day! I think I begin to remember."

He mounted and rode away. "I begin to remember — I begin to remember. The boy and I were not always together upon the main road! Did we part at the guide-post? Then where did we come together again?"

He rode through March wind and sun, by fields where men were ploughing and copses where the bloodroot bloomed, beneath the branches of a great blasted oak, and past a red bank shelving down to the road from the forest above, then on by Red Fields, and so at last into Charlottesville. Here he turned at once to the office of an agent and man of business much respected in Albemarle.

Mr. Smith rubbed his hands and asked what he could do for Mr. Cary — who was looking well, extremely well! "Spring is here, sir, spring is here! We all feel it. On a day like this I cultivate my garden, sir!"

"I also," said Cary. "Mr. Smith, my affair is short. I will thank you to keep it secret also. I want to buy, if possible, a negro boy called Young Isham, who is owned by Lewis Rand. You may offer any price, but my name is not to appear. Manage it skilfully, Mr. Smith, but manage it! I have reasons for wishing to own the boy. You will bear it in mind that my name is not to appear as purchaser."

An hour later, nearing the Greenwood gates, he saw before him another horseman, bent from the saddle and engaged with the fastening. Cary rode up. "Ned Hunter, is it you? Why, man, I have not seen you this long while! Where have you been in hiding?"

"I have visited," answered Mr. Hunter, "New York and the Eastern Shore. You are looking well, Cary; better than you did at Christmas. I was in this quarter, and so I thought I would stop at Greenwood."

The two rode together up the hill, beneath the arching oaks. The servants appeared, the horses were taken, and Cary and his guest entered the quiet old house. A little later, in the drawing-room, over a blazing fire and a bottle of wine, Mr. Hunter laid aside a somewhat quaint air of injured dignity, and condescended to speak of Fontenoy and of how very changed it was since the old days. "Nothing like so bright, sir, nothing like so bright! I have not thought Miss Dandridge looking cheerful for more than a year — and she used to be the gayest thing! always smiling, and with something witty to say every time I came near! I hate changes. This is good wine, Cary."

"Yes. I do not, on the whole, think Fontenoy so changed."

"Don't you? I do. Well, well, it is not the only place that has changed! You've no sign yet, have you, Cary, of the murderer?"

"He still goes free."

"If there's a man in the county that I dislike," remarked Mr. Hunter, "it is Lewis Rand. But if he had taken the river road that day as he said he should, he and your brother might have travelled together, and the two would have been a match for the damned gypsy, or whoever it was, that shot Mr. Cary. Have you ever noticed what little things make all the difference? Shall I pour for you, too?"

"*As he said he should.* How do you know that he said he should?"

"Why, he and I slept the night of the sixth of September at the Cross Roads Inn —"

"Ah!"

"Yes, one gets strange housemates at an inn. Well, after supper I went out on the porch and began calling to the dogs, and he was there sitting on the steps in the dusk. The wind was blowing, and there were fireflies, and the dogs were jumping up and down. 'Down, Rover!' said I, 'Down, Di! Down, Vixen!' And then Rand and I talked a bit, and I said to him, 'The river road's bad, but it's much the shortest.'"

"What," demanded Cary, in a strained voice, — "what did he answer?"

"He answered, 'I shall take the river road.'"

Mr. Hunter helped himself to wine. "I was tired, and he was tired, and I did n't like him anyway, and was n't interested, so I went on calling to the dogs, and we did n't speak again. He and his negro boy went on at dawn, and he took, after all, the main road. He is n't," finished Mr. Hunter, "the kind of person you think of as changeable, and it's a thousand pities he did n't hold to his first idea! Things might have been different."

Cary rose from the table. "Would you swear, Hunter, to what he said?"

"Why, certainly — before all the justices in Virginia. I don't believe," said Mr. Hunter, "that my parents could have had good memories, for somehow things slip away from me — but when I do remember, Cary, I remember for all time!" He drank his wine and looked around him. "I have n't been in this room, I don't believe, for five years! That was before it was all done over like this. What a lot of Carys you've got hanging on the walls — and just one left to sit and look at them! You have n't a portrait of your brother?"

"No. Not upon the walls. If you're not fatigued, would you object to riding with me to West Hill? That's the nearest justice."

"I'm not at all fatigued. But I can't see what you want it taken down for —"

"Perhaps not," answered Cary patiently; "but you'll swear to it, all the same?"

"Why," said Mr. Hunter, "I can have no possible objection to seeing my words in black and white. I'll take another glass, and then I'll ride with you wherever you like."

At sundown Fairfax Cary, returning to Greenwood alone, gave his horse to Eli, and presently entered the library. It was a dim old room, unrenewed and unimproved, but the two brothers had loved and frequented it. Now, in the

March sunset, with the fire upon the hearth, with the dogs that had entered with the master, the shadowy corners, and many books, it had an aspect both rough and gracious. It was a room in which to remember, and it had an air favourable to resolve.

The last of the Greenwood Carys walked to the western window and stood looking out and up. He looked from a hill-top, but the summit upon which lay the Cary burying-ground was higher yet. The flat stones did not show, nor the wild tangle of dark vine, but the trees stood sharp and black against the vivid sky. Cary stood motionless, a hand on either side of the window frame. The colour faded from the sky, and there set in the iron grey of twilight. He left the window, called for candles, and when they had been brought, sat down at the heavy table and began to draw a map of the country between the ford and Red Fields.

Three days later he rode into Charlottesville and stopped at the office of Mr. Smith, whom he found at the back of the house, watching from a chair planted in the sunshine the springing of a line of bulbs. "You see, sir," quoth the agent, "I cultivate my garden! Tulips here, crocus there, yonder hyacinths. Red Chalice has been up two days, and my white Amazon peeped out of the earth yesterday. King Midas and Sulphur and Madame Mère are on the way. Well, Mr. Cary, I tried my level best with that commission of yours, and I failed! The boy is not for sale."

"Ah!" said Cary, and stooped to examine the white Amazon. "I hardly expected, Mr. Smith, that he would be for sale. At no price, I presume?"

"At no price. He is one of the house servants, and his master is attached to him. I am very sorry, sir."

His client rose from the contemplation of the springing hyacinth. "Give yourself no uneasiness, Mr. Smith. I am not disappointed. There are reasons, no doubt, why Mr. Rand declines to part with him. Let us put it out of mind. What a bright little garden you will have, sir, when tulip, crocus, and hyacinth are all in bloom!"

He took his leave, and rode homeward through the keen March weather. "I am beginning to remember quite plainly," he said. "Presently I'll know it like an old refrain — every word, Saladin, every word, every word, down to the last black one."

CHAPTER XXXVII

THE SIMPLE RIGHT

AN important case in a neighbouring county called Lewis Rand from home, and kept him an April week in the court room or in a small town's untidy tavern. It was his habit, known and deferred to, never to accept at such times the hospitality sure to be pressed upon him. The prominent men of his party urged him home with them, but accepted his refusal with a nod of understanding, and rode off strong in the conviction that a man so absorbed, so given over to watching and guarding his client's interests, was assuredly a man to be relied upon in any litigation. A great lawyer was like a great general — headquarters on the field. As for Lewis Rand and the next election — if he wanted to be Governor of Virginia, men who heard him in the court room were not the ones to say him nay! To a rational man his genius vindicated his birth. If he wanted the post, and if it was to the interest of the state, in God's name let him have it — old Gideon to the contrary!

Rand won the case, and turned Selim's head toward Albemarle. There had been a weary half day of thanks and protestations, and he was conscious of a dull relief when the last house was left behind, when the cultivated fields fell away, and the Virginian forest, still so dominant in the landscape, opened its dark arms and drew him in.

He rode slowly now, with drooping head. Young Isham, some yards behind, almost went to sleep in his saddle, so dragging was the tread the mare must follow. The dark aisle of the forest led presently through a gorge where the woods were in effect primeval. Upon the one hand rose a bank, thick with delicate moss and fern and shaded by birch and ash; on the other the ravine fell precipitously to hidden water, and was choked by towering pine and hemlock. The air was heavy, cool, and dank, the sunshine entering sparsely. The place was, however, a haunt of birds, and now a wood robin answered its mate.

Rand rode more and more slowly. The way was narrow, but here and there, between it and the bank, appeared grey boulders sunk in all the fairy growth of early spring. He drew rein, bared his head, and looked about him, then dismounted and spoke to Young Isham, coming up behind. "I will sit here a little and rest, Young Isham. Take Selim with you around the turn and wait for me there. I'm tired, tired, tired!"

The negro obeyed, and the master was left alone. Beside the road, beneath the mossy bank, lay a great fallen rock. Rand flung himself down upon this, and as he did so, he remembered a river-bank, a sycamore, and a rock upon which a boy of fourteen had lain and watched, coming over the hill-top, distinct against the sunset sky, the god from the machine. It was such a stone as this, and it was seventeen years ago. "Seventeen years. And a thousand years in Thy sight —"

The past weeks had seen a change in the condition of his brain. He was yet all but sleepless, and the physical strain had weakened his frame and sharpened his features, but the sheer force of the man, asserting itself, had put down the first wild inner tumult. Imagination was not now whipped to giddy heights; it kept a full, dark level. When, at long intervals, he slept, it was to dream, but not so dreadfully. He had no more visions such as had haunted him in January. The thought of Cary was with him, full and deep, a clean and bitter agony, but he saw him no more save with the eye of the mind. He was as rational as a sleepless man with a murder on his soul might well be, and he suffered as he had hardly suffered before.

With his face buried in his arms he lay very still upon the rock. He lay in shadow, but the sunlight was on the treetops above him. The wood robin yet uttered its bell-like note, the moist wind brought down the bank the fragrance of the fringe tree to blend with the deeper odour of the pine and hemlock. Rand lay without moving, the fingers of one outstretched hand clenched upon the edges of the rock. "A thousand years in Thy sight — and my day is as a thousand years. Oh, my God!"

The minutes passed, deep and grave, slow and full, with the sense of afternoon, of solemn and trackless woods, unbreathed air, silence and high heaven, then the April wind swept up the gorge and brought the sound of water. Rand sat up, resting his head upon his hands, and stared down the shadowy steep. There were flowers growing close to him, violets and anemones, and on a ledge of rock above, the maiden-hair fern. His eyes falling upon them, they brought to his mind, suddenly and sadly enough, Deb and her flower ladies, all in a ring beneath the cedars — Faith and Hope and Charity, Ruth and Esther and the Shulamite.

The recollection of that morning was followed by a thought of the night before — of the Fontenoy drawing-room and of all who had been gathered there. He saw the place again, and he saw every figure within it — the two Churchills, the two Carys, Unity, Jacqueline. "There is not one," he thought, "to whom I've worked no harm. All that I have touched, I have withered."

The wind again rushed up the gorge, a great stir of air that swayed the trees, and filled the ravine with a sound like the sea. Rand listened dully, staring down the steeps of pine and hemlock, giant trees that had dwelt there long. A desolation came upon him. The air appeared to darken and grow cold, the wind passed, and the gorge lay very still. Rand bowed himself together, and at last, with a dull and heavy throb, his heart spoke. "What shall I do," it asked, "O God?"

The Absolute within him made answer. "The simple right."

The wind returned, and the trees of the forest shook to the blast. The simple right! Where was the simple right in so complex a wrong? Step forward, backward, to either side — harm and misery every way! And pride, and ambition, and love, and human company — to close the door, to close the door on all! "No," said Rand, and set his teeth. "No, no!"

The afternoon deepened in the gorge of the Blue Ridge. Now the wind swept it and now the wind was still. The sunlight touched the treetops, or fell through in shafts upon the early flowers. From the mould of a million generations stalk and leaf arose for their brief hour of light and life. When it was spent, they would rest for an æon, then stir again. In the silence was heard the fall of the pine cone.

Rand lay, face down, upon the rock. In his mind there was now no thought of Cary, no thought of Jacqueline, nor of Fairfax Cary, nor of any other of the dead and living. It was the valley of the shadow of death, and his soul was at grips with Apollyon.

He lay there until all the sunlight was withdrawn from the gorge, and until Young Isham, frightened into disobedience, came and touched him upon the shoulder. He lifted a grey and twisted face. "Yes, yes, Young Isham, it is late! Go back, and I will come in a moment."

The negro went, and Rand arose from the rock, crossed

the road, and stood looking down toward the hidden water. From somewhere out of the green gloom sounded the bird's throbbing note, then all again was quiet, dank, and still. He raised his arms, resting them and his face upon them against the red bark of a giant pine. The thought of death in the pool below came to him, but he shook his head. The door was open, truly, but it led nowhere. His soul looked at the chasm it must cross, shuddered, and crossed it. His arms dropped from the tree and he raised his eyes to the blue above. He was yet in a land of effort and anguish, but the god within him saw the light.

CHAPTER XXXVIII

M. DE PINCORNET

MALPLAQUET was a Cary place, leagued in friendship as in blood with Greenwood. For seven months it had esteemed itself in mourning for the kinsman who had ridden from its gates to a violent death. But there were young girls in the house, and now, in the bright May weather, it was hard not to put forth leaf and bud and be gay once more. Actual gayety would not do, the place felt that, and very heartily; but pleasure that was also education, pleasure well within bounds, and education insisted upon, this might now be temperately indulged in. There seemed no good reason why, in mid-spring, the dancing class should not be held at Malplaquet, since it was the most convenient house to a large neighbourhood, and there were in the family three young girls.

The age esteemed dancing a highly necessary accomplishment, and its acquisition meant work, and hard work, no less than delightful play. Half a dozen young people came to stay three days at the house; half a score more drove or rode over in the afternoons, going home after ten by moonlight or by starlight. Their elders came with them; it was a business of minuets and contra-dances, painstakingly performed and solicitously watched. A large old parlour gave its waxed floor, Mr. Pincornet's violin furnished the music, and Mr. Pincornet himself, lately returned to Albemarle from his season in Richmond, imparted instruction and directed the dance. The house was full from garret to cellar, neighbours' horses in the stables, neighbours' servants in the quarter. The long, low brick office standing under the big oaks in the yard made, according to custom, a barracks for the young men who, high of mettle, bold, and gay, rode in from twenty miles around, ready to dance from dusk till dawn, and then, in a bright garden and May weather, to pursue some bits of muslin throughout a morning. Malplaquet was in a state of sober glee when, inconveniently enough, the one Cary whose mourning had not lightened chanced, in ignorance of the dancing class, to ride through the gates and up the hill.

It was his intention, it appeared, to spend the night which was fast falling, and to ride back to Charlottesville in the morning. The head of the Malplaquet Carys met him with affection and apology. "Young people will be young, Fair, and Molly and I thought it best to humour them in this no great thing! It's a mere lesson they're having. But I'm sorry, cousin —"

"You need not be, sir," said the other. "Ludwell would have been the last man on earth to wish their spirit less, or their pleasure less. It's time and the weather, sir, — Malplaquet feels it with all the world. You must not be troubled, and you must not disturb my cousins. I might ride on —"

"No, no, Fair! No, no!"

"Then I won't. Give me a room in the office — I see the house is full — and let Remus bring me supper there. If you'll come over later, sir, we'll talk Embargo, and I'll give you the up-county news. I'll to bed early, I think."

"I wish I could come! By George, it would be a relief to get away from all the bowing and scraping! You're sure you are n't hurt, Fair?"

"Quite sure," answered the other, with his old smile. "I'll go now to the office, if I may. No need even to tell them I am here."

Not to tell them was a thing more easily said than done. Time was when Fairfax Cary would have been hailed delightedly, drawn at once to the centre of things, and kept there by the quick glances of young women, the emulative gaze of neighbourhood gallants, and the approving consideration of the elder folk. His presence was wont to make itself felt. Now, when the news spread that he was at Malplaquet, there was a break in the dance, a pause, a hush. "What shall we do?" asked in distress the daughters of the house.

"Go on dancing," was the reply. "He'll have no difference made. But when the lesson's over, you'll remember, one and all, that he is here."

In the far room of the office, quiet, and with a porch of its own, Cary got rid of the dust of the road, then ate the supper, bountiful and delicate, brought by Remus and presided over by the mistress of the house, who talked to him of Greenwood and of his father. "The best dancer, Fair, and, after Henry Churchill, the handsomest man, — with *the* air, you know, and always brave and gay and true as steel! They said he was a good hater, and I know he was a good friend. You take after him, Fair."

"Ludwell did."

"Yes, I know, I know — but you the most. Ludwell had much from your mother — that strength and patience and grace were Lucy Meade's. Well, well, I cry when I think of it, so I'll not think! Is there nothing more you'll have? Remus is to wait upon you — you hear, Remus? And now, Fair, I'll go back to the children."

Cary kissed her. "Give them all three my love, and tell little Anne to mind her steps. I've got a book to read, and I'll go to bed early."

He sat over his book until nearly ten, then extinguished his candles and stepped out upon the small, moonlit porch.

From the house, a hundred yards away, came the sound of the violin, and of laughter, subdued but genuine. Cary drew a chair to the porch railing and sat down, resting his elbow upon the wood, his cheek upon his hand. The violin brought the thought of Unity. The laughter did not grate upon him. His nature was large, and the mirth at Malplaquet did no unkindness as it meant none. He sat there quietly until the music stopped and the lesson came to an end. The pupils not staying overnight went away, as testified the sound of wheel and stamp of hoof, the laughing voices and lingering good-byes, audible from the front of the house. This noise died, then, after an interval, lights appeared in upper windows. Slender arms and hands, put far out, drew to the wooden shutters; clear, girlish voices said good-night, and were answered by fervent and deeper tones below.

The quiet proper to the hour drew on, the lighted windows darkened one by one, and presently there appeared at the office the master of the house, accompanied by two or three young men. These greeted Cary soberly, but with much kindness. "We've put," said the host, "all the talkative rattlepates away in the house, and given you three sensible men! Mr. Bland has the room at the other end, Jack Minor and Nelson the one next to him, and in the little room beside yours, Fair, we'll stow Mr. Pincornet. They've all danced themselves tired, and the whole place is to have a quiet night." The three sensible men went, after a little, to their several quarters, and the kinsman continued: "The class ends to-night, Fair. To-morrow morning all go away except the Blands and the Morrises and George Harvie's little Dorothea. The house will be quiet, and you are not to ride away from us in the morning! Good-night — God bless you!"

Cary, left alone, watched the lights go out in the rooms of

Mr. Bland, Mr. Minor, and Mr. Nelson. He thought, "I will go to bed and go to sleep"; then, so bright was the moonlight, so sweet and fragrant and now silent the night, that he stayed on upon the little porch, his arms against the railing, his eyes now on the moon, now on the quiet great house and the shadowy clumps of trees. Presently Mr. Pincornet, the moon whitening his old brocade and his curled wig, came from the house, crossed the grass, and mounted to the porch upon which his small room opened.

He started as he saw the figure by the railing. "Who is it?" he demanded, in his high, cracked voice; then, "Ah, I see, I see! A thousand pardons, Mr. Cary,—"

"We are to be neighbours to-night," said Cary. "It has been long since we met, Mr. Pincornet. I am glad to see you again."

"I have been in Richmond," said the dancing master, "since — since September."

Cary touched a chair near him with a gesture of invitation. "Won't you sit down? It is too beautiful a night to go early to bed, and I do not think we will disturb the others' slumbers. But perhaps you are tired —"

"The practice of my art does not tire me," answered Mr. Pincornet. "I will watch the moon with you for as long as you please. We had nights such as this near Aire, when I was young."

He sat down, leaning his chin upon his beruffled hand. The light falling full on his companion showed the dark dress and above it the quiet, much altered face. Mr. Pincornet sighed, and tapped nervously upon the railing with the fingers of his other hand. "Mr. Cary, I have not seen you since — Pray accept my profound condolences, my sympathy, and my admiration."

His old pupil thanked him. "All my brother's friends

and mine are most kind. I should guess that you have yourself seen many sorrows, Mr. Pincornet."

The Frenchman's face twitched. "Many, sir, many. I have experienced the curse of fortune. Eh bien! one pays, and all is said! I have grieved with you, sir, I beg you to believe it. I admired your brother."

"He was worthy of admiration."

"In the south, near Mauléon, I lost such an one — brother not in blood but in friendship, a friendship pure as the flowers of spring and strong as the vintage of autumn. His own troops turned Jacobin and scoundrel, mutinied, shot him down — Ha!" Mr. Pincornet drew out his box and took snuff with trembling fingers. "Well! the King's side was uppermost for a while down there, and we had our revenge — we had our revenge — we had our revenge! But," he ended sadly, "it could not bring back my poor Charles."

"Did you think of it as revenge?"

"No. I thought of it as justice. It was that, sir. Those soldiers paid, but they owed the debt — every sou they owed it! He was," continued Mr. Pincornet, "gallant and brave, a great lover, a great fighter. He was to my heart, though not of my blood —"

"The man that I have lost," said Cary, "was of my blood and to my heart. I am left alone of an old house. And I pursue justice, Mr. Pincornet, I pursue justice, I pursue justice."

Mr. Pincornet looked at the face opposite him. "I think, sir, you will capture that to which you give chase. I have been in town, away from the country, but I hear the talk, and sometimes I read the papers. You have not taken the murderer?"

"No."

"It is strange!" exclaimed the other. "And no one suspected?"

"I suspect," answered Cary sternly, "but the world in general does not, or suspects wrongly. You were not at the inquest which was held?"

The dancing master shook his head. "In your sorrow, sir, such matters were, naturally, not brought to your notice. I fell ill, in the first days of September, at Red Fields, of a cold upon the lungs. I gave up my art and lay at death's door. My head was light; I heard and I thought of nothing but the faces and the voices around about Aire where I was young. I recovered, and, in the stage, I went to Richmond. To ask who is it you suspect would be a question indiscreet —"

Cary sat with his eyes upon the dark azure above the treetops. "Not yet," he said, in a brooding voice; "I have him not yet. Did you, Mr. Pincornet, have any scruple when you took vengeance, near Mauléon?"

"None, sir! I served justice. Soldiers are not levied to murder at once their faith and their officers. No more scruple than is yours in hunting down the wild beast that killed your brother! You have my wishes there for a good hunting!"

The Ancien Régime put up his snuffbox and brushed the fallen grains from his old, old red brocade. "What a night for music and for love! The road down yonder — it is like the silver ribbon they wear — they wore — at court!"

"The road — the road!" exclaimed Cary. "I travel it in my sleep. It haunts me as I haunt it. I know all its long stretches, all its turns —" He sighed, and moved so as to face the whitened ribbon.

"You ride," said the dancing master; "but, for my own convenience, I go afoot, and it is probable that I know it best."

They sat gazing down past garden and hillside to the still

highway. "I have not walked upon it, however," continued Mr. Pincornet reflectively, "since September. I then went afoot from Clover Hill to Red Fields, where I was taken ill. It was the seventh of September."

"The seventh of September!"

"I remember the day," continued Mr. Pincornet, "because I sat down under a tree beside the road to rest, and I had an almanac in my pocket."

"You remember it by nothing else?"

"Why, by one thing more," answered the other. "I sat there, my head on my hand, perhaps thinking of nothing, perhaps thinking of France — an empty road and in the sky black clouds — when suddenly — what do you say? — *clatter, crash!* through the wood opposite and down a tall red bank to the road came another pupil of mine—"

"Yes?" said Cary. "Who?"

"Mr. Lewis Rand."

Something fell to the floor with a slight sound. It was the book that had rested upon Cary's crossed knee. He stooped and picked it up, then, straightening himself, looked again at the silver ribbon. "Black clouds in the sky," he said, in a curious voice, "and the seventh of September, M. de Pincornet?"

"Yes," replied the other, "by the almanac. That was two days, was it not, before your brother's death?"

"My brother, sir, was murdered upon the seventh of September."

"The seventh! The ninth! You mean the ninth! I heard it so when I recovered —"

"You heard it wrongly. It was the seventh."

There was a silence; then, "Indeed," said the dancing master, in a curious dry and shocked voice. "The seventh. At what hour?"

"It is not known. Perhaps about midday, perhaps a little later — when there were black clouds in the sky."

The silence fell again, hard and full of meaning, then Cary leaned forward and laid his hand upon the other's arm. "I've hunted long alone, now we'll hunt for a moment together! Tell me again."

"He came down the bank in a great noise and rolling of stone and earth. There were thick woods on the top of the bank. He came out of them like Pluto out of the earth —"

"He was alone?"

"Alone. But he had a negro waiting for him down the road."

"He told you that?"

"I left my tree and we talked a little. He was torn, he was breathless. He explained that he had started a doe and had followed through the woods. He left me and went down the road to meet his negro. They passed me, and when I came to Red Fields, I was told they had paused there. I said nothing of our meeting. I was very tired and the storm was breaking. Before it was over I was hot and cold and shaking and ill in my bed. I was ill, as I have told you, for a long time. The ninth! I always thought it was the ninth —"

"Would you know again the place where this chase occurred?"

"He came down the bank opposite the blasted oak."

"Ah!" breathed Cary; then, after a moment, "I stopped my horse beneath that tree this morning, and my eyes rested upon that red bank. And I did not know! We are very blind." He rose. "Will you come indoors, sir? I wish to light the candles again."

They entered the small bedroom. Cary lighted the candles, placed them upon the table, and closed the shutters of the one window. From the breast of his riding-coat he took a rolled paper. "This is a map of the country below Red Fields. I made it myself. Now let us see, sir, let us see!"

He pinned the map down with ink-well, sand-box, book, and candlestick, which done, the two bent over it. "Call it," said Cary, "a military map of your country near Mauléon. Now, sir, look! Here is what a man did."

The demonstration proceeded, and it was carried out with keenness and with a very fair approach to accuracy. "Here is Malplaquet, which one passes about nine in the morning, and there by the candlestick is Red Fields, certainly on the main road and certainly paused at by" — he glanced aside at the other's face — "by the murderer, M. de Pincornet! Now let us mark this fox that doubles on himself."

The long, curled wig of the Frenchman and the younger man's handsome head with the hair gathered back into a black ribbon bent lower over the map. "Forrest's forge, the mill, the ford, he passed these places under such and such circumstances — here, where I rest the pen, stands the guide-post. This line is your silvered ribbon, this is the main road that makes a sweep around the broken country. This heavy, black, and jagged line is the river road. They both took the river road, as both had said they would — my brother to me, the murderer to a man at the Cross Roads Inn. The negro boy kept on by the main road. Where is this riven oak?" He dipped the quill into the ink-well. "I correct my map according to my better knowledge. That tree stands two miles below Red Fields, just above the turn where, fifty years ago, was the Indian ambush. We'll mark it here, black and charred. Here is the bank, crowned by woods. The growth is very thick between it and" — his hand, holding the pen, travelled across the sheet — "the river road just east of Indian Run."

He laid down the pen, and turned from the table to the

open door. "The moon is not bright enough, or I would go to-night. I want sunlight, or I want storm-light, for that ride across from road to road! Five hours till morning." He returned to the dancing master. "When, in your country, the man you loved was to be avenged, and his murderers punished, you were glad of aid, were you not? I shall be thankful for every least thing that you can tell me."

"He came," said the émigré, "like Pluto out of the earth. He was breathless as one out of prison — his linen was torn. There was," the narrator's voice halted, then hardened in tone, — "there was blood upon his sleeve. At the time I supposed that, in bursting through that grille of the forest, branch or briar had drawn it. There was blood, sir, about your brother?"

"Yes. If the murderer stooped to know if life was out, it might have happened so."

"He was not pale, I think, but he spoke in a strange voice. 'Ha!' he said, 'I started a doe ten minutes since, and gave her chase through the wood. Now I will rejoin my boy a little way down the road. Are you on your way to Charlottesville?' I told him I would go to Red Fields, upon which he said adieu and turned his horse. A little later he and his boy passed me, riding in a cloud of dust and under black skies." The dancing master raised a glass of water that was upon the table and moistened his lips. "This, Mr. Cary, is all my aid. I admired your brother, and there is, sir, a something about you that returns Charles to my memory. If it pleases you, and if our host will lend me a horse, I will ride with you in the morning, as far at least as the oak and that red bank down which he came."

"I accept your offer, sir," answered the other, "with gratitude. You did not chance to notice his holsters?"

"No — except that his saddle had holsters. I have seen

his pistols. I saw them one night at Monticello. He told me that they were a gift from his patron."

"Yes. They were given by Mr. Jefferson, and the other's name is upon them. Moreover, he travelled armed from Richmond to Roselands. I acquired that knowledge in the autumn. I would that iron could speak — if it could, and if human effort be of avail, I would yet have those pistols in my holding!"

He took the map from the table, rolled it up, and restored it to its place. "It grows late," he said. "Let us to bed and to sleep. It is the eve of a decisive engagement, M. de Pincornet. If you'll permit me, I will call you at five. Remus shall make us coffee, and we'll make free with a horse for you from the stables. Then the road again! but this time I go no farther than the ford, on that white ribbon yonder. You shall keep the highroad, but I will take the river road, and yet I'll hold tryst with you beneath that riven oak!" He began to put out the candles. "I shall sleep and sleep well until dawn, and I wish for you, sir, as good a night. For the aid which you have given me, I am most heartily your servant."

Alone in the little room, he straightened, mechanically, the objects upon the table, paced for a time or two the narrow, cell-like place, then went out again upon the porch and stood with his hands on the railing, and his eyes raised to the white moon, full and serene in the cloudless night. "For without," he said, "are dogs and sorcerers and murderers and whosoever loveth and maketh a lie." He stood for a long while without movement, but at last let fall his hands, turned, and went indoors. When, a little later, he threw himself upon his bed and drew his hand across his eyes, he found that it was wet with tears. He spoke aloud, though hardly above his breath. "No, Ludwell, no! In this sole thing I am right. It is not revenge. I am not vindictive, I am not revengeful.

This is justice, and I can no other than pursue it. It will not grieve you where you are." He turned and buried his face in the pillow. "O brother — O friend —"

The emotion passed and he lay staring at the ceiling, reconstructing midday of September the seventh beside Indian Run.

CHAPTER XXXIX

UNITY AND JACQUELINE

THE library at Fontenoy lay west and north. In the afternoon the sun struck through the windows and through the glass door, brightening the tall clock-face, the faint gilt and brown of old books, and the portrait of Henry Churchill with the swords crossed beneath. Upon the forenoon in question, and even though the month was May, the room looked a sombre place, chill and dusk, shaded and grave as a hermit's cell.

In the great chair upon the hearth sat Colonel Churchill, somewhat bowed together and with his hand over his eyes. By the window stood Major Edward, very upright, very meagre, soldierly, and grey. The northern light was upon him; with his pinned-up sleeve and lifted head he looked a figure of old defeats and indomitable mind. From the middle of the room Fairfax Cary faced both the Churchills.

In his dark riding-dress, standing with his gloved hand upon the table, he gave in look and attitude a suggestion of formality, a subtle conveyance of determination. He had been speaking, and now, after an interruption from one of the brothers, he continued. "That was two weeks ago. I have it clear, and I have my witness. The murderer, leaving the body of my brother beside Indian Run, turned his horse, and, at a point just east of the rock where grows the mountain ash, he quitted the road for the mountain-side. It is desperate riding over that ridge, but he made it as, two weeks ago, I made it, and he came out, as I came out, upon the high bank above the main road, a few yards below the blasted oak. That, Colonel Churchill, is what he did, and what a jury shall see that he did."

Colonel Dick let fall his hand. "Fair, Fair, I never gainsaid that he was a villain —"

"He appeared," continued the younger man, "before my witness, torn and breathless. There was blood upon his sleeve. Now see what he does. He rejoins his negro, and, if I know my man, he intimidates this boy into silence like the grave. Together they pause at Red Fields, a precaution that quite naturally suggests itself to the lawyer mind. But it is in the gloom of the storm, and he does not dismount — a course which, again, he knows to be wise. Apparently Red Fields notices nothing. He rides on. But he has yet to pass through town, to be accosted here, there, at the Eagle, the post-office, to be forced, perhaps, under peril of his refusal being scanned, to get down from his horse, answer questions, drink and talk with acquaintances. He is torn, dishevelled. There is blood upon his sleeve. What does he think as he rides from Red Fields? He thinks, 'Where can I best put myself in order, and remove this witness?' That would be his thought, and he would have the answer ready. He rode on to the edge of town, and there he stopped at Tom Mocket's."

Major Edward left the window. As he passed his brother, he laid for a moment his hand upon the elder's shoulder. The touch was protective, almost tender. "It's a rough wind, Dick! Bow your head and let it go over." He marched away, dragged a chair to the table, and sat down. "Very well," he said. "He stopped at Tom Mocket's."

"Yes, but not merely at the gate, as he testified. He went into the house, and there he washed the blood-stain from his sleeve."

"Can you prove that?"

"I can prove that he went into the house. A negro, running from the storm, saw him enter. When that girl — Vinie Mocket — is put upon the stand, I expect to prove the remainder. Now, the pistol —"

Colonel Dick rose, walked heavily to the glass door, then back to the hearth. "You stand there, as I have seen your father stand. Well, go on! We are men, Edward and I."

"His pistols are handsome ones, the gift of Mr. Jefferson. The murderer's name is engraved upon them. He has made, since September, a number of journeys, and he travels always with holsters to his saddle. Well, not long ago, I bribed the hostler of a tavern where I knew he was to sleep. I have seen the arms he carries. Two holsters, two pistols — but the latter do not match! A different maker, a heavier weight, and the owner's name but indifferently etched. And yet there is in Richmond a man who will swear to Mr. Rand's leaving town with the President's gift intact! The inference is, I think, that somewhere between Indian Run and Roselands the weapon vanished — how and when and where I have yet to find. I expect to recover it, and in the mean time I expect to force an explanation of those mismatched pistols."

He had been standing without motion — manner, voice, and attitude restrained and somewhat formal. He now moved, took his hand from the table, and folded his arms. "I came," he said, "to tell you, Colonel Churchill, and you, Major Edward, you who were my brother's friends and my father's friends, I came to tell you that I shall apply for and obtain a warrant for the arrest of Lewis Rand."

The words fell heavily, and when they were spoken, there was a silence in the library. Major Edward broke it. "You are determined, and I waste no breath in challenging the inevitable. So be it! The child will come home to us, Dick."

The elder brother walked the length of the room and paused before the picture of Henry Churchill. When at last he turned, his ruddy face was pale, his eyes wet. "Henry was a proud man. We grow old, and we grow to be thankful that the dead are dead! Well, Edward, well! we've weathered much — I reckon we can weather more." He halted at the glass door and stared out into the flowering garden. "My little Jack!" he muttered, and drew his hand across his eyes.

Cary spoke from where he yet stood beside the table. "I am aware — how can I be other than aware? — of the sorrow and anxiety which I bring upon this house. As regards myself, you have but to indicate your wishes, sir. I will come no more to Fontenoy, if my coming is unwelcome. One interest here I confidently entrust to your generosity. For the rest I will bow to your decision. If you tell me so, sir, I will come no more — though Fontenoy is well nigh as dear to me as Greenwood, and though I love and honour every inmate here."

His voice broke a little. There was a silence, then Colonel Dick swung around from the glass door. "Don't talk damned nonsense, Fair," he said gruffly.

Major Edward spoke from the old green chair. "We'll bring no unnecessary factors into this business, Fairfax. I don't conceive that it is necessary for us to quarrel. It is not you who have wrought the harm — that burden rests elsewhere. Have you seen Unity?"

"No, sir."

"Then we had better send for her." The Major rose and pulled the bell-rope. "Some one must go to Roselands. When do you propose to act?"

"Very soon, sir. Almost at once. I anticipate no resistance and no flight. I'll give him his due. He is bold and he is ready, and the court room is his chosen field, where his gods fight for him. He'll give battle."

The last of the Greenwood Carys moved from his place,

walked to the window, and stood there in the light from the north. "Before Unity comes, sir, there is something I would like to say. It pertains to myself. You have known me, both of you, all my life, and you knew my father before me. You know what my brother was to me — brother, guardian, friend. You two have lived your life together; think, each of you, how bitter now would be the other's loss. What if all was yet youth and fire and promise — and a villain struck one down, put out life at a blow, and denied the deed! Denied! went on with trumpets to place and honour! What would you do, Colonel Churchill, or you, Major Edward? You would do as I have done, and you would weigh no circumstance, as I have weighed none. Moreover, right is right, and law and justice must not curtsy even to pity for the innocent and tenderness for those who suffer! It is right that this man should feel the hand of Justice. And I can see it as no other than right that I — when all her paid soldiers failed — should have taken it on myself to bring him there, before her bar. It is this which I shall do, and the end is not with me, but with right and law and order, with the weal of society, yes, and with the man's own proper reaping of the harvest which he sowed! Else he also is monstrous, and there is nothing not awry." He paused, made a slight and dignified gesture with his hands, and went on. "I have done that which I had to do. I abide the consequences. But it is hard to bring trouble on you here, and to bring great trouble on — on one other. I wish you to know that, though I go my way, I go with a pained and heavy heart."

He broke off, and stood with his eyes upon the younger of the two brothers; then, after a moment and with a note of appeal in his voice, "Major Edward —"

Major Edward raised his hawk eyes and resolute face. "Trouble enough, yes, heavy trouble — but I should have done as you have done! It is all in the great battle, Fair. We'll be friends still, Fontenoy and Greenwood. There is Unity at the door."

From the Fontenoy coach Unity, who had not been to Roselands since December, regarded the quiet old place through a sudden mist of tears. The driveway from the gate was sunk in green; a hundred trees kept the place secluded, sylvan, and still. Hardly any bloom appeared,— the flowers were all in the quiet garden hidden by the house,— but through a small open space could be seen the giant beech tree by the doorstone.

Unity dried her eyes with her handkerchief, and bit her lips until they were red again. "If you're nothing but a bird of omen," she said to herself, "at least you need n't show it! Oh, this world!" then, "What if he is not from home?"

In the early winter she had advanced several pretexts for not troubling Roselands, had found them accepted by Jacqueline with an utter lack of comment, and had ceased to make them. She kept away, and her cousin made no complaint. What pretext, now, she wondered, would serve to explain this visit? She thought that pretext would be needed at first — just at first. And what if Lewis Rand were at home?

He was not at home. Jacqueline met her upon the great doorstone, kissed her, and held her hand, but made no exclamation of surprise and asked no questions. The coach and four, with old Philip and Mingo, rolled away to the stable, and the cousins entered the cool, wide hall. "You will lay aside your bonnet?" said Jacqueline. "Such a lovely bonnet, Unity! and your blue lutestring! Come to my room."

In the chamber Unity untied her blue bonnet-strings and

laid the huge scoop of straw upon the white counterpane; then, at the mirror, slowly drew off her long gloves, and took from her silken bag her small handkerchief. The action of her hands, now deliberate, now hurried, was strange for Unity, whose habit it was to be light and sure. "Do you remember," she asked, with her face still to the mirror, — "do you remember the last time I wore this gown?"

"You wore it," said Jacqueline, in a trembling voice, "to church, in August — to Saint John's."

"Yes. That Sunday when all the world was there. I smell the honeysuckle again, and hear FitzWhyllson's viol! That was our last old, happy day together."

"Was it?"

"Yes, it was. The very next day the world seemed somehow to change."

"Isn't that a way the world has?" asked Jacqueline. "Change and change and change again —"

"Yes," answered Unity, "but never to the same, never to the same again —"

A silence fell in the room that was all flowered chintz. Unity, raising her eyes to the glass, saw within it her cousin where she leaned against a chair — saw the face, the eyes, the lips — saw the mask off. Unity gasped, wheeled, ran to the chair, and, falling on her knees beside it, clasped her cousin in her arms. "O Jacqueline! O Jacqueline, Jacqueline!"

Jacqueline rested her hands upon the other's shoulders. "Why did you come to-day, Unity? The last time was December."

"I came — I came" — sobbed Unity, "just to bring you their love — Uncle Dick's and Uncle Edward's and Aunt Nancy's — and to say that Fontenoy is still home, and — and —"

"Yes," said Jacqueline. "But this is my home now, Unity.

It has been" — she raised her arms — "it has been my home for many and many a day! You may tell them that; you may tell it to Fairfax Cary."

"Don't — don't think of him as an enemy!"

"I think of him as he is. What is the message, Unity?"

"I have none — I have none," cried Unity, "except that whatever happens — whatever happens, Jacqueline, you are the darling of us all — of the old home and Uncle Dick and Uncle Edward and Aunt Nancy and Deb and me and all the servants! There is none at Fontenoy that does not love and honour you! Think of us, and come to us —"

"When? When, Unity?"

Unity rose. "Now, if you will, darling — dearest —"

Jacqueline smiled. "Now? When you are married, you will find that you cannot leave home so easily." She crossed the bedroom floor to a window, and stood with her hands on either side of the casement, and with her face lifted to the pure blue heaven.

Unity waited with held breath. "She knows — she knows," said her beating heart.

Jacqueline came back to the middle of the room. "Thank them for me, Unity, and tell them that I cannot leave my husband now." Her touch, clay-cold and fluttering, fell upon her cousin's arm. "There are wisdom and goodness in the world, and they wish to see things rightly, if only they had the power. Tell them at Fontenoy, and tell Fairfax Cary, too, that they have not altogether understood! Even he — even the one who is dead — did not quite do that, though he came more nearly than any. It is my hope and my belief that now he understands, forgives, and sees — and sees the dawn in the land!"

She raised her head, and the expression of her face was exquisite. No longer wan, she stood as though the flush of dawn were upon her. It paled, and the air of tragedy enfolded her again, but the light had been there, and it left her majestic. The grace within her and the sweetness were unfailing. She came now to her cousin, put an arm around her, and kissed her on the cheek. "You love truly, too," she whispered. "When trouble comes, you'll understand — you'll understand!"

Unity held her to her and wept. "O Jacqueline! — O Jacqueline!"

"You put on the blue gown to remind me, did n't you?" asked Jacqueline. "I did n't need any reminding, dear. It is all with me, all the old, frank, happy days; all the time when I was a girl and we used to sit, just you and I, by my window and watch the stars come out between the fir branches! And I love you all, every one of you. And I do not blame Fairfax Cary. It is destiny, I think, with us all. But I want you to know — and you can tell them that, too, — that there is one whom I love beyond every one else, beyond life, death, fear, anguish, meeting, and parting. Loving him so, and not despairing of a life to come when we are all washed clean, my dear, when we are all washed clean —"

Her voice broke and she moved again to the window. The clock ticked, the sun came dazzling in, a fly buzzed against the pane. Jacqueline turned. "Tell them that they are all dear to me, but that my home is here with my husband. Tell them that Lewis Rand — that Lewis Rand" — She put her hands to her breast. "No. I have not power to tell you that — not yet, not yet! But this I say — my uncles were soldiers, and they fought bravely and witnessed much, but I have seen a battlefield" — She shuddered strongly and brought her hands together as if to wring them, then let them fall instead and turned upon her cousin a face colourless but almost smiling. "It is strange," she said, "what pain we grow to call

Victory. Let's talk of it no more, Unity." She caressed the other's hand, raised it to her lips, and kissed it.

"I did not come to stay," said Unity brokenly. "You had rather be alone. The evening is falling and they look for me at home. When you call me, I will come again. Are you sure — are you sure, Jacqueline, that you understand what they — what they sent me to say?"

"I understand enough," said Jacqueline, in a very low voice, and kissed her cousin upon the brow.

CHAPTER XL

THE WAY OF THE TRANSGRESSOR

RAND closed the heavy ledger. "It is all straight," he said.

"It's as straight as if 't was a winding-up forever," answered Tom. "Are you going home now?"

"Yes."

"There's almost nothing on the docket. I've seen no such general clearance since you began to practise and took me in. You say you're going to refuse the Amherst case?"

"I have refused it."

"Then," quoth Tom, "I might as well go fishing. The weather's right, and every affair of yours is so cleaned and oiled and put to rights that there's nothing here for a man to do. One might suppose you were going a long journey. If you don't want me to-morrow, I'll call on old Mat Green —"

"Don't go fishing to-morrow, Tom," said Rand from the desk, "but don't come here either. Stay at home with Vinie."

"You won't be coming in from Roselands?"

"I won't be coming here." Rand left the desk and stood at the small window where the roses were now in bloom. "I shall send you a note, Tom, to-morrow morning. It will tell you what" — He paused for a moment. "What comes next," he finished. "There will be a message in it for Vinie." He turned from the window. "I am going home now."

"It's a good time for a holiday," remarked Tom, "and you needn't tell me that you don't need it, Lewis! I'll lock up and go to the Eagle for a while. What are you looking for?"

"Nothing," answered the other. "I was looking at the room itself. I always liked this office, Tom."

As he passed, he touched his subaltern upon the shoulder. There was fondness in the gesture. "Good-bye," he said, and was gone before Tom could answer.

Outside, in the bloom and glow of the May evening, he mounted Selim and rode out of the town. The people whom he met he greeted slightly, but with no change of manner which they afterwards could report. It was sunset when he passed the last houses, and turned toward the west and his own home. He rode slowly, with his eyes upon a great sea of vivid gold. By degrees the brightness faded, changing to an amethyst, out of which suddenly swam the evening star. The land rose into hills, the summits of the highest far and dark against the cold violet of the sky. From the road to Roselands branched the road to Greenwood. It was dusk when horse and rider reached this opening. Selim had come to know the altered grasp upon the rein just here, and now, according to wont, he fell into the slower pace. Rand turned in his saddle and looked across the darkening fields to the low hill, crowned with oaks, from which arose the Greenwood house. He gazed for a full minute, then spoke to his horse and they went on at speed. A little longer and he was at the gates of home.

His wife met him upon the doorstone. "I heard you at the gate —"

He put his arm around her. "What have you been doing all the long day?"

"I worked," she answered, "and saw to the house, and read to Hagar at the quarter. She's going fast. How tired your voice sounds! Come into the light. Supper is ready — and Mammy Chloe has said a charm to make you sleep to-night."

They went indoors to the lighted rooms. "You are wearing your amethysts," said Rand, "and the ribbon in your hair —"

She turned upon him a face exquisite in expression. "They are the jewels that you like — the ribbon as I wore it long ago. Come in — come in to supper."

The brief meal ended, they returned to the drawing-room. Rand stood irresolutely. "I have yet a line to write," he told her. "I will do it here at your desk. When I have finished, Jacqueline, then there is something I must say."

He sat down and began to write. She moved to the window, then restlessly back to the lighted room and sat down before the hearth, but in a moment she left this, too, and moved again through the room. She passed her harp, and as she did so, she drew her hand across the strings. The sweet and liquid sound ran through the room. Rand turned. "I have not heard," he said, in a low voice, — "I have not heard that sound since — since last August. Will you sing to me now?"

She touched the harp again. "Yes, Lewis. What shall I sing?"

He rose, walked to the window, and stood with his face to the night. "Sing those verses you sang that night at Fontenoy"; then, as she struck a chord, "No, not To Althea — the other."

She sang. The noble contralto, pure, rich, and deep, swelled through the room.

> "The thirst that from the soul doth rise
> Doth ask a drink divine" —

Her voice broke and her hands dropped from the strings. She rose quickly and left the harp. "I cannot — I cannot sing to-night. The air is faint — the flowers are too heavy. Come out — come out to the wind and the stars!"

Without the house the evening wind blew cool, moving the long branches of the beech tree, and rustling through the grass. To the west the mountains showed faintly, in the valley a pale streak marked the river. The sky was thick with stars. Behind them, through the open door, they heard the tall clock strike. "I did not tell you," said Jacqueline, "of all my day. Unity was here this afternoon."

"Unity!"

"Yes. For an hour. She came with — with messages. My uncles send me word that they love me, and that Fontenoy is my home always — as it used to be. Whenever I wish, I am to come home."

"What did you answer?"

"I answered that they were all dear to me, but that my home was here with you. I told Unity to tell them that — and to tell it, too, to Fairfax Cary."

There was a silence; then, "It does not matter," said Rand slowly. "Whether it is done my way, or whether it is done his way, Fairfax Cary will not care. He is concerned only that it shall be done. You understood the message, Jacqueline?"

She answered almost inaudibly. "Yes, I understood."

"Seven months — and Ludwell Cary lies unavenged. I have been slow. But I had to break a strong chain, Jacqueline. I had fastened it, link by link, around my soul. It was not easy to break — it was not easy! And I had to find a path in a desert place."

She bowed her head upon her arms. "Do I not know what it was? I have seen — I have seen. O Lewis, Lewis!"

"It is broken," he said, "and though the desert is yet around me, my feet have found the path. To-morrow, Jacqueline, I give myself up."

She uttered a cry, turned, and threw herself into his arms. "To-morrow! O Love!"

He bent over her with broken words of self-reproach. She stopped him with her hand against his lips. "No, I am not

DRINK TO ME ONLY WITH THINE EYES

all unhappy — no, you have not broken my heart — you have not ruined my life! Don't say it — don't think it! I love you as I loved you in the garden at Fontenoy, as I loved on our wedding eve, in the house on the Three-Notched Road! I love you more deeply now than then —"

"I have come," he answered, "to be sorry for almost all my life. Even to my father I might have been a better son. The best friend a young man ever had — that was Mr. Jefferson to me! and it all ended in the letter which he wrote last August. I was a leader in a party in whose principles I believed and still believe, and I betrayed my party. To-night I think I could give my life for one imperilled field, for one green acre of this land — and yet I was willing to bring upon it strife and dissension. Ingrate and traitor — hard words and true, hard words and true! I might have had a friend — and always I knew he was the man I would have wished to be — but, instead, I thought of him as my foe and I killed him. I have brought trouble on many, and good to very few. I have wronged you in very much. But I never wronged you in my love — never, never, Jacqueline! That is my mountain peak — that is my cleansing sea — that is that in my life which needs no repenting, that is true, that is right! Oh, my wife, my wife!"

The night wind blew against them. Fireflies shone and grey moths went by to the lighted windows; above the tree-tops a bat wheeled and wheeled. The clock struck again, then from far away a whippoorwill began to call. They sat side by side upon the doorstone, her head against his shoulder, their hands locked.

"What will you do?" he said. "What will you do? Day and night I think of that!"

"Could I stay on here? I would like to."

"I have put all affairs in order. The place and the servants are yours. I've paid every debt, I think. Mocket knows — he'll show you. But to live on here alone —"

"It will be the less alone. Don't fear for me — don't think for me. I will find courage. To-morrow!"

"It is best," he said, "that I should tell you that which others may think to comfort you with. It is possible, but I do not consider it probable, that the sentence will be death. It will be, I think, the Penitentiary. I had rather it was the other."

After a time she spoke, though with difficulty. "Yes — I had rather — for you. For myself, I feel to-night that just to know you were alive would be happiness enough. Either way — either way — to have loved you has been for me my crown of life!"

"I have written to Colonel Churchill, and a line to Fairfax Cary. There was much to do at the last. Now it is all done, and I will go early in the morning. You knew that it was drawing to this end —"

"Yes, I knew — I knew. Lewis, Lewis! what will you do yonder all the days — the months — the — the years to come? Oh, unendurable! O God, have mercy!"

"I will work," he answered. "It is work, Jacqueline, with me — it is work or die! I will work. That which I have brought upon myself I will try to endure. And out of effort may come at last — I know not what."

They sat still upon the stone. The wind sank, the air grew colder; near and far there gathered a feeling of the north, a sense of loneliness and untrodden space. The whippoorwill called again.

Rand shuddered. "Our last night — it is our last night. Look! — a star shot over the Three-Notched Road."

Jacqueline slipped from his clasp and stood upright, with her hands over her ears. "Come indoors — come indoors! I cannot bear the whippoorwill!"

Early the next morning he rode away. Halfway down the drive he looked back and saw her standing under the beech tree. She raised her hand, her scarf fluttering back from it. It was the gesture of a princess, watching a knight ride from her tower. The green boughs came between them; he was gone, and she sank down upon the bench beneath the tree. It was there that Major Edward found her, an hour later.

Rand passed along the old, familiar road. He travelled neither fast nor slow, and he kept a level gaze. The May morning was fresh and sweet, the land to either side ploughed earth or vernal green, the little stream laughing through the meadow. He passed a field where negroes were transplanting tobacco, and his mind noted the height and nature of the leaf. At the Greenwood road he looked mechanically toward the distant house, but upon this morning he hardly thought of Cary. He thought of Gideon Rand, and of the great casks of tobacco which he and his father used to roll; of the old, strong horses, and of a lean and surly dog that they had owned; of the slow journeys, and of their fires at night, beneath the gum and the pine, beside wastes of broom sedge.

He came into Charlottesville and rode down Main Street to the Eagle, where he dismounted. A negro took his horse. "Put him up," directed Rand, "until he is called for." He kept his hand for a moment upon Selim's neck, then turned and walked down the street and into the Court House yard.

The shady place had always a contingent of happy idlers, men and boys lounging under the trees or upon the Court House steps. These greeted Lewis Rand with deference, and turned from their bountiful lack of occupation to watch him cross the grass and enter the Court House. "He's gone," remarked one, "straight to the sheriff's office. What's his business there?"

The next day and the next the idlers in the Court House yard knew all the business, and rolled it under their tongues. They loved a tragedy, and this curtain had gone up with promise. Had they not seen Lewis Rand walk into the yard — had they not spoken to him and he to them — had they not watched him enter the Court House? The boy who minded the sheriff's door found himself a hero, and the words treasured that fell from his tongue. It was true that he had been sent away and so had heard but little, but the increasing crowd found that little of interest. "Yes, sir, that's what he said, and just as quiet as you are! 'Is the sheriff in, Michael?' he asked. 'Tell him, please, that I want to see him.' That's what he said, and Mr. Garrett he calls out, 'Come in, Mr. Rand, come in!'"

Other voices claimed attention. "And when they dragged Indian Run yesterday, there was the pistol at the bottom of a pool — his name upon it, just as he told them it would be —"

"Fairfax Cary was in the court room yesterday when he was committed. He and Lewis Rand spoke to each other, but no one heard what they said."

The boy came to the front again. "I did n't hear much that morning before Mr. Garrett sent me away, but I heard why he gave himself up. I thought it was n't much of a reason —"

The crowd pressed closer, "What was it, Michael, what was it?"

"It sounds foolish," answered the boy, "but I've got it right. He said he must have sleep."